JOUST

JOUST

MERCEDES LACKEY

DAW BOOKS, INC.

DONALD A. WOLLHEIM, FOUNDER
375 Hudson Street, New York, NY 10014

ELIZABETH R. WOLLHEIM
SHEILA E. GILBERT
PUBLISHERS

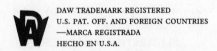

Dedicated to the memory of those lost
NYFD Ladder Companies: 9/11/01

LADDER 2
Frederick III, Jr.
Michael Clarke
George DiPasquale
Denis Germain
Daniel Harlin
Carl Molinaro
Dennis Mulligan

LADDER 3
Patrick Brown
Kevin Donnelly
James Coyle
Gerard Dewan
Jeffrey Giordano
Joseph Maloney
John McAvoy
Timothy McSweeney
Joseph Ogren
Steven Olson

LADDER 4
David Wooley
Michael Brennan
Joseph Angelini Jr.
Michael Haub
Michael Lynch
Samuel Oitice
John Tipping II

LADDER 5
Michael Warchola
Vincent Giammona
Louis Arena
Andrew Brunn
Thomas Hannafin
Paul Keating
John Santore
Gregory Saucedo

LADDER 7
Vernon Richard
George Cain
Charles Mendez
Richard Muldowney, Jr.
Vincent Princiotta

LADDER 8
Vincent Halloran

LADDER 9
Gerald Baptiste
John Tierney
Jeffrey Walz

LADDER 10
Sean Tallon

LADDER 11
Michael Quilty
Michael Cammarata
John Heffernan
Richard Kelly, Jr.
Matthew Rogan

LADDER 12
Angel Juarbe, Jr.
Michael Mullan

LADDER 13
Walter Hynes
Thomas Hetzel
Dennis McHugh
Thomas Sabella
Gregory Stajk

LADDER 15
Joseph Leavey
Richard Allen
Arthur Barry
Thomas Kelly
Scott Kopytko
Scott Larsen
Douglas Oelschlager
Eric Olsen

LADDER 16
Raymond Murphy
Robert Curatolo

LADDER 20
John Fischer
John Burnside
James Gray
Sean Hanley
Robert Linnane
David LaForge
Robert McMahon

LADDER 21
Gerald Atwood
Gerard Duffy
Keith Glascoe
Joseph Henry
William Krukowski
Benjamin Suarez

LADDER 24
Stephen Belson
Daniel Brethel

LADDER 25
Matthew Barnes
John Collins
Kenneth Kumpel
Robert Minara
Joseph Rivelli, Jr.
Paul Ruback
Glenn Perry

LADDER 27
John Marshall

LADDER 35
James Giberson
Vincent Morello
Michael Otten
Michael Roberts
Frank Callahan

LADDER 38
Joseph Spor

LADDER 42
Peter Bielfield

LADDER 101
Joseph Gullickson
Patrick Byrne
Salvatore Calabro
Brian Cannizzaro
Thomas Kennedy
Joseph Maffeo
Terence McShane

LADDER 105
Vincent Brunton
Thomas Kelly
Henry Miller, Jr.
Denis Oberg
Frank Palombo

LADDER 111
Christopher Sullivan

LADDER 118
Joseph Agnello
Vernon Cherry
Scott Davidson
Leon Smith, Jr.
Peter Vega
Robert Regan

LADDER 131
Christian Regenhard

LADDER 132
Andrew Jordan
Michael Kiefer
Thomas Mingione
John Vigiano II
Sergio Villanueva

LADDER 136
Michael Cawley

LADDER 166
William X. Wren, Retired

JOUST

ONE

THE hot wind out of the desert withered everything in its path—including anyone so foolish as to be out in the sun at midday. It carried reddish dust and sand on its wings, and used both to scour whatever it did not wither.

It did not howl, for it had no need to howl and rage for its power to be felt. It only needed to be what it was: relentless, inescapable, implacable, and ceaseless. This was the dry season, the season when the wind called *kamiseen* was king. It swept out of the sea of sand, bearing with it the furnace heat that drove man and beast into shelter if they were wise, and sucked the moisture and life out of everything. The earth was baked as hard as bricks, as hot beneath a bare foot as the inside of an oven. Add to that the hammer of the sun, which joined with the *kamiseen* in a conspiracy to dry up all life; nothing moved during the *kamiseen* at midday, not even slaves.

Except serfs, like Vetch. Altan serfs, the spoils of war, who were less valuable than slaves.

Little Vetch hunched his shoulders against the pitiless glare of the sun above him, and licked lips gone dry and cracked in the heat, as dry and cracked as the earth under his feet.

The walls of his master's compound offered some protection from the wind, but none from the sun. To his left, the back wall of tan mud brick around Khefti-the-Fat's workshop and house cast no shade at all on the path upon which he trudged. To his right, lower walls of the same material surrounded his master's *tala* field.

Calling it a "field," however, was something of an exaggeration. It could not have held more than five hundred *tala* plants, a single green oasis in the sand and baked earth, all of them heavy with unripe berries. It was here, only a few steps from the village where Khefti had his workshop, for two reasons. The first was that *tala* had to be irrigated during the dry season if it was to bear any amount of fruit at all. The second was that Khefti would never have let anything as valuable as a *tala* plant grow where he could not put his eye upon it on a regular basis. Vetch was fairly certain that Khefti counted the berries themselves twice daily. Fortunately, the husbandry of the precious *tala* was not his concern, for Khefti would never have entrusted anything so important to a serf. He was not even allowed to set foot inside the enclosure.

Vetch kept his head bent down as he heaved his heavy leather water bucket along. His arms and shoulders ached and burned with fatigue, and his stomach with hunger; his eyes stung with the sweat that dripped and the dust that blew into them, his mouth was dry, full of *kamiseen* grit, yet he dared not take a mouthful of the water in his bucket or use it to wash the sand from his eyes. That water was for the *tala* plants, not to quench the burning thirst of a mere serf.

He kept his eyes fastened on the hard-packed, sandy clay of the path under his dirty, bare feet. This was not because he was afraid to look up, and possibly incur the wrath of any freeborn Tian who might happen by for showing "insolence." He was watching for a particular little spot on the path that led from Khefti-the-Fat's well inside his compound, to the cistern that irrigated his *tala* field. This spot was marked only by the fact that the soil there was a slightly different color than the rest.

He wanted so badly to put the bucket down; the rope handle cut into his hands cruelly. It was all that kept him going, knowing that spot was there, marked by the dirt he'd dug up and replaced last night.

Ah. There it was. He fastened his gaze on it, and labored toward it, trying not to pant, which would only dry his mouth further.

Vetch made no outward sign that he had noted the place, for the last thing he wanted anyone to think was that there was anything unusual about the spot. He couldn't have sped up if he'd had to. The water bucket that had been tossed at him by his master this morning was unwieldy, and quite full. If he wasn't careful, most of what was in it would slosh out before he got to the cistern.

The bucket was far too big and heavy when full for someone as small as he was to carry easily. Not that he had a choice. Serfs made do with the tools they were given, and kept silent about any complaints they might have in the presence of their masters, or they suffered whatever consequences the master chose to mete out. A man might hesitate to scar a slave who had cost him money to buy, and might earn him more money when sold. He would have no such compunctions about a serf, who only cost him money in the housing and feeding, who could not be sold unless the land to which the serf was attached was sold also. How many times had Khefti told Vetch that? *"You're of cursed little use to me alive, insect!"* he would say. *"Your death would mean nothing, except that I need not waste my bread in the mouth of one so useless as you!"* He sometimes wondered why Khefti kept him alive at all, except that Khefti-the-Fat was so grasping that he never willingly let go of *anything* he owned, no matter how useless or worn out it was. Every scrap, every bone, even the ashes from his fires were used until there was nothing left. So that was probably it; Khefti was determined to use Vetch up, as he did everything else.

There were laws regarding the treatment of slaves. There were no such laws protecting serfs, for serfs were Altan, and the enemy: spoils of war, prisoners of war.

Even when they were only little boys.

And in Vetch's case, *very* little boys indeed.

He had never been big, but now he hardly seemed to grow anymore, on the poor fare that Khefti-the-Fat allotted him. A weedy little boy he was, named for a weedy little plant the Tians judged not even fit for fodder. Not fit for *anything*, as his master would say. And never mind that it was Altan custom to give their boy children unpleasant names while they were young to mislead the night-walking ghosts into thinking they were worthless rather than snatching them up in the darkness. "Vetch" he was on the Tian inventory rolls, and "Vetch" he would now remain for as long as he lived. And properly named, too, according to Khefti-the-Fat.

"What have you done to earn your bread?" the master would say, his fat belly shaking with rage, his pendulous jowls trembling, as he delivered another blow to a back already scarred. *"You steal from me, you are a thief, who takes my food and gives me nothing in return!"* This was usually right after Vetch had attempted and failed at some task, and Khefti was beating him to teach him to do better.

This was, often as not, some chore that *should* have been given to a man, or at least, a larger boy—but that was never an excuse for failure, and took not so much as a single stripe from Vetch's chastisement.

Teach with the rod, for stripes improve the memory, said one proverb, *A boy's ears are on his back, he hears better when beaten* ran another. These were Khefti's mottoes, and he lived by them. He even beat his apprentices just as much as the law and their parents permitted, though them, he dared not starve. But he saved the heaviest punishments for Vetch.

Vetch deviated from the center of the path just a little, and shortened his steps so that he was able to come down—hard—on the off-color spot.

Upon Khefti-the-Fat, every misfortune will fall. My sandal to grind his head into the dust, he chanted to himself, just as he had chanted over the finger-long *abshati* figure he'd made out of river clay yesterday in the image of his master. *My foot to break his back. The thorns of the acacia to pierce his belly, and the food turn to thistle in his mouth.* Cursing a master was a thing absolutely forbidden; if he were caught doing so, any beating he'd had before this would seem as nothing. He knew that, but if he could not curse Khefti, there would be nothing in his life worth getting up for in the morning.

Not that he had any real faith that his curses would come to pass. Khefti-the-Fat had too many charms hung about his person and his house for the curses of one small serf boy to fly past them and strike home. But it was something to curse the master, a small blow, if only a symbolic one, something more than merely enduring. And there was always the chance that Vetch would, by sheer dint of repetition, or the chance that he contrived a curse that Khefti *didn't* have a charm against, get some small crumb of discomfort to plague his master past all the protections.

That one small hope was really all that Vetch had, and it was what he lived for.

Yesterday, when Khefti had gone to sleep for his afternoon nap without assigning Vetch a task to follow filling the cistern, Vetch had seized the opportunity to run down to the river and dig raw *latas* roots to hide under his pallet to eat later. Now, in the dry season, the Great Mother River had shrunk from a fruitful matron to the slimmest of dancing girls, and a languid one at that. The *latas* was easier to reach, the roots now buried in the mud flats rather than waist-deep in the river water, and crocodiles disinclined to pursue potential prey over the mud flats when so many fish were stranded in ever-shallower pools left behind by the receding Great Mother River. While the *latas* had been in bloom, the glorious blue flowers rising on their waving stems above the surface of the river, Vetch had mentally noted every patch, so he knew where even the smallest and least accessible clumps were. He had to; he was in competition with every other hungry mouth in the village. Perhaps none were as starved as he, but unlike onions and barley, the roots were free for the digging, and all it took was a stick and determination to get them.

In digging up the roots, he had come across a generous lump of nearly-pure clay, of the sort that Khefti would have been very pleased to see. To Vetch, it had been a treasure as fine as the roots he carried home, for any time that Vetch got his hands on clay, he would make an *abshati* figure to use to curse Khefti-the-Fat.

He certainly knew most of what there was to know about molding *abshati* figures, for he heard the instructions bellowed in the ears of Khefti's apprentices, day in, day out. The making of such figures was usually for funerary purposes, not cursing—there was a good living in the making of *abshatis* to represent the deceased or to supply the spirit with servants in the next life. A good half of Khefti's pottery income came from funerary wares, or replacing such items as went into the tomb from the household stores. Vetch probably could have made *abshatis* as good as any of those turned out by the apprentices, had Khefti allowed him. But no one would purchase an *abshati* made by a serf, an Altan, the enemy, lest it carry some sort of subtle curse against Tians that would render the magic the priests would say over it ineffective.

Ordinary mud would not hold the detail he needed to make a good figure, nor would it shatter the way a well-dried statue of clay would. But although his master was a potter, there was no way for Vetch to purloin *his* clay, for he guarded it as jealously as his *tala*. Good clay was valuable, and a careful accounting was made of every weighable scrap of it.

This time, through some quirk of good fortune, the figure Vetch had modeled was a particularly good one. He had managed to get the limbs all in the right proportions, and Khefti's bulging belly, ugly frown and perpetually-creased brows just right. Perhaps it was crude, and the face a bit blobby, but anyone who looked at it would surely recognize who it was meant to be. While it was still wet, he had filled the mouth with bits of thistle, and shoved acacia thorns deep into the belly. Then he had set it up on top of the wall in a hidden corner to dry hard in the sun and the *kamiseen*, and when all of the work was done for the day, because it was such a good likeness, he decided that instead of merely grinding the thing under his heel while chanting his curses, he would try something different.

He had dug a hole in the path in the moonlight and put the figure in it. That way he could tread on it with every bucket hauled to and from the well, reciting the curses in his head. Maybe if he did *that* enough, one of them would fly home and strike true. Knowing he would put his foot on his master each time he traveled the path kept him going, even in this heat.

The dust that flew up in a puff from under his bare foot as he planted it on the burial spot was nearly the same no-color as his foot itself, coated with dried clay and dust as it was. All the better; cursing was earth-magic, and maybe this time the links would be strong enough to make the curse stick. Vetch had tried, and more than once, to get something of his master's person to put into the figures he made. But Khefti was a coward, always afraid of magic and curses, and was so careful of such things that he never pared his nails without counting all the bits before burning them, and even made his barber burn the hair he'd scraped off the master's misshapen head before Khefti would leave the shop. Well, Khefti was not well-beloved among his neighbors, so perhaps he was right to be so concerned.

Vetch reluctantly took his heel from the spot where the figure lay buried, and heaved the bucket forward another step. His arms ached so much, and his legs were so wobbly from exhaustion that it was all he could do to keep from dropping to his knees in the dust, but he dared not set the bucket down for an actual rest. At any moment, Khefti might awaken from his nap and look out to see if Vetch was working.

Every morning and every afternoon, as long as the *kamiseen* blew, he filled the drip-cistern that fed the fragile pottery pipes that in turn watered his Tian master's *tala* plants. The only source of water for the cistern was the Great Mother River or the master's well, and neither was easier than the other to get water from.

If he fetched water from the well, it meant pulling up the water one bucket at a time, bringing up the rope, hand over hand, with the bucket feeling as though it was getting heavier all the time. And the well was (of course) nearly as far from the cistern as the river, though in the opposite direction. The river was marginally farther away, though he would not have to drag the weighty bucket up its rope. But the clear water from the well wouldn't clog the pottery pipes the way that muddy water from the river would, unless Vetch was very careful when he filled the bucket. Being "very careful" meant wading out into the river, up to his knees—which put him in the way of the crocodiles, who would not turn down prey that came so obligingly within their reach.

Vetch hated this bucket, too heavy, too big, too awkward, and if he'd dared, he'd have put a hole in the bottom of it. But if he did, Khefti would probably find something worse for him to use— bigger and heavier, or so small as to be nearly useless.

Tala could only be grown during the dry season, after the Great Mother River had shrunk to a shadow of her wet-season greatness. It only set its berries after the sun-baked fields of wheat and barley were harvested and reduced to bleached stubble and the earth beneath the stubble was riddled with cracks as wide as a man's hand. But *tala* fruits were worth their weight in electrum, for *tala* fruits gave the Jousters their ability to control their great dragons.

Dragons . . . dragons and *tala* were inseparable. The only reason to grow the *tala* was because of the dragons, the creatures that were the greatest weapons that the Tians had. Vetch had only ever seen the dragons at a far distance, overhead, flying out from the city of Mefis a little up the river, gold and scarlet, blue and green against the hard, bright blue of the sky. They would have been beautiful, if they were not so terrible.

Dragons—well, in part, they were responsible for his being a serf. The war would not have gone so badly for Alta if the Tians hadn't had so many more dragons and Jousters. He supposed, dully, that he should be cursing them, too—but he could only focus his hate on one target at a time, and at the moment, that target was Khefti.

Vetch stumbled over a clod and trod down hard on a stone, saving the bucket from going over at the last moment. "Night-demons take you!" he cursed the clod and stone alike, and thought, resentfully, that if Khefti were to allow him the clothing that were allotted to a slave, he would have straw sandals, and he would be saved stone bruises, saved the burning heat that came up through his hardened soles. Khefti's paths were like Khefti's heart; hard and uncaring. What could it *possibly* cost to permit his one serf a simple pair of sandals?

That was the moment when a revelation, and a sickening one, came to him. And he realized that one of his errors in cursing Khefti might have been in the phrasing of the first part of the curse. He had specifically said *my* sandal *to grind his head into the dust.* But Vetch wasn't wearing sandals, didn't own sandals (not even the cheapest, woven-straw kind every slave got) and likely never would own sandals. Granted, that was the way that the magician Vetch had spied on had phrased *his* curse for his customer, but the customer *had* worn sandals.

Vetch ground his teeth in frustration, and jerked at the rope handle of the bucket. Well, he would continue the cursing for the entire three days, but *how* could he have overlooked something so simple?

Better he should have cursed the *tala* fields—

But that would be a dangerous thing to do as well as an audacious one, potentially more dangerous than cursing his master.

Granted, the mud-brick wall held little shrines to every god that could be invoked, and plenty of talismans for growth and plenty, which should have prevented any harm whatsoever from coming to the fields, but if Khefti even *thought* that Vetch was cursing the fields, his stick would be out and drumming a beat on Vetch's back for days.

Besides, Vetch wanted to hurt Khefti directly, not indirectly. And anyway, as the son of a farmer, someone who loved and served the land, something within Vetch shrank from wishing harm even on a tiny plot of *tala* plants.

Vetch's master was not a farmer; he was a potter and the master of a brick yard. Nevertheless, he made a great deal of money from his little *tala* field; his workshops were for his daily bread, but his *tala* bought him luxuries that his neighbors envied. A harvest like this one would bring more than enough to pay for a rock-carved tomb in the Valley of Artisans, a tomb he could not otherwise have afforded, and for which his apprentices were making a veritable army of *abshati* servants and pottery funerary wares fit for a man far above Khefti's station. It also paid for all manner of luxuries: fine linen kilts, many jars of good date wine every day, melons, honey cakes, and roast duck on his table on a regular basis. Khefti even had a melon cooling in his well at this moment, a true luxury in the dry season.

Oh, melon. . . .

Just the thought of a melon made Vetch's stomach cry out with hunger. He hadn't even tasted a melon *rind* in an age. Khefti thriftily had his cook pickle the rinds from his melons, in keeping with his parsimonious nature.

And that thought led down the well-worn path of food. Good bread and beer, melon and dates and pomegranate, honey and fish; all the things that Vetch had not tasted since he became a serf. For that matter, he had not had *enough* to fill his belly since the last of the great Temple Festivals at the beginning of the growing season, and that was only because it was the Temple of Hamun that provided the bounty. The raw *latas* roots Vetch had eaten this morning (in addition to his allotted stale loaf end) had helped with the never-ending hunger, but nothing would ever make it stop altogether.

From the moment Vetch had entered Khefti's service, he was *always* hungry; as the savory aromas from Khefti's kitchen tantalized his nose, he would be making a scanty meal of whatever Khefti allotted him. Breakfast, a palm-sized loaf of yesterday's dark barley bread (he could have eaten half a dozen of the same size), or supper, a tiny bowl of pottage *his* family wouldn't have fed to a pig and another little loaf of stale bread. Sometimes the fare was varied by the addition of an onion beginning to go bad. Lunch was whatever *he* could find, in the hour when Khefti slept—a handful of wild lettuce, *latas* roots grubbed out of the riverbank and eaten raw, wild onions so strong they made the eyes water. Sometimes he found wild duck eggs in season; sometimes there were berries or palm fruits, or dates fallen to the ground. Mostly, he got only what Khefti gave him. He hadn't seen cheese or meat or honey cakes since the farm was taken. He dreamed about food all the time, and there was never a moment when his stomach wasn't empty. He went to sleep, curled around his hunger, and woke with it gnawing at his spine.

The only thing that ever really competed with the hunger was anger.

And anger was as constant a companion as hunger. Not that he could *do* anything about his anger, but at least when he was angry, sometimes he'd get so worked up that he'd upset his stomach, and then the hunger would go away for a little.

And when he was angry, he could make the loneliness and the pain and the fear recede for a little. When he was angry, he wasn't on the verge of the tears that often threatened to overwhelm him. Sometimes, anger was the only defense he had— when the village boys plagued him and threw stones at him, when Khefti beat him. He couldn't strike back, but at least he could keep from weeping, giving them the satisfaction of knowing that they hurt him. Crying would make him into a greater target for torment than he already was; tears were a sign of weakness he couldn't afford.

But he was truly the most miserable of boys, and sometimes he thought that anger was the only possession he had that could not be taken from him.

And anger was, perhaps, the only thing that kept him alive, in the midst of a life hardly worth living.

He slept on a pile of reeds *he* had cut, under the same awning that sheltered the wood for the bread oven from rain, in the outer back court, beyond the kitchen court. His clothing was a loinwrap of whatever rags were deemed unsuitable even for household use, and only when it was little more than a collection of holes held together by dirt and threads like spider's silk was it ever replaced. Thus Khefti gave lip service to the provision of "food and shelter" for his serf. Under Khefti, Vetch had nothing that was not scant, except for anger and hunger.

Well, one thing more, perhaps. He had hatred.

He hated Khefti with a despairing, dull hatred that was as constant as the anger and hunger and was surpassed only by the fear that Khefti inspired.

His stomach growled again, and grated painfully. Sweat prickled Vetch's scalp, and a drop of sweat trickled down his temple, down his face, and down his neck, leaving behind a trail of mud in the dust that coated him. But the hot, dry wind swiftly dried it before he could free a hand to wipe it away, adding one more itch to all of the insect bites and healing scratches he was always plagued with. His stomach pressed urgently against his backbone, and he was tired, so tired—even that anger that never left him was not enough to overcome how tired he was.

What had *he* done that the gods should treat him so?

How was it fair, that Khefti claimed him and could work him like a mangy donkey because he had bought the house and a thin strip of the land that had once belonged to Vetch's father? How was it right, that the Tian thieves had taken the farm that had been Vetch's home from those who had lived and worked it for generations? What justified what had been done to Vetch's family, to a man who had not so much as raised a hand in self-defense against the Tians?

Anger lived in his belly, waking and sleeping, but it was an impotent anger with nowhere to go. And at times like this, it was a weary anger that had worn itself out on the unyielding stone of his life.

A few steps more, and he made it to the side of the above-ground stone cistern. With a sigh of relief, he eased the bucket to the ground, and went up the two steps that allowed a little fellow like him to reach the cistern lid. He slid the wooden cover aside, pausing for just a second to savor the momentary breath of cool damp that escaped, then groped behind him for the bucket handle, ready to haul it up again.

It wasn't there.

The anger in him roused, and gave him a flare of energy. Vetch whirled, expecting to find that one of the Tian boys who apprenticed with his master had tilted the bucket on its side, allowing it to spill its precious burden into the thirsty, hard-packed earth. Or worse, had stolen the bucket—which would force him to go to Khefti, who would beat him for losing it. Then he would have to fill the cistern with whatever Khefti gave him, crippled by a back aching and raw.

Someone had taken the bucket, all right, but it wasn't an apprentice.

Behind him, a tall, muscular Tian—a warrior, by his build, and one of the elite Jousters, by the heavy linen kilt, the wide brown leather belt, and the empty leather lance socket hanging from it—held the heavy bucket to his lips, gulping down the master's well water with the fervor of one who was perishing of thirst. Vetch stared at him, the surge of anger he'd felt at having his bucket stolen by yet another Tian overcome with sheer astonishment at seeing one of the Jousters *here*. He had never seen a Jouster so close before, not even an Altan Jouster.

Where there was a Jouster, could his dragon be far away?

Vetch looked wildly about, then a snort made him look *up,* to the roof of the pottery-drying shed inside Khefti's walls, and there was the great dragon itself, looking down at him with an aloof gaze remarkably like that of one of the pampered cats that swarmed the Temple of Pashet.

Vetch gaped; the dragon was a thing of multicolored, jeweled beauty, slim and supple, and quite as large as the shed it perched upon. A narrow, golden, large-eyed head oddly reminiscent of a well-bred horse's, with the same slim muzzle, dished nose, and broad forehead was surmounted by a bony crest that shaded from deep gold into a pale electrum, as pale and translucent as the finest alabaster. That elegant golden head rose on a long, flexible neck that shaded from emerald to blue. The wings, of blue shading into purple, rising from muscular shoulders twice the bulk of the hindquarters, were spread to catch the sun. The long, whiplike tail, which reversed the shading of the neck, going from green into gold, was curled around the cruel golden talons of the forefeet, as the dragon lounged comfortably on the flat roof of the shed. The eyes, though, they were was what caught you and held you—slit-pupiled and the deep crimson of the finest rubies—

Not that Vetch had ever seen the finest rubies, or indeed, any rubies. But that was what people said, and certainly the colors sported by this beast were every bit as gorgeous as the magnificent wall paintings in even the poorest Tian temples depicting the jewels worn by gods and kings.

Such beauty—it was hard to look at the dragon and remember that he should hate it.

The Jouster finished his drink and dumped the rest of the bucket of water over his head without even bothering to take off his helmet, and the anger awoke again, at the wanton wastage of what had taken Vetch so long to haul. Vetch made an involuntary whimper of suppressed rage in the back of his throat as the man tossed the bucket aside, as if it was something of no account, to be discarded.

Which meant, of course, that if Khefti came out at this moment and saw him without the bucket in his hands—

Now anger turned to panic. Vetch scrambled after the bucket just as his master, the *last* creature he wanted to see at this moment, appeared in the door of his courtyard. Khefti was huge and terrifying; his size alone was intimidating, for he must have weighed twice as much as this Jouster. His gut bulged over his dingy, grease-stained linen kilt, his fat hands were quick with a blow, and his doughy face wore a perpetual scowl beneath his striped headdress.

He could not have chosen a worse moment to wake up from his nap and come a-prowling—exactly as Vetch had feared.

Khefti-the-Fat was the worst master Vetch had ever had, for though most of them had regarded their serfs as of less importance than a donkey, none had been cruel. Vetch was the only one of his family left with Khefti; the Tian who had originally taken control of their land along with that of their neighbors, had sold it in turn to another prosperous Tian, who in his turn broke it up into smaller portions and sold them. Each time it was sold, Vetch's family got a new set of masters, but at least they had been allowed to remain together, working the earth still—for the owners had all agreed that it would be in their best interest to farm it communally, using the combined labor of Vetch and his family, which after all, cost nothing. This went on for several years, until at last, came the purchasers that included Khefti. Khefti had specifically bought the house itself, and the family vegetable garden. And Khefti was not inclined to farm the land communally with the others, as every other owner had been; in fact, he was not inclined to farm at all. He wished to enlarge his fortunes by becoming an absentee landlord.

This had resulted in the actual dispersal of all of the remaining members of Vetch's family—his three sisters, mother, and grandmother. Khefti kept only Vetch. What happened to the rest of them, Vetch had no idea; Khefti had taken him to his own house in this village on the outskirts of Mefis, and had rented out Vetch's home and its tiny garden to yet another Tian. *Taken* was perhaps too mild a word; Vetch had been dragged away from his family, literally kicking and screaming, as the girls were led away weeping by their new masters. Grandmother had given him a last look that told Vetch she knew that she would never see him again, then shuffled off after her new master, head bowed, with every fiber of her registering defeat. The last Vetch saw of his mother was a final glimpse of her collapsing to the earth. Then Khefti had begun beating him to make him stop screaming, which was the last thing that Vetch remembered before waking up to a bucket of water poured on his head and being tied to the back of Khefti's cart to follow along as he could.

Why Khefti had kept Vetch at all, the boy had no idea. Perhaps it had only been for the sake of the records; certainly a man with the look of a tax collector came every so often and Vetch was trotted out for his inspection. Perhaps in order to hold any land, you had to have at least one of the serfs that came with it.

If that was true—then what would happen when he and his family were all dead? Vetch didn't know that either. He didn't really want to think about the alternative—that his sisters and his mother would become "breeding stock," producing a bloodline linked to the property, to allow the new owners to hold it, giving them more hands to work it. . . .

But why Khefti had decided to keep Vetch, rather than one of the girls or Vetch's mother—that was something only Khefti knew. Not that Vetch would have wanted to see his sisters or mother or grandmother under Khefti's untender care. No, better it was him, not them.

Better that Khefti hadn't gotten the idea to produce the bloodline. . . .

Best of all that the need to keep a serf ended when the serf was dead. And perhaps that was why Khefti had kept Vetch; smallest of the lot, cheapest to keep, and likely the quickest to die of ill treatment. Too bad for Khefti, Vetch was tougher than he looked; he was never sick, no matter what trash Khefti fed him.

Vetch had never thought he would ever envy the lot of a slave, but he had learned better, under Khefti. For slaves, there was always the possibility of freedom; a master might free them at his death, or a slave might earn his freedom in some way. Not so for a serf; tied to the land they were, from birth to death, and tied to the master that owned the land. As property that could be bought and sold readily, slaves were as valuable as any other livestock. Not so for serfs; they came with the land, and one could not sell them without selling the land. Khefti could never realize a profit by having Vetch trained to some skill or great strength and selling him at a profit.

Khefti had no reason to do more than keep Vetch alive, and work him as hard as possible. Vetch would never be worth more to him than he was at this moment. And from the look on Khefti's face as he glared at a Vetch who was *not* at this moment working, his value had just dropped again.

Khefti had not seen the Jouster; he certainly hadn't seen the dragon. All he saw was Vetch, standing on the steps of the cistern with empty hands and no bucket in sight.

With an inarticulate roar, Khefti snatched up the little whip that never left his side, and descended on Vetch. For all his bulk, Khefti-the-Fat moved surprisingly fast; Vetch only had time enough to crouch down and cover his head with his hands when the quirt descended on his shoulders, leaving a stripe of fire across his back that made him gasp with pain.

Once. Twice. Vetch squeezed his eyes shut, ducked his head further, stuffed both hands in his mouth and bit his knuckles, strangling his cries with his hands. Khefti never delivered fewer than a dozen blows even at the best of times, but sooner or later he *had* to see the Jouster, and then he would stop, if only to gape in shock. If Vetch could just hold on without fainting until his master realized they were not alone—

But the third blow never came.

Vetch risked a glance backward over his shoulder, and saw, with astonishment, that the Jouster had caught the wrist of

Khefti's whip hand and was holding it effortlessly at shoulder height. Never quick-witted, Khefti's expression was frozen between the moment of rage when his hand had been caught and the dawning realization of just *who* and *what* had stopped him from beating his property.

The Jouster's helmet concealed most of his face. Vetch could not see enough to read his expression.

But *why* had he stopped Khefti from striking?

"The boy is not at fault," the Jouster said, in a mild voice, "I took his bucket to quench my thirst. He could hardly take it away from me."

Vetch's mouth dropped open with astonishment so great that the pain of his two stripes seemed to fade. The *most* he had hoped for was that Khefti would be too embarrassed to beat him in front of the Jouster, which would give Vetch a chance to explain himself. He had hardly thought the Jouster would take his part!

Khefti went red-faced and spluttering, but what could he say? Nothing, of course; the Jousters were a kind of nobility, and certainly outranked a mere *tala* farmer, potter, and brick maker. Nor would he dare do anything further to Vetch while the Jouster was there, since the Jouster had so forcibly expressed his disapproval.

Once he was gone, however, he would certainly extract a double dose of punishment out of Vetch, for having looked a fool in front of a Jouster. Unless—

Unless the Jouster continued to speak with his master. Then, perhaps Vetch could slip away, get the bucket, and go back to his task again while Khefti was talking to the Jouster. If Khefti saw that Vetch had run back to his appointed labors at the very first moment possible, he might feel the beating he'd already given Vetch was enough. Vetch kept one eye on them both, and eased one foot down the stair.

The dragon snorted again, and the Jouster looked up at it, then down at Khefti. "From the look of things," he continued, in that same mild voice, "you've been abusing and neglecting the Great King's property. This boy looks half starved, half beaten, and treated like a masterless cur. You do remember, don't you, that serfs are the *Great King's* property, and not yours? Or is it possible you had forgotten that little detail?"

Khefti went from red to white, all the blood draining from his skin until he looked like an enormous damp, white grub.

The Jouster turned his gaze from Khefti to Vetch. "I need a boy," he said casually, as if it were no great importance to him. "And if you're getting *any* amount of work from one that starved, he must be remarkable. I'll have him."

Khefti's jaw dropped. "But!" he protested. "But—but—"

"*As you know,* a Jouster can requisition any of the Great King's property within reason, if it is to serve him and his dragon." The Jouster shrugged. "One small boy—three-quarters starved—is certainly within reason. You will speak to the King's assessor when he comes to see if the King will permit you to continue holding the land to which the boy was tied. Or, of course, you could see if there is some other member of his family available—but if there is, I suggest that you treat the new acquisition better than this one. The assessor's eye will certainly be on you now."

He let go of Khefti's wrist, and Khefti dropped to the ground, to lie there like a quivering, misshapen, unbaked loaf. "But—" Khefti burbled. "B–b–b–but—"

The Jouster ignored him. Instead, he looked up at his dragon again, which uncoiled itself and stepped carefully down into the yard. The roof of the drying shed creaked as the dragon removed its weight from the structure. The dragon stretched a wing lazily out to its fullest extent, then pulled it in, and yawned. It moved up beside the Jouster just as a faithful dog would come to heel, then bent its forequarters so that its shoulders were even with the Jouster's chest. The Jouster grabbed the back of Vetch's loincloth as if he was a parcel, and heaved him up over the dragon's shoulder.

The band of his loincloth cut painfully into his stomach, though Vetch more than half expected it to give way and tear. Vetch landed stomach-down on the dragon's neck, but the Jouster had not thrown him hard, and his breath was not driven out of him. He'd landed on a sort of carry pad of stuffed leather in front of the Jouster's saddle, and he clung to it like a lizard on a ceiling as the Jouster leaped into the saddle itself.

Then the dragon tensed himself all over, stretched his wings wide, and with a leap and a tremendous beat of those wings, took to the sky with a frightening lurch. The sudden upward movement pressed Vetch into the carry pad, and he felt the Jouster seize the band of his loincloth again, and for the second time in his life, *fear* replaced every other sensation; the fear that he was falling, falling!

But he fought back the fear, and clung to the pad. A second wing beat drove them higher—through a storm of dust kicked up by the wind of those wings, Vetch watched Khefti's striped canvas awnings over the woodpile, the kitchen court, and the summer pavilion on the roof go ripping loose and flying off.

Below them, Khefti lifted his arms to the sky and began to howl like a jackal.

A third wing beat, a third tremendous gust, and half the thatch of the drying shed tore loose as well, and the furnishings from the rooftop tumbled over the edge into the street. Fashionable light wickerwork chairs and tables, palm-frond mats and pillows stuffed with duck- and goosedown came off the roof like a shower of gifts from a generous noble; passersby scrambled after the bounty and carried off everything they could seize. Khefti was not well-beloved . . . he could count on never seeing so much as a stray feather again. His howls were mingled with curses and entreaties to the gods—who, with luck, were deaf to his pleas.

And the last of Vetch's fear evaporated in half-mad glee at the sight.

A fourth wing beat, and Vetch could no longer see the house of his former master, only hear his thin wailing from below as he lamented his losses and called upon the gods to witness his ruin.

The ground whirled away as the dragon wheeled, the fear returned, redoubled, and Vetch closed his eyes and hung on with all his might.

He had no illusion that this was rescue; he had merely traded one master for another. But this one, at least, had chided Khefti for starving and mistreating him. So perhaps this master would be better than Khefti.

At least he would be different.

At least, life would be different.

And to that thought, he clung, as he clung to the saddle-pad, and with much of the same desperation.

TWO

GLEE could not hold back the terror for long. In all of his life, Vetch had never been higher off the ground than the top of a wall; now he was so far above the earth that the tiniest glimpse of it getting farther and farther away made him feel sick and dizzy.

And this, evidently was only the beginning.

When he'd seen dragons passing overhead, it had never occurred to him how *high* they were. Now he knew—oh, *how* he knew!—and the knowledge was enough to scare him witless.

The dragon continued to rise, surging upward and upward, so high that Vetch squeezed his eyes closed again, for he could not bear the sight of villagers reduced to the size of ants, and the mud-brick houses of the nameless hamlet on the outskirts of Mefis to the size of the pebbles that the ants swarmed around. This was bad enough, *would* have been bad enough had the flight been as smooth as those his spirit took in dreams.

But no. With every wing beat, the dragon lurched skyward, then dropped back a little, convincing Vetch's stomach that they were all about to plummet to the ground. If he'd had anything in his stomach, he would have lost it within the first few moments. As it was, his gorge rose, and there was a musty, sour taste in the back of his throat to accompany the nausea. Vetch kept his eyes squeezed shut.

Finally, they stopped lurching and bounding, and Vetch cracked his right eye open a trifle to see that the dragon was gliding out in level flight. This was only *relatively* level; it still rose and fell again with each wing beat, except when it was gliding. When the dragon glided, his stomach was a hard, cold knot of agony, certain that they were about to fall out of the sky. When it beat its wings, his stomach turned over again.

In the first moments of the flight, he vowed that if he ever set foot upon the ground again, he would never leave it . . . and once they reached the height that the Jouster wanted, he vowed that if he lived through this experience, he would dig a hole in the ground and live in it for the rest of his life. Eyes shut, or eyes open? Both states left him in a state of panic.

When his mind unfroze enough for him to notice anything but fear, the first thing that struck him was the extraordinary *heat* of the dragon's body, hot as the hottest sand at midday during the dry season, hotter than the furnace wind of the *kamiseen*, heat that came up through the pad he clung to. Which was just as well, as he was shivering in a cold sweat. The other was the feeling of the Jouster's hard, strong hand in the small of his back, once again holding to the belt of his loincloth. Never once did that grip weaken; Khefti-the-Fat might have been strong beneath the blubber, but this man was ten times stronger. And after a few moments of "level flight," Vetch began to believe that at least the Jouster wasn't going to let him fall.

Not that he was enjoying the experience. Given his face-down position, he couldn't open his eyes without staring down—a very, very long way down—at the ground that was now so horribly far beneath them. And he couldn't close his eyes without being horribly aware of every little lurch and lean of the dragon that carried him. His heart was pounding so hard with fear that he thought it might burst through his chest; the wind of the dragon's wing beats drowned out every other sound, and now the pain of those two stripes burned all across the stretched skin of his back, adding to the ache of his fingers, arms, and legs as he clung to the pad.

Of the two options, he finally decided that *not looking* was the lesser of the two evils. So he squeezed his eyes tight anyway and prayed; there wasn't much else he *could* do. He prayed to Altan and Tian gods both, though the prayers were anything but articulate, and certainly not even close to the proper forms, consisting of all the gods' names jumbled up together with *get me down!*

But the gods were with him, it seemed; the flight wasn't a long one. Just about the time when Vetch's muscles were starting to cramp and hurt from the strain of holding on, he felt the dragon dropping, and this time, the falling sensation didn't end in an upward lurch. He cracked open one eye, to see the ground rushing up at them, and squeezed both of them as tightly shut again as he could. If anything, seeing that they were hurtling back *toward* the ground was worse than seeing it so far below them. His heart seemed to stop as the fall went on, and on, and suddenly he couldn't breathe.

Now the great wings thundered all around him, fiercely beating the air, and Vetch redoubled his grip on the pad. He braced for the impact of hitting the ground—

But it never came—

Only sudden stillness, and the snap of wings folding, like canvas or leather snapping in a high wind.

And no movement, no movement at all.

Was it over?

Vetch's eyes flew open involuntarily.

Face-down on the pad as he was, the first thing he saw was the dragon's shoulder, the folded wing, and then, the ground, a *proper* distance away, with a beetle crawling across it that was a real beetle, not an ox reduced to the size of a beetle by distance.

The ground! Never had he been so happy to see a stretch of earth!

The Jouster's hand loosened on Vetch's belt, and without being prompted, Vetch let go of the pad and slid down the dragon's hot, smooth shoulder to the earth. His feet hit the ground together, his legs buckled under him, and he landed on his rump, but he scrambled to his feet quickly, his eyes never leaving his new master, much though he *wanted* to just lie on the ground and embrace it. The Jouster tossed his leg over the saddle and the dragon's neck, and jumped lightly down, giving his dragon a hearty slap on the shoulder. The dragon snorted, and tossed his head a little.

"Now what've you brought back, Ari?" asked a gruff voice from behind Vetch's back. "This can't be a prisoner of your arm, and I doubt it's a spy either."

Vetch didn't turn, though he started a little, and pain arced across his back, marking the path of those stripes; the Jouster had claimed him, the Jouster was his master, and a serf never turned his back on his master (except to be whipped), a lesson that Khefti had driven home with a heavy hand. However, the voice sounded mildly irritated, and the underlying tone conveyed that it was someone in authority.

The Jouster pulled off his helmet, revealing a handsome, if melancholy face, square-jawed, with a great beak of a nose and high cheekbones, brown of eye, and black of hair, as all Tians. He spoke to whoever was behind Vetch; at least Vetch now knew his master's name. *Ari*. "This is my new dragon boy, Haraket. Serf. I claimed him from his master already, so you'll have to send to the Palace to handle the accounting; the boy can probably tell you who the fat blob was. Seems a likely child; he was working like a little ant, when I saw him, filling a cistern with a bucket too big for him. He wasn't afraid of Kashet, anyway, and that's a head start, so far as I'm concerned."

"Not some street trash?" the voice replied dubiously. "He's got fresh stripes—"

"I'm not blind, Haraket, I was there when he got them, for 'letting' me take his bucket and quench my thirst," Ari replied, putting the helmet down, then turning to unbuckle the throat-strap of the saddle. He sounded a trifle irritated, then unexpectedly, the Jouster laughed. "No, he's a serf, not a thief, not a gutter brat. Now the fat slug that was beating him is going to have to find another in his bloodline if the lazy lout wants to hold the land the boy was tied to."

Vetch blinked, to hear his own speculation borne out. So *that* was, indeed, why Khefti had taken him!

Somehow, that only made him feel angrier.

The Jouster's voice took on an interesting tone, very faintly—malicious?—as he continued unbuckling the dragon's saddle straps. "You know, if whoever sold the land divided up it up too much, the other landholders might not have spare serfs in his line to give up to anyone else. He might lose that land when the assessor comes to see about it."

With a fierce surge of longing, Vetch *wished* he could be there when the assessor came. He wanted, *oh*, how he wanted to see Khefti squirm, prevaricate, and sweat! He had sunk all of his savings into that house—or at least, he'd told Vetch that often enough. So if he lost it only because he did not have Vetch anymore, what a supreme bit of revenge that would be!

"But a serf—why not a free boy?" the voice complained. "There must be dozens of free boys you could have from their parents for the asking!"

"Because I'm tired of replacing free boys when they get haughty airs and decide they ought to be something better than 'just' a dragon boy!" Ari snapped, and unbuckled the last strap. He pulled the saddle and the pad that Vetch had clung to off the dragon's back. He turned with it in his hands, and looped all of the straps around it into a compact bundle with a swift and practiced motion.

He dropped the whole thing in Vetch's arms; Vetch had been expecting this from the moment he'd heard what he was to become. A serf, after all, was for the bearing of burdens. He caught it as it dropped, though one of the strap ends hit the ground and his stripes burned again. He was used to working, and working hard, with more whip cuts on his back than two.

The saddle was heavy, at least for him, and he staggered for a moment beneath its weight. It had an additional scent besides that of leather—a hot, metallic scent, with an overtone of spice. The scent of the dragon?

"There, boy—" the Jouster said, in a tone of dismissal, as he bent to pick up his helmet and tuck it under his arm. "You go with Haraket; he'll teach you your business. You'll be living here now."

Jouster Ari stalked off without a backward look, and Vetch turned, the saddle in his arms, to face the person he had not yet seen.

Haraket. Who must be an Overseer.

The man wore a simple white linen kilt, augmented by one striped, multicolored sash around his waist and a second that ran from his right shoulder, across a chest as muscular as any warrior, to the opposite hip. His square head was shaven, though he did not wear a wig, his skin as browned and weathered as that of any farmer, and he wore a hawk-eye amulet of glazed pottery around his neck. He gazed down on Vetch with resignation from beneath a pair of heavy, black eyebrows. But at least he didn't look angry. And he wasn't wearing a whip at his waist either.

"Come on, you," he said, with a sigh. "Since I'm to teach you your business, the best time to start is now." Vetch ducked his head obediently, silently telling himself not to look sullen, and followed as the man strode off across the beaten earth of the courtyard. But he stopped dead at the sound of something large and heavy following *him.*

He turned. The dragon stared down at him, cocking its head quizzically; it had been right on his heels.

"Come *on,* serf boy!" the man snarled, when *he* turned to discover that Vetch was not behind him anymore. "Kashet will come along without being led, much less leashed or chained. He follows me and Ari like a dog, and in time, he'll follow you. Kashet isn't like other dragons, and that's something you'd better keep in mind from this moment on. Ari doesn't need *tala* to control him. You're damned lucky to be Ari's boy; Kashet is a *neferek* to handle compared with the others."

He turned abruptly and strode off again, and Vetch hurried to catch up with him, the dragon following along like a hound. For the moment, the ever-present anger that burned in his belly had retreated before his feeling of complete dislocation and bewilderment.

The dragon had landed in a huge courtyard with enormously high limestone walls around it, "paved" with pale beige earth pounded hard and as flat as a smooth mud brick. There were four entrances or gates to this courtyard, square arches each surmounted by a sculpted and painted symbol of a god, each one right in the middle of each wall. All were tall enough to allow a dragon to pass through them, and broad enough for three. The man marched straight through the one nearest them, which had a hawk eye painted in blue, red, and black carved into the top; Vetch followed, and the dragon followed him.

The colors were bright enough to dazzle the eye; there was nothing like these painted walls in Khefti's village. The painted images leaped out at Vetch, dazzling him. Even Khefti's apprentices never worked with such wonderful colors!

On the other side of the wall were—more limestone-faced walls, equally dazzling in their whiteness. They formed a sort of alley or corridor stretching in either direction; the area was also open to the sky. These walls were not as tall as the ones around the courtyard, and dragon heads peeked over the tops at intervals, peering at them with some unreadable emotion. They weren't all the green and gold of Kashet; there were blue ones in all shades from dark to light, red ones, a purple color, and a pale gold and silver. The colors were dazzling, gorgeous, and they filled his eyes the way that a fine meal filled the appetite. Already, Vetch could tell there was a profound difference between these dragons and Kashet. Ari's dragon had some friendly interest in his eyes when he looked at Vetch—these dragons had the eyes of a feral cat, wary and wild.

He expected noise out of them, based on the way the oxen and donkeys of his father's farm behaved when a stranger came into their yard; to his surprise, there was very little. The dragons hissed and snorted, but there was no bellowing, no growling.

Perhaps they didn't make any louder sound; perhaps they couldn't.

They came to an intersection, and the bald man turned the corner to lead him down another corridor, then another—and just as Vetch thought he was totally lost, turned a final corner that brought them inside another courtyard. He stumbled forward on momentum and blundered into a huge pit that formed the center of the courtyard, a pit that was knee-deep in soft, hot sand. He floundered in the stuff, helplessly, and the man reached out a long arm and hauled him back onto the hard verge. Again, the whip cuts on his back reminded him they were there.

"Stay on the walkway around the edge, boy," the man said, but not unkindly. "That sand will burn you, else, until you're used to it. You'll need to toughen your skin to it."

He'd already found that out; the sand radiated heat upward, as hot as the sun overhead, hotter than the *kamiseen*. His legs stung a little, though he wouldn't have called it a burn, exactly. His feet were too callused to feel much, even heat, from so brief an encounter.

"Put the saddle over there," Haraket continued, pointing to a wooden rack mounted on the wall nearest Vetch. "Untangle the straps and drape them over the rack to dry—dragons don't sweat, but Jousters do. Kashet doesn't need to be chained the way the others do, so you leave him free."

The dragon, ignoring both of them, plunged past them into the center of the room to wallow into the hot sand. Vetch heaved the saddle up onto the rack as he'd been told to do. Under Haraket's watchful eye, he arranged the saddle straps over the bars of the rack, untangling them as he did so. Something told him that the straps shouldn't touch the ground, so he took care that they did not do so. The *kamiseen* did not venture down here, for a wonder, though he could hear it whining above the walls. Not that it was cooler here; not with those hot sands contributing to the fire of the sun overhead.

When he turned to face his instructor, he thought that the man was not displeased. He looked up into Haraket's face, and waited for more instruction. It was not long in coming.

"The first thing you need to get into your mind is this: Kashet and his Jouster will be your sole concern from morning to night," Haraket told him, crossing his muscular arms over his chest, and looking down at him, examining, weighing, assessing. "A dragon boy not only tends to his dragon, he tends to the Jouster that rides him. No one can give you orders but your Jouster and me, unless Ari or I tell you otherwise."

Vetch bobbed his head. "Yes, Overseer," he replied.

Haraket grunted. "Here is the next thing; your Jouster can probably find plenty of other servants if he needs them, but *you* are the only one who is to tend to his dragon. If you have to choose between tending the dragon or the Jouster, there is no choice for you: tend the dragon."

Vetch blinked, but again nodded obediently.

"Now, the first thing you must do, this very moment, is to feed Kashet so that he knows you. Only a dragon boy, or at need, the Overseer or the Jouster will feed a dragon. They are too valuable to let anyone else meddle with them—" Haraket hesitated, then added, "—and other than Kashet, a dragon sharp-set with hunger might—savage—anyone he didn't know who came to feed him. They're wild beasts, very large and very powerful. Don't ever forget that, not for a moment."

Other than Kashet. . . . Well, that was *some* comfort. But the thought still made Vetch gulp nervously. And the way that Haraket had hesitated over his choice of words made him wonder if the man had substituted "savage" for "devour."

Not a comfortable thought at all. What had he fallen into?

"But you'll never need worry about Kashet." That was said with a certainty that quelled a little of Vetch's unease. "Now, come with me. The only way to learn how to feed him is to do so."

Haraket turned and went out the doorway, and Vetch followed. Shortly the man was leading him at a trot down the corridors; Vetch was hard-put to keep up with the Overseer's long legs. But those words worried him. *Only the Jouster or the Overseer or the dragon boy feed a dragon.* So now, he was probably going to be in competition with another boy—who, from the sound of it, would be freeborn—to take care of Ari and his dragon. That could spell nothing but trouble.

"Sir?" he panted, literally the first question he had asked of anyone since the Jouster arrived at the cistern. He had to cough to clear his dry throat, for he still had gotten nothing to drink. "Sir, who is Kashet's dragon boy?"

The Overseer looked down at him, his lips tightening; Vetch flinched. He couldn't imagine how a simple question had made the Overseer so annoyed. "Imbecile," Haraket muttered, and answered more loudly, "*You* are Kashet's boy. Haven't you been listening to me?"

He almost dared to hope. Was it possible? Did this mean that Kashet's care was going to depend entirely on *him?* And if so—

—surely not. Surely, there was someone else, a rival, who would be very angry when he saw that Vetch was a serf. And it could be worse than that, much worse, given what the Jouster had said about "boys getting airs." Perhaps he had selected Vetch in order to humiliate this other boy—who would, of course, take out his humiliation on Vetch whenever the masters' backs were turned. When Khefti beat his apprentices, the apprentices pulled evil tricks on Vetch, it followed as surely as the sun rose. And that was without Vetch being a rival!

"Sir—I meant—who is Kashet's *other* dragon boy?" In his heart was the dread he would have to face a rival who would share his duties and, without a doubt, attempt to make sure that everything that went right reflected to his credit, and all the blame for whatever went wrong landed on Vetch. Some of that must have shown in his expression, as the Overseer's face cleared, and he grunted.

"There is no other dragon boy for Kashet. Jouster Ari and I have been caring for him of late." He grunted again, this time with a distinct tone of disdain. "Jouster Ari's previous boy elected to accept a position in the King's army without notice, and left us cursed shorthanded."

Now all that business about serfs and free boys made sense. . . .

Soldiers had higher status than mere servants . . . and certainly fewer menial duties. *So that's what he meant by "getting airs. . . ."* It would make sense that the Jouster would now prefer to find a boy who had no choice, who could not go elsewhere, except, perhaps, back to Khefti. Which of course, was no choice at all.

"Here—down this way is where the servants from all of the temples bring the sacrifices," Haraket said, making another abrupt turn. This was an alley that looked like a street in the village in a way, though the walls were much taller than any village structures, and the unbroken stretches of wall argued for something the size of a major temple! But the walls along this stretch had doorways and clerestory windows, so it seemed that here the walls *were* part of huge buildings.

Haraket stopped in front of a real, closed door rather than an open archway or simple gap in the walls. He opened it, and with his hand on Vetch's shoulders, shoved him through.

On the other side—

Vetch *almost* broke and ran at the vision of carnage that met his eyes.

The air was full of the metallic scent of blood, so thick he could practically *taste* it, and everywhere he looked there were dead animals . . . *hundreds* of dead animals. Working here were butchers, a dozen of them, naked to the waist, smeared in drying blood, dismembering the corpses and throwing the pieces into bins or barrows beside them.

He was no stranger to the slaughter of farm stock but never on a scale like this, and never anything bigger than a goat.

There were carcasses of enormous cattle, goats, sheep, stacked up as casually as mud bricks, being hacked up by the butchers into hand-sized and head-sized chunks, and the sight made him feel sick and dizzy.

And for a moment, all he could think of was the last sight of his father, covered with his own blood—and the anger surged, but the fear and sickness that followed buried it, and he had to clutch the wall and put his burning back up against it to keep from fainting.

But curiously, as the shock wore off, he saw there was no blood, or very little. "This is all fresh from the Temple sacrifices," Haraket was saying, quite as if he had not noticed Vetch's reaction, as the nearest of the butchers tossed chunks of meat, bone-in, skin-on, into a barrow parked next to his chopping block. "It's a nice piece of economy when you think about it. Every day, hundreds of animals are sacrificed to the gods or cut up for divination ceremonies, but there's no use for the bodies when the blood and spirit have drained away."

As Haraket spoke, Vetch began to get control of himself again. It was only meat. No animals were being killed here. It was only meat.

Of course, the Tians believed that the gods required only the blood and the *mana* of the creatures sacrificed on the altars. There were so many gods, and so many people who needed their favor—he had never actually been to the Avenue of Temples in Mefis, but he had heard tales, heard that there were a hundred gods or more, and almost as many temples, and all of them got sacrifices daily. Not just the bread and beer and honey, the flowers, and the occasional fowl of the little Temple of Hamun, Siris, and Iris in the village, but live beasts, and entire herds of them.

"There aren't enough priests in the world to consume all that flesh," Haraket continued, "Even if they were as fat as houses. So it comes to us, who can certainly use it. That's why they built the Jouster's Compound on the Temple Road. So—ah, he's filled that barrow, now you take it."

The barrow was heavy and hard to push, but Vetch was accustomed to be ordered to do things that were difficult. Haraket watched critically as he grabbed the handles and started shoving, then took the lead. Vetch kept the barrow rolling, following Haraket back to Kashet's pen at a much slower pace than they had taken to get to the butchers' place. Haraket kept his strides short, although he did not bother to look at Vetch more than once or twice.

Already, though, things were profoundly different than they had been under Khefti. The Overseer was not chiding him nor punishing him for taking too long with the barrow. Not once had he been cuffed for stupidity, or had his ears boxed for asking a question. Once again, Vetch dared to hope.

Kashet was watching for them; Vetch saw the now-familiar head peering over the walls long before they got to the opening of the pen. Kashet didn't wait for him to bring the food all the way into the pen either; no sooner had Vetch gotten to the part of the corridor immediately outside the entrance than the dragon snaked his neck out of the doorway and snatched a chunk of meat from the barrow in his powerful jaws, startling Vetch so that he jumped and squeaked involuntarily.

But Haraket gave him a long and measuring look, and after a pause while his heart pounded, Vetch continued pushing the barrow forward, telling himself that if Kashet had wanted to eat *him*, he'd have gone down that long throat while he was still struggling with the saddle.

Kashet plucked chunks from the barrow three more times before Vetch parked it where Haraket pointed. He ate neatly, if voraciously, snatching up a chunk of meat, tossing back his head, and swallowing it whole. Vetch could even see it traveling down his long neck by the bulge it caused.

But he never so much as gave Vetch a threatening or speculative look. Haraket stood at the side of the sand pit with his arms crossed casually over his massive chest, completely relaxed. Vetch tried to copy his example, though his heart raced in his chest.

But Kashet was not in the least interested in Vetch, only what was in the barrow. And in fact, the dragon began to remind Vetch of a falcon, a little, in the neat single-mindedness with which he filled his belly.

"He's an easy charge, so long as you do well by him," Haraket said, speaking quietly. "The only time he's even offered a snap at someone was when the idiot boy forgot his evening feed and he didn't get a meal until morning. By the God Haras, I'd have snapped, too! And the fool blubbed at me after, and thought I'd feel sorry for him!" Haraket snorted. "I pitched *that* one out on his ear myself."

Vetch vowed never to be so much as a moment late with one of Kashet's meals.

Haraket frowned, though not at Vetch. "That was Kashet's first boy; two dragon boys we've lost now, and Kashet's the easiest beast in the compound! He takes a bit more *time* in tending perhaps, but by the gods, it isn't the kind of time you waste with one who's hell-bent on not going where you want him to!" The Overseer sighed. "Maybe it's Ari. He doesn't pet and praise his boys, take them along to feasts, the way some of the others do. And there's no profit to be made out of him. . . ." Haraket turned, ever so slightly, and looked out of the corner of his eye at Vetch.

Vetch kept his mouth shut. Haraket was telling him this for a reason, and if he didn't yet know what the reason was, soon or late he'd find out about it.

Besides, that angry little voice inside him reminded him, *it isn't as if you have a choice. It's here, or Khefti.*

When the barrow was empty, Kashet heaved an enormous sigh, and returned to the hot sand. This time he dug himself a depression in the middle of it, and stretched his entire length within it. Within moments, he was, to Vetch's astonishment, deeply asleep.

"He'll sleep like that until it's time to go out again this afternoon," Haraket said, with a little noise that *sounded* like a fond chuckle. "You couldn't wake him now if you tried. Ari was back early from his patrol—so we've just enough time to get you kitted up and clean and fed before I show you the afternoon jobs." He paused, and raised an eyebrow. "And I believe we should do something about those stripes of yours, too."

Vetch almost gaped at him in shock. Never, ever, had one of his masters offered to do anything about the marks of a beating!

With that, they left Kashet wallowing in the sand, sleeping off his meal in the noontime sun that beat straight down on him, met by the heat radiating up from the sand. Haraket hustled Vetch off again, again to a room, and not an open-air courtyard, though it was not nearly as huge as the butchery. This was a very fine room indeed, with plain, honey-colored limestone walls, narrow openings near the ceiling to bring in air and light while excluding the full cruelty of the sun and the *kamiseen*. It even had a stone floor. The only buildings that Vetch had ever seen that were made of stone like this were temples, and he found himself trying not to gape. Along one side of this room were ranged full terra-cotta jars of water as tall as Vetch was, with wooden or horn ladles hung on their sides. There were also neatly-folded piles of fabric on shelves above the jars, what looked like smaller pottery jars of unguents and possibly soap. And to clinch that this room was for bathing, there was a drain in the center of the floor.

Haraket shoved him inside as he stood hesitantly on the threshold. "Strip," he ordered Vetch, abruptly. "I hope you know how to wash."

He sounded dubious, which woke some smoldering resentment, but Vetch didn't have to be told what to do twice. The last proper bath he'd had was—

He cut off the unwanted memory—of washing off blood. His father's blood. . . .

It was enough that he would have a proper bath *now*.

He pulled off the rope belt and the rags, and hesitated with them in one hand. Surely he should wash them?

"Feh, boy, you don't think that's worth *saving*, do you?" Haraket barked with distaste. "Throw it there, and get on with it!"

He pointed to a rubbish pile, and not at all loath to rid himself of the rags, Vetch tossed them aside. He headed straight for the water jars and ladled dipperfuls of water over himself, scrubbing himself down with a handful of lye soap and a loofah sponge. And he scrubbed every inch of himself as well, fingernails, toenails, even his back, though the soap got in the cuts and stung until he had to bite his lip, trying to get stains off his legs, wishing he had a razor so he could shave his skull bare as his father had used to do for him. . . .

He scrubbed himself twice over, rinsing himself with more water from the jars, and was about to start on a third round when Haraket grunted. "That'll do, boy. Any more, and you'll have the skin off. I want you clean, not raw."

Haraket tossed him a folded piece of cloth to dry himself with, then another bundle of fabric when he'd done with that; he caught it, and unfolded it to find, not just a loincloth, but a proper linen kilt, such as he had not worn in—

—in too long. Not since the moment he had been made a serf.

But he still remembered how to wrap a simple kilt, or his hands did, anyway. Then, skin tingling and arrayed in that real linen kilt of his own, he turned obediently to the Overseer for the expected inspection.

Haraket surveyed him, and nodded with satisfaction. "Not so bad," he said, with reluctant approval. "You clean up better than I'd have guessed. By the way, dragon boys don't wear sandals; you'd lose them in the sand wallows. From the look of your feet, they're tough enough. Now, turn your back to me."

Vetch did so, as Haraket got one of the jars of unguent from a shelf, and applied it generously to the whip marks.

And the pain vanished, replaced entirely by a cool tingling.

Vetch couldn't believe it, and as Haraket put the jar back on the shelf, he turned, wondering if he should thank the Overseer.

But Haraket forestalled him with a question. "Hungry?"

Vetch tried, tried *so* hard, not to look too eager, but—

—well, he was only a little boy, after all, and not too practiced in disguising his expression except by the simple expedient of staring at his feet. Haraket, for the first time that day, actually smiled.

"Now it is me who is the fool. Of course you are. You look like a sack of gnawed bones. Come along."

Haraket strode out of the bathing chamber and Vetch scrambled after him, beginning to feel very dazed by this marked change in his fortunes. This morning, he had been filthy, starving, and about to be beaten. Now he was clean, well-clothed, and so far, he hadn't encountered anyone who was likely to have as heavy a hand with the stick as Khefti.

"What's your name, boy?" the Overseer asked gruffly. "I can't keep calling you 'boy,' or I'll have half the compound answering when I shout at you."

"Vetch, sir," Vetch replied, taking two steps for every one of Haraket's.

"And who was your master, Vetch? Ari's going to want that assessor out on him by tomorrow, I expect, so I had better get that sorted by this afternoon." Haraket gave Vetch another of those sidelong looks. "That's what I'm for; seeing the tallies are all correct, all the chickens put to roost."

"Khefti-the-Fat, sir. He's a potter and brick maker with six apprentices, and he has a *tala* field outside his house in the village of Mu-asen—" for a moment, Vetch worried that this wouldn't be enough to identify his former master, but Haraket interrupted him.

"That's enough, Vetch. There can't be more than one fat potter with a *tala* field within a hop of Mefis. The King's assessor will find him."

And then, as Haraket turned to open yet another door and he

followed, he discovered that he had been led straight into paradise.

Or if not *quite* paradise, it was as near as Vetch had ever been to it.

"Paradise" was a kitchen courtyard of lime-washed mud-brick walls, shaded from the pitiless sun by bleached canvas awnings strung between the courtyard walls, additionally supported by ropes crossing underneath them, tethered to the other walls. It was full of simple wooden benches and tables set with reed baskets heaped with bread, pottery jars of beer with the sides beaded with condensation, wooden platters of cheese, baked latas roots, and sweet onions. And little bowls of the juice and fat of roast duck, goose, and chicken, such as he had not tasted since the moment he became a serf. The aroma of all that food made him feel faint and dizzy again.

He stared at it, not daring to go near, hoping beyond hope that he would be allowed the remains whenever Haraket and the other masters were finished eating.

And then his stomach growled, and hurt so much it brought tears to his eyes for a moment. And the anger returned, anger at these arrogant Tians for making him stand in the presence of plenty that *he* wasn't to touch—

"Well, what are you waiting for, boy?" Haraket said impatiently. "Sit down! Eat! You do me no good by fainting from hunger!"

And he shoved Vetch forward with a hand between his shoulders, making it very clear that this was not some cruel joke.

Vetch stumbled toward the table and took a seat on the end of the nearest bench, hardly daring to believe what he'd heard.

He looked up at Haraket again, just to be sure. The Overseer made an abrupt gesture with one hand; Vetch took that as assent.

He managed, somehow, to react like a civilized and mannerly farm boy and not cram his mouth full with both his hands. It took all of the restraint he had learned at Khefti's hands, though, for the aromas filled his nose, and the nearest platter of loaves filled his sight, and his mouth was watering so much he had to keep swallowing or he'd drool like a hungry dog.

He took one of the little loaves though his hands shook, tore it neatly in half. Helped himself to a single piece of cheese, to *latas* and onion, and a small jar of beer. He laid all of this on the wooden table in front of him, and only then began eating; the taste of fresh bread nearly made him weep with pleasure. It was still warm from the oven, the crust crisp and not stale, the insides tender and not dry, and it was three times the size of his ration under Khefti. Then he dipped the other half of the bread in the rich fat, and took a bite, and *did* weep, for the taste exploded on his tongue, and with it came all the memories of what home on a feast day had been like. . . .

He glanced back at Haraket, but the man was gone. Which meant—his mind reeled with the thought—which meant that he was *expected* to eat his fill, and no one would stop him!

But the memory of a day during the rains when he'd found a discarded basket of water-soaked loaves in the market warned him against gorging. That day had been a disaster; he'd eaten himself sick, and had spent a horrible night, stifling his groans as his belly ached. He'd gotten punished twice, in fact, once with a bellyache, and the next day when his exhaustion made him sluggish and he'd soon collected a set of stripes from Khefti. He would eat slowly, and yes, eat his fill (or as near as he was allowed) but he would not stuff himself, or he would be very sick, and his new masters would surely be angry at him. So far, no one had been ready to add to his stripes. He would not let his greed give them an opportunity.

When he'd finished the first round of bread, he started on the cheese and onions, and about that point, the other dragon boys started coming in.

A group of four came in together, chattering away. Like him, all were clothed in simple linen kilts and barefoot. Like Haraket, all wore a hawk-eye talisman at their throats. They were older, taller and stronger than Vetch was, though; and well-fed, and moving with the kind of casual freedom that no serf or slave ever displayed. And unlike him, if their hair wasn't cut short, their heads were shaved altogether. That was the mark of an Altan serf; long, unbarbered hair, like some wild barbarian tribesman from the desert, like one of the Bedu, the nomads who had no king, only tribal rulers. Tians, the masters, shaved their heads, or trimmed their hair at chin length.

He made himself as small as he could on the bench.

They stopped dead at the sight of him, and eyed him with curiosity. "Who's that?" one asked of the largest of the four.

"Kashet's boy," said the other, with a knowing glance. "I heard Jouster Ari brought in a serf over his saddle bow that he'd decided to make into his new dragon boy."

"Huh," the first replied, and looked down his long nose at Vetch, his black eyes narrowing with superior arrogance. "Mind your manners, Kashet's boy," he said loftily to Vetch. "We're all free here but you, so remember your place."

Vetch ducked his head. "Yes, sir," he murmured, and that seemed to satisfy the other, for he crowded onto the bench near his friend and paid no more heed to Vetch.

Vetch felt his anger churn inside him again. They were *just* like Khefti's apprentices, worthless lot that they were! They thought that the worst of them was superior enough that Vetch should offer his head to their feet! None of *them*, likely, had ever been landowners! Had he not been born free, as free as any of them, and son to a family who had owned their land for generations?

But he had not lived the last few seasons without learning that when a freeman and a serf had conflicts, it was always the serf who lost.

So he kept his eyes fastened on his food, kept his anger in check, and hastened to make himself even smaller. He watched the others when he went for more food, always snatching his hand back empty if it looked as if one of the free boys was interested in the platter or basket that he was reaching for.

But even so, for the first time in a very, very long time, he was able to eat as much as he wanted. In fact, he had not really eaten like this very often back when his father was alive, for even a farmer did not have the means to produce a seemingly never-ending stream of food and drink at a meal. Only a great village feast would bring forth this sort of abundance. Kitchen girls—slaves, he thought by their neck rings, though they were the sleekest and best-looking such slaves *he* had ever seen—kept coming out of the kitchen with more food, more beer; no matter how much the boys ate, there was always more. One of the older girls seemed to have taken a liking to him; she made certain that there were platters within his reach, and replaced the empty jar at his hand with a full one. He thanked her shyly, and she winked at him and hurried back into the kitchen.

Haraket came for him about the time that he had decided he couldn't safely eat another morsel. That was long before the other boys finished—but then, he'd had a head start on them, and *they* were lingering over their food.

The boys hushed their chatter when Haraket appeared in the doorway, and watched as Vetch scrambled to his feet in response to the beckoning hand. The chatter began again as soon as Vetch cleared the doorframe, following Haraket, and his ears burned with embarrassment and resentment, imagining what they were saying about him. Making fun of his looks, his intelligence, his imagined habits. Comparing him to the brutes of the desert, the beasts of the fields.

It doesn't matter, he told himself, though in truth, it did. They were no better born than he! Tians were by no means morally or mentally superior to Altans! The Altans were the older race, and were dwelling in civilized surroundings when the Tians were grubbing *latas* roots with pointed sticks!

But—"Don't pay any attention to those idle lizards," Haraket said dismissively. "There are three creatures here you have to please; Jouster Ari, myself, and Kashet. No one else matters."

Easy for him to say, Vetch thought, recalling all the nasty tricks that used to be played on him by Khefti's apprentices and the freeborn boys of the village. He was surely in for more of the same from this lot.

But Haraket might have had the mind-reading power of a Clear-Sighted Priestess, for he seemed to pluck *that* thought right out of Vetch's skull. "Freeborn, serf, or slave, a dragon boy is a dragon boy, and if they try any tricks with you, *you* come to *me*," Haraket said, with some little force. "Remember what I said; your duty is your Jouster and Kashet, first to last. Anything, *anything*, that interferes with you doing that duty is an offense against your Jouster and his dragon, and believe me, boy, we take that *very* seriously. Beating is the least of what I'll deal out to a troublemaker."

"What?" he blurted, so taken aback that he spoke the word aloud. And winced involuntarily, expecting a buffet for his insubordination.

But Haraket didn't cuff him. "You please me, your Jouster, and your dragon," he repeated once again. "And that is all you need to concern yourself with. *But* don't antagonize the brats," Haraket added. "Have the proper attitude. They *are* freeborn, and you're not."

"Yes, sir," he murmured. That was more like what he'd expected to hear. . . .

"But if you're keeping your proper place, and *they* interfere with you, I'll give them something to weep about," Haraket said, and it sounded to Vetch as if a tinge of grim satisfaction colored the words. "They'll be cherishing stripes for a week, if they harm you. But enough of that; you'd best be sure you're pleasing me and Ari and Kashet," Haraket continued. "And believe me, there's a lot to do to please us."

Of that, at least, he had no doubt.

THREE

BACK and forth Haraket led him, showing him where the Jousters' quarters were, the armory, the little Temple of the god Haras, the Jousters' particular patron. Vetch was beginning to get the sense of how to navigate around the complex; really, once he got over his bedazzlement at the size and scale and luxury of this place, it wasn't any more difficult than negotiating the tangle of streets and houses of Khefti's village. It had, at first blush, seemed a maze, but now he realized that the dragon pens, at least, were all at the eastern end of the compound, with the great landing court right in the middle of them. Everything else was west of the pens and court, and the area closest to the pens was devoted to the butchery. So long as he kept going east from wherever he started, he'd come into the area where the dragons were housed, so even though the complex was the size of several villages, he couldn't get entirely lost.

And the walls were not bare and featureless either; he hadn't paid much attention before because he had been concentrating on Haraket, but now he saw that at every intersection of corridors, on the walls at the corners, there were engraved images of gods, all different. Nearest to Kashet's pen, where there was an inter-section of two corridors, the gods upon the east-running corridor were the fat little dwarf god of good fortune and fertility, Khas, and on the north-running one the charming little goddess of the dawn, Noshet, with her beautifully plumed wings spread wide against the sand-colored wall. It wasn't lost on him, when he real-ized each corridor was marked by a god, that he could navigate among this maze of corridors by means of these carvings.

The dragons were not peering over their walls now; in fact, there was no sign of them at all, and when Haraket beckoned to him to follow into his own dragon's pen, he saw that Kashet was still drowsing in his sand wallow. "It will shortly be time for the Jousters to take their second patrols of the day, since there is not, at the moment, any actual *war* taking place."

Tell that to my people, Vetch thought, the anger that was always with him sullenly flaring. But Haraket was still speaking—ordering him, rather.

"Now, *you* come saddle Kashet again," Haraket told him, as Vetch stood gingerly on the edge of the sand wallow. Kashet was already easing himself up out of the hot sand, slowly and reluc-tantly, making little grunting sounds. "Go over to the saddle stand and call him. Say, 'Kashet, stand,' and make it sound like you mean it."

Vetch took his place beside the wooden rack holding the saddle and harness. He glanced at Haraket, but got no clues from the overseer's expression. *Make it sound like you mean it.* Well, order-ing an ox around, or a goat, you had to sound firm. But it had been very, very long since he had been permitted to give orders even to an animal. He wasn't even used to raising his voice. . . .

Finally, he tried to imagine how he would feel if *he* were the master, and it was one of those boys who had sneered at him back at the kitchen who was the serf. He tried to think of himself order-ing the boy to fetch something. "Kashet!" he called, his voice sounding shrill in his own ears. But at least it didn't sound uncer-tain. "Stand!"

Kashet snorted; the snort sounded amused. But the dragon came readily enough, and stood towering above him, neck craned over, head looking curiously down at him. Again, he was struck by the heat of the dragon's body; it was as if he stood beside a clay bread oven during the baking.

Kashet looked even taller than he recalled. He couldn't have touched the dragon's shoulder even if he'd stood on tiptoe.

Now, how was he going to get the saddle on the beast when Kashet's shoulder was higher than Haraket's head?

Haraket watched him, eyes narrowed, waiting—for what? The overseer passed a hand over the top of his shaved head, and Vetch *knew* that he was waiting for Vetch to do something.

Was Haraket waiting for him to deduce how to handle the dragon from the clues he'd been given?

It wasn't fair—but it *was* a test of whether or not he could think for himself. He looked around, and couldn't see anything to climb onto in order to get the saddle onto the dragon's back. If he couldn't get the saddle *up* on Kashet's back, could he get Kashet to come *down* to him?

"Kashet!" he shouted, hearing his voice squeak a little at the end. "Down!"

And that, it seemed, was the answer.

With a grunt, the dragon knelt at the side of the sand pit, just the forequarters, putting his back just low enough for Vetch to reach. He heaved the saddle off the rack, taking care not to tangle the straps. He remembered how it had lain on the dragon's back, just in front of the wings; he thought he remembered how all of the straps buckled. He manhandled the saddle over Kashet's neck, wiped sweat from his forehead with the back of his hand, and took a quick glance at Haraket.

The overseer looked satisfied. Or at least, he wasn't frowning. So that was probably it; but Haraket wasn't going to give him any more clues. He would either manage to carry his orders out on his own, or—

—or back to Khefti.

But it couldn't be that hard; it couldn't be any more complicated than harnessing a donkey to carry a load, or an ox to the plow. It ought to be logical. There were just not that many ways that you could buckle a harness!

He didn't think Haraket expected or wanted him to fail, either, which was a refreshing change. No, he got the feeling that Haraket merely wanted to see if he could do the job, how quickly, and how much help he would need.

Maybe, whispered that angry voice, *he expects that you're going to botch it because you're an Altan barbarian. . . .*

Well, if that was the case—Haraket would find out he was better and smarter than those freeborn Tians.

While Kashet was still crouched, Vetch took the opportunity to buckle the highest neck strap on the saddle, the one that carried what he thought was the breast strap fastened in the middle of it. Then he ordered, this time with more confidence, "Kashet! Up!"

The dragon stood, and Vetch puzzled out the straps that fastened the front of the saddle at the neck and throat. But the rest of the harness was not immediately clear, and he paused with a strap in his hand. There were a *lot* of straps.

Maybe there were a lot of different ways you could fasten a harness. Or, at least, this particular harness.

"Find the mate on the other side," Haraket prompted. "And bring them under the forelegs to that breastband that's sewn to the neckband. That's the fat strap that should follow his keelbone. After you fasten the neckband, the straps are always in pairs."

So Haraket *was* going to give him some hints! He wouldn't have guessed *that* from the Overseer's stony expression. He relaxed a little, and continued his task with more confidence.

With a few more such hints, Vetch got the harness fastened, then without further prompting, went over all the straps again, cinching them down as he recalled his father harnessing the donkey for carrying a load to market. When he glanced again at Haraket, the overseer wasn't frowning at all; in fact, there was no mistaking his look of satisfaction.

When Vetch finished, Haraket came over and double-checked the fit of each strap. Some he tightened further, but the ones across the neck, he loosened.

"Here, the neckband—it's more to carry the breastband than anything else," Haraket told him. "You want it loose enough to slip two fingers under it. But here—" he moved down to two of the straps that passed in front of Kashet's legs. "—these need to be as tight as you can pull them. This one here, too—" Vetch watched him closely, making mental notes. What he *wanted* was to be free of masters, but—short of a miracle—that wasn't going to happen. Failing that, this was the best place he'd ever been in, and he *did not* want to be sent away.

Especially not back to Khefti, for he was fairly certain that if Khefti was ever presented with the opportunity to get his hands on Vetch again, what he would contrive for the remainder of Vetch's life did not bear thinking about. It would be so bad, in fact, that Vetch's previous existence as Khefti's serf would seem pleasant in comparison.

So I will serve Kashet, and my Jouster, and they will never want another dragon boy, he vowed to himself, watching how Haraket slid two fingers between the harness and Kashet's neck to check the fit.

Jouster Ari reappeared at that point, and Haraket stepped back abruptly. Vetch scrambled back out of the way, certain that the Jouster would find something wrong. All of this would come tumbling down, and with a word the Jouster would send him back to Khefti, or at least order Haraket to beat him.

But after an inspection of the harness, Ari gave a brief nod to Haraket, handed the Overseer his lance, and slapped Kashet on the shoulder. Without a command, Kashet extended his foreleg to the Jouster; Ari used it as a step, and with its aid, vaulted into the saddle. Haraket handed the lance back to Ari, and the Jouster set the lance into the socket at his belt, and took a firm grip on the handhold at the front of the saddle.

Warned now by his own experience, Vetch shielded his eyes;

Kashet spread his wings and leaped upward, and in a storm of sand and hot wind that buffeted Vetch and made him shelter his face in the crook of his elbow, the dragon vaulted into the clear blue of the heavens. The dragon and rider wheeled above the pen for a moment as Kashet gained height, looking like a jewel-bright painting against the cloudless blue of the heavens.

Then, abruptly, they side-slipped to the north and were gone.

"Don't just stand there gawking, get that shovel!" Haraket barked, and Vetch hastily looked back down and saw where the overseer was pointing. "Once Kashet's out of the pen, you clean it, clean it thoroughly, and immediately!"

At Haraket's direction, Vetch got the shovel and the barrow he'd used to bring the meat, and began the cleaning. Kashet used a second pit cut into the earth and rock to one side of the huge wallow, smaller than the wallow and not nearly as hot, for a privy. Like a cat, perhaps, for the droppings were neatly buried and the smell minimal. Not unpleasant either; they smelled a bit acrid, but not fetid. The droppings themselves, black, hard as stones and round, were about the size and weight of a melon.

"Don't touch those with your bare hands," Haraket warned, as he carried one in the shovel to the barrow. "Something about them burns the skin."

He took Haraket's word for it, though he was surprised, and couldn't imagine what could do the burning. The droppings were actually cooler than the nesting sand, so it evidently wasn't heat that would burn the skin. Perhaps it was something like natron, only stronger.

"This stuff is worth its weight in silver," Haraket said warningly, as Vetch pushed the barrow at his direction. "You account for every dropping to me, and *I* account for it to the priests; whatever they use it for, it's important to them. There's a tally board where you'll be taking it."

So there was; Vetch unloaded his barrow, and put a mark on the board for every dropping before he went back for a second load. There weren't nearly enough droppings piled in the courtyard where he upended his barrow, given all of the dragons that were here; someone must come and take the stuff away pretty promptly.

Vetch didn't ask what dragon dung was good for; if it was priestly business, it was just as well not to know, and that was doubly true when the priests were Tian. They were likely to take an innocent question poorly if it came from someone like him.

The sun, which had been directly overhead when he began the task of cleaning out the pen, had traveled westward, and the corridors were now shadowed by the high walls. That certainly made his job a little easier, although the *kamiseen* managed to drop down and began to scour its way through the complex, bringing the fire of the desert with it. Still, he was not looking forward to nightfall, for it was as cold at night during the dry season as it was hot during the day. Once the sun god left for his nightly journey through the underworld, he took all of the warmth with him.

I wonder where I'm to sleep? he thought, suddenly, when it occurred to him that the day was more than half spent. He hadn't seen anything that looked like a sleeping pallet since he'd arrived here. He really didn't want to sleep where the rest of the dragon boys slept; he'd lie awake all night waiting for them to do something to him. But he probably wasn't going to get a choice about it either. Unless—they might have other serfs here, or they might have him sleep with the slaves. That wouldn't be bad. At least they wouldn't have a reason to plague him.

When he tipped out the last of the droppings on the pile, Haraket signed to him to leave the barrow over to one side of the room. "Someone else will clean the barrow. Now *you* have lessons that go along with tending your dragon. You'll be seeing to Kashet's harness and saddle, so now it's time for you to begin to learn to clean and mend harness," said Haraket, and led him off again into the maze of corridors.

At the very edge of the area of the pens, just past the butchery, where pens and open courtyards gave way to real buildings with roofs and doors, was his next destination. Now that the noon meal was over, there was more activity here, and along the corridor marked by the sign of Teleth, the wise god of scribes and engravers, it now appeared that the doors there marked a series of workshops. This was where Haraket led Vetch, who was certain now that he could at least find his way back to Kashet's pen from where he was.

"Hu, Shobek," Haraket called, pushing open a door to a dim room, full of shadows, that smelled of leather and leather oil. It was also full of dragon boys, presided over by a dour old man.

"Hu, Haraket," replied the old man, a thin and wiry individual with a leather cap fitted over his shaven skull. "The new one?"

"The same," Haraket replied, and before Vetch could ask anything, turned on his heel and strode away, leaving Vetch standing just inside the doorway.

This time, it appeared, his work was to be accomplished under someone else's supervision besides Haraket. The old man examined Vetch for a moment; the other dragon boys here were ranged in neat rows all down the room, each sitting cross-legged on a brown reed mat, each one with his hands full of some piece of harness or other leather work, head bent in concentration. Clearly this man Shobek had charge over them all, and enforced discipline completely. The other boys might glance up at Vetch, but it was a brief glance, and each one quickly returned his gaze to the work in his hands, lest the Overseer of this workshop catch him staring too long. The air was redolent with the pleasant smell of new leather, of leather oil, and of some spice he couldn't identify.

"Ever worked leather?" the old man growled. And when Vetch shook his head, he just sighed, as if he had not expected any other answer. "You are the newest and most ignorant of everyone here, boy," the man said roughly. "You have a lot to learn, and you'd better make up your mind to learn it quickly. I'll have no idlers in my workshop. Show me your hands."

Quickly, Vetch stretched out both his hands, grateful that he'd gotten that bath. His nails might be broken, his palms callused hard, but at least both were clean. The old man grunted.

"Good. You're no stranger to work. And you've got clever, small hands. I can make some use of you now, so mind what you're told, for I won't tell you twice."

Within moments, Vetch was sitting cross-legged on a reed mat of his own, discharging the dirtiest job of all, that of cleaning the saddles.

Old saddles, actually, with the leather cracking and going dry; evidently he wasn't to be trusted yet with saddles that weren't all but ruined.

"No one is using these at the moment," Shobek said, as he piled four of them beside Vetch's mat. "Clean and get these fit to repair, and then I'll put you on Kashet's spare harnesses."

As Shobek instructed him, he was relieved to find that there was not much that was going to be *difficult* about this job. His first job was to clean the saddles, using some concoction in a pottery jar, his second, to oil, and try and revive the elderly leather by rubbing in a compound of wax and tallow, with precious myrrh added to give it fragrance.

And it was myrrh that his nose had detected, though he hadn't recognized what it was at first, for its signature aroma had been mingled with the honey scent of wax and the heavy scent of the oil.

It wasn't the hardest task he had ever had, by any stretch of the imagination. And although at this point, the hottest part of the day, anyone who wasn't a servant was lying down in a cool room or trying to cool off by bathing in a pool, this wasn't a *bad* job. He was sitting down; he was in a cool, dim room. The thick mud-brick walls kept the heat out, and the stone floor cooled things further. There was a certain sensuous pleasure in working with the leather, watching it slowly revive under his attentions, the fragrant myrrh soothing his senses. He knew what myrrh was, of course; on feast days even Khefti would get a cone of perfume scented with it or some other fragrance and wear it all day on top of his coarse, braided horsehair wig. The Tians loved perfumes and unguents, and someone who did not bathe at least twice daily and who smelled of grease and sweat as Khefti did was regarded with unconcealed disdain. So on festival days, in the hopes of mingling with his betters, Khefti would bathe like a concubine and lavish as much myrrh on himself as he could afford. Not that it did much good. Not all the perfume cones in the world could cover up the rancid scent of Khefti-the-Fat. . . .

There were other spices in the wax as well, though none as strong as the myrrh. Perhaps this was what gave the dragons their pleasant scent.

The saddles were not large or heavy, as Vetch already knew; nothing like the kind of bulky chair he would have envisioned for riding a dragon. Instead, they were a kind of thick pad of kapok-stuffed leather molded by time and use to the shape of a particular dragon's shoulders, with straps and braces, handholds, carry pads and harness straps firmly sewn onto them. The ones in his charge were very old and much abused; stiff and dried out, the pale brown leather cut up here and there, the harnesses snapped, the sinew stitching torn loose, the stuffing coming out in places. The other boys were doing the skilled work, that of replacing harness straps and restitching and patching. All he had to do was to untangle straps, which were generally stiff and dried hard, then remove as many of the broken ones as he could, and get the leather clean and supple again.

It wasn't easy work, cleaning these filthy saddles and harnesses, but compared to hauling water in the full sun and the *kamiseen* wind to nourish the *tala*, it was practically like having a holiday. For once, he wasn't concentrating on the curse on Khefti, nor on not spilling a bucket. He found himself half entranced while he worked, thinking of nothing at all, merely listening to the other dragon boys chatter softly to one another. Evidently, so long as they got their quota of mending done and didn't talk too loudly, their Overseer didn't care if they gabbled away.

But then, they were all freeborn. Freeborn boys obviously had fewer constraints on their behavior, even when working at a task, than serfs. There were limits on how much they could be pun-

ished, and for what infractions; freeborn boys could leave an ap-
prenticeship if their parents agreed, so a Master had better not
beat them more often than their fathers did if he wanted to keep
them. The more difficult the job they were apprenticed to, the
more freedom they tended to have, so given how difficult the
dragons were to work with, the dragon boys probably got away
with a great deal.

Of Khefti's apprentices, two were learning the skilled trade of
the potter, the other four, the far-less-skilled task of the brick
maker. The pottery apprentices lorded it over the other four, who
got no relief even when Khefti took his daily nap. They had a
canopy to work under; Khefti deemed that sufficient for their
needs.

Vetch wondered, though, whether *dragon boy* counted as being
an apprentice, or being a real job. Or were there degrees within
the task—that you were the equivalent of an apprentice until you
became an Overseer, or even a Jouster? There certainly weren't
any dragon boys over the age of fifteen or sixteen, not if he was
any judge of ages.

This lot ignored his presence altogether, which suited him.
They spoke of other boys, of their families, of what they planned
to do this evening when the dragons slept and their duties were
over. It astonished him, a little, to hear how *very* much they were
allowed to do in their free time, for Khefti's apprentices were permitted to leave their Master's home only to go straight back to
their own.

But the dragons didn't fly by night. Perhaps they couldn't.
When the sun-god descended, and it grew cold, perhaps they
slept. That would mean that there wasn't much in the way of
duties for a dragon-boy after sundown.

Certainly all of them had plans to enjoy themselves. Some of
them planned to bathe in certain pools in the complex, some to
fish by moonlight, and a favored few, older, and who actually had
real money to spend, intended to visit a wine house outside the
complex.

Then some of the talk turned to certain dragons and Jousters, and the nobles of the King's court who had an interest in them.

"The next time Lord Seftu invites Kest-eman for a feast, I'm to come along," boasted one, to the apparent envy of his peers.

"Lord Seftu!" exclaimed a boy with who should not have adopted the shaved-head style, for it made his exceedingly round head look like a grape on a slender stem. "They say he has acrobats *and* dancers *and* musicians at all of his feasts! And river horse, and bustard and sturgeon and honeyed dates stuffed with nuts—"

"And boating on his pleasure lake by moonlight," chimed in another, enviously. "And every guest has a serving maid of his own."

"He's been to every practice," the first boy said smugly. "And he's won a great deal of money on Besere, thanks to what *I* told him. He told Besere that he wants to reward both of us."

"On top of what he's given you already?" exclaimed the round-headed boy. "Shekabis, when we're done, can I touch you? Maybe some of that luck will rub off!"

Vetch learned massive amounts about the Jousters and their lives just by listening. The nobles, it seemed—some of them, anyway—found it entertaining to watch the jousting practices. They would wager on the Jousters as they practiced the skills that made them what they were, sometimes tipping the dragon boys for information on the health and temper of dragons and their riders. Now Vetch had at least one minor question answered. So *that* was where boys were getting their money!

And—as he stretched his ears shamelessly to listen—he soon found that wasn't the only way they got money to spend.

"Lady Heetah's getting desperate. She gave me a whole silver piece to carry a message to Ari this morning," one of the older boys said, with a sly grin for the others. Even Vetch knew what that meant. Ladies didn't ask boys to carry messages to men unless they were in the midst of (or wanted to instigate) a love affair. It sounded as if this Lady Heetah was in the latter position.

"And did you?" asked the round-headed boy, with a lift of his lip that suggested that Lady Heetah was throwing away good money on a hopeless cause.

"I left it in his rooms, when I went to clean Abat-nam's." The first boy shrugged. "Who's to say if he even looked at it? Or cared, if he saw it. She should have learned better by now; she sent me on a fool's errand, that one. But she pays well."

"Besotted." The second shook his head. "Stupid women. As well court the image of Ta-Roketh in the Temple of Kernak as Ari. Actually, you'd be better off courting the statue. You might get a miracle and the image might fill with the god and respond to your invitation."

"That's what Lesoth says," another of the older boys nodded wisely. "Ari's never paid attention to court ladies. Oh, he likes his women, well enough—he's never even looked at a pretty boy— but the court ladies haven't a chance with him. Paid night blossoms, yes; Ari is like any other man with them."

One who had been silent until then rolled his eyes. "Like any other man? Like a Bull of Hamun, you mean! Lesoth says that Ari's got a mighty reputation in Seles-teri's wine shop! The dancing girls there all know *him* well!"

The others laughed knowingly, and Vetch gathered from that comment that "Seles-teri's wine shop" was one of those where the dancing girls performed horizontally as well as vertically.

"But ladies," the boy continued, shaking his head. "Ladies might as well throw their silver down a well as waste it on paying us to take love poems to Ari. Married or not, it doesn't matter. He won't so much as look at them, no matter how they fling themselves at him."

"So they might as well give their silver to us as not," a third put in, impudently. "It doesn't hurt Ari, and a foolish woman can't hold onto money anyway. *I'll* carry love poems for them, aye, and even put them in his bed!"

A fourth snorted. "No more chance of that with the new boy around. It's *him* who'll get the silver now."

But the second shook his head. "Na, na, the silver will stay in their purses, worse luck. You know they won't trouble to bribe a serf, they'll just order him to do what they want. Not that it'll make any difference. Four years, I've served Jouster Kelandek, and *he* says that Ari's the smartest of the whole pack of Jousters. That Ari prefers paid women, because he can send them off when his pleasures are over, and no jealousies and weeping, after, and that if *he* had any sense, he'd follow Ari's example, instead of getting entangled with spoiled cats."

They seemed to have forgotten Vetch's presence entirely—or else, because he was a serf, they paid no more heed to him than if he'd been a piece of furniture. Which was fine by Vetch. The more he could overhear about his new master, the better.

And the boys continued on in that vein, each one with another tidbit or two, about the ladies who had tried to attract Ari's attentions, about the dancing girls and pleasure women (the higher-class ones, called "night blossoms") that Ari had brought back to his rooms after an evening spent outside the compound or when a troupe was sent in by the Great King or the Vizier to entertain the Jousters as a reward. It was very soon apparent to Vetch, though, that despite all the innuendoes and sly hints, the other dragon boys knew little more about what happened in Ari's quarters then than did the ladies who sought in vain for the Jouster's favors. There was much speculation and very little substance in what they said.

It was also quite clear that this—the carrying of messages from ladies who sought the company of a Jouster—was the easiest source of some, if not all, of the dragon boys' ready money. The messages were clandestine, of course. Those ladies that were married needed to take care that their lords and husbands didn't find out that they fancied a Jouster. Those that were concubines needed to be nearly as careful, for though they might not have the position of wife, their lords would take it very much amiss to discover they were offering those favors to another which should have been reserved to their lord and master. Only the unmarried and unmated ladies could distribute their favors freely, and even then, care had to be taken that a jealous suitor or wrathful father did not get wind of a romance. The Jousters were a class apart, but that didn't mean that parents of rank wanted a love affair going on with one. Jousters had no real wealth of their own unless it came to them from their fathers, no land, no property, nothing of substance to offer a wife and her family in the way of an alliance. Everything they enjoyed was provided by the King, and came back to the King if they died. They might, if they were notable fighters, survive long enough to get the Gold of Favor as well as the Gold of Honor, and perhaps be ennobled and be given a house and land. But given the nature of the way that they fought, defeat was usually fatal, and few lived to retire with honor.

All this, Vetch had already known; the Jousters were famous across the length and breadth of Tia, and if they weren't individually public heroes, lionized and lauded whenever they set foot outside the compound, it was because the Great King wished them to be thought of as his personal force, much like the King's Regiment, not as individuals. In the rigid hierarchy of Tian society, the Jousters were unique and occupied a niche that was only just short of ennobilization, had many of the material privileges of being noble, yet were utterly dependent on the King for those privileges.

It slowly dawned on Vetch that the Jousters were, in their way, no freer than he was. If he was tied to a piece of land, *they* were tied to the dragons. They could serve only the Great King, and all that they had, they owed to him. They actually *owned* very little, for most of what they had was also the Great King's. And if they lived in great luxury, well, they paid for that in the risking of their lives every day.

As the others nattered on, Vetch gleaned some idea of just what that meant.

A lucky shot from below, or a particularly skilled marksman could bring a rider down. When dragons ventured too near the ground, they could be hurt, and when injured, not all the *tala* in the world would control them—and usually the first thing to go was the saddle and rider. Riders simply fell from the backs of their dragons all the time; sometimes in combat with the Jousters of Alta, but just as often in simple practice. The dragons did not always cooperate with their riders; sometimes riders were thrown, and sometimes there were midair collisions, in the course of which a Jouster could be thrown from his saddle.

He gathered that there were nets of some sort intended to catch a downed Jouster if he fell in practice, but sometimes the accidents happened when the Jousters weren't over the nets.

And of course, there were the clashes with the Jousters of Alta, as each rider attempted to deliberately unseat the other with his lance.

"Is Lesoth still trying to find a way to use a bow?" asked the round-headed boy.

"No. He gave that up yesterday when he finally got tired of Nem-teth snapping at his arrows when he loosed them," the other answered. "Jouster Ari finally took him aside and warned him that he could choose between Nem-teth catching all of *his* arrows, or breaking Nem-teth of catching *all* arrows."

"Ouch." The round-headed boy winced. "That would be bad."

"Believe it," the boy nodded. "As it is, it takes a lucky shot to hit a Jouster. If his dragon stopped snapping at arrows, though—" He made a strangling noise, evidently intending to convey— quietly—the desired effect.

So—*that* was why they didn't try to use bows themselves, and why they weren't being shot out of the sky on a regular basis!

He was learning an awful lot just by sitting here, cleaning leather.

Thinking it over, it seemed as if a lance was the only really practical weapon since a bow was out of the question. A club— well, you couldn't get close enough to use a club. You couldn't throw a spear, not with the dragon's wings flailing away on either side of you. A sling—well, that took a lot of skill. A sword pre- sented the same problems as a club. Which left the lance. . . .

In the case of a lance strike in a real Joust, a fall in that case was invariably fatal; the dragon, if not captured by another Jouster, might or might not return to its pen. Other than Kashet, the dragons' only loyalty lay in that they were fed regularly, and that was not necessarily enough to bring a riderless dragon back to his pen when they were far from home and the mountains so temptingly near.

Though, in fact, one *had* returned from combat this very day. Its dragon boy was *not* envied; a dragon without a Jouster didn't get regular exercise, and it was prone to get irritated or sluggish under such circumstances. If the former, well, it was the boy that the dragon took his ill temper out on. And if the latter, when the dragon *did* get a new Jouster, it would become irritable when forced to exercise and lose the fat that it had gained in the interim.

The boys' talk concentrated on the dragon that had returned, and commiseration with its boy, not the rider that had fallen. In fact, they didn't even once mention his name. That was not callousness on their part, in fact, Vetch considered such caution very wise; too much talk of him might bring his spirit *here*, instead of it staying properly in his tomb.

Night-walking spirits were not known for their gentleness. A hungry ghost might remember old grievances, or feel jealous of the living. There were a hundred ways such a ghost could revenge himself on the living. He could bring fever spirits, or the demons of ill luck; he could plague the sleep with nightmares. He could even lead stronger spirits to the sleeping victim, or drive one mad.

So the fallen Jouster would be remembered, oh my yes—with proper offerings and sacrifices in the Jousters' little Temple, tonight; the Temple was consecrated ground, and the Priest of Haras knew how to propitiate a spirit and give it a resting place it would be content with while it waited for proper housing.

Then all that was right and proper would be accomplished at the Tomb of the Jousters when his body was finished with the forty days of embalming. But that would be across the Great Mother River, in the Vale of the Noble Dead, and was the duty of the mortuary priests. The Tians believed that to enter into the Summer Country, the deceased must have a proper anchoring in an embalmed body, and proper offerings for at least forty days, and more offerings to take with it when it crossed the Sky River. If this was not done, it wandered. If it was not done properly, it wandered, and the longer it wandered, the angrier it became.

That was why it was not a good idea for the living to walk about at night, for fear of encountering angry or hungry spirits, the more especially if someone who actively hated you had ever died. Khefti, for instance, had made so many enemies that he hardly dared stir at night, and on the few occasions that he *did* leave the safety of his house after sundown, he was so hung about with charms and amulets that he looked like an amulet hawker, and he rattled with every step.

Vetch had no experience one way or another with spirits; with Khefti for a master, by the time *he* was let go for the day, he was so weary he always fell dead asleep. He had tried to set up a tiny shrine for his father, but it kept getting swept away when he was at his labors, and anyway, he didn't have anything to spare for offerings but the clay loaves and beer jars and other goods he molded in miniature and left there.

Certainly his father's spirit had never returned to give him any signs . . . there were tales of that, as well, of spirits that returned to help the living. Though in truth, those tales were fewer than the tales of vengeful ghosts.

But then, how would his father even know how to get here, or even where Vetch was? In all of his lifetime, his father had never been farther from his farm than the village.

"Haraket ordered her fed up and given a double dose of *tala*," the boy who was in charge of that returned dragon said. "So she won't be much of a handful for a while. And I heard straight from him that he's got a new Jouster for her, so she won't get a chance to go sour. I can handle her."

"There's a lot of new Jousters coming, I heard," one of the younger boys ventured cautiously.

"You heard right. The Great King, may he live a thousand years, wants the number increased," replied the boy who seemed to know everything—or at least wanted the others to think he did. "There's more hunters out looking for fledglings, and more Jousters being trained. And more of us, of course. That's probably why Ari came in with a serf on his own so he could free up Haraket from tending Kashet; Haraket's not going to have the time to tend Kashet pretty soon, what with all of that going on."

Now a glance of speculation was cast in his direction, but when he saw the way the conversation was going, Vetch had quickly dropped his gaze to his work.

"Think they'll put more serfs in as dragon boys if this one does all right?" asked a new voice.

The leader sounded as if he wasn't opposed to that idea. "Probably. I'll tell you what, though, that might be a good thing. I mean, think about it, new Jousters have to come from *somewhere*, so why not us, on a regular basis, instead of only now and again? After all, we know as much about the dragons as the Jousters, and we spend *more* time with them. Ari was a dragon boy, they say, or maybe a scribe, before he tamed Kashet. In fact, that was why they *made* him a Jouster."

"So why don't all the dragon boys tame dragons?" someone else asked. "Then we could all be Jousters instead of shoveling dung!"

But the knowing one laughed. "Tame a dragon? Are you mad? You think tending the old ones is work—try taming one from the shell! It's too much work, *much* too much work! If you think you work hard now, just think what it would be like to tend *two* dragons instead of one, *and* spend all of your free time with the baby so he thought of you as his mama, *and* help him with his fledging, *and* train him to saddle before he actually flew! You'd be so busy you'd meet yourself coming and going! Don't think they'd let you off of tending your Jouster's dragon, because they wouldn't!"

"Yes, but—Kashet's so tame, so easy to work with—wouldn't it be worth it?" the other persisted.

"Not if the King wants Jousters, and wants them now," replied another of the older boys. "Training takes long enough as it is, and the only people that *really* benefit from a tame dragon are the dragon boys. While the *tala* makes dragons tractable, why bother?"

The talk turned to other things, then—mostly about girls outside the compound—and Vetch lost interest. But what he'd heard had been very useful.

Now he knew why both Ari and Kashet were different. Why Ari was so particular about his dragon boy, and why, at the same time, he was surprisingly considerate to Vetch.

So, the Jouster had been in Vetch's shoes before he'd tamed his dragon. And he hadn't just gotten a fledgling from the hunters, he'd somehow raised one from the egg!

Vetch had been allowed to make a single goose into a particular pet when he'd been deemed old enough; a goose that was guaranteed never to go into the pot (or at least, not until it had died of an honorable old age or accident). *He* had been given a hatching egg, so that the first thing that the baby had seen was him. It hadn't been a case of *taming* the gosling so much as *raising* it.

And Ari had done that. With a dragon. Which must, based on how much food the young gosling ate, and all the care and brooding it required, have been a phenomenal amount of work!

Small wonder the King wasn't willing to train dragons for the Jousters that way. . . .

For not just anyone could train the young hatchlings that way. The gosling hadn't followed *any* human as its mother, it had only followed Vetch. No, that task would have to be taken on by the Jouster who meant to fly that particular dragon. Which meant that the Jouster could not be fighting at the same time, because bringing in regular meals to keep a baby dragon's belly full would be a full-time job. As well as the cleanup, afterward.

Not that Vetch particularly wanted to see more Jousters in the air; not when they were leading the fight against *his* people. . . .

It made him feel very queasy inside, to be reminded of that. Here he was, serving the enemy—

—not that he had a choice.

Not if he wanted to live, eat—not, in particular, if he wanted to do more than eke out a miserable existence.

He shook his head a little. *Too many complicated things!* he told himself fiercely, redoubling his efforts on the saddles. And what was the point of thinking about it, for what could he do? He was only a little boy. No matter what he did, no matter what became of him, nothing in the greater world would change. The war would still go on, and Ari would just find another boy for Kashet.

Shobek came over at that moment to inspect what he'd done. and grunted his satisfaction with the work.

Vetch noticed then that the other boys were putting their work aside for Shobek to inspect and gather up. Some he nodded over, some he scolded for shoddy workmanship. "You'll only get it to do over again tomorrow," he said crossly, as one of the boys looked sullen. "Haven't you gotten that through your thick skull yet? Well?"

"Yes, Shobek," the boy replied.

"Then if you *don't* want to keep seeing the same job on the same saddle again, over and over for the rest of your life, do it *right* tomorrow!" He looked around at the rest of the boys, whose attitude had changed, and who all looked eager to be gone from there. "Well, off with you."

They were off, like a shot. Vetch didn't know *what* to do, but he was saved from having to ask by the arrival of Haraket.

"You, Kashet's boy—remember that you are to come here right after pen cleaning after the noon meal," the old man said, as Haraket took possession of him. "Remember! Every day!"

"Yes, sir—" he called back over his shoulder, though he wasn't certain the old man heard him, for a new crop of six or eight boys came crowding in to fill the small room.

"Now," Haraket said, as he led Vetch down a corridor decorated with royal hawks, the token of the god Haras. "You will learn what it means to serve your Jouster as well as your dragon."

FOUR

VERY shortly, Vetch had a good idea where he was. They had gone this way earlier, in Vetch's whirlwind tour of the compound. This corridor, where the Temple of Haras also stood, marked, in fact, by the images of the god Haras, led to the Jousters' private quarters. This place wasn't so difficult to find his way around in after all!

The Jousters' importance would have been evident even to someone who didn't know what they were, just by virtue of the wall decorations on this corridor. Rather than simple carved images at the intersections of other corridors, the walls here were adorned with stunning, brilliantly colored paintings of the god Haras, in his falcon-headed human form, in his falcon form, in his form of Haras-re, the falcon of the sun. These paintings were huge, covering the entire wall, from top to bottom, and Vetch had never seen anything like them for sheer beauty. Certainly nothing could compare to them, even in the Temples he had been in. If this was what the corridor outside the Jousters' quarters looked like, what must the palace of the Great King be like? Were *his* paintings not paintings at all, but inlaid with precious materials?

They ended up at the doorway arch leading to the Jouster's quarters. This was a very large opening, with the royal hawks carved into the limestone wall in bas-relief on either side, and a third hawk with wings spread wide carved over the lintel, all so incredibly painted he expected them to spring to life at any moment.

Why not a dragon? he wondered. But this was not the time to ask. "Here," Haraket said, but not to Vetch, "This is Ari's new boy. His name is Vetch. Ari chose him himself."

"So I've heard," replied the resplendent personage at the door. The person to whom Haraket was speaking was in every possible way the opposite of Haraket. Where Haraket was muscular, this man was thin as a reed; where Haraket was bald and apparently disdained the use of a head covering altogether, this man wore an elaborately braided and beaded wig—though truth to tell, beneath the wig, he was likely shaved bald as well. This was no coarse, horse-hair or linen-thread wig. This was a wig made of human hair, dark and lustrous, each tiny braid no thicker than the cords of a snare, and ending in a turquoise, gold, or carnelian bead. It made Vetch's head spin to think how much it must have cost— and this Overseer was wearing it as an everyday ornament!

Haraket was brisk, but not entirely unfriendly; this fellow was haughty and cold. Haraket's clothing was simple; this man had an ornately pleated kilt of fine linen and a belt, armbands, and collar of faience and woven beads, as well as ornamented sandals. His collar featured the royal hawk with outstretched wings, rather than merely a faience ornament of the hawk's eye, and he clutched a gilded, carnelian-tipped wand of office as if he feared to permit it to leave his hand.

The man looked down at Vetch with a thinly veiled sneer. "And this—is to tend to Jouster Ari."

Haraket shrugged; he looked indifferent, but Vetch sensed an undercurrent of disdain and dislike—not for him, but aimed at the other man. He also had the feeling that Haraket understood this haughty fellow much better than the fellow understood Haraket.

"He may surprise you; they tell me he's surprised everyone else today with how diligent a worker he is."

"A serf?" the other man's eyebrow raised.

Haraket made a noncommittal sound. "We all know how phenomenally lucky Ari is, maybe he's the kind that can look into the muck of a newly-flooded field and find the Gold of Honor."

The other Overseer looked pained. Haraket ignored him, and tapped Vetch on the shoulder.

"Vetch, this is Te-Velethat, the Overseer in charge of the Jousters' personal quarters. You do what he tells you, until he sends you back to me or I come to fetch you." Haraket still sounded indifferent, but Vetch read the warning in his words. Haraket had no power here; this was Te-Velethat's realm, not his. It was up to Vetch to keep himself out of trouble and satisfy the Overseer of the Jousters' quarters.

Well, *this* was familiar territory. There was only one way to satisfy someone like Te-Velethat.

Grovel and work. Grovel a very great deal, with such subservience that he might just as well offer his head to the Overseer's sandal, and work as hard as ever he had for Khefti. Well, he could do that. He had a great deal of practice at both by now.

Vetch bowed, as low and as well as he possibly could, noticing as he did so that the skin of his back felt tight, but not sore. Whatever Haraket had rubbed on the whip cuts had worked a wonder!

Te-Velethat sighed theatrically, but didn't seem displeased by the exaggerated display of subservience.

Haraket took that as a signal to depart, and did so; he turned on his heel and stalked off as quickly as he could without it looking like a retreat. Vetch didn't blame him.

But at least he knew *exactly* where he was with Te-Velethat. The man was probably a freed slave; he was certainly desperate that his status be noted and acknowledged by *anyone* he considered to be his inferior. And that was precisely how to get along with such a man; Te-Velethat was far less of an enigma to Vetch than Haraket and Jouster Ari were.

In that, he was, thus far, a typical, arrogant Tian.

Vetch hated him, of course.

Vetch also knew better than to show that hatred. Like Khefti, the man would not hesitate to punish the least sign of insubordination. And Haraket would not defend Vetch in such a case, for the welfare of Kashet was not at stake here, and obeying this Overseer *was*. Though Haraket might dislike Te-Velethat, Vetch expected that he would certainly feel Te-Velethat was justified in punishing the rebellion of an Altan serf.

So Vetch kept his eyes down and his hatred to himself. He reminded himself that all he had to do was obey orders, which would not, could not, be as onerous as the tasks Khefti routinely set him. When he'd served Khefti, he'd come to regard cleaning as almost a holiday. He would *not* be slaving in the hot sun at midday, and Te-Velethat could only claim his time until Kashet returned.

The Overseer waved impatiently at him. "All right—boy. Come along." Te-Velethat might look an indolent sort, but he wasted no time; he turned abruptly and strode off with the fast, jerky pace of a stork in a hurry, and obviously expected Vetch to follow. Vetch did, running to keep up; he had the feeling that there was no way that he could appear to be *too* subservient.

The plan of the Jousters' section of this maze was clear once they passed that doorway. It consisted of a series of courtyards, each centered by a pool for bathing or with ornamental fish and *latas* in it, with the Jousters' personal rooms arranged around the courtyards. Each courtyard was linked to the next by a covered hallway that pierced each room-ringed court like a needle so that the squares of courtyard and rooms lay along the hall like beads on a string. At this hour, evidently, all the quarters were deserted by their tenants, though there were several boys to be seen, busy cleaning rooms.

The haughty fellow eventually stopped at one of the quietest of the courtyards. The pool here, although there were blue *latas* growing at one end, was clearly used both for swimming and as an ornament; the *latas* were planted in their own section, separated from the swimming portion of the pool by a raised wall just under the surface of the water, and the rest was tiled in white and green. A canvas shade had been stretched from one side of the courtyard to the other at one end, giving some relief from the heat of the sun. The courtyard was paved with stone, and there were small date palms, some bearing fruit, planted in enormous terra-cotta pots arranged at intervals around the central pool. There seemed to be four suites of rooms in this court. The Overseer stopped at the entrance to one of those suites, and looked down at Vetch as if expecting him to stand there like an idiot.

Or, perhaps, waiting for an excuse to use the little whip that was fastened to the beaded belt at his side. That too-familiar smoldering in the pit of his belly warned Vetch; he must not give the Overseer an excuse, not only to beat him, but to dismiss him altogether.

He was not anxious to lose a place where he was being fed as much as he could eat, he had clean clothing and baths, and there was no Khefti.

Especially not over something as ridiculous as not being able to do a little cleaning properly.

Khefti had been too miserly to hire many servants or purchase slaves, so Vetch had done just about every task in the household that didn't require special training. Including a great deal of cleaning.

Vetch took a step or two inside the doorway, and let his eyes adjust to the gloom. This was a simple enough set of rooms; that was something of a surprise. Vetch would have expected a great deal more in the way of luxury, but there was nothing elaborate but the wall paintings, really. There were three rooms in a row across this side of the courtyard, with a small storage room to the left of the central one in which Vetch now stood, and what was probably the bedroom to the right. Only the outer wall facing the pool was faced with limestone; the rest was sensibly constructed of mud brick with a layer of thick sand-colored plaster covering the brickwork, leaving a smooth surface for the wall paintings. The walls themselves were as thick as Vetch's forearm, with horizontal slit-windows up near the ceiling. Every Tian house, other than the simplest mud-brick huts, had those, meant to provide means for a cooling breeze to flow through, though at the moment, what was whining through them was the *kamiseen*.

Te-Velethat waited, just as Haraket had waited, presumably to see if Vetch would act on his own initiative. Without being ordered, Vetch entered the main room and immediately began picking up discarded clothing, tidying away scrolls and rolls of reed paper, capping a bottle of ink left open—after all, that was what those other boys had been doing, in other rooms in this same complex. If Te-Velethat thought he was a stupid barbarian who had to be explicitly ordered what to do, he was going to be surprised.

With a look of relief, the Overseer left him alone without another word to him, either of instruction or of warning. Now that, in its way, was something of a trap. Vetch had no doubt that Te-Velethat would be back to check on his work—and would also be looking sharp for anything missing that Vetch might have tried to steal. That was fine; the day Vetch couldn't manage a little simple cleaning was a day when crocodiles would turn to *latas* roots for their sustenance. And Te-Velethat could look in vain for signs that Vetch had stolen anything. Stealing from Ari, besides being just plain *wrong*, would also be stupid; Vetch would be willing to bet that the Jousters' property had plenty of precautionary curses on it, and anyone who stole anything of theirs would live just long enough to regret it.

This was a curious set of rooms. Vetch was acquainted with farmhouse comfort, and Khefti's idea of luxury; this didn't match either of those models. With Te-Velethat out of the way, he spent a little time exploring it.

Ari not only had his set of three rooms, on the other side of the bedroom, in what would be a corner room, he had a bathing room shared with another set of rooms. Presumably those rooms were just now empty, since when Vetch poked his nose curiously in there, he saw there were no personal possessions in them. The storeroom was just that; it contained chests, boxes and jars, two bolts of linen, rolls of paper, a few oddments, all on wooden shelves. The room that opened out into the courtyard held a charcoal brazier, a writing desk and a flat cushion to sit on, stools, a low table and chair beside it, a couch with another little table and an alabaster lamp, and a large chest of scrolls. The lamp was a simple, thin cup, meant to hold oil and a floating wick. Spare furnishings, to Vetch's mind, and the furnishings themselves were plain and virtually unornamented. The plastered walls, however, were covered with beautiful paintings; in the central room, these paintings featured scenes from court life. On the first wall, lithe little dancers wearing nothing more than jewelry; on the second, musicians, a harper, a woman with a drum, a flute player, and two girls with sistrums. A set of shaven-headed acrobats cavorted on the third, and a group of men with the hawk-eye amulets were lounging at a feast on the fourth. The paintings were life-sized and wonderfully done, in fine, clear colors.

The sleeping chamber held Ari's bed and headrest, two chests that held clothing, an armor stand (now empty), a rack for the lances that gave the Jouster his title, and a rack that held both the short and the long bow, and quivers of arrows for each. The last was interesting, given what Vetch had learned today about why Jousters didn't use bows. Did Ari hunt? If so, what, and when?

The bed was a simple, elegant frame with a woven lattice for maximum coolness; the headrest an elegant, but unadorned curve of wood. There was a table beside the bed with an oil lamp on it, another with a round mirror and a pot of kohl for lining the eyes as well as a razor. No Tian would do without kohl; it protected the eyes from the glare of the sun. There were some cushions and some good rugs on the floor, but not a great deal else. In the sleeping chamber, scenes of nature adorned the walls; the river, with blossoming reeds and *latas*, horses racing across the desert, birds flying above a field—and on the wall most visible to the bed, a great dragon, wings spread. There was no doubt that the dragon was meant to be Kashet, for it had his coloring.

These were paintings that, if Vetch was any judge, were worthy of a palace. Yet there were few other signs of luxury; in the main chamber, nothing much ornamental but that truly handsome alabaster lamp made in the shape of three *latas* flowers, each of which would hold oil and a floating wick. In the bedchamber, only what Vetch had found, no jewelry chest, only another fine lamp. There wasn't even a board for hounds and hares, or the pebble game, which adorned nearly every other home Vetch had ever seen.

It seemed strange to Vetch that one as exalted in rank as a Jouster should live in quarters that were furnished more simply than Khefti's—but at least that made it easier to clean them.

He started with the bathing room; it was much like the one where Haraket had ordered him to strip down. Since mud brick would fare poorly around water, it was faced and floored with limestone, with jars of water and dippers, and on a limestone shelf, jars of soaps and oils, sponges. There was a bench upon which one could lie to be massaged by an attendant. Another shelf held folded piles of soft linen cloths, and two of those were crumpled on the floor. Vetch picked them up and set them outside the door.

A Jouster also apparently had his choice of scented unguents when he was clean; there was quite a selection of clay and stone unguent jars lined up on another shelf above that massage bench, though truth to tell, most of them looked unopened.

Well, if Ari chose to live simply, that just made it easier to take care of his things. Vetch got a broom from the storage closet and swept out the bathing room, for with the *kamiseen* blowing, there was sand in everything, and there was no point in doing more than to try to keep it under control. He then used one of the jars of water to wash down the floor for good measure. For a moment he wondered if he should use the water of the pool to refill the jars—but that seemed dubious. He thought he remembered a well nearby, in the passageway, in fact, so that it was handy to two of the courtyards, and sheltered from the sand-laden wind.

He had recalled correctly, and went through the all-too-familiar ritual of hauling water. Only this time it was with a bucket that suited his size, and he only had to refill the bath jars and two smaller ones that held drinking water.

Then he swept up the bedroom, collecting a discarded kilt and loincloth as he did so, and adding them to the pile of linen towels. The outer room was already tidied, so he swept it before turning his attention to the lamps, refilling their oil reservoirs from one of the jars in the storage room. As his last task, he went insect hunting, looking in every nook and cranny, under every bit of furniture, lifting every jar and chest, looking for the insects that often sought shelter there. Most especially he looked for scorpions, those deadly and silent desert creatures, which could hide almost anywhere. He finally found a little one in the bathing room, and smashed it with the butt of the broom before washing it down the drain with a cup of water.

He was standing in the middle of the now-clean outer room with a bundle of Ari's soiled linen in his hands wondering what to do with it when Haraket came for him again. "Put those there," the overseer said, pointing to a basket just outside the door. "Someone collects dirty clothing and linen once a day to take it to the laundry women."

He nodded; well, at least he wasn't going to be expected to do the laundry, too! "Is there anything else I should do?" he ventured diffidently. It would have choked him to have asked Te-Velethat for further instruction, but he trusted Haraket to tell him the truth.

Haraket gave a brief inspection of his work, and shook his head. "Just what you've done, and this will be a part of your duties every day. The courtyard servants are all body servants; too lofty to clean. While Ari did without a dragon boy, they had to share out the cleaning, and let everyone know how they felt about such demeaning tasks." Haraket's tone of contempt spoke volumes about what he thought of those servants. "One thing to remember, though, there are a number of Jousters, including the other two on this court, who would rather see as little as possible of the boys; keep that in mind when you encounter one. Ari's not like that, but assume anyone else will be."

So—even the oh-so-superior freeborn dragon boys were not as welcome to the Jousters as their attitude would have led Vetch to believe! That *was* something to keep in mind, though not for the reason Haraket meant. Vetch ducked his head in answer, and followed Haraket out of the courtyard.

"Kashet will be returning shortly, and that is when you will give him his evening sand bath and his supper," Haraket continued, shooing Vetch along with an impatient gesture. "After sundown your time is your own, but between dawn and dusk you'd best be prepared to hustle."

It *was* a great deal of work, but it was also nothing nearly as hard as Khefti's assigned chores. And Khefti had him working from *before* dawn to *after* dusk, doing it all on less than half the food in a day that Vetch had gotten at a single meal here. Thus far, Vetch had absolutely nothing to complain of.

By the time they got to Kashet's pen, the dragon was already there; Ari just gave Haraket an exhausted nod in greeting, and dropped what remained of a lance on the ground as he left, presumably heading for his quarters.

What *remained* of a lance . . . which meant that Ari had been in a fight with one of the Altan Jousters. Their numbers were far smaller than the Tians, but they were a factor in the ongoing conflict; they certainly kept the Tian Jousters from having everything their own way. Vetch picked up the macerated lance and deposited it where the rest of the trash was collected, with very mixed feelings.

He didn't want any harm to come to Ari—not the least because if Ari was killed, he'd have no need for a dragon boy, and even if Kashet was drugged by *tala* into accepting another

Jouster, it wasn't likely that the new man would be as tolerant of having a mere serf serve him as Ari was.

On the other hand, he couldn't help but hope that the Altan Jouster had at least given Ari something to think about. *Can a Jouster be beaten without being killed?* Vetch didn't know, but if that *could* happen—

At least, for Ari, if he's defeated, let it be without him being hurt, he prayed fiercely. *I don't care about any other Jouster, but as long as Ari's kept safe, let there be an Altan who can win in the Jousts!*

Ari presumably felt that Kashet was in reliable hands now, for he'd left without a single backward glance. That left Vetch, under Haraket's supervision, to take the saddle and harness off Kashet. This time Haraket didn't lift a finger; he left it to Vetch to manage by himself.

But at least, he gave some signs of approval when Vetch did everything, did it correctly, and without guidance.

"Now bring him along, and follow me," Haraket decreed, and strode off, expecting Vetch to keep up. He put one hand on Kashet's shoulder, as he had seen Ari do, and set off after the Overseer.

Kashet didn't need any encouragement; wherever they were going, it was a place that Kashet liked. The dragon nearly bowled them both over in his eagerness to reach it.

They remained within the area of the pens, but this time they followed an east-west corridor with the cat-goddess Pashet on the walls. Eventually. when they reached what must have been the southeast corner of the complex, Haraket turned into another open-roofed area.

"This is the buffing pen, where you'll give Kashet his sand baths," Haraket said, leading them both inside. "Every day at this time, in fact."

This was another open-air court, a place of huge stalls, like those for horses, but big enough for dragons. Haraket guided Kashet into one of them. There were rings here for chaining the dragons, but of course, that was not a precaution that Vetch needed to use with Kashet.

"Go get one of those buckets of sand," Haraket said, pointing to a place where buckets—yes, full of sand—were lined up against the wall. Vetch did as he was told, while Haraket got a basket heaped with soft cloths from a storage shed. Then Haraket showed him how to take a handful of sand and polish the dragon's hide with it. Kashet seemed to love it, leaning into the grit like a dog being scratched. The sand polished off dirt and anything else that had stuck to the scales. And the sand was particularly good at cleaning the hide of the wings.

Those peculiar wings . . . they weren't like the wings of any other creature that Vetch had ever seen. Certainly not like bird wings, nor like bats, nor like insects. They had many peculiar folds and planes, layers of skin and flexible tendons and thin, flat bones that were almost as flexible as the tendons. But all of those surfaces made for places where itchy things could lodge, so Vetch set to scrubbing with a will.

Kashet wasn't scaled everywhere; the wing webbings were made of tough, thin skin, there was skin at the eyes and nostrils, and in the joints. All of the skin needed oiling, when he was done scrubbing Kashet with the sand. The oil soaked in quickly, leaving the hide softer and more flexible; in fact, it vanished so quickly that not one grain of sand stuck to the hide afterward. His beautiful blue scales were like the curved, shiny iridescent wing covers of beetles, they shone with a deep and luminous color so rich it was like nothing in Vetch's experience.

And Kashet adored it; loved every bit of attention, and even helped Vetch to get to inaccessible spots by crouching down or contorting himself to bring some area where Vetch could reach it. Vetch burnished him with sand first, then at Haraket's direction, with soft, oil-soaked cloths, until the dragon gleamed. While he worked, other boys brought in their dragons, until all the other dragons were in the buffing pens as well, and the whole place was full.

He couldn't help but notice that every other boy brought in his dragon with a heavy collar around its neck, and a strong chain attached to the collar. The least tug on the chain would somehow close the collar down around the dragon's throat, cutting off his breath.

So *that* was how a mere boy could control a huge creature like a dragon!

"Only Kashet is safe to handle without chains when he's around the others," Haraket observed, as another dragon boy brought his charge into the pen, but not as Haraket had, with only a hand on his shoulder. "They're like dogs sometimes, snappish and quarrelsome. That's why the walls of the pens are so thick, so they can't reach each other over them."

This green-bronze dragon wore her chain around her neck like the others; just at that moment, she balked and tried to pull the chain loose from the boy. He gave the chain a yank, and the collar closed down around her windpipe, choking her for an instant. She wheezed for a moment, and then subsided; the boy gave the chain a flip to loosen it, and continued where he'd been heading to chain his charge to a post at the far wall of the pen. "Right now, Par-kisha is sated by the *tala* on her food, but he's wise to chain her," Haraket observed. "Fights between dragons are impossible for anyone but the Jousters to break up, and—" he fixed Vetch with a knife-sharp glance, "—remember this, boy. Fights are generally fatal to handlers caught in the middle."

Vetch nodded, and gulped.

But Kashet was nothing like the half-wild thing chained to the post next to him; he had turned into a veritable puddle of dragon, leaning into each buffing stroke with his eyes half closed. Like an enormous cat, he loved grooming and being groomed. Oh, the others enjoyed it, too, but not to the extent that Kashet did.

Finally Haraket deemed the task done even to *his* exacting standards, and allowed Vetch to lead the dragon back to his pen for the last time that day. Leaving Kashet to bask in the sun while his hide absorbed the oil—which imparted that spicy scent to him—Vetch got another barrowful of meat.

By now, drowsy and relaxed and more certain of his new dragon boy, Kashet was not so impatient to be fed. He ate in a leisurely fashion, while Haraket and Vetch watched.

"The other dragons all get *tala* mixed with their meat at every meal; make sure you never get one of those barrows," Haraket cautioned. "Kashet is *never* to have *tala*. Not even at morning feed—and believe me, when you see the others snapping at their boys, you'll be grateful that you've got Kashet, and not mind the extra work he makes for you. Maybe the other boys will have less work than you, but yours will be easier. And Ari's a good master."

With Kashet fed and digging himself a hollow in the sand in which to sleep, Haraket gave Vetch a grudging smile.

"All right, serf boy," he said gruffly. "You've done as well as anyone else his first day. You're finished until morning. Go back to the kitchen and get your supper, and you're free to do whatever you wish until dawn. You'll sleep on a pallet in here with Kashet, though, and not with the other boys. Ari's particular about Kashet, and he wants someone with him all the time."

"Yes, sir," Vetch said feeling that for once he'd encountered Tians who deserved being called "sir."

And he was going to sleep here, away from the other boys—potential tormentors. He felt another burden of worry ease away from him.

"You're how old, boy?" Haraket demanded suddenly. "And what in Tophet were you before you were bound to the land?"

"Ten or eleven, sir, though I'm not sure." He'd lost track of the seasons, really, it wasn't hard to do so when your days were exhausting and the work never ending. "Maybe older." Maybe much older, but he wasn't going to say that. Much older, and he might be deemed too old for this task. "My father was a farmer," Vetch stammered, surprised by the abrupt demand. Masters did not, in his experience, give a toss about how old you were, or what you'd been when you were free.

"Not too old, not too young. Good." Haraket nodded. "Right. Off with you; get that dinner. I'll have the pallet brought here for you; it will be waiting for you when you're ready to sleep." With that, he left Vetch at the door to Kashet's pen, stalking off with his long, ground-eating strides. Vetch gathered his courage, and looked for the kitchen.

By now, he had a rough map of the place in his mind, and he found the kitchen by dead reckoning and following his nose. This time he was not the first one to reach the place. There were other boys there already, but they were largely too full of themselves and their doings to pay much attention to him, particularly as he settled himself at a table out of their way.

The sun was just setting, and torches were being lit, so he was left to himself at first. But there was already food on the table, as before, so he didn't mind. Wonderful bread, stewed greens and fresh onions, boiled *latas* roots; all of it fresh and cooked *well*, not burned, not left over. There were more little bowls of fat, too, for dipping bread into, and a spiced paste of ground chickpeas. Eventually one of the girls serving drink noticed him. She slapped down a pottery jar of beer in front of him in an absentminded sort of way and nodded to another, who left him a hot terra-cotta bowl of pottage. Then, as he was scooping up pottage in pieces torn from a piece of flatbread, came the surprise.

Because the next thing that was left at his table was a plate full of meat.

Now, Vetch hadn't had meat in—well, longer than he could remember, because even a farmer as his father had been didn't slaughter his animals very often. In fact, the meat he'd gotten most often had been wild duck, goose, and hare, except on one memorable occasion when someone's ox had broken a leg, and the whole village had a feast before the meat went bad.

This was a whole platter of sliced beef, cooked until it was just barely pink, and oozing juices. He stared at it dumbfounded. Why, this was the sort of thing that only rich men ate at dinner!

But then it dawned on him *why* they all got meat—all the sacrifices from the Temples, of course! And why not? Compared to what the dragons ate, the amount of meat that would be cooked and served at a single meal was trivial. So why shouldn't the Jousters and their staff share in the bounty?

Nevertheless, Vetch wasted no time in helping himself, tearing the slices apart with his fingers. He stuffed the first bite into his mouth, and closed his eyes in purest pleasure.

This wasn't like that long-remembered stewed beef. This was better; incomparably, amazingly better! The salt-sweet meat practically melted on his tongue, bombarding him with a savory complex of flavors that made his toes curl with delight.

Well, and *of course* it was better—you didn't offer the gods your old, work-worn ox or a cow aged and tough with bearing calves and producing milk! You brought the gods a fine, young bull or heifer, or even a tender calf. You'd be stupid to do otherwise! The best of the best came to the gods, who drank in the blood and the essence, which left all that perfectly wonderful meat for mortal enjoyment.

If *this* was what the dragon boys and other slaves and servants got who were last on the chain—after the priests had taken their pick, then the Jousters, then the dragons—what must the priests be feasting on every night?

No wonder no one ever sees a skinny priest. . . .

But there; it was dangerous, serving the gods. Sometimes it was deemed necessary that someone go to serve them in person . . . then there would be a sacrifice that would not be passed on to the Jousters' compound.

At least, the Altan gods were that way, and if anything, the Tians were even more bloody-minded.

Vetch shuddered, and pushed the thought from his mind, concentrating on the savor of every morsel. It was only priests that were sacrificed, anyway; slaves were deemed too lowly to please

the gods, and serfs were the enemy, and who would send an important message via one's enemy?

The sky darkened, and someone went around the periphery of
the court, lighting the rest of the lamps, while someone else pulled
back the awning. Others came to sit at his table—servants within
the complex, he thought, not other dragon boys. Some were
probably serfs, but there was no way to tell which were and
which were not, for slaves as well as serfs went with uncut hair
and unshaven scalps. They didn't talk to him, but that could simply be because they were stuffing food into their mouths with
evident enjoyment.

Then, when he thought he could not possibly be more satisfied,
the serving girl plunked down another pottery platter in front
of him.

Honey cakes.

Fresh-baked, crisp and flaky, with the honey glaze on their tops
shining in the torchlight, the sweet aroma rose to his nostrils and
tickled his appetite all over again. He fell to with a will, much to
the open delight of the serving girl.

Finally, feeling as stuffed as a festival goose, he reluctantly got
up from the table, the last of the dragon boys to leave, though
servants were still coming in to eat.

But even then, he was in for one final surprise.

Just before he left the kitchen courtyard, that same serving girl
intercepted him. She was not so much a girl, he noticed now; it
was just that she didn't have that *worn-out* look that serf women
and slaves got; he thought she might have been close to the age
of his own mother.

"Here," she said, pressing a package wrapped in a broad leaf of
the kind fish were baked in into his hand. "Take this with you.
Little boys get hungry in the night, and you look three-quarters
starved, anyway. We Altans have to stick together."

So she was another Altan serf! He tried to give it back to her,
alarmed at the thought that he might be getting her into trouble.
"I don't—" he began. "You'll get—"

But she laughed and closed both his hands around it. "Ah, nothing of the sort!" she said cheerfully. "Even if we didn't have so much food here that we give what's left to the beggars after every meal, *you* are a dragon boy, and Kashet's boy at that; I'd be in trouble if I *didn't* make certain you had plenty to eat, not for sending you off with something extra!" She turned him around and gave him a little shove. "Off with you; I've work to do."

So, clutching a packet that held more food in it than he got out of Khefti in three days—and that was by weight alone, no telling what was actually in the packet—he made his way back to Kashet's pen. When he thought about all the times he'd been unable to sleep because his belly was aching with hunger, or when he'd managed to get to sleep, only to have hunger pangs wake him in the middle of the night—well, he could hardly believe his luck.

Torches placed at intervals along the walls and at each intersection showed him the pictures on the walls clearly. He did get lost going back, but eventually he righted himself, and followed the pictures to the pens. The torches burned brightly, with the faint scent of incense to them, and not a great deal of smoke. The yellow light they gave off was clear and strong; the walls here were high enough that the *kamiseen* didn't blow them out, only made them waver and flicker now and again, as a gust or two got past the wind baffles. His eyes were light dazzled so that when he looked up, he couldn't make out the stars, though, which was what had led to his getting a little lost, for he couldn't tell east from west in this maze without seeing the sun or stars. Or the moon, but it was rising late tonight, and wouldn't even begin to peek up above the walls until after he found Kashet's pen. He could hear the sounds of the other boys chattering together somewhere. And for a moment, he felt a strange emptiness inside of him that no amount of bread could touch.

But then he turned the corner into Kashet's pen. He stood in the soft darkness for a moment, and let his eyes adjust to the dimmer light, for there were no torches in here. When he was able to make out details, he saw the pallet waiting for him beneath the awning that protected the saddle and harness. At that moment, all he could think of was sleep.

Tia was a desert land, and the desert was as cold by night as it was hot by day. Now the hot sands where Kashet rested were a source of comfort, a radiating warmth better than the wall Vetch used to sleep beside, for this warmth wouldn't fade before the night was half over. Vetch was happy enough to spread out on his pallet and settle down beside the lightly snoring dragon. The dragon was fast asleep in his wallow, and it didn't look as if Vetch could have awakened him if he'd tried. With no torches in here, once Vetch's eyes had gotten used to the darkness, he looked past the awning over his head to the stars.

In the darkness of his old sleeping place in Khefti's back kitchen, Vetch had spent many an unhappy night on his pile of reeds, shivering in his rags. This pallet was, he thought, made of a thick mattress of straw inside a covering of fleece, all of that covered with heavy linen. There were two blankets as well, and an Altan pillow rather than a Tian headrest. It felt strange to stretch out and not have scratchy straw sticking into him, or feel the stone through the straw. It felt as if he was stretched out on a cloud.

He carefully put his food packet near at hand, but inside an upturned bucket that he vermin-proofed with a brick to hold it down. Then he laid himself down on his pallet, warm, full, and trying to figure out what he had done to warrant this sudden change in his fortunes. He looked up at the stars for a clue, but the stars weren't in the mood to answer, it seemed.

From somewhere in the distance came the sounds of a celebration in progress, and the occasional note of a flute or throbbing of a drum. He wondered what was being celebrated.

Not another Tian victory—

But no one had said anything about it, so perhaps it was something else. Maybe it was nothing more than a party. When you were as rich as these people were, you could have little feasts and celebrations all the time, for no particular reason.

He felt odd. He wanted to hate the Tians, even the ones here.

After all, weren't *they* taking the place of dozens, even hundreds, of warriors? Weren't they the reason why the conflict was going so badly for the Altans?

Oh, he wanted to hate them! But that meant hating Jouster Ari, who had saved him from Khefti, and Haraket, who had been decent to him.

But the stars were very bright, and very distant, and though he tried to open his mind and heart to the gods for guidance, he heard nothing counseling revenge. He pulled the blanket up to his chin, and wriggled his toes, sleepily. The pallet beneath him was soft and wonderful, so superior to a pile of reeds that there was no comparison.

He yawned. Yes, he would hate the Tians. All of them.

Tomorrow. . . .

He closed his eyes, and drifted into sleep, with Kashet snoring in his ears. And for once, he did not dream.

FIVE

HARAKET came to rouse him in the morning, as Nofet, the Goddess of Night, was just pulling in her skirts to make way for Re-Haket, the Sun God. He woke at the first sound of a footfall and all at once; it had been Khefti's habit to wake him with a kick to the ribs, if he were not already scrambling to his feet when his fat master lumbered into the kitchen courtyard. For all that Khefti was lazy, he still rose with the first light, in order to get the most possible work out of his serf and few servants and apprentices in the course of the day. So Vetch slept lightly, and the soft sound of Haraket's step woke him completely.

He was not confused as to his whereabouts, though; he knew perfectly well where he was the moment he opened his eyes, and as he unwound himself from his blanket and set his gaze on Haraket's unlovely face, his heart lifted. There would be no beatings today, no empty belly, no burdens too heavy, or work too much for his strength. He was a dragon boy, now, and had the sort of life he could not have dreamed of having even this time yesterday. He felt his lips stretching involuntarily, and for a moment, did not understand what his face was doing. He was startled, an instant later, when he saw a slow, slight smile on Haraket's face, to realize that *he* was smiling, and Haraket was smiling back.

How long had it been since he had last smiled? He couldn't remember . . . feeling extremely odd, he covered his confusion by bending to fold up his blankets and roll up the pallet.

The barge of the sun god was not yet above the horizon, but the beams of his light were streaking the sky. The air was cold enough to make Vetch shiver, the *kamiseen* already whining around the tops of the buildings. Soon enough, though, Lord Re-Haket would begin to hammer his power down upon the land, and upon anyone not fortunate enough to be able to remain in shade or indoors.

Re-Haket was *not* the chief god of the Tians, as he was for the Altans, perhaps because although he gave life to this land, he also brought death in the dry season. *Tians'* greatest deity was Hamun, the ram-headed Lord of Storms and the Stars, said by them to be the father of all the gods. Among the Altans, Hamun was nothing more than the god of the shepherds.

"Up with the sun lord, are you?" Haraket said, with a lift of one corner of his mouth. "Well, good. Today, I want you to try and make your way through your duties without me. You *ought* to be able to; for one thing, you can follow the others around if you need to find things. For another, the corridors are clearly marked."

Vetch nodded, though his stomach fluttered a little with nervousness. He did not really want to follow the others about. He had the feeling that they would make things hard for him if he tried. Maybe they wouldn't be allowed to hurt him, but they could do other things to make his life difficult. "Yes, sir," he replied, and hesitated. There were a hundred questions he wanted to ask, a hundred reassurances he wanted to beg for.

Haraket read all that in his face, and shrugged. "Somebody will put you right if you ask. You'll have to learn quickly, but you aren't stupid, boy. You can manage."

Vetch didn't much like the sound of that, but it wasn't as if he had any choice in the matter.

Well, actually, he did. He could make a mess of his duties, and be sent back to Khefti.

But he was just one serf, after all, a single unimportant serf. How could he expect an Overseer to devote any amount of time to herding him about in his duties? Haraket had already spent an incredible amount of time on him yesterday, and that was probably only because he was making sure he would not have to send Vetch away. If he was to succeed, he would have to be better, smarter, and more diligent than the freeborn boys here.

Haraket's face took on an expression Vetch didn't recognize. "Look, boy, I *can't* lead you around as if you were a Palace brat needing a nursemaid. If I do, it'll only make things difficult for you with the other boys; they'll think I'm playing favorites, and *then* there'll be hell to pay. You're in a bad place, and so am I, and you'll just have to jump into the river and hope Lord Haras' amulet protects you from crocodiles."

Vetch swallowed, but this, he understood. Haraket was right.

"Now, listen, you know what to do in the afternoon—so these are your morning duties. The very first thing you do every morning is to feed Kashet. That is of first importance; Kashet will have gone all night without eating, and you should know by now how much a dragon has to eat; he'll be starving as soon as he's thoroughly awake."

They both looked over their shoulders at that; Kashet was barely stirring, and raised his head to blink sleepily at them. Obviously, he was *not* thoroughly awake yet.

"Once you've done that, then saddle and harness him," Haraket continued. "Jouster Ari will be here as soon as he thinks Kashet will be ready; he's the first in the air, you can count on him for that. Once Ari and Kashet are away, *then* you can get your breakfast, and follow the other boys and do what they do."

"Yes, sir," he repeated, and Haraket strode off on some duty of his own. Kashet had put his head back down and had gone back to sleep, torpid despite the rising sun.

So it looked as if he had some breathing space before Kashet started looking for his food.

Vetch gave himself a good stretch, shook out and rewrapped his kilt, then went to fetch Kashet's breakfast of meat. But this time he found himself showing up at the butchers along with many other dragon boys. Haraket was already there, and while Vetch was waiting his turn for a barrow, he kept one eye on the Overseer.

Haraket watched each boy fill his barrow with a critical eye; twice he stopped a boy from leaving without truly filling his barrow, and once he stopped a boy who was trying to stagger off with *too* much. He scooped half of the meat into another boy's barrow, with the admonition, "Dump that in front of her and come back for a second trip, Waset. If you hurt yourself trying to carry too much, you'll get no sympathy from me."

Vetch had to line up for the butchers once he got his barrow, but once he had it, and loaded it up with as much as he could carry safely, Haraket waved him past a station where the other boys were scooping powder atop the meat and mixing it in.

"That's the *tala*," the Overseer warned. "Remember, not even a *touch* of *tala* for Kashet. Ari would have my hide, and I'd have yours."

Well, Vetch didn't doubt *that* one bit.

Haraket left him in the next moment, to go and scold yet another boy for loading his barrow too lightly. Vetch could still hear him roaring at the other lad as he pushed his barrow away down the corridor. "How *dare* you short your dragon because you're too lazy to carry him a full meal! How *dare* you overseason with *tala* to make up for it! You young bastard, are you trying to kill your Jouster? Don't you know what will happen? If his dragon—"

The sense of the words was lost as Vetch pushed his barrow around another corner, but he wondered what *would* happen to an underfed, overdrugged dragon. Would it be so weakened that it couldn't fly properly? Would it just not have enough energy to fly a combat? Would too much *tala* make it drunk, or stupid? Or if it got *really* hungry, would it turn on its Jouster? Wild dragons could and did eat humans. . . .

He shuddered a little, and hurried on. The east was getting brighter, with long streaks of light shining up across the blue sky, the hands of the God reaching out to touch the land. He found himself humming the morning hymn to Re-Haket for the first time in so very long . . . perhaps for as long as it had been since the last time he remembered smiling. He was smiling now as he whispered the words of the hymn to himself. *How beautiful art Thou, bringer of life, shining-winged one . . . how beautiful with morning's banners, streaming forth in glory.*

Kashet was restive and a little waspish after the long night without food, but in the other pens, Vetch heard hisses and whines, the snapping of jaws, and the curses of the dragon boys. He knew then that he was very lucky to have Kashet as his dragon. All Kashet did was to play his favorite trick for snatching meat from the barrow, snaking his head around the corner again once he spotted Vetch coming from his vantage point over the wall. Vetch been more than half expecting it, so this time he didn't jump. In fact—the dragon gave him such an amusing sidelong glance as he grabbed his treat that Vetch had to laugh.

So that was three things he hadn't done in . . . forever. He had smiled, sung, and laughed, all in the same morning, before breakfast. He felt a little dizzy with amazement. Yesterday, he had nothing to look forward to but misery. Today—

How beautiful art Thou, radiant with banners!

Kashet ate faster than he had at the two previous meals, probably because he was so hungry. He tossed the meat chunks down his throat as fast as he could without choking, and the barrow was already half empty.

Watching how much Kashet was eating, Vetch made a decision; he dumped what was left in the barrow on the ledge beside the sand wallow, and went back for another half a load. Haraket was still there, and gave him a surprised look and a raised eyebrow when he saw Vetch again. "Kashet's really hungry," Vetch said diffidently to the Overseer. "I thought—should I bring him extra?"

"Not just before a flight—but feed him extra when he comes back in, as much as he'll take," Haraket decreed, with a thoughtful nod. Then he muttered, as if to himself, "Huh. He may be putting on a growth spurt; they never actually stop growing, after all."

Vetch waited; he had the feeling that Haraket was making up his mind about something.

"Hmm," Haraket mused, then did make up his mind. "Wait a moment, boy—Notan!"

The Overseer waved at one of the butchers. "Bring me a basket of hearts for this boy!"

The butcher nodded, and brought over what had been requested, dumping the organs into Vetch's barrow.

"Now, you go give those to Kashet," Haraket ordered. "If he's really putting on a growth spurt—that's not impossible, even though he's mature—even though he's going to be flying shortly, we need to do something about it. So whenever he starts eating like a pig, but he's going to be going straight out, you ask for a basket of hearts. That's dense meat; it'll give him strength without weighing him down. Now, off with you—and Vetch?"

Vetch was already halfway to the door, but he turned obediently at that. "Sir?" he asked.

Haraket was actually smiling, broadly. It quite transformed his face. "Good lad. You're thinking. Keep it up. *Ask* me first, before you do anything with Kashet, but keep thinking."

"Yes, sir," he said, feeling a flush of pride warming his cheeks and ears. He all but ran back to the pen, pushing the much-lighter barrow before him.

Kashet dove on the hearts as if he hadn't just eaten a full barrow load of meat. Clearly, they were a great treat for the dragon. Vetch had to laugh, though, at the playful way he would pick one out of the barrow, toss it into the air, and catch it before it hit the ground; Kashet seemed to enjoy the sound of his laughter, too, for he curved his neck and regarded his dragon boy with a sparkling eye that seemed, at least to Vetch, to have a great deal of good-natured humor in it.

Kashet ate every scrap of meat that Vetch had brought, but the last few hearts he ate daintily, taking time to enjoy them. Vetch saddled the now-sated dragon, and the Jouster arrived just as he finished tightening the last of the straps. Kashet cooperated beautifully, dropping and rising on Vetch's commands as if he had been doing so for years. Once again, Vetch could overhear what was going on in the nearer pens, and it seemed that the other dragons were finally being less obstinate, but only just. Presumably the *tala* made them more obedient. But the other dragon boys had to shout their orders over and over before the dragons obeyed, so Vetch was quite finished long before they got their dragons all buckled and cinched down.

Ari didn't say anything, but he did give Vetch an abstracted nod when he arrived; after a brief and approving inspection of the harness, Ari patted Vetch on the back in an absentminded way and climbed into his saddle, and a moment later, he and Kashet were hardly more than a little dot in the sky.

By now, the sun was well up and it was beginning to get warm; not all the heat was coming from the sand in Kashet's wallow. The *kamiseen* whined around the tops of the walls, bringing with it the scent of the desert, and overhead, a vulture circled. And Vetch was beginning to get hungry, despite the packet of bread and meat and honey cake he'd been given last night.

Well, the sooner he got the pen clean, the sooner he could get something to eat.

He got to work, not only cleaning out the droppings, but giving everything a good stir about with a rake that he found. Yesterday at this time, he'd been hauling water and clay and river mud for Khefti's pottery and the brick yard, with nothing more than a loaf end in his stomach. He'd have done ten times the work he'd done this morning, with more in front of him, and the promise of no reward at all.

This—well, *he* got to judge the size of his loads, the tools were the right size for someone as little as he, and the raking was no work at all compared with *anything* Khefti set him to do.

At last, with the sun now well above the walls of the compound, and casting long slants of golden light on the sand of the pen, he put the rake away. The light had not yet made its way down into the corridors between the pens, but certainly he had done enough by now to justify getting his breakfast.

Had no trouble finding his way to the kitchen court this time. Just as he got there, one of the girls was pulling the awning across the courtyard and he watched with curiosity. *Now* he realized what that bunched canvas was across the top of one of the walls of Kashet's pen—it was a similar awning! But it couldn't be to shelter the dragon from the sun, not when they needed and craved heat so much. . . .

Maybe it's to keep the rain off? That actually made sense. It wouldn't be dry season forever. Soon enough the winter rains would start; however the sands were heated, rain wouldn't do them any good.

When the serving girl was done, he sat down at what was beginning to be his usual seat at the farthest end of the farthest table, and got his breakfast of hot bread and barley broth with the other boys. Once again, there were others besides the dragon boys eating there, and they were the ones who sat at his table. Many appeared to be servants or craftsmen of one sort or another.

There were a great many of them; more people than lived in both his old village and Khefti's combined.

He thought about that as he ate, watching the others at the tables around him. He finally decided that it probably took a lot of people to keep this place running: servants for the Jousters and Overseers; leather craftsmen for the saddles and harnesses; wood workers to supply furniture and do repairs; weapons makers to make the lances and clubs that the Jousters used; laundry women; cooks and bakers; seamstresses; stonemasons and brickmakers . . . this place was a little world unto itself.

The other dragon boys, however, had not softened their attitude toward him. Free and Tian, and so far above *him* that he might as well be a beetle for all of the attention they were carefully *not* paying him, they were very blatantly excluding him from their company.

Except that they kept looking at him out of the corners of their eyes, and whispering to each other as they did so. It made the wonderful, soft bread form a lump in his throat. He could tell that they would neither forget nor forgive his inferior race and status.

He was an interloper among them, unwelcome. There would be no friends here.

Once again, he got that hollow feeling as he watched them chatting and laughing with each other, and pointedly closing *him* out of their circle.

He should not have expected anything else, and in his heart, he knew that.

Not even slaving for Khefti had he felt quite so alone. It was worse than having tricks pulled on him. They were all doing the same job, after all, he and they. It wasn't as if he was going to be doing less than any of them. It wasn't as if he was going to be especially favored by any of the Overseers. If anything, he could count on Te-Velethat being harder on him than on anyone else! *Why* couldn't they at least be willing to talk to him, a little? He hadn't had a real friend in so long. . . .

Small wonder Haraket wanted him to sleep with Kashet. At least the dragon was willing to be his friend.

He clenched his jaw, and turned to his surest defense.

Anger.

What makes them *the lords of the world, anyway? Just the luck of being born Tian, that's all! If the war was going differently—any of* them *could be serfs, now, this moment. They don't deserve their good luck.*

He filled the hollow with anger, but it was a slim bulwark against the loneliness. The bread turned as dry as old reeds in his mouth, the broth might as well have been water. It was very hard to swallow, and he stared down into his bowl to avoid their smug glances.

It had been so long since he'd had a friend . . . bleakness made his eyes sting and he closed them, lest he betray himself with a tear.

But perhaps—

A thought occurred to him, and his eyes stopped stinging, and the lump in his throat diminished.

Perhaps, given Haraket's tirade against one of *them* this morning—he might not be the only serf as a dragon boy for long. Boys could be dismissed; Haraket had made that abundantly clear. So if *he* did well, maybe one or more of the other Jousters would follow Ari's example?

Boys "got airs," and left of their own accord as well. Who was to say that a Jouster who'd been left in the lurch would not decide it would be much better to have a boy who *could not* leave?

That made him feel a little better; in fact, it made him feel a bit more courageous. Good enough that, although he did not trade hauteur for hauteur, he lifted his head and straightened his back, concentrating on his hands. *Let* them pretend they were better than he was! *Haraket* had shown that he approved of how Vetch was doing. It was Haraket and Ari he had to please, not them. He *would* do better than they; no matter what they did, he would be better at it. He would tend to Kashet until he glowed with health; he would labor at the leather work and do twice as much as any of them. He would show all of them up for the lazy louts they were, and shame them all!

And damned if he would ask anything of any of them. But by the time he was settled here, *their* Jousters would be asking them, "Why can't you be like Kashet's boy?"

After breakfast, he trailed behind the others, having gathered from what he overheard that it was time to get a bath and a new kilt. They all went straight to the same bathing room where Hara-ket had taken him when he first arrived. He debated loitering until the others were done, then decided to edge inside and hope they ignored him.

They did; and despite some horseplay and a little shoving amongst themselves, the presence of another adult Overseer who was handing out clean, white-linen kilts and inspecting the boys for cleanliness must have kept them on good behavior. He *did* loiter just long enough for the greater part of them to clear out, taking the opportunity to scrub himself really well, much to the evident satisfaction of the watching Overseer. "Very good," the man said, as he handed Vetch a loincloth, a kilt and a leather thong with the glazed-faience talisman of a hawk eye on it that he had seen around everyone else's neck here. "Kashet's boy, aren't you? Jouster Ari is a stickler for cleanliness; I'm pleased to see that you are, as well."

"Yes, sir," Vetch replied, and ventured, "Could someone cut my hair, sir?" He didn't mean to cut it *off*, of course, but he hoped it might be trimmed up a bit. . . .

Evidently he wasn't even to be allowed that much.

"You're not freeborn, boy," the Overseer rebuked him. "But—here—" He handed Vetch a coarse shell comb and another bit of leather thong, and at least Vetch was able to get the knots out of his hair for the first time in months and months, and braid it.

He handed the comb back to the Overseer, who stowed it away, wishing he could shave his head altogether. But only a free-born boy could shave his head and wear a wig; a serf was branded as such by his own hair, long and uncut. It was the easiest and cheapest way to mark a serf. Shaving took time, the resource of a good, sharp razor, and had to be done every day.

Hair damp, freshly kilted, wearing the glazed hawk-eye talis-man, he followed in the wake of the last of the boys, knowing there were other chores that needed doing between now and when the dragons returned. So long as the others didn't notice his presence—

He felt better with the hawk eye around his neck; such talismans kept the night-walking spirits away, and demons, as well as guarding him from the crocodiles of Great Mother River. It wasn't the talisman that he would have chosen—he'd have taken one of Nofret's stars, if he'd had a choice, or better still, the sun-disk of Hakat-Re—but it was good to have it. The talisman wasn't only for luck; it marked him, should he ever need to leave the compound, as a servant of the Jousters. No one would interfere with him while he was wearing it. No one who was not of the Jousters wore the hawk eye; if a talisman of the God Haras was wanted, it would be one of the God Himself.

And yes, he learned as he walked boldly behind the last three boys into yet another chamber, that there were plenty of tasks to be done. For the first time, he found himself taking a place among *all* of the other dragon boys, who were lined up in front of some racks of equipment.

This was yet another proper room, a large one, smelling of oil and fresh wood, and yet another Overseer, this one a hard-looking man of a kind with Haraket, only leaner. This room was lined with rack upon rack of the lances that all Jousters used.

The Overseer intercepted him as he entered the doorway, stopping him by the simple expedient of stretching his arm out to keep Vetch from passing. "Jouster Ari's boy. Vetch—"

Caught off-guard, he bobbed his head nervously. "Yes, sir," he managed.

"This way." He pulled Vetch off to the side, with one hard hand on his shoulder. He stationed Vetch in front of a rack of lances. Vetch could feel the eyes of every boy in the chamber on him, and it was all he could do to keep from cringing. He reminded himself of their scorn, and of his vow to be better than any of them. He *would* prove that an Altan was better than any two Tians put together!

He fastened his gaze on the rack of weapons, as he was no doubt intended to do. Now, except for that mashed lance of Ari's which had hardly been recognizable as such, this was the first time that Vetch had ever seen these lances up close, and much to his surprise, they appeared to be made, not of wood, but of bundles of reeds or papyrus somehow bound and glued together into a whole. The surface was very shiny, the bindings of linen thread wrapped in intricate patterns and varnished into place with a lacquer that turned everything shiny gold.

"Vetch, this is important; I want you to check each one of these. Because this is your first time here, I've set this up as a learning exercise. I put some damaged ones in this rack to show you what to look for and how to check the lances for breakage and weak spots. Here; this is a good one." He thrust the lance, which was just a little longer than he was tall, into Vetch's hands. It was astonishingly light, and even more astonishingly strong. "First, flex it, like this—" he gestured with his hands to illustrate, and Vetch tried. Another surprise; the thing was springy, much more so than wood. And *strong*.

"You feel that? That's how a good lance should behave. If it doesn't flex like that, it's gone dead; toss it." He handed Vetch a "dead" lance, which had nothing like the flexion of the first; after trying it, Vetch obediently tossed it onto a pile of other discards.

Behind him, he heard the other boys at work at their own racks; presumably they already knew what they were doing.

Learn quickly, he reminded himself.

The Overseer showed Vetch other defects to look for; broken tips—they weren't so much *broken* as crushed—weakened spots, which were soft and gave when poked, lances gone out of true. So this was one of the important jobs of the morning, and Vetch could see why it was vital.

He could figure out why the lances would have broken or had gotten weak places by himself; after all, the lances weren't for show, the Jousters used them to fight with. But he couldn't reckon why they'd go dead, or out of true.

Well, that wasn't his job. *His* job was to pull them off the racks when they did.

There were a lot of lances, and each one had to be inspected minutely. Furthermore, *every* boy had to inspect *every* lance that passed, and the Overseer followed behind them inspecting every one that they all passed, sometimes discarding one for no reason that Vetch could fathom. Perhaps it had something to do with magic. Perhaps it had more to do with caution and experience. A Jouster's life could depend on his lance, and whether or not it held up in combat. It didn't take *long,* but by having the boys look the weapons over and discard the ones with obvious flaws, it surely must save the Overseer a great deal of time.

When they were all done with the lances for the day, they filed off in a group for another task that required all their hands. He trailed along behind, not too close, not so far that he would lose them at a turning. They ignored him.

This one took them to a huge walled court, filled with coarse linen cloths, loosely woven, stretched over frames that were held above the ground on wooden legs, at about the same height as a sleeping couch. And on the linen cloths, were the very familiar yellow-green, rounded shapes of ripened *tala* fruit.

This time he didn't have to be told what to do; a farmer's child knew drying racks when he saw them. He went straight to the baskets of *tala* waiting to be spread out on the racks, and took one to the nearest empty cloth waiting to be filled.

Not hard or difficult work, but it was hot out here, and the sun bore down on him without mercy. Nor was his task over when the last of the fruits were spread out on the linen; then he must go to the other racks to turn the fruits so that they dried evenly. Each thumb-sized fruit had to be turned by hand, of course; a rake would have damaged the coarsely-woven sheets.

That wasn't the end of his involvement with the *tala* either. Next he was sent with a dozen of the others to pound *tala* berries that were fully dried into the familiar powder that was mixed with the meat. Each of them stood at a heavy stone mortar the size of a bucket. The mortars stood on the floor in a row, each with a wooden pestle as tall as he was waiting in it, ready to make the *tala* into the form in which it controlled the dragons.

He was no stranger to grinding things either; when you were a serf, tending the land, you either ground the grain you were allowed to glean after the harvest into flour for yourself, or you did without bread. The scent of the *tala* filled the air, green and bitter, a little like gall, but without the acrid aftertaste. He pounded the pestle into the stone mortar at his feet in rhythm with the other boys, thinking as he did so that this was not as bad as it might have been. They were allowed to take a break for a drink of cool water from jars along the wall whenever they needed one, which was far more than Khefti had ever allowed, and although the drying chamber was in full sun, the mortars were ranged under shade. No, this was not as bad as it could have been, though the other boys complained loudly that they were ill-used. He simply set himself to produce more of the powder than any of them.

Then, at long last, when even his work-toughened arms were tired, came lunch.

He was more thirsty than hungry, and drank an entire jar of beer before he even touched a bite of food. While he drank it, though, he kept his eyes on the table in front of him, but kept his ears open wide.

"Going to come fishing with us after supper, Hafer?" asked one of the boys whose piping soprano betrayed that he could not be too much older than Vetch.

"Not unless you can promise more sport than last time," Hafer replied. "Joset and Mata are going bird hunting, and said they'd take me along to hold their throwing sticks. They almost always get ducks." He smacked his lips ostentatiously.

But the other boy only laughed. "Ducks! Nasty little mud hens, more like! You can have my share! Grilled fish, now that's more what I like."

For a moment he was surprised, but then he realized that *of course* fish would be a rarity on the table here, despite the abundance of other luxuries. You couldn't sacrifice a fish to the gods, after all. So what was common fare for practically anyone else with the time to spend on the river was a treat for the dragon boys.

A discussion of the superiority of grilling over coals versus baking in mud ensued, and when another conversation caught his ear, held in the deeper voices of a couple of older boys, he switched his attention to that.

"—and I've two copper coins, which ought to be plenty," one said. "You can drink like the Great King himself at Neferetu's beer shop on two coppers."

"Your Jouster won't care if you go into Mefis to spend it?" the speaker sounded envious. "Mine's afraid if I go into the city, I'll decide this is too tame a life. He doesn't mind my hunting and fishing, but—"

"—but carousing in beer shops is out of bounds, eh? Worse luck for you!" Out of the corner of his eye, Vetch saw one of the older boys slap the shoulder of the other in a gesture of commiseration.

Well, after yesterday, he knew where they got the money to spend. Fortunate creatures. Dragon boys weren't paid anything so far as he could tell; the generous allowances of food, clothing and (presumably) lodging would be more than most apprentices could dream of, and apprentices weren't paid anything either.

But perhaps dragon boys didn't count as apprentices, or more likely, once they got older, perhaps they—the freeborn ones, anyway—were counted among the servants. In which case, they *would* get a wage. All but Vetch, of course. Serfs worked for nothing.

So perhaps that was another reason why Ari had plucked him from Khefti's grip; the Jouster wouldn't have to part with wages for his dragon boy.

That put a bit of a change in the complexion of things . . . if true.

Still, Vetch was the *only* serf here, and it didn't seem as if having a serf as a dragon boy had ever been a common thing among the Jousters. So maybe saving money wasn't the reason, or at least, not the whole of it.

He kept thinking that there were uglier reasons for Ari taking him on, but he kept coming back to the conclusion that it was nothing more than he'd been told. Ari wanted a reliable boy who wouldn't leave, and was prepared to give him the same treatment every other boy got.

And he'd seen Ari's quarters; the man lived frugally, yet he didn't strike Vetch as being a miserly sort. So what, if anything, was he saving money for by having a serf to serve him? No, money probably didn't enter into it.

He finished his meal and hurried back to Kashet's pen; if his timing was right, this was just about the point yesterday when Ari had turned up at Khefti's cistern. So he and Kashet should be returning at any moment.

He was, in fact, not far off. He did a bit of sweeping and tidying around the pen, when he heard the clatter of claws on stone in the corridor, and saw Kashet's head rising above the walls of the pens, looking alertly toward his own. Shortly after that, the dragon, with Ari walking at his shoulder, strode into the pen and positioned himself next to the saddle stand.

And at that, Ari, though clearly weary and nursing a bruised shoulder—and carrying a broken lance—laughed aloud. "Well, Vetch, I think you've passed Kashet's test. He doesn't line up alongside the stand for anyone but me. Not even Haraket gets *that* sort of cooperation."

Vetch was already ducking under Kashet's chest to undo the bellyband when Ari's words made him blink. How was he supposed to respond to *that*?

The words were out of his mouth before he thought about them. "I like Kashet, sir. Animals can tell when you like them."

"So they can." Ari tossed the useless lance aside. "Which means I can leave you both in safe keeping." With an affection slap of Kashet's shoulder, the Jouster strode out, without even looking back to see if Vetch was doing everything properly.

Vetch looked after him with mouth agape for a moment.

Never, once, in all of the time that he had served Khefti, had the Fat One ever left him unsupervised after only two times at a task.

But Kashet's snort into Vetch's hair quickly recaptured his attention. The dragon's breath was very hot; hotter, in fact, than the sun on his skin. It was just short of painful; Vetch took that as a rebuke and hurried to divest Kashet of harness and saddle.

Other dragons were coming in now, and with irritated hisses and whines, they paraded past Kashet's pen, their dragon boys keeping them on the shortened chains that would choke them if they tried to get away. Meanwhile Kashet paid no attention to their protests; with the harness off, he dove into his sand wallow, where he rolled and writhed, as if he itched.

Well, if he was putting on a growth spurt, perhaps he did. Maybe his skin felt too tight. Did dragons shed their skins as they grew, or not?

Which reminded him, though Kashet had not been so unmannerly as to do so himself—he needed to get Kashet's food!

He hurried off to the butchers; Kashet would have a good, long nap in the heat of the day, so this might be the time to give him that extra feeding.

Haraket was there, monitoring the amount each boy took in his barrow and the amount of *tala* he mixed in. "Two barrows for Kashet, sir?" Vetch asked diffidently, as he rolled his own barrow past the *tala* bin.

"Hrmm. Yes. He'll have a chance to sleep most of it off," Haraket replied, and the briefest of smiles crossed his face. "Just a bare day here, and you're acting and thinking like a seasoned hand! Keep this up, boy, and it'd take the Great King's personal order to pry you away from me and out of Ari's service."

Well, Vetch had no particular objections to that. If he *had* to serve his enemies . . . at least this lot of enemies wasn't striping his back until it was raw, and fed and housed and clothed him well.

Kashet was more than ready for his midday meal, and climbed out of his wallow with eagerness when Vetch dumped the barrowful out on the stone verge. Vetch went back for the second load, returning as quickly as he could; the dragon saw the supplement to his repast arriving, and there was no doubt in Vetch's mind that he was ready for it by the way he pounced on the contents of the barrow.

When the last morsel was nothing but a lump in Kashet's throat, the dragon returned to his sands, and quickly buried himself in them, and in mere moments was sound asleep. Vetch absented himself, but only after a moment of his own; the sleeping dragon was an amazing sight, and Vetch drank it in, hardly able to believe that he, *he,* could command such a creature and be obeyed. Not like Ari, of course, but still. . . .

Enough. He left Kashet. He couldn't afford for anyone to think he was lazing about.

The remainder of the day followed on the same pattern as yesterday had, except that he didn't bother to present himself to the Overseer of the Jousters' quarters this time, he just slipped inside and found Ari's rooms and did his cleaning. The Overseer actually came by while he was in the middle of it and did a kind of double-take that was so funny that Vetch had to turn his head away and turn his sudden laugh into a cough to cover it. Evidently the man wasn't expecting Vetch to be there this early. Or, perhaps, at all.

Well, he was. And what was more, Vetch wasn't going to give him a single excuse to use his lash.

Not then. Not *ever.*

By supper, it was evident that the other boys had determined the pattern for their treatment of Vetch, at least for now. They pretended he didn't exist.

And some of the other servants followed the boys' lead. This left Vetch sitting with a couple of burly, silent, and rather intimidating laborers, who had evidently been hired for their muscles, not their minds, for they never spoke a single word all through the meal. But at least the friendly serving woman was still there, and though she hadn't time to talk to him, every time she passed, she gave him an encouraging wink.

He had been the first to sit down for dinner, and he was the first to leave as well, once again bearing a little packet of food for a later snack. He went back to Kashet's pen as the last of the light faded from the western sky. The dragon raised his head a little and blinked sleepily at him, but didn't move. Their quarters became quiet as the dragons settled into their nighttime torpor and the boys themselves either settled into their shared rooms, or went out. This afternoon, with a little time to spare, he had determined that the dragon boys had a little court of their own, with a pool in it for swimming, and tiny rooms that they shared, four or six to a room. Not as luxurious as a Jouster's quarters . . . and to Vetch's mind, not much different from a pallet in the dragon pen. Maybe a little inferior; *they* had no privacy to speak of.

He walked about the dragon compound until dusk, familiarizing himself with the place. The dragon pens were ranged about the landing courtyard, with long, narrow store-rooms between each pen so that the dragons couldn't reach each other over the walls. There were far more pens than there were dragons, though even the unused ones had sand wallows that were every bit as hot as Kashet's. On the west side were the Jousters' quarters and the kitchens, on the north and south, those of their servants and slaves and the dragon boys, and on the east, the armory, the saddlers, and the butchery where the sacrifices were cut up, treated, and distributed. It was quite easy to figure out once you understood the pattern. Vetch didn't venture into the Jousters' quarters, which were lit with torches and lanterns. Servants entered with food and drink and departed with empty platters, and there was a scent of incense and perfume on the night breeze. There was a great deal of talk and laughter going on in there, and Vetch elected not to try and peek in. He got the distinct impression that he definitely would get into trouble if he did. A freeborn boy might get away with spying on the pleasures of his masters—a serf, never.

At length he returned to Kashet's pen, and unwound his kilt, laying it aside. Vetch settled into his corner on his pallet, but he wasn't sleepy yet. As the gloom of dusk settled over the pen, he looked up at the robe of Nofet, spangled with the gold beads that were the stars.

He tilted his head to the side, listening, and heard a hum of muted voices from the other parts of the compound, occasionally someone laughing loudly—both male and female voices. And music, and a woman's voice, singing. Since it wasn't likely that it was the servants and slaves who were laughing like people at a feast, it was probably visitors. Very particular sorts of visitors. Well, the Jousters were the Tians' great weapon, the reason why they had conquered as much as they had, so it was only reasonable that they should have what they wanted. Including women, dancing girls, singing women and—other women.

Vetch was no stranger to why men wanted women. There were the farm animals he'd lived with, after all. And though Khefti could not have gotten a woman without paying for one, well, there were other men in the neighborhood, and there was a little nearby beer house where certain kinds of women plied a trade other than serving beer and food—and when they got a client, they took him wherever they needed to, including the alley just off the kitchen court where Vetch slept.

So the Jousters apparently got whatever rewards they wished to claim. They were heroes after all; much admired and lionized. In fact, some of those women were probably the ladies of the Great King's court, taking the pleasure here they did not find there.

The Tian Jousters were worth a small army in and of themselves, so Vetch had been told. When they swooped down on an Altan village, carrying fire pots to drop on the granaries and strawstacks, they brought terror to the Altan heartland. When they descended on the chariots of the Altan army, terrifying the horses and sending them back through their own lines, there to wreak sheer havoc as they careened though the packed fighters, they disrupted the most successful of Altan tactics, the chariot charge. But worst of all was the tactic that struck true fear into the heart of every Altan officer: when the dragons plunged out of the sky, seized an officer or commander in their talons, lifted him into the air—and dropped him. Vetch had never seen this himself, of course, but everyone had heard the stories. He couldn't imagine how the Altan leaders were keeping officers in the field, when at any moment they might find themselves being dragged into the air, then plunging to their deaths. . . .

Not that he had ever been within miles of the fighting; even the village where he lived had never seen a dragon except at a remote distance, high in the sky. His father's farm had been only that, a farm, and not some enemy stronghold to warrant the attentions of a dragon.

Just a farm, of no tremendous value, except to those who lived there, whose sweat had watered the fields for generations, who had nurtured the soil since time out of mind.

The sound of footsteps just outside the pen broke into his thoughts; he looked up and saw someone standing in the doorway.

It was Ari.

SIX

VETCH had no source of light here in the pen, but there were, of course, the torches in the corridor outside. It was easy enough to recognize Ari's profile against the flickering illumination pouring in the doorway, light that came spilling in through the open arch of the doorway from the torch placed directly across on the corridor wall.

"Kashet—" the Jouster called softly. There was a sibilant sound as the dragon shifted in his sand wallow, and then the dark wedge of Kashet's head loomed above the Jouster's. Vetch was surprised; he hadn't thought that Kashet could be roused once he settled for the night.

The dragon lowered his head and butted it up against Ari's chest. The Jouster staggered a little, then began rubbing the hide between his eyes. "I raised him," Ari said aloud, making Vetch jump. "That's why he's different; that's why *we* are different. The rest were all taken from their nests just before they were going to fly, or just after, when they are too clumsy to avoid the netters, but I hatched Kashet myself, just as a mother dragon would."

"How?" Vetch asked.

Ari chuckled. "I got an egg, I buried it in the hot sands of one of the pens, I turned it three times a day. I talked to him every day, too, while I turned him, because I've heard the mothers mutter to their eggs when they turn them, so I supposed that the sound might be important. I was there when he hatched, and fed him myself, and when he made his first flight, we flew together."

Vetch considered that. "Do you think he thinks that you're his mother?" he asked, tentatively.

"Perhaps at first," Ari replied. "But he's an adult now, and I doubt that he does anymore. I suppose you could say that we're friends; I understand him, and he understands me. Oh, not in *words*, of course, and it isn't as if we hear what the other is thinking, though some people believe that is what we do. We just know one another very well. It's a little like having a falcon, or a hunting pard, or a wild dog that you've raised from infancy. You become accustomed to one another's habits, and able to anticipate what the other is going to do." He paused. "I'm pleased, I'm *very* pleased, that you are getting along with him, and he with you. He doesn't take to just anyone. Haraket can handle him, but it's clearly a case that he tolerates Haraket, rather than likes him. He actually likes you."

That explained a great deal about why Kashet was so unique among the other dragons, and so tame. Ari had actually *hatched* Kashet; the great dragon hadn't been "tamed," because he was tame from the beginning. There was no doubt in Vetch's mind that Ari was right about why Kashet behaved so differently from the other dragons; feral kittens taken half grown from a farmyard never would properly tame down to become quiet, even-tempered pets, even though they were the same breed as, and in all ways identical with, the pampered and aristocratic temple cats. But a kitten from a perfectly feral mother, taken before its eyes were open and fed on goat's milk, became as tame as any temple cat. Most wise farmers had at least one such cat in the household, often more.

Vetch's mother had always made it her business to have a pet cat in the household. She'd said it was to keep the house clean of vermin, but Vetch recalled many evenings in the winter when she would sit beside the charcoal brazier in the twilight, cat on her lap, petting it while Vetch's father mended some small item or other. . . .

Resolutely, he turned his mind away from the memory. What good did it do to remember such things? Better to keep his thoughts on the here and now.

Well, *this* was why Kashet didn't need *tala*. This was why he was so trustworthy. Yes, he had something of a mind of his own, and probably had a temper as well, but he wasn't *fighting* his handlers all the time, and he was tame. True, Vetch had spent much longer on the sand bath than the other boys because it was quite clear that Kashet was not going to leave until *he* was satisfied, but so what? And he would probably need to be played with during times of idleness, and apparently needed to have a human with him at night, but Vetch couldn't see how that could really be counted as "work." To Vetch, knowing now why Kashet was so easy to handle, it seemed ridiculous that Ari was the only Jouster with a truly tame dragon. "Why doesn't everyone do that?" Vetch asked, after a while. "Get eggs, I mean. If it makes that big a difference?"

Ari sighed; it sounded weary. "Because it isn't the tradition, I suppose. Or because it is a great deal less heroic to take an egg than a fighting, hissing nestling that is a few days from flight—or one that *is* flying and might turn and savage you. Or, most likely, because tending an egg and the nestling that hatches is a great deal of work that *must* be done by the man who intends to ride the dragon. It can't be done by anyone else, for the dragon bonds with the person who tends him from the egg. I *know* Kashet would never let Haraket ride him, and I'm not entirely sure he'd ever let anyone other than me in the saddle. And you would have to get an egg freshly-laid and move it in the heat of the day in order to move it without killing the dragonet inside. Why go to all that work when the *tala* keeps the dragons tame enough to ride?" He made a bit of a scornful noise. "My fellow Jousters, I suspect, would rather think of themselves as dragon masters or dragon tamers than dragon nursemaids."

Vetch held his peace; the Jouster didn't seem to expect an answer. He continued to scratch Kashet, who was making burbling sounds in the bottom of his throat. "I am somewhat out of place among our mighty warriors, I fear," Ari said after another, much longer interval. "I was never a soldier, never ambitious to be a warrior. I was trained as a scribe; it is only by virtue of the fact that I ride Kashet that I am a Jouster. The others—well, they are fighters, always intended to be, and never thought of any other life." He coughed a little. "In fact, I suspect that they actually *think* as little as possible."

"I guess that's good in a warrior," Vetch said, feeling obscurely troubled. "A warrior is only supposed to obey orders, not think about them."

Ari coughed again. "You could be right. Haraket says that I think too much, and I probably do."

Vetch sensed something that he couldn't quite put into words; he strained after it, but it eluded him. "Maybe Haraket is wrong. It's important to think before you say or do something," he said finally. "That was what my father always said—"

Ari's head came up, like a hound scenting something interesting. "Your father, the farmer? That is, since you are a serf, I assume your father was a farmer. . . . Did he own his land, before we came and took it away from him? Or was he already a serf to an Altan master, so that our coming made little difference to him?"

Strange questions, certainly not ones that any Tian had ever asked Vetch before. Dangerous questions to answer, if the anger got the better of him. But the darkness made Vetch feel bold, and the calm and curious sadness in Ari's voice cooled his ever-present anger, and he answered, though only after trying to keep his father's advice in mind. "We—our family—held our land for five hundred years," he said, with painful pride.

"Five hundred years." A sigh in the darkness. "And did your father take arms against us? Or your brother? Or were you tilling the soil in peace, far from any battlefield, and never thought about war until the day someone came and told him that his land was no longer his and made you all servants where you had once been masters?"

Vetch felt his mouth falling open. Never, once, had any Tian *ever* said anything to indicate that the theft of the family land had been anything other than absolutely justified, the proper desserts for having been on the wrong side in the war. Just who and what *was* Ari?

He felt impelled to answer. "My father—my father didn't know anything about fighting," he said, his throat growing tight. "We knew there was a war, because so much of our crops went in taxes to feed the King's soldiers, but we never saw any fighting."

No, one long, slow year rolled into the next, and the time was marked by planting, growing, harvest, dry, winter, and flood, the six seasons of the year. No one but the tax collectors ever came to the village, for they were *so* far out of the way. Their farm was on the very edge of the swamp where the land became untillable unless you filled it in, one basket of earth at a time. And people did that; in fact, that was how Vetch's forefathers had gained their land, they had won it from the swamp an inch at a time. There was fever there, and the insects were a constant plague, but the land itself was generous and offered abundance to those who cared for it.

The cruel memories came flooding back, and he stared at the darkness of the far wall, feeling his stomach and throat tighten as he spoke. "It was planting season. Father wouldn't leave the farm at planting season, so I *know* he didn't go to fight the Tians. And I never had any brothers, only sisters."

Sisters who were surprisingly tolerant of the small brother who plagued them with tricks, his mother's darling, his father's pride.

Mother, father, sisters, and grandmother; all had lived in relative harmony in the mud-brick house that had been added onto by generations going back decades. Vetch remembered every room of that house, the kitchen at the rear, that was the heart of the house, the little room with his mother's loom, the storerooms, and that luxury of luxuries, separate little sleeping rooms for each of them. He remembered how, in the worst heat, they used to sleep on the roof at night for the sake of the breeze. He remembered how the sun used to pierce the high windows in his bedroom at dawn, and write a bright streak of light across the top of the opposite wall. The room was just big enough for his pallet—raised above the floor by a wood-and-rope frame—and a chest that held his clothing. But it was his, and when he dropped the curtain over the door, he could be quite alone with his dreams. That was when he still had dreams. . . .

Only the freeborn can afford to have dreams.

"I don't think my father ever saw a sword, much less ever held one," he said, his throat tight. "The sharpest thing on the farm was his scythe." He had to stop and swallow. "The war never even came near us; we just heard that the army was retreating, but we weren't near the big road, so we never saw it going. I don't think my father ever even thought about it; he was too busy worrying about the seeds and the seedlings."

His throat grew tighter, his stomach ached, and his eyes burned. Vetch didn't want to think about when it all ended; didn't want to remember the day that the strangers came, with their bronze swords and leather shields, their long spears—how they spoke to his father as if he were a slave. He still didn't know exactly what they had said; his mother had all of them sheltered in the house with her, when his father had ordered them there, she'd scolded as she *never* scolded until they all went into hiding.

But the memories came anyway, and once again, he was *there*, back in that kitchen, where the bread was burning on the hearth and his mother was paying no attention to it, though it filled the room with the scent of ruin. He was peeking around the edge of a door, and saw how the strangers demanded that his father kneel to them, like a serf. Saw how he cursed them, and picked up a sickle—

It wasn't the anger that came, it was the grief. His throat swelled, and he wanted to howl out his loss like the jackals of the desert. But he didn't dare. He stuffed his hand in his mouth, to stifle his sobs, and even his anger was not proof against the sorrow that threatened to overwhelm him.

One moment, and his tall, strong father had been standing, defying the men who—he now knew—had come to steal the land that had been theirs for centuries. In the next instant, he was on the ground, and his mother had burst out of their futile "hiding place"—as if the Tians hadn't known they were there all along!—to fling herself over his body. Vetch saw it before his eyes as if it was playing out all over again; his mother was running toward the twitching body of his father, screaming, and his sisters followed her, adding their wails to hers, while he stood frozen in the doorway for a moment, before following *them*.

And there was red blood everywhere; it was saturating the front of his father's kilt, pouring into the dust beneath his feet, a single drop on the cheek of his killer, a smear on the blade of the murderous sword.

He didn't remember leaving the house, but he was running, too, not thinking, only screaming at the top of his lungs, screaming at the soldiers. Then, horror on top of horror, the Tian soldiers grabbed her, grabbed him, grabbed his sisters, with the remote indifference of a housewife taking up a chicken for the pot.

Grabbed them, throwing them down beside the road, in the dust, and if any of them tried to rise, they were kicked or clubbed with the butt of a spear until they stayed prostrate. He remembered the taste of dirt and tears, of the blood from his split lip, remembered how his youngest sister wouldn't stop screaming and the soldiers kicked her in the head until they knocked her unconscious.

She was never right after that. . . .

He couldn't get any words past his closed throat, but Ari was just as silent. In a way, he was glad, because if Ari had spoken a single word, he might have flown at him in a rage, and then—

—well, he didn't know what would happen. He certainly wouldn't hurt the Jouster, no more than he had had any chance of hurting the soldier who had killed his father. But in another way, it left him alone in the dark with unbearable memories.

He remembered how, once he was face-down in the dirt, he shook all over; he recalled, viscerally, how he was afraid even to look up, while the sun baked down on his back, and flies buzzed in his father's blood. He remembered that sound, that horrible sound; he was never able to bear the sound of flies after that. He remembered the bruises on his arms where the soldiers had grabbed him, on his ribs where they kicked him, the hundred and one scrapes and cuts where he'd been flung into the ground, the painful bump on his head where one of them had hit him with a spear.

But most of all, he remembered the terrible grief, and the help-lessness. Grief that nearly strangled him, and fear, for the bottom had dropped out of the universe and everything he had trusted in was gone.

The soldiers made them lie there in the dirt beside the road as another stranger arrived, this one with a family and a wagonload of furnishings.

Then the soldiers dragged them off their faces, all but Dershela, who lay on her side, her face black and blue. Her, they picked up by her sheath, which tore, leaving one breast exposed, and dropped her behind the rest of them. The soldiers made them all kneel and watch as the strangers invaded their home, and went through the house, pulling out everything they owned.

Had owned.

And before long, it was unrecognizable.

Every article was picked over; the little that the soldiers consid-ered worth taking was pocketed, and the rest destroyed. Every bit of pottery was smashed, every scrap of fabric torn up, every bit of wood splintered and chopped to bits. Every possession was reduced to trash, then tossed onto the dust heap.

But not before his father's body was thrown there first, with less ceremony than if it had been the carcass of a pariah dog, then covered with the trash that had been his possessions and pride. There was no burial ceremony for his father, no offerings, no prayers, no shrine. His ghost would roam the night, unhomed, rootless, unable to find its way to the Summer Country across the Star Bridge.

And then that Tian family took possession of the house that had been home to his father's line, unbroken, for long, long years. As the strange furnishings moved in, the man's wife began berating the servants that they had brought with them—and criticizing the house at the top of her lungs. Her shrill cries filled the air like the calling of a quarrelsome goose as she bullied her servants into emptying the wagon into the house that was rapidly becoming unrecognizable.

Only then was Vetch's family hauled to their collective feet (except for poor Deshara, who was still unconscious) while the officer explained to them what all this meant—that they had been punished for harboring enemies of the Tians, for *being* enemies of the Tians, for attacking the Tians. That their land was confiscated, and they were graciously being allowed to live, even though their lives were forfeit because the male of the house had attacked an officer of the Tian army.

And that was when they learned what the word "serf" meant.

He could not remember the exact words, only the sense of it, but then again, the sense of it had been beaten into him for so many years that it hardly mattered. That he was bound to the land, and bound to serve the ones who owned it. That he had no rights, except that of being fed and housed. That he was of less import than the kitchen cat, who at least, was of a sacred line going back to the Pashet, the cat goddess.

And last of all, that within the space of a morning, he and his family had been reduced to chattel. They could own nothing, earn nothing, be nothing. They had become possessions, and ones of little value.

Then, after seeing their husband and father murdered for no reason, after lying without food or water in the hot sun for hours, after watching everything they had ever known utterly and wantonly destroyed, they were permitted to rise and start their new lives. They were allowed to make their beds out of whatever they could get from the discards and what they could gather with their own two hands among the weeds and along the riverbank. They were permitted to lodge in what had been the cattleshed, to work their own land without profit or payment.

He choked on his tears now, as he had then, when he had curled into a ball on the malodorous pile of river reeds, and wept himself into exhaustion.

And he remembered how from that day onward, he had eaten what scraps were given to him in bitterness, flavored with tears, seasoned with grief too deep for words.

He didn't want to remember. But he could never forget.

"Five hundred years ago, boy," Ari said softly, breaking the horrible silence, "Five hundred years ago, a people called the Heyksin came to Tia. Did you know that? To us, they are the Cursed People, the Nameless Ones, because of what they did to us. Only scribes, priests, and a few fools who call themselves scholars still know what they called themselves. And they destroyed our army, killed our King and our nobles, and sent their people to take the farms and livelihoods of Tians who had lived in their little mud-brick houses for hundreds of years."

He paused, and breathed into Kashet's nostrils. "So. Does that story sound familiar to you?"

"I—" Vetch couldn't speak.

"Well, perhaps if I continue," Ari replied, as if he had not heard that faltering reply. "Yes, they sent their people to become the owners and masters of homes they themselves had not built, had not tilled. And the Tians who had called those places home now served the newcomers as slaves. When the Tians rebelled, they

were beaten and suffered further depredations, when they dared
to strike against their overlords, dozens of innocents were slaughtered in retribution. That was what was happening to us, five
hundred years ago, when your grandfather's grandfather's grandfather was settling his little farm, winning it from the swamp beside the Great Mother River. Then we Tians learned to ride
dragons, to drive chariots, and to make bronze swords and spear-
heads, and we rose up and drove the Heyksin out. There are
those who even say that it was from the Altans that we learned
to do these things, though most would deny this, or say that it
was the gods themselves who taught us. Oh, we were *so* proud
of ourselves! We were sure that the gods had blessed us, and that
we were destined to create a great nation."

"But what happened? If it was Altans who taught—" He
stopped; he couldn't go on.

Ari bent his head over Kashet's. "Well, it depends upon who
you ask. Some say that your people attacked ours. And that might
very well be true—and it may not. I think it more likely that as we
pressed northward, the Altans were pressing south, and we met
and quarreled over the spoils. And perhaps it was only a matter of
your kings hating ours, and ours despising yours. I think—only
think, mind, that the Altans probably *did* attack us when we grew
strong enough to threaten them. I believe that they originally
hoped to put us, the younger kingdom, in our place. And Vetch,
they *do* continue to attack us, there is no denying that; they do
send young warriors into our villages to kill the important men or
the Great King's officials there. They set ambushes on the road to
murder and rob. And we use this as a reason to muster the army
and press northward again, to 'pacify the countryside.' The
wrongs are so tangled up now that there is no disentangling them.
The problem is, we did—and are doing—to you what the Heyksin
did to us. The problem is, because we cannot catch the agents
and soldiers, we take out our wrath upon those Altans we
can catch."

Once more Vetch had the sense of something very important

that was just out of his grasp. But the grief and rage, the terrible emotion that Ari had roused in him—it was too raw, too painful to permit him to think about anything else. Tears cut down his cheeks, hot and bitter, his gut was a mass of knots, and his throat was swollen with grief. But he had learned since that terrible day how to cry without a sound, not even a sniffle, though his eyes burned and ached and his throat closed up completely and his gut was cramped with holding in the sobs he dared not release. Not even in front of this man, who had been absently kind, who spoke as if he might understand.

Ari shook his head, and reached up to pat Kashet's neck. "And none of that matters to you, I suppose," he sighed. "It certainly doesn't matter to the other Jousters. It doesn't seem to matter to anyone but me that Tians are doing to Altans precisely what we claimed were the most heinous of crimes when the Heyksin inflicted them upon us. It doesn't seem to concern anyone that *we* have become what we most despised. Haraket is right. I think too much."

He patted Kashet again, and the dragon nuzzled him, then pulled away, settling back into the sand. And without another word, Ari turned and left the pen. Vetch was alone in the darkness, with a slumbering dragon, a sorrow too deep and wide to leave room for anything else, and his memories. And an anger that built walls as high as his sorrow was deep.

His throat felt raw, and his gut ached. In a way, it had been easier when he had served Khefti. He'd been too exhausted to be troubled by his memories at night, and his hatred for Khefti had eclipsed all other emotions.

Now—now he lay and watched the moon rise above the pen walls, and when he closed his eyes—

—he watched his father, a quiet, dignified man, face the captain of the soldiers. Kiron Dorian had been a strong, but very lean farmer, bronze skin turned the color of smoothly-tanned leather by the sun; Altans were a trifle paler than Tians, but other than that, there was little difference between the peoples of the two

Kingdoms. Like all Altans, he cut his hair short, just above the ears, and he wore the short, unpleated kilt that all Altan farmers sported. In all other ways, he and the soldiers could have been cousins, with the same black hair and dark eyes, the same jutting chins, the same beak-like noses. . . .

There were those who said that the Altans and Tians sprang from the same stock, although both sides would vehemently have denied any such thing. But this had been Vetch's first sight of a Tian and—and he could not tell the difference between these men and the folk of his own village.

Other than the fact that they were a shade or so darker than his father, and the difference in clothing, of course, and the rest of their dress. And the weapons.

Why, *why* had Kiron reached for his sickle? He had stuck it in his waistband when the captain approached him, but *why* had he drawn it?

Or had he only reacted instinctively, in anger, to protect his land and his family?

Vetch tried to remember what it was that he had heard the captain say—the soldiers had spoken in broken Altan, with a heavy accent. There had been the insults, of course, and the orders—

But surely Kiron had known he could not prevail against an entire band of soldiers.

Maybe he hadn't cared. Or maybe he had just reacted instinctively, as any man would, when faced with a threat. He had tried to drive out the interlopers, to defend what was his.

And died for it.

Vetch squeezed his eyes shut, and curled himself up to muffle his sobs, and for the first time since his father had died, wept himself to sleep.

The days settled into a pattern of meals, work, and sleep. Within a week, the other dragon boys got used to Vetch's presence, and went from ostentatiously ignoring him to absentmindedly ignoring him, the latter being much easier to bear. At least there was no overt hostility, and the tricks and "pranks" he had dreaded never occurred. He wondered if Haraket or some other Overseer had given them an actual warning about mischief, though that might have been waving a red rag at a bull. After all, the surest way to make a boy do something is to forbid him to do it.

He never asked; he was just grateful to be left in peace. Once in a while, one of them would actually speak directly to him, though it tended to be a command rather than a comment or a pleasantry; Vetch ignored the commands as he had ignored the hostility, for he was not *theirs* to command.

The attitude that he *was*, however, rankled, and grew worse, not better, over time. By the time the *kamiseen* died, it was clear even to Te-Velethat that Vetch was a superior worker, and even the sour Overseer of the Household was willing to give him grudging credit for his work. So being told to fetch and carry by someone too lazy to do his own work—with an air of lofty superiority—made his blood boil. Such incidents gave his hatred fresh fuel to feed upon, fuel which was otherwise—lacking.

Haraket was unfailingly just, the Overseer of the Household scarcely ever set eyes on Ari's quarters anymore, and thus Vetch seldom saw him, and the other servants, slaves, and serfs treated him no differently than any other dragon boy. His fingers no longer itched for clay to make a cursing figure from. In fact, he could go for half a day without being consciously angry.

And as for Ari—well. During the daylight hours, the Jouster was kind, in an austere and distant fashion, courteous and polite. But every so often, the Jouster would come to Kashet's pen late at night, and the most extraordinary exchanges took place. . . .

Vetch learned very little about Ari's childhood; only how he had apprenticed as a scribe. He did learn a great deal about dragons, for Ari had studied them extensively. In their behavior, at least according to Ari, they were most like the great cats of the desert, with a great deal of hawklike behavior, especially when young, thrown in.

"Their eyesight is much better than ours, but not as good as a falcon's," Ari said one night, as Vetch sat a little apart from him, both of them with their feet and ankles in the hot sand of Kashet's wallow to keep off the nighttime chill. Kashet's head was actually in Ari's lap. "I've seen a falcon come down out of the sky from so high up that he wasn't even a speck, to take a bustard crouched in the desert a few feet in front of me that I couldn't see. A dragon's eyesight isn't nearly that keen. But they are hunters, like the falcons, and when they get prey in sight and they're hungry, you haven't a chance of diverting them from it. Not all the *tala* in the world can overcome their instincts when they're hungry."

Vetch thought back to his first day, and Haraket berating one of the boys for feeding his dragon too lightly. "What'll they do?" he asked. "If it's a Jouster's dragon that's very hungry, I mean?"

"Hunt," Ari said shortly. "Probably *not* their rider; they haven't had a chance to learn that we can be food. But they'll hunt things they've seen brought to them as food by their mother and father. Once they're old enough to feed themselves, their parents bring them whole animals and don't tear bits off to feed to them. And at the end, just before the youngsters make their first flight, sometimes the parents bring in prey that isn't quite dead, so the dragonets get the experience of seeing their dinner alive and moving, and make a first kill early on. So they'll have seen sheep, goats, rabbits, maybe even fowl. A hungry dragon will ignore his training to hunt, and his rider had better hang on or he'll be thrown. And if that should happen in the middle of a fight or a flight, too bad. I've known of a rider to be killed by Altan archers while his dragon was on the ground, feeding, and he was sitting in the saddle, an easy target."

"And if a dragon ever does learn that humans can be food?" he asked.

"That dragon is destroyed," Ari replied flatly. "That's happened, too, in training—stupid Jousters in training who let themselves get slashed or bitten, and their dragon gets the taste of human blood. You can see it in their eyes; they've made the connection, and no human is safe. We call them 'mar dragons,' and no amount of *tala* can make them forget. We can't turn them loose because they've lost all fear of men, but we can't keep them, either."

"Would that happen with Kashet?" he wondered aloud.

Ari started to answer him, then paused. "Huh. I don't know. Dragons don't consider each other as prey, and I suppose Kashet thinks that we are dragons. It's not an experiment I'd care to try."

Vetch enjoyed listening to Ari talk. He'd been a little worried at first, when Ari turned up after dark, wondering if Ari had something else in mind besides talking, but no more. And if he enjoyed listening, Ari appeared to enjoy having someone who would listen intelligently.

Whatever the reason, at least he felt less alone.

Vetch was surprised one noontide to find Haraket *not* overseeing the boys as they collected their meat; he was even more surprised to discover him testing the temperature of Kashet's sand wallow with his hand and forearm. At least, that was what he *thought* Haraket was doing; he couldn't imagine any other reason why the Overseer would be kneeling at the verge with his arm plunged into the sand.

Vetch did not stop to question him, however, for Kashet was tossing his head impatiently, wanting his meal.

But Haraket was frowning as he got back to his feet, and he strode over to Vetch, still frowning.

"Get the pen completely cleaned when Kashet's away," Haraket ordered. "I mean *completely*. Tidy everything up. This entire row of sand wallows needs the heating spells renewed on them, and the Ghed priests mustn't be offended by anything that isn't spotless and utterly neatened."

He glanced significantly at Vetch's pallet and his few belongings, and Vetch understood immediately. *Tidy everything up* meant to hide the reminders that this dragon was tended, not by a free-born dragon boy who lived with the others, but a serf. The Ghed priests were notorious sticklers for tradition, and tireless enforcers of custom.

So he hid everything that belonged to him in the storage room, as well as anything else that happened to be lying about in the pen for good measure. Then he cleaned out wallow and "privy"—or at least raked out the top layer of sand in the wallow—and by the time the priests arrived, there was no sign even that Kashet's pen was in use.

Wild with curiosity by this time, he hid in the storage room with the door curtain held down with a weighted bar across the bottom so that it couldn't get caught by an ill-timed breeze to reveal where he was. He peeked carefully through a tiny gap between the curtain and the doorpost, as he heard the chiming sound of sistrums and the footsteps of many people.

He waited there while they did—whatever it was that they were doing—in the next pen over. It was hot and very close inside the storeroom, which lacked the roofline windows of a room that was going to be used by people. Sweat prickled his scalp, and a drop slid down his back as he waited. Finally Haraket led four priests and four little priestesses in a kind of solemn procession in through the door to the pen, and they arranged themselves around the wallow, a priest to each corner, the four priestesses in a line across the back wall, Haraket near the door.

They were colorful figures; all four of the priests went shaven-headed, without a wig, but where their heads were bare, their bodies were anything but. Rather than the kilt of most men, they wore long robes of finely pleated white linen; not one robe, but three of them. The first reached to the ground, the second to the calf, and the third to the knee. Their sandals were ornamented with turquoise, and like Haraket they wore a striped sash around their waists and another running from left shoulder to right hip. But *their* sashes were embroidered and beaded in red, yellow, and green, and were twice as wide as Haraket's. The four young priestesses dressed in robes of whitest mist linen with wreaths of blue *latas* flowers about their heads, and beads of gold and carnelian at the ends of each of the hundreds of braids in their wigs. They appeared to be not much older than Vetch. Their eyes were lined with kohl and shaded with malachite, and they each wore cones of perfume atop their fine wigs.

All four priests raised their hands together, and began to chant in time to the chiming of the sistrums shaken by the priestesses. They looked so identical at that moment that they might have been paintings on a wall done by the same artist.

The spell was an intricate one, not some simple cursing. Vetch listened avidly as they began with a long, protracted invocation to the gods, Ghed in particular.

Then began the real work of the spell, and that was where Vetch lost track of what they were doing completely. It *seemed* to involve the sand wallow, but also the Great King's palace. Both were described in exquisite detail, and the God Ghed was enjoined to *take*—something—from the palace, and put that same something here in the wallow. But what that was, Vetch could not make out.

Whatever they were doing took a lot of time, though, a great deal of chanting *and* effort, and the priests' pleated robes were beginning to wilt a little before they were done.

Inside the stifling storage room, Vetch was feeling a bit wilted himself.

Finally, though, they finished. With a last shake of the sistrums, the priests dropped their arms as one, and filed out the door, as solemnly as they had come. Haraket followed them out, and Vetch heard the chiming and footsteps moving on to the next pen.

Nevertheless, he waited until the chanting on the other side of the walls had started up again before venturing out.

There was *no* doubt that their magic had worked, and worked well. The sands were hotter than ever, and as Vetch hauled all of the things *out* of storage that he'd so hastily shoved *in,* he saw a heat shimmer playing over the top of the wallow. He had to work quickly; he was already a little late to clean Ari's quarters. Fortunately, that hardly mattered; there just wasn't that much work to be done there, and he had gotten it down to an art.

Kashet greeted the change in his wallow with a surprised snort, then gleefully plunged in. Ari raised his eyebrow, and paused for a moment instead of heading straight for his quarters.

"Were the Ghed priests here?" he asked.

Vetch nodded. He was still alive with curiosity. "Haraket said the magic needed renewing."

"I thought things were getting a little cooler than Kashet prefers," Ari replied, and allowed his eyebrow to drop again. "Good."

"Ah—" Vetch wasn't sure he should be asking the question, but he couldn't bear not to. "What were they *doing*, anyway? I mean, how do they make things hotter?"

Ari had half-turned away, on his way out the door. Now he turned back and gave Vetch a long, level look. "You were listening, weren't you."

It wasn't a question. Vetch looked at his feet, then at Ari, and swallowed. He was about to be punished. He knew it, he just knew it. "Yes, sir," he admitted.

"Don't tell anyone else. The Ghed priests would have a litter of kittens over the idea that an Altan serf was inside their sacred square." But Ari's normally solemn, brown eyes were full of amusement, and Vetch took heart again. "As to how they did it—if I knew, I'd be a priest-mage, not a Jouster. But I know *what* they do, because I've copied out the rituals and spells for them before. Have you ever been to the Great King's palace?"

Before Vetch could shake his head—after all, why would *he* get into a palace!—Ari was going on.

"If you had, the first thing that would strike you is that while everything else is hot enough to bake bread, inside the walls of the palace it's cool enough for the ladies to wear lambswool mantles. And that is because the Ghed priests, with their magic, are taking the heat from there, and putting it in our sand wallows. That's what the spell is for; it's like an irrigation ditch that allows the heat to flow from there to here."

Vetch stared at him. He'd have doubted Ari's sanity, except that there was no reason to disbelieve the Jouster. "But," he said, "what about in winter? You wouldn't want to make it colder." It was the only thing he could think of.

"In winter, they take it from somewhere else. My *guess* would be forges, bakehouses, places where there is a lot of heat it would be good to get rid of, even in winter. In fact, since the winter rains aren't far off now, they probably did just that this time around, rather than come back a second time to recast the spell." Ari shrugged. "They might even take it from the fire vents and lava cones out there past the desert; I might have copied some of their spells, but magic is something it's best not to know too much about. Now—*don't* let anyone know you watched the magic, and don't let anyone know I told you how the spell works."

And with that, he *was* gone, leaving Vetch with quite a bit more to think about.

That night, when Ari appeared to tend to Kashet, not a word was spoken about magic. But now Vetch was curious about other things that were not so dangerous to know.

The weather was about to turn; the nights were more than chill, they were *cold*, and Kashet was very happy with his sand wallow this evening.

"There are hot sands that the wild dragons use?" he said, making it a question, as Ari rubbed under Kashet's chin.

"Of course there are—though, mind, dragons also use the heat of their own bodies to hatch their eggs. Wild dragons take it turn and turn about, males and females, to brood the eggs. That way they both can eat and drink. At night, when it's coldest, they brood the eggs together."

Vetch considered this. "How do you know that?" he asked, finally.

Ari chuckled. "Because, fool that I was, I went out and watched them. And yes, I could very easily have ended up going down one of those long throats. But I was young and immortal, and I was very, very tired of sitting about and writing, endless copies of things no one cared about. Even when I came here, I was the unconsidered copyist. I wanted to do something different, something that would be read for the next hundred years." He chuckled again. "Actually, although I didn't really want to be a scribe, my uncle wouldn't hear of anything else, and after my father died, he was the head of our household when he made my mother his second wife. He was always quoting the sages to me. 'The metalworker has fingers like crocodile hide, and stinks worse than fish eggs. The fisherman wears little but net, and eats only what he cannot sell. The farmer labors from dawn to dusk, serving only the tax collector, the embalmer is shunned by all, the brick maker is as filthy as a pig, the soldier lives every day never knowing if it will be his last. But the scribe never goes hungry; he can aspire to the halls of the great ones, and his is the only profession wherein he himself is the overseer.' Except that, of course, that last isn't true at all, and most scribes spend their lives, not in the halls of the great ones, but sitting in a marketplace, waiting for anyone who wants a letter written, or bent over a desk in his lap, copying copies of copies of things so tedious they send him to sleep."

Vetch sighed. Whoever had written that hadn't known anything about farmers. . . .

Then again, whoever had written that was, without a doubt, trained as a scribe originally. He started to ask about Ari's parents, but Ari continued before he could say anything.

"When I came here to serve the Jousters, I decided to learn as much as I could about the dragons, and I decided that the best way to do so was to study the wild ones. I watched them courting in the sky, and although I never actually caught one laying an egg, I did know within a day when one *was* laid, because I took to watching particular natural sand wallows. Which wasn't easy!

Dragons only use the wallows that are sheltered to lay their eggs in, usually in caves.''

Vetch shivered, thinking that "wasn't easy" was assuredly an understatement. What had Ari done? Had he actually been brave enough to slip into the caves to see if eggs had been laid?

Ari had warmed to his subject; it seemed that whenever the subject was "dragons," Ari could always stir up enthusiasm. "The mother doesn't start brooding until her clutch is laid, so it wasn't particularly hard to sneak into her cave to see if she'd left anything.''

Not particularly hard. Vetch managed not to snort. But he did say, judiciously, "I couldn't have done that."

This time Ari laughed aloud, and ruffled Vetch's hair. It was curious; at first, Vetch had been very wary of Ari, knowing, as he did only too well, that some men . . . well. But Ari had never given him a moment of unease. The physical demonstrations had all been—

—*safe.* That was the word. Brotherly, perhaps. That was close enough to the word he didn't want to think of—

—*fatherly.*

Fortunately, Ari was still merrily talking away. "They usually court and lay just at the start of the dry, and the egg hatches when the rains begin. They feed and grow all during the winter and spring, and fledge when the dry comes again. They're still small, *far* too small to joust with, far too small to carry a rider for long, but as you'll hear Haraket say a thousand times, 'Neither Jouster nor dragon are made in a season.' Kashet, of course, began carrying me from the beginning.''

"Is that why he's so strong?" Vetch ventured.

"It could be," Ari agreed, and yawned. "Vetch, if you want to hear more about Kashet—"

"Yes!" Vetch interrupted.

Once again, Ari laughed. "Then we'll have more time after the rains start—which they will within a day or so, or at least, that's what the Nuth priests are saying. Then our patrols will be cut to one a day, because the dragons will not want to fly. Until then, Kashet and I need to get in as much flying time as we can, so I am going to sleep. And you should, too."

Ari gently moved Kashet's head from his lap; the dragon grumbled, but shifted so that all of him was in the wallow. Then Ari stood up.

"Thank you for listening to me babble, Vetch. My fellow Jousters are more than tired of hearing me."

He heard the faint echo of loneliness in Ari's voice, and quickly said, "I'm not!"

Ari ruffled his hair again. "I should hope not," he replied with mock sternness. "Dragons in general, and Kashet in particular, are your business, young dragon boy. Get some sleep, now."

Ari went off to his own quarters then, and Vetch took his advice. He went to sleep quickly, dreaming of a sky filled with dragons.

SEVEN

IT was the business of the priests and priestesses of the goddess Nuth—or, more accurately, the Seers among those priests and priestesses—to predict the start of the season of winter rains. This was of vital importance to the Jousters, for once the rains began, their work would be much curtailed. Dragons didn't like the cold and performed sluggishly when the temperature dropped—and although you could get them to fly in the rain, not even *tala* would keep them in the air for long. So as the end of the dry season neared, the more closely the compound watched the Temple of Nuth for word. Haraket sent messengers daily, asking if a date had been Foreseen. Anxiety mounted, in no small part because the Jousters, and their dragons, were tired. They needed this respite, and needed it badly.

They need not have been concerned. Precisely when the Nuth priests said they would, the rains came.

Three messages arrived from the Avenue of Temples before Haraket could send his daily request; the first gave warning that the rains would certainly begin the next day, the second gave the exact hour (which was the second hour of dawn), and the third, that the first storm would be unusually heavy. Vetch and the rest of the dragon boys had all rehearsed what they were to do, and after the sun set and all the dragons had settled, they had gone down every row of pens and pulled the canvas awnings over every one of the sand wallows. There was no point in allowing even the unused wallows to become pits of hot sand soup, for green muck would grow in it if the water didn't steam away in time, and that would mean digging out all of the mucky sand and replacing it with clean.

When the rains actually began, Vetch was sound asleep. He woke to the sound of distant thunder and within an hour, rain poured out of the sky and drummed down on the awnings; it was still so dark that he couldn't even see his hand in front of his face, and the first rush of water put out the torches in the corridor outside. It was quite a storm, and he was glad to be under cover when it came, although all of the lightning stayed up in the clouds, and the thunder never was more than a rumble overhead. Still, as hard as the water was pouring down out of the sky, the roar as it hit the canvas and the ground was enough to drown out everything but that thunder. He couldn't help but contrast his position now with the same time last year, when he had actually climbed up onto the woodpile in Khefti's back courtyard to shelter under the canvas covering it—for he was not permitted an awning to keep *him* dry.

These rains would actually do very little for the state of the Great Mother River, for the annual flood that enriched the fields with a thick carpet of rich silt were caused by rain that fell in the lands of the headwaters, much farther south. And the winter rains in Tia were nothing like the ones in Vetch's home in Alta; storms could last for many days without a pause up there, but were gentle things, as much mist as rain.

The floods had less effect in Alta as well. By the time the Great Mother River reached Alta, she had spread out into the flatlands and swamps, and there was more room for the floodwaters to go.

On the first day of the rains, dawn did not truly arrive; the darkness merely lightened, gradually, to gray. The awnings were cleverly made to dump the rain into channels that carried the water away from the sand wallow; very little got into the hot sand, and most of that quickly steamed away. Kashet showed no signs of wanting to move; in point of fact, it looked to Vetch as if nothing short of an earthquake would budge the dragon from his wallow. Not that Vetch blamed him; he wished *he* could stay warm and dry—but the rains didn't stop the chores from needing to be done, so he would have to get up and join the other boys at their daily tasks.

He wrapped his woolen mantle about his shoulders, and left the shelter of the awnings for the corridor—

—where he promptly got soaked. No awnings there; it would have been a shocking waste of canvas, even for so prosperous a place as the Jousters' compound. The best he could hope for would be that he'd get to spend most of his time inside rooms rather than courtyards. At least the wool of his mantle stayed warm, though wet. The linen kilt went sodden and cold and distinctly unpleasant, it clung to him clammily and only impeded his walking.

He got Kashet's breakfast; the other boys were straggling in, as reluctant to leave their quarters as he was, and for once, they didn't pointedly ignore him. Shared misery was making for a semblance of amity, anyway. Haraket was there as usual, and made sure that each of the boys covered the meat in their barrows with much-stained squares of scrap canvas, hide, or some other covering from a pile of such things beside the *tala*-bin. Vetch did the same, although his load did not have *tala* on it; that was the main concern, that the *tala* not wash off. The dragons would be reacting to the onset of the rains according to their natures; some would be surly, some languid, some edgy, and the surly and edgy ones would need that *tala* if their boys were to handle them safely in their enforced confinement. He pulled his mantle over his head, squared his shoulders, and trundled his barrow back to the pen through the downpour.

Kashet raised his head lazily from the wallow when he entered the pen, and took his time in eating his meat. Perhaps he already knew that there would be no flying today; he was certainly clever enough to know that when the rains began, work ended. Kashet seemed to savor each bite, rather than bolting his food, but Vetch didn't care that the dragon lingered over his meal; he took the opportunity to bury his chilled feet in the hot sand, and spread his soaking mantle over the top of the wallow out of Kashet's way. The wool began to steam immediately, and the hot sand felt so good on his cold feet that he left the verge and sat himself right down in the sand himself, wrapping his skinny arms around his knees and resting his chin atop them. Long before Kashet finished his meal, Vetch stopped shivering and began to warm up.

Kashet paused when the barrow was just about half emptied, and craned his neck over to look at Vetch curiously as the boy joined the dragon in the sand, but did nothing more than snort, then went back to his food. It occurred to Vetch then that this was an entirely unanticipated benefit of having Kashet as his dragon—*some* of them were very territorial about their wallows, and it would have been sheer torture to have to stand there shivering, *knowing* how nice and hot the sand was, and not daring to put so much as a toe into it.

Once fed, Kashet buried himself in his sand again, with his wings tucked in tightly to his body. Vetch cleaned the litter pit without Kashet even stirring. Presumably the other boys were having no more trouble with their beasts than he was with Kashet, since he didn't hear the usual cursing, hissing, and rattling chains from the pens of some of the troublemakers.

He breathed a sigh of relief. He might not care much for any of them, but one thing that the rains were going to do was leave the others plenty of idle moments, and he really would rather that nothing increased their irritation. The rains had always been the *worst* time for mean tricks from Khefti's apprentices, because the apprentices, too, were cold and wet and miserable, and inclined to try and make anyone inferior to them even more miserable than they were. If the other dragon boys were having an easy time of it, they'd be less likely to have anything to take out on Vetch.

He hated to leave Kashet's pen and the heat radiating up from the sand wallow, but he didn't have much choice in the matter. Perhaps the dragons weren't going to fly, but there were plenty of chores that still had to be done.

But as he reported to his various stations, he learned that he was getting a bit more leisure than he'd thought. There was no need to check over the lances, for instance, and the last few baskets of the ripened *tala*, the fruits of the end of the season, had to be discarded, for it could not be dried now. Nor could it be pounded to powder in weather like this; so much dampness in the air would ruin it. And as for tidying the Jousters' quarters, well, that depended on the Jouster in question. Most of them did not want to be disturbed, which meant that the dragon boys got to sit around idle—though it was an enforced idleness that none of them really enjoyed. Yes, they could go out hunting in the marsh, or fishing—in the cold, soaking rain, which took all the joy out of such pastimes, and turned them into labor. They could go into the city, but even with coins to spend, there was no great joy for them there, for the beer shops were colder than their own quarters, suffered from floors that turned into mud, and were crowded with laborers who got the lion's share of attention from the serving girls and entertainers. Only the nobles and the wealthy got to spend the winter rains in an endless round of feasting and merriment indoors. The rest of the city went about its business in wet, cold misery. No one went out of doors unless he had to, and those who did were not happy about it.

So the leisure hours of the winter rains were spent confined to their courtyard, playing what games they had, huddled around charcoal braziers. So far as Vetch was concerned, charcoal braziers were a poor substitute for the hot sands. Since Kashet didn't object, just after the noon meal, he actually moved his pallet down onto the wallow, for sand in his bedding was a small price to pay for the added warmth.

Ari was one of those who had told his dragon boy not to trouble
with tidying up that afternoon, which meant that Vetch would
have the entire time free. After feeding Kashet at noon, Vetch
stretched himself out on his pallet to soak in the heat. He might
not have done as much actual *work* today as he usually did, but
the cold was as punishing as physical labor, and he felt absolutely
drained. Not sleepy, just exhausted.

In weather like this, Khefti would have him running about on a
hundred tasks, mostly concerned with leaks and mud—mopping
up water that came through the roof, going up on the roof to
find and stop the leaks, and cleaning up the mud that Khefti, his
apprentices, his customers, and his household tracked in everywhere. During the rains, Vetch's life seemed to revolve around
mud, cold, and wet, adding wretchedness to the perpetual misery
of his empty belly. Khefti would lurch between two moods during
the rains. In his first mood, he would be pleased, because, after
all, rains in a place made of mud-brick buildings would mean more
business for him afterward. Rain *would* get past the plastering if it
wasn't properly kept up, and then Khefti would get his business.
Vetch sometimes wondered, if, now and again, Khefti didn't pay
his apprentices to go about just before the rains and put a little
damage on the homes of those Khefti determined could afford
some rebuilding. . . .

But *during* the rains, only the pottery was working; he couldn't
make brick until the rains *and* the flood stopped. So in his second
mood, Khefti would be glum and angry, impatient for the rains to
stop so that he could get to making those bricks, angry that four
of his six apprentices were idle, counting up the cost in fuel and
food with no income from the brickworks coming in. Furthermore, Khefti would be as miserable as everyone else with the cold
and wet, and would take it out on the nearest object, which was
usually Vetch.

Which was hardly fair, but "fair" wasn't a word that could ever
be applied to Khefti.

Vetch had Khefti on his mind a great deal today, which didn't necessarily make him feel safe. There was always the feeling that Khefti hadn't finished with him.

He had just started to get warm, and to think about what he might do to occupy his time, when he heard someone at the entrance to the pen, and looked up.

It was Haraket. He sat up with a start of guilt, wondering if putting his pallet in the wallow was something forbidden, or if he had somehow forgotten a chore that should have been done. The Overseer gestured to him as he scrambled to his feet and up onto the stone verge, and his alarm increased when he saw Ari was with Haraket. Both were wrapped in dripping mantles, as if they had just come a long distance down the uncovered corridors.

"Here, boy—" Haraket thrust another mantle at him, this one adult-sized. "Wrap up in that and come along. You've been called up before the magistrate; he's waiting at the Dragon Hall."

What? Vetch was so shocked by that statement that all he could do was stand stark still and gape at the two of them, the mantle dangling loosely in his hands.

"Better say, *we* have been called up," Ari corrected. "Vetch is the object of disputation. It seems your former master is not letting go of you without a fight."

Vetch felt his heart plummet right down to the ground, and he went cold all over. Khefti? Oh, gods—

I knew it. I just knew it. This was too good to last—

And Khefti would never, ever, give up anything that he thought was his by right.

"Hah. Neither are we, and the law's on our side," Haraket said, with a certain grim glee. "The magistrate's come here with the fat slug in tow, rather than summoning us to his own Court; the magistrate knows who has the rights here. So come along. And don't look like a gazelle in the jaws of a lion, boy!"

But he couldn't help *feeling* like a gazelle in the jaws of a lion! His stomach had gone into knots and was hurting, and not all of his shivers were due to the cold as he followed Haraket and Ari.

They led him right out of the corridors he knew, into a part of the compound where he had never been before, right past all of the Jousters' Courts.

And all the while, Vetch was in agony. They didn't *know* Khefti—they didn't *know* how grasping-clever he could be! If he was here, it was because he had found a law that would give him possession of Vetch again. Khefti would never attempt anything that he thought would fail. If he'd come for Vetch, it was because he already knew that he would win.

Haraket herded him down a dead-end corridor that terminated in an enormous sandstone building, the largest that Vetch had ever seen, which would have been a pale gold in the sunshine, but was a rich brown with the rain soaking into its face. It was easily four stories tall, and must surely be the tallest structure in the compound. The Haras-falcon of the Jousters, painted in red and blue and green, spread his wings above the bronze door, and two seated statues of the Great King Hamunshet, he who had driven the Heyksin out of Tia, and who had, so Ari said, been a Jouster himself, flanked the doorway. They stared off majestically into space, ignoring the mere mortals who passed between them.

Inside, the building was even more splendid than the outside, with wonderful, brilliantly-colored wall paintings of Jousters on their dragons flying above chariots, being led by the Great King Hamunshet, wearing the blue war crown, and mounted on his own malachite-green dragon, driving against the barbarians that had thought to hold Tia.

These were not paintings designed to make Vetch feel like anything other than the foreigner he was. At least it wasn't pictures of some other Great King leading his armies against the Altans.

An avenue of brightly painted and carved stone pillars, formed to look like bundles of *latas* flowers, led to the dais at the other end of the building. Immense torches in sconces shaped like *tala* branches mounted onto the pillars provided plenty of light. On the dais was an old man in an immaculate white pleated-linen robe belted with a plain scarlet sash, and a wig of many shoulder-length plaits each ending in a small golden bead. He wore a pectoral necklace of the truth goddess Mhat in gold enameled in scarlet and blue around his neck. Although his garments were anything but ostentatious, he held a little gold whip against his chest, showing that he was the Great King's representative. This, then, was the magistrate.

Below him was Khefti-the-Fat, who looked a bit *less* fat than he had when Vetch had last seen him. He also looked a bit more tired, and very haggard. But he was dressed as Khefti always dressed when he was trying to impress someone, in a pleated linen kilt and overrobe of wool (which barely confined his belly), and a collar of faience beads, and his best short horsehair wig. "That's him!" his voice shrilled out as soon as Vetch came into view. "That's the boy! And that's the Jouster who took him!"

"Are you certain?" the magistrate asked mildly, as if he was totally uninterested in the answer. "You will swear to this, by the good goddess Mhat?"

"Absolutely," Khefti replied instantly.

"That's a fascinating observation, since until this moment, this *gentleman* hasn't heard my voice today, and I was wearing my Jousting helmet at the time I took possession of the boy," Ari said, his tone one of reason tempered by just a touch of scorn. "If this man is so prescient as to be able to see my face within that helmet, then perhaps he should be examined by the Thet priests. Tia could use one whose eyes are not deceived by outward appearances and can see through metal and leather."

Khefti set his jaw, and did not answer. The magistrate's face remained as a mask; Vetch could not tell if he was affected by Khefti's falsehood or not.

"Haraket, Overseer of the Dragon Courts, this man tells me that your Jouster carried off this boy that was in his custody, the serf called Vetch, who is linked to a house and garden in the north." The magistrate's voice was completely without inflection. Nothing whatsoever was to be read in it, and Vetch felt his heart shrinking within him.

"That is entirely true, my lord," Haraket said, not at all dismayed. "It is also true that all serfs are the Great King's, and that a Jouster may requisition anything belonging to the Great King within reason."

"Within reason! But this was *not* within reason!" Khefti shrilled, his voice awakening unpleasant echoes in the hall. "I have no other serf of that bloodline, nor can I obtain one! The assessor has said that I may no longer hold that house and land as a result, a house and land which I got lawfully, and which I have much improved! I have spent every groat of my savings improving it! Am I to lose the price of it and all of my investment as well? It is not reasonable to take this serf from me!"

The magistrate raised one eyebrow slowly. "It is the Great King's to say what is reasonable and what is not," he said in a cold voice. "And I am his voice in this matter."

Khefti did not take warning from that tone. "Then I call upon you, Magistrate, to judge accordingly!" Khefti demanded. "Every grain of barley, every groat in my possession, I have invested in this house and land to which the serf is bloodbound. I, who am the sole support of my aged and infirm mother! And I depend upon the labor of this serf, feeble-minded as he is, to tend to the work of my home, for I have not the means to hire servants or purchase slaves, with all my spare income bound up in that house. No one else would take him so stupid and clumsy that he is—"

Vetch shook inwardly, certain that Khefti would outmaneuver Ari and Haraket. He'd have laughed, if he had not been so full of dread that a black weight hung over his heart. Aged and infirm mother, indeed—aged, yes, Khefti's mother was certainly that, but not infirm, and possessed of property of her own which she would not let Khefti "manage" for her. As for being the obedient son, had he not, in Vetch's hearing, referred to her as "the withered old bat" and prayed to the gods to take her before she drove him mad?

As for the rest of Khefti's lies and half truths, once they would have awakened a fire of rage in his heart. But not now. Now, he had something to lose, and there was room in him for nothing but terror.

"I swear upon my honor, that this serf was being badly neglected, Magistrate," Ari said, with a little bow of deference. "The proof of that lies in the scars upon his back—and the simple fact that in the short time that he has been with us, he has near-doubled his weight. All the serfs are, as you have rightly reminded us, the property of the Great King and as such may not be abused."

"Turn about, boy," the magistrate ordered distantly. Vetch dropped his mantle at his feet, and did so, turning *away* from Khefti. He dared not meet his former master's eyes, or he would not be able to stop his trembling. "It appears, from the number of scars upon this boy's back, that he has been punished far in excess of what I would deem reasonable. Also, I have no doubt that Jouster Ari is speaking the truth about his starved condition, which is also not reasonable. Have you anything to say about this, Potter Khefti?"

"The boy is a fool, Magistrate!" Khefti protested. "Almost an idiot! He would spoil good food rather than eat it, and the only way to correct him was to beat him! I tell you, no one else would take him when the time came to apportion the serfs to the land! He is as ignorant as a desert rat, and as stupid as a stone! He scarcely understands the simplest of orders!"

That—lying beast! Vetch's indignation almost overcame his fear as Khefti painted him to be utterly worthless, naturally brutish, wantonly foul, unfit to be in the company of anyone civilized. He made up an entire litany of things Vetch had supposedly done: objects broken, items spoiled, the trail of mischief and malicious ruin he supposedly left behind him. He wove his lies cunningly—

And above all, he had the advantage of being Tian, free, and a craftsman.

And as a serf, Vetch could not even speak for himself, in his own defense.

"Why, how very interesting *that* is—since he has become one of the most competent dragon boys in the Courts in the short time that he has been with us," Haraket exclaimed, when Khefti ran out of vile things to accuse Vetch of. Haraket's voice was even a little higher than usual, as if he was shocked by Khefti's statements.

"Furthermore, my dragon Kashet will not do without him, Magistrate," Ari added. "My dragon has never been so well tended. In fact, thanks to this one, I have been able to take over the full patrol of any ailing or incapacitated Jouster we might have, as well as my own, so well-tended Kashet is."

"Oh?" Vetch turned round about again at Haraket's prodding; the magistrate seemed interested now. "The skill of this dragon boy with his charge has relevance to this case. We must see this."

Ari smiled. "Vetch," he said, with calm confidence, "Please go and bring Kashet back to the Dragon Hall."

Vetch made an awkward little bow and scuttled off. But not before he overheard the magistrate say to Ari, "If that boy can budge a dragon in this weather, he must be the most remarkable dragon boy in the compound."

Vetch ran out into the rain, and wondered as he passed through the doors just how he was expected to get Kashet into the building, but at the moment, that hardly mattered. As long as he *could* get the dragon here, that was all he needed to do. *His* problem was going to be getting Kashet out of his hot wallow and into the cold rain. Kashet liked the rain as little as Vetch did, and if Kashet didn't care to budge, there wasn't going to be a great deal that Vetch could do about it.

If he couldn't manage to get Kashet to obey, would the case be lost? Would he have to go back to Khefti? He'd never had to ask Kashet to do something that the dragon really didn't want to do—until now.

His feet slapped on the wet floor of the corridor, splashing through little puddles standing here and there. The rain was *not* going to quit, and Kashet had made it very plain this morning that the dragon did *not* like the rain, at all. If Vetch's stomach had hurt before, it felt as if there was a cold rock in it now. His shoulders were so tight that he was afraid to turn his head too quickly, lest his neck lock in place. And when he reached Kashet's pen, the rain was still coming down as hard and as cold as ever, maybe harder, and the dragon had not moved since he'd left.

That was not a good sign. What if Kashet had gone torpid? What if he was so deeply asleep that nothing would wake him?

Sprinting to the front of the wallow where Kashet's head rested, he saw with relief that at least the dragon's eyes were open. So he wasn't asleep, and he wasn't torpid.

"Kashet!" he shouted, hearing his own voice going shrill with nervousness in his ears. "Kashet, up!"

Kashet raised his head and swiveled it down to stare at him, his huge eyes focused and wide. Vetch thought that the dragon looked incredulous, as if he could not believe that Vetch was ordering him out of his wallow. And he showed no signs of intending to obey the order.

"Kashet, *up!*" he repeated, feeling desperation eat at him. This could go badly so easily! What if he couldn't get the dragon to his feet? What would he do then? He felt his throat tighten and his stomach began knotting even more. *"Please,* Kashet!" he begged shamelessly, feeling his eyes sting as he tried not to blubber. "Please, Kashet! Stand!" He got an idea—if ever there was a time to see whether the dragon understood more than simple commands, now was the moment to test that hypotheses. "Ari, Kashet!" he cried, "We need to go to Ari! *Up!*"

Whether Kashet understood him, understood the desperation in his voice, or just elected to be obedient, Vetch couldn't tell. All that mattered was that after a moment that seemed to last a year, the dragon sighed, heaved himself out of the wallow with a groan, ducking his head to avoid the canvas awning, and stepped up onto the stone verge. He gave Vetch a sorrowful, long-suffering look as the first drop of rain hit his nose, and he tucked his wings in close to his body, the first sign, so Ari had said, of an unhappy dragon.

"I know," Vetch said, feeling terribly sorry for his charge. If the air and rain were cold to *him*, what must Kashet be feeling? "I know, it's horrible. But please, Kashet, we have to go to the Dragon Hall. We have to go to Ari. Kashet, come—"

He put one hand on Kashet's shoulder, as always, and stepped forward, not knowing if the dragon was really going to follow, and terrified that he would not.

But after only a slight hesitation, Kashet paced unhappily forward.

They made their way along mostly-deserted corridors; the rain was keeping everyone with any sense in under a roof. Kashet looked longingly back a time or two, and made false starts off toward the familiar destination of the buffing pens, but when Vetch didn't veer in that direction, he heaved another pained sigh and kept going with his wings clamped tightly to his body, head down, rain dripping from his nose and wings, the very picture of one who is imparting the greatest of favors by going along with something he doesn't want to do, and not enjoying it one bit.

Vetch's heart was in his mouth with every step they took. The farther they got from the pen, the more likely it was that Kashet would decide that he had had enough of the cold and the rain, and rebel. It would be perfectly logical for Kashet to decide he'd had enough of this nonsense, and turn back to the pen. Vetch didn't have a chain or a collar on the dragon; he had no way whatsoever of controlling him. In the urgency of the moment, it hadn't even occurred to him to go look for a chain and collar, and now it was too late.

Too late to do anything but hope that the habit of obedience was strong enough to overcome Kashet's distaste for the cold and wet, that the dragon understood he was to go to his beloved Jouster, that Kashet really *did* feel enough affection for his dragon boy that he would obey in the face of discomfort, or all three.

And he dreaded the moment when they turned down that corridor that ended in the Dragon Hall, for when Kashet saw the dead end, he would be all too likely to turn back. How was he going to stop the dragon? Would Kashet respond to another shouted order, or would he just ignore Vetch and go back to his pen?

Kashet's head came up, though, the moment that they turned into the dead-end corridor where the Dragon Hall stood. Vetch saw at the very same time that the little door he had gone through had simply been inset in a much larger door that *would* admit a dragon, and that this door now stood open wide, though how anyone could move something that *big* was a mystery to him. Kashet's nostrils flared, and he picked up his pace, then craned his neck forward, peering through the rain, and increased it again, until Vetch was running to keep up alongside him—

Of course, by Kashet's standards, it was still nothing but a fast walk.

And as Vetch peered through the curtain of rain, he saw what Kashet had alerted on—Ari, standing just inside the door. *Of course! Kashet must have scented Ari before he saw him—* Vetch felt a rush of relief that the Jouster had thought of coming out where the dragon could scent and hear him.

Ari retreated back into the building, but Kashet had seen enough. He knew where Ari was, now, and no matter how much he wanted to go back to his wallow, Ari's presence was a more powerful draw than the now-distant sands of his pen.

When Vetch and Kashet entered the shelter of the Dragon Hall, Ari was back at the foot of the dais with Haraket, the magistrate looking on with interest. Kashet paused for a moment in the relative dimness, probably so that his eyes could adjust, then resumed his walk toward his Jouster—but now that he was in more confined surroundings, and out of the rain, he proceeded at a ponderous walk that Vetch easily matched.

As they neared the dais, Khefti was moving, too, backing up, eyes wide, one crablike step at a time, until his back was against a pillar and he could go no further. The magistrate, however, showed no signs of alarm, and appeared to be as easy in the presence of dragons as Haraket.

When they got within speaking distance of the group, Vetch noticed that Ari's lips were moving in an exaggerated fashion, as he mouthed something, as if he was trying to tell Vetch something he didn't want to say aloud. Vetch narrowed his eyes, and tried to make it out.

One word.

Down.

Ah! Of course—he needed to demonstrate that he could command Kashet without chains and other devices. "Kashet, *down!*" he ordered, and Kashet obeyed, ponderously dropping both fore- and hindquarters down onto the sandstone paving squares. Only then did Ari come forward to take his place on the opposite side of the dragon from Vetch, and Kashet curved his neck around and brought his head down for a well-deserved scratch from his beloved Jouster. His wet scales gleamed in the torchlight like an enormous pile of gemstones, and he shone in this opulent setting as beautifully as any exquisite jewel. If the magistrate was looking for evidence of a well-cared-for dragon, Kashet's appearance was certainly that.

"Well," the magistrate said, his voice taking on a slight tinge of warmth, as his lips curved in the faintest of smiles. "No collar, no chain, brought here all the way through the rain—this *is* the most remarkable dragon boy in the compound. He definitely serves the Great King far better in this position than any other." He chewed on his lower lip for a moment, then seemed to make up his mind about something. "In fact, I cannot see how he could be replaced. The Great King requires his services here."

"*No!*" Khefti shouted, his face purple with rage, as he lost all control, seeing his property slipping through his fingers. "*No! He is* mine, *mine by* right!" And he lunged toward Vetch, who reacted instantly out of long habit by cringing back against Kashet's side.

All of Kashet's languor vanished. He shot to his feet and spread his wings, cupping them over Vetch, then snapped out his neck parallel to the ground as far as it would go. He made one angry bite at the air in warning, and hissed at Khefti with the sound of water hitting white-hot stone.

Khefti yelped with sheer terror, and lurched backward as quickly as he'd lunged forward. Kashet didn't—quite—snap his jaws a second time at the swiftly-retreating brick maker, but it certainly looked as if he wanted to.

"Most interesting," was all the magistrate said, as Ari slapped Kashet's neck to get his attention, and ordered him down again. Khefti remained where he was, warily out of reach.

"Magistrate!" the brick maker called desperately. "It isn't *just* the land—property into which, I say *again,* I have invested all that I own, property which was to support me and mine in my honorable age, when I can no longer ply my lawful trade! This boy is—was—all I have to tend my *tala* field! I cannot tend it and attend to my apprentices at the same time! Where will the *tala* for the Great King's Jousters come from, if my field withers for lack of tending?"

"There are other fields," Ari said, making his annoyance at Khefti's attempt to play at blackmail very evident. But a shaven-headed, white-kilted scribe who had been standing at the side of the dais, hidden in the shadows until now, came forward at that, and whispered in the magistrate's ear. The old man listened carefully, nodding—then smiled.

Smiled benevolently at Ari and Haraket—then turned the smile on Khefti. But when he did so, the smile was—less benevolent. Vetch might, if he'd been asked to describe it, call it "vindictive." And it came to him in that moment that the magistrate had taken more of a dislike to Khefti than Vetch could have ever thought possible, that he would not, would *never,* exceed the bounds of justice and the law, but when justice and the law handed him a means to deliver Khefti a blow, he was not above taking joy in the fact that it had done so.

"Of course we cannot allow a *tala* field to fail," he said, in so smooth a voice that not even the finest cream could have been smoother. "Nor can we deprive you of the investment you made to sustain you in your age. Not when there is a simple solution available to us."

He stepped back a pace, and held up his little whip. "Therefore, in the name of the Great King, I decree that there shall be a transfer of attachment. This serf is no longer bound to the house and land of his bloodline, and Khefti the brick maker now owns these properties outright, to do with as he pleases."

Khefti was not given time to react to this, for the magistrate followed this pronouncement with another.

"And since he has declared he cannot sustain his *tala* field without the labor of the serf, in the name of the Great King, I bind this same serf boy to the *tala* field formerly owned by Khefti the brick maker, and take this property into the hands of the Great King's overseers, to be administered by them on behalf of the Great King and his Jousters." The magistrate's smile widened as Khefti's cry of pleasure turned to a gasp of loss and dismay, and Vetch was reminded irresistibly of a crocodile. . . .

A crocodile that has just swallowed a large and particularly tasty meal. "The Great King has simple serfs in plenty to tend this field, and it will be efficient for the *tala* to come directly into the hands of the Great King rather than through an intermediary."

Efficient? Hah! It means the tala *will come to the Great King for nothing, save only the labor of a serf or slave!* Vetch was dazzled by the beauty of it all; the scribe had surely told the magistrate that Khefti's *tala* field was—as simple property—worth less than the house and land stolen from Vetch's family. So Khefti could not even protest that he was being cheated—he now *owned* that house and garden, rather than merely holding them, a right which could have been revoked at any time. He could sell them at a profit, he could do anything with them that he chose. But the value of the *tala* that had come and would come in the future from that tiny field would far exceed that of the property now given to him, and Khefti very well knew it. There would be no more duck on Khefti's table, no more palm wine, no more little luxuries. And the Great King would have the yield of one more *tala* field without the need to pay for it.

"And meanwhile," the magistrate concluded, "this serf, who clearly cannot be spared, will be permanently assigned to the Jouster's Compound in the service of Jouster Ari and his dragon."

Khefti whimpered, and dropped to his knees, as the magistrate moved his whip out from his chest, until his arm was completely outstretched, in the ritual motion that signified that the judgment had been passed and there was no use in protesting it. "So let it be written," he intoned. "So let it be done."

Ari and Haraket bowed as the magistrate turned to the side and strode out of the hall, his scribe in close attendance. Khefti remained where he was, his face a study in tragedy; Ari signaled to Vetch with a sideways nod of his head, and he and Vetch turned and moved out of the hall again, with Kashet pacing happily between them. The dragon seemed to understand that something good had just happened, and that it was due to something *he* had done. He arched his neck, and his eyes sparkled; he carried his tail high and his wings half-furled over his shoulders.

Vetch was nearly beside himself with joy. No one could possibly have devised a more perfect revenge! Why, this could be the manifestation of Vetch's own curse! Surely Khefti's food *would* be as thistles in his mouth, and his belly cramp as if it were pierced with thorns on a daily basis! All of his own ploys had been turned as weapons against him! He had lost, lost the income from the *tala* field that kept him in luxuries, lost the services of Vetch which had cost him nothing (and now would probably have to hire a servant or buy a slave to take care of the things that Vetch used to), lost the *tala* field itself, and would have to look upon it *every single day* as the serfs or slaves of the Great King tended it in Vetch's place! And all because of the words out of his very own mouth, because of his own actions! Vetch skipped along beside Kashet, feeling as if it was he, and not the dragon, that had the wings.

"Well, are you satisfied?" Ari asked, when they were several corridors away, amusement in his voice.

"Yes!" was all that Vetch could get out around the happiness that tightened his chest.

"Good." Ari patted Kashet's shoulder. "It's nearly time for Kashet's last feeding. Get him a basket of hearts, will you?"

And with that, he left from the two of them, heading back toward his own quarters in the pouring rain. Kashet hesitated, looking after him for a moment.

"Dinner, Kashet," Vetch reminded the dragon, soothingly. That was all it took. Once again, he had to run to keep up. But it was a run that he was happy to make.

Ari did not come to the pen that night—not that Vetch blamed him, for the rain continued to come down until long after darkness fell, and it would have been a miserable journey. Vetch fell asleep on his pallet in Kashet's wallow, with the dragon an arm's length away, both of them basking in the warmth. But the next day, although the skies did not clear very much, the rain stopped, and Ari arrived in the afternoon.

The Jousters still did not fly, for it was all too possible for them to come to grief in the uncertain winds around the storms, or to be struck by lightning. So Ari arrived after Kashet's second feeding, wrapped in his woolen mantle against the cold, and sat down to bury his feet in the hot sand.

"This is better than any brazier," he said contentedly. "I always spend a lot of time here with Kashet in the rains."

He looked over to the far end of the wallow, where Vetch's pallet still lay, and nodded with approval. "Very smart. My last dragon boy was too afraid of Kashet to move his bed where it was warmer; I could never understand that. If the dignity of a Jouster permitted it, I'd sleep *here* every night of the winter, and not in my quarters. Every rainy season I find myself regretting that I am a Jouster, and not tending my hatchling anymore." He turned his gaze toward Vetch and smiled apologetically. "I'm afraid I have to ask you to go tidy my rooms while I'm here of an afternoon. Otherwise Te-Velethat will be angry with you for shirking your duties, and the other Jousters will be angry with *me* for not insisting that you do them."

Vetch read a world of implications in those few words—as he was probably meant to. The others would, of course, have heard all about Khefti and the magistrate. Initially, of course, they would have been outraged that a mere brick maker dared to set himself against a Jouster, and they would have been pleased at Khefti's thorough trouncing. But then, once they'd had a chance to mull it all over, some of them would be sure that this incident would "spoil" Vetch, or that Ari was overindulging him. Bad enough in a free Tian boy—but not to be thought of in a serf. Anyone in the compound who had their doubts about Ari's choice of dragon boy would be watching Vetch as a falcon watched a bird, and they would be just as ready to pounce on any suspicion of poor performance.

Vetch jumped to his feet as suddenly as if he had sat on a wasp. "Of course, sir!" he exclaimed. At this point, after the scene in the Dragon Hall yesterday, if Ari had asked him to fling himself into a crocodile's jaws, he probably would have done it joyfully. Well, perhaps not *joyfully*, but he wouldn't have hesitated.

He ran off without another word, and as usual, found that there really was not a great deal to do except that his usual chore of *sweeping* out had turned to one of *mopping* out—cleaning up the mud that had been tracked everywhere.

Given that he was being watched, he elected to clean the mud out of the courtyard as well, even though that wasn't technically his task. Not that it was a quarter as much work as the same task had been for Khefti-the-Fat . . . and Vetch grinned the whole time he was doing the job, startling the life out of Te-Velethat, who looked in to see that he *was* there and doing his job. He was picturing Khefti doing the job for himself, for surely he had not yet managed to hire a servant nor buy a slave.

No, the wages he'll offer will be too small by half, and no one will take them, Vetch thought gleefully. *And the price he'll be willing to pay for a slave won't get him anything. He'll have to wait until some dealer comes by with a lot of slaves that nobody else wants, and even then, he'll end up paying twice what he wants to.*

The picture of Khefti with a mop was so delicious that he undertook to move every stick of furniture and clean under and behind it, startling Te-Velethat when he came, once again, to check on Vetch's progress. Vetch didn't care what the Overseer thought, so long as he was impressed with Vetch's diligence.

Nothing could spoil his pleasure today, nor for many days to come. Khefti-the-Fat had brought Vetch's curses down on his own head with the words of his own mouth.

Life was very, very good.

EIGHT

AFTER that first afternoon, Ari spent time with Kashet—and indirectly, with Vetch—nearly *every* afternoon
during the rains. The mornings, though, proceeded nearly as they
had during the dry; mornings were spent in training flights, if there
was no wind and no storm directly overhead. If the rain was going
to stop at all, it usually did so during the hours of the morning, and
training was vital for the dragons, no matter what season it was.
They needed practice even though they weren't fighting, as did
all warriors, but more than that, in the rains, when it was impossible for armies to move and difficult for even individual fighters,
the dragons needed exercise. In the wild, dragons would be going
about their business, hunting, mating, teaching their young the
business of being the largest predator in the hills. Dragons in the
compound didn't need to do any of those things. Their meals
were brought to them, they were prevented from mating; therefore, at all times, but especially in the rains when they were confined to the area around the compound, they had to fly and
get plenty of vigorous exercise, or they would get fat, spoiled,
and stale.

Now, the dragons themselves were not at all in favor of this. *They* saw no reason to bestir themselves. Like Kashet, they hated the rain and the cold, and there was a lot of protesting from the pens as they were led out to the landing court in the morning. Kashet protested, too, but it was mostly a token.

"He takes forever to get up in the morning," Vetch noted one morning, near the end of the rainy season. "But once I get him up, he doesn't hiss and moan about flying off the way the others do. The others—you'd think they were going off to be whipped!"

"He enjoys the training," Ari explained. "He likes the training a lot more than the patrolling."

Or the fighting? Vetch wondered. Well, Kashet would truly enjoy himself for some time, then. Spring and the Flood were not far off; already the Haph priests were going down to the measuring stone three times daily, to see if the waters had begun to rise. No less than the season of rains, the season of flood was one in which it was difficult for armies and individuals to move about. And Kashet would surely enjoy the fact that the days would soon be getting longer and warmer, and the rains would stop.

Ari was giving Kashet's eye ridges a good scratch, unaware of Vetch's thoughts. "He likes the kinds of things that we do in training, and he always has."

"He probably likes being able to outfly any other dragon," Vetch observed, as he buckled a chest strap. Ari laughed.

"He probably does," the Jouster agreed. "Now, I wonder what the morning holds for us—" Ari lifted his head and took a deep breath, testing the air like a hound; he was almost as good as a priest for being able to predict weather in the short-term. "No scent of rain; we should be all right and get the full morning to work out in. Are the other boys leaving you alone?"

Vetch was getting used to Ari's sudden changes in subject, though not quite used to Ari's personal interest in him. He ducked his head to avoid looking into the Jouster's eyes. "I'm all right," he said softly. "They don't bother me."

"But they don't make friends with you either."

Vetch shrugged, as if he felt nothing more than indifference, but that was a third thing that he wasn't used to—Ari's uncanny ability to know pretty much what was going on in his life. "It doesn't matter as long as they don't bother me," he said firmly.

"Vetch, look at me," Ari ordered.

Feeling distinctly uncomfortable now, Vetch stopped what he was doing and obeyed the order. Ari had a very sharp, very direct gaze; those dark eyes seemed to look through everything. Ari's mouth thinned; it wasn't quite a frown, but it was clear to Vetch that he was not entirely happy.

When Ari had begun showing this—interest—in him, Vetch had been nervous. But Ari had never displayed anything but concern for his welfare—as if he felt responsible for Vetch in some way. Vetch still didn't understand it, and he still wasn't comfortable with the attention, but that was mostly because he just didn't like telling anyone as much about himself as Ari wanted to know. There was no reason for a Tian to want to know a serf's inner thoughts! Everything he had learned about the masters made him very nervous when they started probing. And even if Ari had never once been less than fair with him, it *still* made him nervous when it was Ari.

"You have no friends among them, and that disturbs me." Now Ari frowned faintly. "It isn't right; even *I* had a few friends when I was your age, and not just among the other scribes. You shouldn't be so alone."

"I'm not alone. I have Kashet," Vetch replied, trying to sound as if he was perfectly happy with the situation. "I didn't have any friends when Khefti was my master, and *his* apprentices, the boys I had to work around, were always trying nasty tricks on me. It's *much* better here; no one dares do anything to me, especially after what happened to Khefti. Maybe they don't think I'm the proper rank to be allowed to be a dragon boy, but they can't do anything about that as long as Haraket is satisfied. And as long as you are."

And really, he *was* happy, mostly. Contented, at least. He was getting enough to eat and plenty of sleep in a warm and quiet place, he was clothed well, he wasn't exhausted and cold all the time, and Ari was kind to him.

In fact, Ari was more than kind; he was learning from Ari, learning as Ari spent long hours talking to him about dragons, which was proving to be very important to him. For Vetch had conceived a passion for dragons that surprised even him. He *liked* them, even the dragons that were not as special as Kashet. Now and again, when their boys weren't around, he would poke his head into a pen and speak soothingly to one that was restless, or look one over to make sure it was getting properly fed. He felt a kind of proprietary interest in all of them. He had learned from Ari about every step in a dragon's development, from egg to full-grown dragon. He had learned a very great deal about Kashet specifically, which only helped him when it came to handling the great beast. And as for Kashet—well, no boy could have had a better creature to care for.

"You're sure?" Ari persisted. "You're certain that you're happy here, even though the boys aren't being friendly with you."

"Serfs," Vetch said, with so much unexpected bitterness that it surprised even *him* when it came out, "are not supposed to be happy."

"Serfs are not supposed to be treated like chattel," Ari said, with surprising gentleness. "They are involuntary war captives, by no fault of their own. And to me, that means that, within the limit of what I can do, any serfs under *my* orders *are* supposed to be happy."

Vetch bit back the things he might have said, because Ari deserved none of them. "I haven't been happier than I am here since my father died," he said instead.

"That is not precisely a recommendation," the Jouster replied dryly.

"Well, then—I'm not likelier to *get* happier," Vetch said firmly. But in a sudden burst of inspiration, he added, "And all I have to do is think about Khefti on his knees, wailing like a baby over a stolen honey cake, to make me *very* happy."

As he hoped, Ari laughed, and threw up his hands, acknowledging that Vetch had the right of it. "Well enough. It's no bad thing to have true justice delivered to you by a magistrate with no interest in seeing you get it. If you are content, then I suppose I must keep my own opinions to myself."

Then he left Vetch alone with his thoughts, which was a great relief to Vetch.

Over the past weeks, Ari had somehow managed to coax all of Vetch's life story from him—what there was of it, that is. It hadn't all come out at once; more in bits and pieces, the story of the day that the Tian soldiers came and the death of Kiron coming out last of all.

Perhaps it was easier because when Ari put questions to Vetch, instead of the other way around, it was in the evenings, when Ari came to bask in the heat of the sand wallow before going back to his rooms to sleep. It was always dark, there was usually rain coming down on the canvas awnings, drowning out the sounds from beyond the immediate vicinity of the pen. He would pet Kashet, who was like a great cat in the way he liked being scratched and caressed when he was feeling sleepy. There, in the darkness, Ari was hardly more than a shadow, and halfway across the pen; he never offered to approach Vetch or his sleeping pallet. It was Vetch who would come to sit next to the Jouster, if he chose. It was unreal, as if Vetch was talking to a ghost, or as if he was asleep and talking in a dream.

It was at those moments when Ari would say things that would leave Vetch wondering and thinking long after he had left. Sometimes it was news. Ari preferred to tell Vetch things that were bad news for any Altans before Vetch heard about them in a taunt from one of the other boys. That a tax collector had been murdered in some occupied village, and Altan men and boys had been crippled or even killed outright as the soldiers tried to find out who did it. That another village had been taken, had resisted, and been razed to the ground. That a well had been poisoned, and all of the villagers made to drink the water afterward, to ferret out the one who had done it by seeing who was too afraid to drink. . . .

The Tian response to revolt was to try to make it too expensive for Altans under occupation to be willing to hazard it again. That the ploy wasn't working seemed to have escaped them utterly.

"No one seems to have worked out that your people have nothing left to lose," Ari had said, only last night, "And that is a position you *never* want to put someone in. When you've nothing left to lose, there's no reason *not* to try whatever you can to win something back. The Heyksin learned that lesson from us, to their cost. I find it difficult to understand why we have not made the connection for ourselves."

Vetch thought about that all during his chores, and wondered just what he might have tried out of desperation, if he'd still been under Khefti, and was older. Probably just about anything, for nothing short of death could have been worse than the conditions he'd been living under.

Maybe that was why the other boys would have nothing to do with him. Under their taunts, they were afraid. They didn't know what he might do; they didn't realize that there wasn't a chance that he would jeopardize what he had here. He was worse than a wild dragon to them, unpredictable and possibly dangerous.

In a way, that cheered him up a little, and yet, for some reason he could not understand, it also made him—sad.

"I've been doing some reading in the law scrolls," Ari said that night, with the great delicacy he always used when he was going to talk about Vetch's past, "Perhaps a bit dry, but it seemed to me that I ought to make certain what protections the law provides you, given what your former master attempted to try. It seems that there are laws about the Altan farmers—that there are treaties, that we can't just come in and confiscate land unless there's proof that the landowner in question fought against us or harbors and gives protection to enemy fighters."

"Those laws didn't protect my father," Vetch replied bitterly.

"And it doesn't sound as if they are protecting anyone else either."

"Well, you know, *if* I were someone unscrupulous and I wanted a rich farm in a recently-annexed territory," Ari said, after a long silence. "I believe that I would bribe the Commander of Hundreds to send out some Captain that was a friend of mine to investigate farms and farmers on newly-won lands. And I believe I'd tell that friend that it would be to his advantage if, on one particular farm, there happened to be an incident. After all, if a farmer flies into a rage and attacks the Captain of Ten in full view of his own men, well . . . at that point the law doesn't protect him, and his lands are clearly going to be legally confiscated."

"I suppose," was all Vetch replied, feeling the all-too-familiar knot in his stomach. Then Kashet gave him a reason to change the subject to a more comfortable one, by making a peculiar, hollow whistle in his throat, a mournful sound that made both of them jump. "Why does he *do* that?" Vetch asked.

"I think," Ari replied, as an answering whistle came from the next occupied pen, "it's so that they all know where each of the dragons in the flock are, even at night when they're asleep. Ah, Vetch, speaking of knowing where someone is, I won't be coming tomorrow afternoon, but I'd like you to come clean my quarters anyway. I'm going into the Mefis markets to get a few things. It won't be long before the rains stop, the Flood comes and goes, and we have to go back on full duty."

Ari didn't said anything more on the subject of the laws regarding farms in conquered land, but that had left Vetch wide awake and staring at the stars of Nofret's Robe long into the night. It made sense; it made hideous sense. And, in a curious way, it settled his mind, for if this was the true answer, it wouldn't have mattered *how* hard Kiron tried to keep his temper when the soldiers came. No matter what happened, the whole scene had been scripted beforehand. No matter how reasonable he had tried to be, it was fore-ordained that Vetch's father would be forced into a position where he would *have* to attack the officer. The provocation would have gone on until the desired result was achieved.

Maybe Kiron had even sacrificed himself for the good of his family, or thought he had. Vetch really didn't know (other than the insults) everything that had been said to his father on that fateful day. Maybe the Captain had threatened awful things to Vetch's mother and sisters. Maybe the insults had just hit Kiron on a raw nerve. Vetch would never know.

But the next afternoon when he returned from cleaning the Jouster's quarters, he found that Ari had brought something back from the market that wasn't for himself or for Kashet, and had left it under the awning where Vetch kept his few belongings.

It was a funerary shrine, a tiny thing no bigger than the box that held a scribe's tools and also served as a desk. With it was a small *sebti*-figure painted like a prosperous Altan farmer.

It wasn't a Tian shrine either; it was Altan. Such things were not outlawed, after all, for it would be futile to try and prevent even a conquered people from worshiping the gods they'd known all their lives. Futile and stupid, for doing so would guarantee that the worship would go on underground, and probably would result in riots eventually. Besides, the Altan and Tian gods were hardly incompatible; in some cases they differed only in name, and that slightly.

But the Tians believed that a dead man's body must be preserved in order for him to enjoy his life across the Star River, and that grave goods *here* meant possessions *there*. For the Altans, even if the body was not preserved, nor given a proper funeral, all could still be well if one of the family or friends saw to it that there was a shrine, a *sebti* figure properly named, *representations* of offerings, and the proper prayers. All of which, of course, had been denied to Kiron.

Until now, that is.

Vetch stared at the beautifully made object with his mouth dropping open. Step by step, he ventured to his corner and squatted beside the little shrine. It was basically a box, with a hinged lid, and a series of compartments inside. One held a sarcophagus to put the *sebti* in, another a set of farming implements in miniature, then came a pair of oxen, an entire herd of goats, a flock of geese, another of chickens, tiny beer jars, minuscule bread loaves, cheeses, bunches of onions, sacks of grain, even a pair of blank-faced nameless *shapti*-figures to serve as servants. It was perfectly appointed in every way for a farmer's life in the Summer Country; in fact, it must have cost more than a cow in milk or a herd of goats to purchase such fine workmanship. On the top of the shrine when it was closed, there was a niche for the *sebti*, a bowl for offerings, and best of all, since Vetch didn't *know* most of the prayers for the dead, the prayers were graven into every surface of the shrine itself.

With hands that shook, Vetch picked up the figurine, and named it; placed it in the niche, and began reciting as much of the proper prayers as he could remember. It wasn't as if he hadn't done all of this before—but the mud figures he made would crumble, or melt in the rains, and worst of all, he simply didn't know the vast majority of the all-important prayers. He couldn't have been older than five or six when his father died; how *could* he have memorized the prayers?

But it didn't matter now if *he* recalled them imperfectly or not at all, for the prayers were *there*, carved into the shrine, perfect and magical, and anything that Vetch did would only reinforce what had already been set in motion once the figure was in its niche, or tucked away in the sarcophagus inside. In his mind's eye, he could see the bridge across the Star River being formed of the magical words, see the Silver Road stretching out from Kiron's feet to the bridge and over it, see his father wake as from a nightmare of wandering, look down and see his way to that paradise in the stars made clear. . . .

And if he wept as he tried to chant, and found the mist mingling with tears that choked his voice, well, there was no one to see him or mock him for his womanish behavior.

Ari said absolutely nothing about the shrine, nor did Haraket;

in fact, they paid no more attention to the shrine and to the offerings that Vetch laid fresh in the bowl every morning, than they did to the pallet. But with the shrine and the *sebti*, even without the proper funeral and tomb, Vetch's father would no longer be a hungry, homeless ghost, wandering the world, unnamed, impotent, alone.

It was impossible to hate Ari after that. Absolutely impossible.

Vetch's hatred of all things Tian began to shrink and chill. Not that it went away, far from it. It was still there, but it was no longer quite so all-encompassing and all-consuming. He no longer began and ended his days in hate; he woke thinking of other things—some special duty, or some possible amusement—and he went to sleep with the prayers for the dead on his lips, instead of curses. And with those prayers, there was generally one for Ari.

Keep him safe, he would plead with the Altan gods. *Defeat him, but don't hurt him, don't hurt Kashet. Make them dizzy, make them ill, but don't hurt them.*

He included Kashet in his prayers because he knew that if anything were to happen to Kashet, Ari would be shattered. For that matter, so would Vetch himself.

There was no doubt that there was a real bond now between Kashet and his dragon boy, a mutual bond. Kashet would often solicit attention from him, and even became playful around him, engaging in a tug-of-war with a spare leather strap he liked to toy with, or throwing it into the air with a toss of his head for Vetch to catch. These days of relative peace, with more leisure time, meant that he and Kashet spent more time together—and *he* had more time and opportunity to learn about his charge from Ari. The more he learned about dragons, the more he found himself wanting to learn—and it was certainly a subject that Ari never got tired of talking about.

But the rains couldn't last forever, much as he would have liked them to. Two days after Ari left the shrine for him, the compound was a-buzz with the word that the waters of the Great Mother River were rising at last. The Flood had begun, that would cover all of the arable land—if the gods were kind—with the silt that made Tian land so fertile. The same Floods would proceed down-river toward Alta, isolating it, and making it impossible for any fighting to take place until the waters receded.

"Patrols will begin very soon," Ari said absently, when Vetch gave him the news that morning.

Vetch didn't want to think about that, so he changed the subject.

"Haraket said before the rains that he thought Kashet was put-ting on a growth spurt, but he's fully grown *now,*" Vetch said, as Ari scratched just under Kashet's chin. "How can it be that he's growing, if he's already adult?"

"They never do actually stop growing," Ari replied. "In fact, I'm pleased to hear that; Kashet's a bit leaner than some of the others, and I've been concerned about that. Is he eating more?"

"A *lot* more," Vetch said ruefully—since he was the one who had to haul the extra, twice daily. "And I've had to let out his chest straps."

"Good; he's putting on the muscle I think he needs, then." There was clear satisfaction in Ari's voice.

What Ari didn't know about dragons wasn't worth knowing, and Vetch wanted to know it all, too. It wasn't enough for him, as it seemed to be for the other dragon boys, just to feed and groom Kashet. And today, with the resumption of Ari's duties looming ahead, he threw caution to the wind and piled question atop question, for when patrols began, who knew when Ari would be available to answer those questions again?

What did the *tala* do to the other dragons? What was a starving dragon likely to do? How long did dragons live? If they kept on growing, were there bigger dragons out there than the ones that the Jousters flew?

"*Tala* acts a little like beer, and a little like poppy, but most like *khat.* It makes a dragon quiet without putting them to sleep, un-less you give them too much. It wears off quickly, though, which is why the boys have to dose each meal with it. A starving dragon will go hunting, and nothing a rider can do will turn him back to his pen. He's likely to throw off his Jouster because if he's that hungry, the *tala* wears off quickly, and it will occur to him that he *can* be rid of the rider. And since he'll do that when he's flying and not when he's on the ground—well—" Ari shook his head. "Then he'll escape back to the wild dragons, and eventually be rid of his saddle and harness as well. And yes, there are bigger dragons out there, *much* bigger. To tell the truth, I suspect most of them are escapees, because a dragon that's been ridden knows about arrows, javelins, spears—and knows that humans are to be avoided. Such a dragon will grow to be old and wise and very large indeed."

Ari answered every question he had, with patience and interest of his own. It was the longest actual conversation that Vetch had ever had with the Jouster, and it seemed as if Ari was actually enjoying it. He only called a halt when his own stomach rumbled, a growl that made both of them laugh.

If he had to be a serf, then this was the best place he could have found himself. Now he just had to keep Ari and Kashet safe, so he could continue to stay here, even if it meant laying siege to the gods with his prayers.

Jousters were called by that name because they were *not* utterly unopposed in the air—because they did, in fact, *joust* with other dragon warriors. The Altans had dragon riders just as Tia did—in fact, more than once, Ari had said that it was supposedly the Altans who had taught the trick of capturing and taming dragons to ride to the Tians.

Unfortunately for Alta, the number of Jousters that the Altans could field was much fewer than the Tians, and their training didn't seem as good. That might have had something to do with the dragons themselves; they were desert creatures, and Alta was mostly swamp, river delta, and island. Perhaps it was harder to find them, and harder to keep them under such conditions.

When two Jousters met in the air above a battle, they dueled for supremacy with the same short lances that Vetch spent so much time inspecting for flaws; weapons that were blunt rather than pointed, made to knock the rider from his saddle, or at least to knock him unconscious.

Ari was, presumably, very good at this. That had not changed. What *had* changed was that now Vetch had gradually stopped praying that he be defeated—in any way. Now he was torn between wanting him to be better than anyone else, and wanting his own people to start winning against the Tians. Jousting was deadly; an unseated Jouster was generally a dead Jouster. Every Jouster that Ari defeated was probably a severe loss to the Altans. But for Ari to be defeated did not bear thinking about.

By the time Ari went back to his patrols, Vetch was trusted to leave the compound itself alone and unsupervised, which meant that if his duties took him there, he *could* go out to the training ground beyond the walls.

And one bright, warm, humid day, when Vetch had been serving Ari and Kashet for a little more than half a year, Haraket sent him to the training grounds with a message, and Vetch got to see precisely what Jousting really looked like—and how very dangerous it could be, even in practice.

The Floods had peaked. It would be a good year, for the waters covered all of the arable land, but had not ventured where they were not wanted. Although in Khefti's village and many others there was water up to the very doorsteps and people waded ankle- and knee-deep in the streets, the only houses or storehouses that had flooded were ones built by incredibly foolish folk who had not the sense to listen to the priests. The compound and the training ground, of course, were built on land that could not be farmed, and hence, flooded only in years of a disaster. In fact, other than the green-water smell in the air, there was no sign of flooding as Vetch stepped outside the walls.

He'd never been to the practice grounds before during training; he'd always been kept busy at his assigned tasks when the Jousters were practicing. He'd never even seen the empty grounds, actually, and he'd had to ask what gate to leave by to find them. To tell the truth, he had not really wanted to see the Jousters in action; it would only remind him of his divided loyalties and make his stomach hurt.

The practice grounds stood well outside the final wall of the Jousters' compound. The first—and very odd—sight that marked them for what they were was the nets. Fishing nets were strung between strong poles or palm trees, so that they hung parallel to the ground and well above it. He had not expected that; it had honestly never occurred to him that the Jousters would have something in place that would let them practice aerial combat without fatal consequences. He'd somehow assumed that they *didn't* practice actual fighting while aloft, only flying maneuvers, and the passes that would allow them to get close enough for blows.

Several dragons and riders were on the ground, watching those that were in the air. Vetch scanned those grounded first for Ari and Kashet, and didn't find them. *Then* he looked up, and saw that they were hovering in place high in the air above the middle of one of these nets, as Ari shouted directions to two more Jousters who were sparring above the net next to his with the blunted lances. To Vetch's surprise, there were a lot of onlookers off to one side, and many of them seemed to be wealthy or of noble birth. They had their servants with them, holding colored sunshades above their heads, fanning them, offering them cooling drinks, whisking insects away. They looked like a garden of pampered flowers.

He hadn't expected that either. The world of the Jousters within the compound was as isolated as that of any Temple—*he* had never seen anyone who wasn't associated with the Jousters, and although he had overheard plenty from the other boys about the many feasts, entertainments, and gatherings at which there were outsiders, he hadn't attended any himself. He'd *heard* them, in the distance, some nights, particularly during the rains—music and laughter, sometimes raucous, sometimes drunken and quarrelsome. For whatever reason, Ari kept him away from such things, though other boys were sometimes permitted to attend as auxiliary servants or hangers-on to their Jousters.

Now here were spectators who were clearly of the elite of the Tians of Mefis. They glittered in the sun, all of them sporting armbands and wrist cuffs of gold, and collars of gemstone beads, fine wigs or elaborate headcloths, and linen kilts of the best fabric with sashes and belts richly embroidered. There was even a woman among them, dressed in a tightly-pleated, transparent linen dress with a sheath made of a net of turquoise-colored beads over it, holding the folds of the linen close to her body. She was attended by no less than four servants, one with a sunshade, one with a fan, one to carry a chair for her, and one to supply her with cooling drinks.

These, then, were the people that the boys had spoken of, who gave them money to carry letters to the Jousters, who bet upon the outcome of their combats, who desired their presence at their entertainments, as if the Jousters were themselves some form of entertainer. And something else occurred to Vetch at that moment, as he watched their avid faces. They did not go to war themselves, but they certainly profited from it; they did no fighting, yet when the fighting was over, it was they who had gained— more land, more goods, more money in their coffers.

He found himself suddenly filled with such hatred that he had to look away from them lest by his expression he betray himself. Not that he *cared* if they knew he hated them, but he might get Ari into endless trouble.

So he looked back up at the dueling Jousters being instructed by Ari. This practice session didn't look very dangerous, for even Vetch could tell that these two weren't very good at the Jousting. Their dragons would not come close enough to permit any real combat, and although they heaved at the guiding reins, the dragons stubbornly fought their riders.

When they did "close in," they got nowhere near enough to actually make an exchange of blows. The dragons made very clumsy passes at each other, one high, the other low, while the Jousters were flailing at the air yards away from one another.

It was partly the fault of the dragons, and partly of the riders, who (he suspected) were afraid of getting close enough to be hit themselves.

Vetch knew all the dragons by sight now, and it wasn't hard to tell which the two Jousters rode, even if he didn't know the names of the men themselves. That was a failing among the dragon boys, to know the dragon and refer to the Jouster as "So-and-so's rider." One of the dragons was Seftu, a handsome, if irritable crimson male, and the other was Coresan, a female of a deeper hue and notoriously whippy tail. Coresan was usually mild-mannered in nature, or at least, she didn't give any more trouble than any other dragon, excepting only that she was known to leave her dragon boy with black-and-blue calves and thighs with that unpredictable tail. But something had her on edge the last week; from what Vetch had been hearing, her dragon boy was half afraid to go in her pen of a morning, and kept her chained as short as he dared. He'd been tempted to go look in on her himself, but his own duties had kept him so busy that he hadn't had the time.

Their Jousters were the newest of the group, barely out of ground training, and certainly it was going to be a very long time before they were the masters of either their weapons or their dragons. Ari was getting very frustrated, and no wonder; the dragons were giving most of their attention to each other and very little of it to their riders now—and were circling each other in a peculiar fashion that reminded Vetch of something. . . .

And just when he realized what it reminded him *of*, Seftu's rider finally got close enough to deliver a sideswipe with his lance to Coresan's Jouster. The latter was momentarily distracted from the job at hand, since Coresan chose that moment to curvet side-ways in the air, toward Seftu.

Close enough to actually land a blow, for the first time since

Vetch had started watching. Only this was a blow for which neither the attacker nor the defender were prepared.

The lance connected—*hard*—

With a terrible *crack*, it connected with the Jouster's skull; the lance bent in the middle, the sign that it had hit with enough impact to be ruined, all of the fibers pulped.

And that was nothing to what must have happened to the rider's head. Not even the Jousting helmet could have saved him from that blow.

Vetch caught his breath, and his heart stopped.

As if a god had waved his hand to slow time itself, everything froze for a horrible moment.

The Jouster hung in his saddle—*hung* there, balanced only because he hadn't yet *un*balanced. Then his lance dropped from a hand gone limp; the broken lance followed it, falling down . . . down. . . .

Vetch's mind hadn't caught up with what was happening, but his *gut* felt that *crack*, and knew exactly what it meant before his thoughts could form.

Then, in painfully slow motion, Coresan's Jouster bent over the saddle.

Then *went* over the saddle, in a slow forward somersault.

And continued to roll, tumbling right *out* of his saddle.

As Vetch's heart clenched, he plunged toward the net below. But he wasn't falling right, there was something horribly wrong. He was limp, limbs sagging, and Vetch felt his stomach lurch as he realized that not only was the man not conscious, but that he was going to miss the net entirely.

The Jouster was Tian; the enemy. Vetch didn't even know his name. Vetch should have been silently cheering the demise of one of the people who was responsible for all the horrible things that had happened to his land and his family.

Should have, perhaps—but couldn't. All he could see was the body dropping straight to his death; all he could hear was the cry from above where the second Jouster still flew, a cry of desperation, thin and filled with utter terror.

Everyone else watching seemed to realize the same thing at the same moment; there were gasps and cries of horror, and the sharp scream of the woman cut across the heat-shimmering air.

Vetch's stomach lurched again. He wanted to look away, but he couldn't. He seemed to be paralyzed as the body hurtled towards the earth, unchecked. In a moment, there would be a spreading stain of red on the pale, baked earth—

—*like Kiron's blood*—

—and the smell of death—

—*when his father lay despised in the yard of his own house*—

—and the buzzing of flies coming for the blood—

—*as they came to feast on Kiron's*—

Then a flash of blue-green swept across the sky, and with it came the sound of dragon wings, a thunder and a wind that shivered across the ground, driving the dust before it—

It all happened so quickly that it was over before Vetch registered *what* had happened. But the Jouster was no longer tumbling down through the air, nor was he lying in a smashed heap on the ground.

The Jouster was lying across Ari's saddle, draped over Kashet's neck.

Vetch thought his eyes were going to bulge out of his head in startlement. For Ari had—somehow—saved him.

NINE

THE unconscious Jouster lay across the front of Ari's saddle, draped over Kashet's neck like a half-filled grain sack.
How, *how* had Ari and Kashet caught him? For that was the only
possible explanation, though Vetch could hardly believe his eyes. It
seemed nothing short of a miracle. Had the god Haras, the especial
god of the Jousters, spread his wings over them both? Had he given
Ari some special power that he could do something like this? Had
there been an especially gifted priest in the crowd of onlookers,
able to work some powerful magic to make this happen?

But he shook off his shock; this wasn't the time for him to
think—there was need of him, and now, for Ari and Kashet were
coming slowly in to land.

Serve your dragon; serve your Jouster.

Kashet dropped down with a thunder of wings that drove up so
much dust that the gawkers had to shield their faces and look
away. Ari wasn't being any too careful about *where* they came
down, so long as it wasn't actually on top of anyone. And if the
folk who were *in* the way could scramble out of the way in time,
then it wouldn't be on top of them. . . .

There *was* a mad dash by servants and spectators alike to get out of the way. They scattered like a covey of quail, and Kashet landed heavily in a cloud of dust.

Vetch ran for his master, and the rest of the onlookers surged forward behind him and overtook him, enveloping him, swallowing him up. Ari didn't so much as glance at any of them; his attention was on the servants—Jousters' servants, who must have been out of Vetch's sight behind the crowd of dragons and riders—who had reacted faster than anyone but Vetch. They were already at Kashet's side, and were taking the unconscious Jouster from Kashet's saddle. He slid down limply into their arms, but as far as Vetch could tell, he was still alive and breathing.

The crowd erupted in cheers and surged against the ring of servants, trying to get closer to the dragon and Jouster. They surrounded Kashet and Ari in a circle of enthusiastic—even hysterical—joy, shouting at the tops of their lungs. Kashet, normally the most placid of creatures, reared back, eyes widening with alarm, nostrils dilating in distaste.

Vetch was caught up in the crush, between the servants trying to take the Jouster away, and all of the well-wishers. But somehow Ari saw him, and roared an order to let him through, pointing and waving imperiously with one hand.

The order had no effect at first, and Vetch jabbed with his elbows at those he dared to, and tried desperately to push past those he dared not offend. After a moment of confusion in which he tried to no avail to get through the spectators—some of them wealthy, powerful, dangerous—they realized who Ari was shouting for and parted for him. Kohl-rimmed eyes both knowing and haughty stared at him as he shoved past; once his hand brushed against a garment of linen so fine that the rough skin of his hand snagged it. He just barely noticed; he shook free, and shoved his way to Kashet's side.

"Haraket sent me. Haraket says—" Vetch panted, staring up at his Jouster with mingled awe and disbelief, and trying mightily to remember his message. "Haraket says—"

"Never mind what Haraket says—this isn't over yet." Ari looked up with a scowl, and Vetch followed his gaze.

The two dragons were whirling together now, in the mating dance that Vetch had instinctively recognized, and Seftu's rider, a tiny dot at this distance, was clinging on for dear life. Another high, thin wail of pure fear drifted down from above. Vetch was not surprised. Not only was the novice Jouster no longer in control of his dragon, he was going to be lucky to stay in the saddle. And he was very, very lucky that *his* dragon was the male. If he'd been riding the female, and a male dragon found an inconvenient little human in his way—

A single *snap*, and the inconvenience would be gone.

"Idiots!" Ari snarled. "If they paid *half* as much attention to their dragons as they did to the vintage of the date wine they drank last night, they'd have *known* this was coming on and ordered extra *tala*. Vetch!"

Vetch snapped to attention.

"Run and tell Haraket what just happened. Tell him that Kashet and I will bring Coresan in when the mating's over; she'll be tractable then, and there's no point in losing a dragon because her Jouster was an imbecile. Seftu's rider will have to bring his male in by himself, unless Haraket wants to send a couple of others up to herd him in when he's done."

"Yes, sir!" Vetch said, instantly, and started to turn to run.

But Ari held up his hand; he wasn't finished, and Vetch froze. "Tell him that I think her Jouster got the kind of crack to the head that breaks the skull, so Haraket had better send to the Temple of Teth for a trepanning priest at least, to lift the bone, and perhaps one with Healing magic, just in case. You go run ahead now—" He raised his voice as Vetch whirled and broke into a mad dash for the compound. His voice rang out behind Vetch, as he commanded the servants over the babbling of the crowd. "You lot! Stretch him on that bench—*carefully*, now—and carry him *on* the bench to the compound and Overseer Haraket!"

Vetch couldn't do anything about the injured Jouster—and in

any case, now that he wasn't going to have to watch him die horribly, he didn't really *care* what happened to the man—but he did care about Ari, and what Ari proposed to do. He couldn't imagine trying to come between two mating dragons. It was dangerous enough bringing a bull to a cow, or a stallion to a mare!

But—no, Ari wasn't going to come *between* them, he proposed to bring Coresan in once the mating was over. It was just as well that he was going to leave Seftu to Seftu's own Jouster, and serve the man right if he had to ride the dragon until Seftu was exhausted, or at least until near nightfall, when Seftu would want his dinner and his own comfortable sand wallow for the night.

So would Ari, when all of this was over. And Haraket had to know exactly what had happened, right now.

So he ran, ran as hard as ever he could, pelting down the training field, through the huge sandstone gates, and into the corridor beyond. His bare feet pounded along the ground in time with his pounding heart as he searched for Haraket.

But he didn't have to search long. Haraket had already seen the dragons in the sky and knew that there was a mating going on, even if he had not seen the accident, nor the aftermath. He had certainly seen that one of the dragons was riderless, and was on the way, expecting the worst.

Vetch literally *ran* into him, and bounced off Haraket's stomach, landing on his backside in the middle of the corridor.

"Coresan's Jouster is hurt!" he blurted, looking up at the surprised Overseer. "They were trying to mate, I mean the dragons, and he got hit! He got a lance to the back of his head and fell off, but Ari caught him! Ari brought him down, he's at the practice ground, and Ari says to tell you he's going to bring Coresan in— the servants are bringing the Jouster—Ari says get priests—"

Haraket had wits like a striking cobra, somehow he made sense of what Vetch was babbling. "Hah. *You*—" he snapped, pointing a finger to one of the two men with him. "To the Temple of Teth. I want a Healing-Priest and a trepanner. *You* to ready Jouster Ari's quarters, wine and food, for by the gods, he'll want them when he comes back in. And a massage slave. And a hot bath. Move!"

They moved, all right; they turned and ran off in opposite directions, running just as fast as Vetch had. So did Haraket, leaving Vetch gaping at them from the dust of the corridor.

After a moment he scrambled to his feet, realizing that his initial errand was discharged.

Serve your Jouster. Serve your dragon.

He had to know what they were doing, first.

Will they be all right? Will Seftu or Coresan try to attack them? The thought put a shiver up his back. Surely not. Ari knew dragons as no one else in the compound did. Surely he would never do something that would cause the mating dragons to turn on him and Kashet.

He ran on, his side beginning to ache now, to the landing court where he could see the dragons in the sky clearly, without the interference of walls. They were still wheeling and whirling around each other in a complicated ritual that was the equal of anything a bird could do. They soared and plunged, they twined around each other and broke apart.

Mostly, Seftu chased Coresan, and she evaded him only enough to make it clear she was going to see just what he was made of before she let him mate with her. Then, finally, after a series of three heart-stopping lunges, as Seftu herded the scarlet female higher and higher in the sky, they began an ever-tightening spiral that took them still higher, up into the cloud-studded sky, until they were scarcely larger than ants.

Then—then they lunged for one another with a ferocity indistinguishable from rage.

The lunge ended in a tangle of locked claws and a plunge to earth that must have terrified Seftu's rider out of a dozen years of life. How he stayed in the saddle, Vetch could not even begin to guess.

Caught together, neither willing to let go, paralyzed by the rapture of mating, they spun around a common center, whirling, wings held half outspread at a peculiar angle. They plunged, on and on, down to the unforgiving earth, while Vetch and everyone else in the court held their breath. And just behind them plunged a blue-green streak that was Kashet, paralleling their fall.

At the very last moment, just before the impact, they broke their hold on each other.

Their wings snapped open completely at the same moment, and the vertical plunge suddenly became horizontal as they tumbled from the fall into a ground-brushing flight, and streaked off in opposite directions, parallel to the ground.

Vetch wasn't interested in what happened to Seftu; presumably his Jouster would get him back under control and bring him in without help. He had eyes only for Ari and Kashet, who had followed the entwined dragons down in their deadly plunge, and now deftly herded Coresan away from the eastern hills across the river, above the King's Valley where all the Great Kings had their tombs—where she *wanted* to go—and towards the compound. And she didn't want to go there; she kept snaking her head back and trying to snap at them. But Ari and Kashet were more clever than she.

They managed to keep their "superior" position in the air, staying above her all the time. Kashet didn't even have to do more than threaten; a dragon's one vulnerability was his wings, and Kashet could slash Coresan's with his claws very easily from where he was. Coresan didn't dare chance it, and was herded where Ari wanted to go as Kashet feinted strikes at her wings.

At that point, a dragon landed in the court; it was Seftu, and his rider looked as if he must have been near to soiling himself with fear. Vetch ignored Seftu and the Jouster; some other dragon boys *did* run to help the man lead a reluctant Seftu away, but Vetch's charges were still in the sky, and he was not going to leave the court until they were safely down.

Haraket had arrived without him noticing, and stood just behind Vetch. He grunted when he saw Seftu land. "The priests lifted the bone; the fool will be well enough, idiot that he is," Haraket said to no one in particular, though Vetch knew his words were meant for Ari's ears, via Vetch. "A few weeks, and he'll be healed up, though if he hadn't been seen right away—well, he'd not have had a chance."

Coresan was coming back now, in the direction of the compound. Once she was turned, they started forcing her down. By getting and staying above her, they forced her to fly lower and lower, and slower and slower as well, until she couldn't stay in the air any longer. And at that very moment, they were above the landing court, and her training took over and she came in to ground.

The moment Coresan touched the earth, Haraket was there with two of the strongest slaves in the compound and three leading chains. Vetch started to help them, but Haraket waved him off.

"Keep off, boy! This is not work for you!" he shouted, and then turned his attention back to the angry dragon. He needed to; that tail was whipping back and forth with deadly force until a third slave came up and flung himself bodily on it, pinning it to the earth. She hissed and tossed her head—but she was also tired, and probably hungry, and unlike a wild dragon, did not think of humans as *food* but as *those who brought food*. Haraket and one of the other slaves plunged under her snapping jaws and grabbed her harness and hung on it until she stopped tossing her head and lunging. She didn't surrender, then, but she did stop fighting. With Ari and Kashet hovering above to keep her from taking off again, Haraket hooked his chain into the ring on the front of her harness and the two slaves hooked theirs into the foot loops on either side of the saddle. Then, last of all, Haraket whipped a choke collar around her neck, and that was that.

Serve your dragon. Serve your Jouster.

Vetch wanted to watch. But his time was not his own at the moment. As soon as Kashet came in, he and Ari would need taking care of. Vetch sprinted for the gate nearest Kashet's pen.

When Ari and Kashet landed, they'd need—and deserve—careful attention, and *he* was going to be the one to give it to them.

At the exact moment he began to run, Coresan resigned herself, and with a final hiss, allowed herself to be led away. The third slave freed her tail at Haraket's signal. Together Haraket and his two helpers led the dragon to her pen, while Ari and Kashet rose again, to hover a little higher for a moment while they picked a good landing spot. Then they landed, nearest to the gate that led to Kashet's enclosure.

By that time Vetch's last glimpse of them was as he sprinted through the gate in the wall, going for Kashet's pen himself. Seftu's dragon boy was in the corridor, laden with food and drink; Vetch snatched what he wanted from the provender over the other boy's vehement protests, which he ignored. After all, the novice rider didn't *deserve* it; wasn't he half responsible for the near disaster? Seftu's Jouster could bloody well *wait* for his wine. If Vetch were to have a choice, he'd get stale river water, thick with flood-time mud, and be grateful for that much.

When Ari and Kashet stumbled into Kashet's pen, Vetch was there ahead of them, waiting with a skin flask of palm wine for Ari and a bucket of water for Kashet. But Ari waved off the wine and took the bucket of water instead, drinking as he had that day that Vetch had first seen him, and pouring the rest over his head and shoulders. Kashet went straight to his trough, which, as always, was also full of clean water, and drank as deeply as his Jouster; Vetch was unharnessing him as soon as he reached the trough and stopped moving forward. The dragon not only felt as hot as a furnace, he *smelled* hot, and Ari smelled like his dragon. Both of them looked utterly spent; the kohl around Ari's eyes was smeared, making his eyes look like holes burned in his face, and Kashet's eyes were dull with fatigue.

Ari shook his head like a dog, sending droplets of water flying in the bright sunlight. Vetch cast a glance at him as his own fingers unfastened buckles and pulled away harness; he looked *terrible*.

Weary and ill, and not at all as triumphant as Vetch thought he should be—

"Etat save me from ever having to do *that* again," he said, and sat down, right on the edge of the sand pit, head and shoulders sagging.

Vetch was torn between going to him and continuing to get the harness off of Kashet; he compromised by unbuckling the last strap and letting the saddle drop to the side, then going to Ari.

"Sir?" he ventured, not daring to touch the Jouster.

"I'll have that wine now, boy," came the muffled reply.

Vetch put the skin in his hand; he fully expected Ari to drain it, but the Jouster again surprised him, taking only a single mouthful before handing it back.

"That's better." He raised his head. "How is Reaten?"

That was Coresan's Jouster; Vetch recalled it as soon as Ari spoke the name. And he had news, startled out of Seftu's dragon boy. "He has a cracked skull, and it would have been very, very bad if he hadn't been seen to right away, but the priest is certain that he will be all right eventually," Vetch told him. "The trepanning priest is lifting the bone right now; he should be all right once the incision heals."

"Teh and Teth be thanked," Ari sighed, and Vetch had no doubt that the words were more than half prayer. "And Haras, who puts the wind beneath our wings. The gods truly look after the fools of the world." And he shook his head, slowly, and took another mouthful of wine. "That so little permanent harm has come of this is more than either of those two deserve."

Vetch couldn't help himself; he was bursting with curiosity, and with no little awe. "Sir—how did you *do* that? One moment he was falling, the next, he was across your saddle! It looked like magic!"

"It's all Kashet's doing," Ari replied, but he looked up, then, and behind the weariness, seemed very pleased at Vetch's wide-eyed admiration. "I'll admit we've practiced just that move, in case something like this happened. This was the first time we've caught a man, though—it's always been bags of chaff before this. Have you ever seen a dragon take a goose in flight?"

He waited for Vetch to reply; Vetch shook his head.

"No? Well, it's something they do in the wild, pulling their head and neck back, then snapping it forward while flying, like a heron catching a fish. I've taught Kashet to do that, only to bring his head in *under* what we're trying to catch rather than snapping at it with his jaws, then to raise his head and fly up a little at the same time. If we've got the balance right, what we're aiming for slides right down his neck onto my saddle where I can steady it." Ari shook his head, and Vetch gaped as he tried to imagine just how much control and coordination—and cooperation on Kashet's part!—that would take. "Needless to say, no one else can do it. Another of my little eccentricities that the others put up with in the past; none of them ever had the imagination to see that it could be used to rescue a falling rider. I suspect there won't be any more sniping remarks about it after this, though."

Sniping remarks? Never had it even passed Vetch's mind that his own Jouster, so highly thought of by Haraket, might be on the receiving end of *any* criticism. After all, from what he had overheard, Ari was widely thought of to be the most skilled rider and Jouster in the compound. So why would anyone criticize him?

But it appeared that Ari's unorthodox ways were enough to make him as much of an outsider among the Jousters as Vetch was among the dragon boys.

Vetch snapped his mouth shut, and nodded, and watched as Kashet left his water trough half-emptied, dove into the sand, and rolled wearily in his hot sand wallow. "Reaten won't be flying for weeks," he offered. "So the priest says."

"The Commander of Dragons will have a few choice words with him before he's able to fly," Ari said with grim satisfaction. "And I suspect that he'll consider himself lucky to have that crack over the back of his head; the Commander just *might* take pity on him because of it."

"What's going to happen to him?" Vetch asked.

"At the least, they'll both be personally reprimanded by the Great King's Commander of Dragons and *might* be dismissed as Jousters for their carelessness." Ari's lips thinned, and his jaw tightened; Vetch had seldom seen him angry before this, but he was definitely angry now. "As raw as they are, it isn't as if they can't be replaced. They both should have known better, but of the two, Seftu's rider is the most to blame. A male shows the mating urge much more graphically than a female. *I* would have seen it, if they hadn't only just gotten up into the air. I thought all that jockeying about was Reaten and Horeb trying to impress me with fancy flying, and having no luck at it."

Ari paused, and Vetch wordlessly handed him the wine for another small, moderate mouthful.

"In fact, *anyone* who had anything to do with Seftu and Coresan should have seen the signs," Ari continued. "There's going to be some sharp words all around before this affair is over, and maybe some dismissals."

Seftu's dragon boy probably knew that; he'd been tending Seftu for the last two years at least, and should know all of the protocol and rules that governed not only the Jousters themselves, but everyone connected with them. Certainly he knew more about it than Vetch did. That was probably why he hadn't done more than protest weakly when Vetch robbed him of his burden; shock, and the fear of being dismissed, had left him so stunned he completely forget Vetch's lowly status.

Or else, being dragon boy to the hero of the hour had suddenly *raised* Vetch's status.

"Seftu's safe enough; back in his pen," Vetch was able to report. "His rider—Horeb—I don't know where he is, but his dragon boy was on the way to the Jousters' Courts with food and wine." Dangerous to go further than that, or mention any speculations of his own. He *was* still just a serf, after all. Anything more, well, that could be taken as gossip about his masters, and even Ari, tolerant as the Jouster was, might feel he had to take some sort of action at that point. So he kept himself quiet.

"Well, it wouldn't surprise me if Horeb was at least demoted back to the training classes. Reaten just might find himself sent back to the ranks, too, no matter how much the Commander pities him. In any event, he's going to be bedridden for a while. Which will mean that Coresan won't be ridden for weeks. Just as well. Coresan will be impossible to handle for that long, or at least until she rids herself of her eggs." Ari closed his eyes and held out his hand; Vetch put the wineskin into it, and Ari took another mouthful. This time, he kept the wineskin. "It could be worse. Let's hope the others have learned a lesson about paying attention to their dragons' behavior, anyway." Ari had a fourth, very long pull on the wineskin; Vetch thought there was a grim satisfaction in his expression. But he was more interested in what Ari had said than in what his expression might imply.

"Eggs?" Vetch asked, as a wild thought entered into his mind. Dared he think *he* might be able to get hold of one—if there were any at all? But if he could—after all he'd been learning from Ari— "She'll lay eggs now? How many? Who's going to mind them?"

"Nobody," Ari sighed, and his shoulders sagged. "I would, if I could, but no man can tend and fly more than one dragon at a time if it's to be done raising the dragons from the egg. What a waste! Of course, they'll probably be sterile—wild dragons mate a dozen times or more for a clutch of two or three and Coresan only mated once today—but you'd think that *someone* would be interested in trying to duplicate what I did when I was Haraket's helper! But no. This has happened before, although without the accident, and other than the one egg that hatched Kashet, the eggs were just taken away and left on the refuse heap." His gaze turned scornful. "Of course, *warriors* can't be bothered with playing nursemaid to an egg and a dragonet, and they can't simply assign the task to their dragon boy and expect to come take over from him when the dragon fledges."

"They can't?" Vetch breathed, hearing his own wild thoughts confirmed, hearing that the sudden plan that had burst into his mind *might* be more than a mad dream.

"No, they can't, not when a dragon's been raised from the egg by a man," Ari replied. "Not even if you drugged him with *tala*. A dragon raised wild thinks all humans are the same human; a dragon raised from the egg knows better." He turned a fond gaze on Kashet, who was now stretched out flat on the top of the sand, spread out like a rug. It was a very peculiar posture, one that said volumes about how tired and cold Kashet was after that flight. Vetch couldn't imagine how Coresan had had any fight in her at all, after the mating, if Kashet was so exhausted. "The dragon that's raised from the egg is a dragon that won't fly for just any-one, will he, Kashet?"

The dragon raised his head, just a little, and sighed.

Ari laughed. "Like a falcon egg-reared, or a cheetah taken be-fore his eyes are open, a dragon hand-reared is loyal only to the one who nurtures him—a hand-reared dragon is *not* like a dog, who will hunt with any man who knows his commands."

Kashet rolled over on his back and twisted his long neck around, eying Ari for a moment, then snorted with what sounded like amusement.

At that moment, a number of disparate bits of information came together for Vetch, like broken bits of a wine jar flying back together again and giving him the shape of the thing.

First—Ari had studied to be a scribe, and *as* a scribe, had been sent here to serve in the compound. A scribe was needed here, certainly, but he must have had a great deal of free time. Many Jousters could read and write on their own, and wouldn't need his services.

Second—Vetch recalled Ari had said that he had "found" a dragon egg—and after all he had learned, Vetch couldn't imagine anyone climbing into a nest after a dragon egg! He already knew, of course, that Ari's education had been cut short before he could be recruited into one of the Temples. *He* had thought that it was because Ari had hatched Kashet, but what if he had things back-ward, that Ari had been bound over to work here *first*, and only after serving as the compound's junior scribe and learning all he could about dragons, had he hatched Kashet?

Third—Vetch had the key fact that he had not known before this, that a Jousting dragon had escaped to mate and lay eggs at least once before today. That changed the shape of his speculations, entirely.

Ari *must* have served here and become interested in the dragons for their own sake, then perhaps he rose to become one of Haraket's helpers, either in his capacity as scribe or because of his interest in the dragons and their ways; that would account for the unspoken bond between the men.

But more times than not, any boy in training to be a scribe ended up attached to a temple, not attached to the Jousters' Compound. What had led to Ari's needing to leave his studies? Because he wasn't that old, yet he had been flying Kashet for years—so he *had* to have hatched Kashet while he was in his teens. So he couldn't have truly finished his education as a scribe.

Unless perhaps he had been attending one of the temple schools, when his family fell on hard times and could no longer pay for the schooling. Hadn't he said once that he was the youngest boy, and it was his uncle who was the head of the household? He had—he'd said his uncle, also a scribe, had made Ari's mother his second wife after Ari's father died.

Yes; that must have been it. All the pieces fell neatly into place. Vetch could picture it in his mind's eye. Ari's father sending him to school, dying, leaving his widow and son to be supported by his uncle, who eventually married her. Then, the additional strain of a second wife and children on the family finances forced Ari to become a "common" scribe before his education was complete, and he took a position here in the Jousters' Compound. Ari must have gotten hold of a fertile egg from one of those chance matings, perhaps from the dragon of a Jouster he had served as a scribe, or gotten directly from Haraket as an experiment, or perhaps just because he'd been bold enough to take one before they put it on the midden.

Vetch knew better than to blurt out his conclusion, though. Nor did he blurt out *his* reaction—that what Ari had done, *he*, Vetch, could do. "You should rest, Master," was what he said instead. "Your room is ready; Haraket has already seen to that."

"And whatever Haraket sent you to tell me originally is now of minimal importance, compared with the impact all of this will have on affairs in the entire compound," Ari said, and shook his head, crossly. "Evil spirits plague Reaten with boils! I'll have to take *his* patrols now, doubtless, while *he* lies abed, being made much of by all his noble friends!"

Then, perhaps, he bethought him of what Vetch had told him, and his irritation eased a little. "Or perhaps not. It's an interesting thing with noble friends; when your star is rising they are all for standing near you and bathing in your reflected glory. But when your star falls, no one can escape from your vicinity fast enough."

Vetch just nodded; agreeing was harmless enough, but he must not *say* anything that could be construed as criticism of his masters.

Ari patted Vetch on the head. "Get Kashet an extra treat; you know, bullock hearts, if there are any. He more than deserves them. Then go to the kitchen and tell them I want my dinner in my room."

"Haraket's seen to that, sir," Vetch said. "And he said something about a hot bath and a massage slave."

Now Ari smiled, just a little. "Good old Haraket! Well, I'll take him up on all of it; I'm for a cool swim first, in the Atet pool, and perhaps after that I'll feel less like strangling Reaten, then finding Horeb, ripping off his arm, and beating him to death with it." The corners of his mouth turned up a little more. "After all, it would be ill-done of me to deprive both the Commander of Dragons and Haraket of that privilege."

He levered himself up off the edge of the sandpit, and as he stalked off out of the pen, Vetch noticed that he was favoring one leg. He must have injured it somehow—either in the rescue, or when he and Kashet were bringing Coresan to earth. Typical of him not to have mentioned it.

Haraket will have had a massage slave sent, he remembered. *And perhaps that will help.*

Vetch did as he was told, and while he was getting Kashet's treat, he heard that, not unexpectedly, the request for someone to bring Ari his supper and someone else to see to a massage nearly brought on a fight among the servants over who was to have the honor. Ari's very self-effacement in *not* lingering to be made a hero of, had had the effect of making him more of a hero than he would have been if he *had* stayed about to preen rather than bringing Coresan in. Or at least that was true among the servants. What those wealthy spectators had thought of Ari's heroic efforts today—well, Vetch couldn't begin to guess.

But there was another repercussion to all of this. When Vetch went back to the butchers to return the barrow for Kashet's feed and his treat, there was a drama being enacted right in the center of the court.

It was Sobek, Reaten's dragon boy, who was causing all the fuss. With all the other boys around him, he refused, sweating and trembling, to go anywhere near his charge. He described, at the top of his lungs, to an enraptured and credulous audience in the butcher court, how she had snapped at him and—so he claimed—nearly taken his leg off.

"Like a mad thing!" he cried, his voice cracking. "Mark me, she'll *eat* anyone she gets hold of! She nearly ate *me!* I swear it!"

"That is because she mistook you for a goat, with all of your silly bleating," Haraket boomed from the door to the courtyard, where he stood, legs braced slightly apart, arms crossed over his chest, a fierce and disapproving frown on his face. Vetch shrank back against the wall, but already his mind was a-whirl with a possible idea. "What is all of this foolishness, Sobek?" Haraket continued. "*And* disobedience—saying you will not tend to your dragon—"

"And I won't!" Sobek cried hysterically, both hands clenched into fists, his face a contorted mask of fear and defiance. "I won't, you hear me! My father is a priest in the Temple of Epis, and he'll have something to say about this!"

"Your father is a cleaner of temple floors, and *you* may go back to him in disgrace if you say one word further," Haraket thundered dangerously, his eyes flashing and his brow as black as a rainy-season storm. Vetch sucked in a breath; Haraket annoyed was dangerous enough, but Haraket enraged? *Was* he about to see Sobek beaten? If so, it would be the first time he'd seen *anyone* beaten, even the slaves, since he came to the compound.

But Sobek had been pushed too far; his fear was no act, and he had gone over the edge from fear into panic. He snatched the eye amulet off his neck, and threw it to the pavement, where it shattered into a thousand pieces. The noise of it shattering could not possibly have been as loud as it *seemed*. It sent a shiver over all of the dragon boys and servants crowded into the court, and even Vetch was not immune. "Send me back, then!" he screeched, as the shattered pieces glittered on the stone. "Go ahead! Better that, than to be torn apart! I care not, Haraket, I will cut papyrus, I will beg for my bread, rather than go into *that* killer's pen!"

But if Sobek had been pressed too far on this day, so had Haraket. And Haraket had authority.

"Out!" Haraket roared, *"Out of my compound, out of my life!"* Step by step he advanced on Sobek, his face red with anger, so outraged by the dragon boy's rebellion that he was about to lose control of himself. "You are *dismissed*, dragon boy, *little* boy, little *coward!* Run back to your father, pathetic scum! Go and cut papyrus for a pittance, for that is the only position you will ever hold to put bread in your mouth!"

His arm shot out, pointing toward the door. The hand trembled, with suppressed rage. "Run away like the frightened child you are, before I lose my mind and beat you black and blue to give you bruises to take back with you! Run! *Run!*"

Sobek ran; bolted for his life past Haraket, bare feet slapping on the stone, fleeing for the outside world and presumed safety.

Silence fell over the courtyard, a silence broken only by the shuffling feet of the other dragon boys. Hanging in the silence was the certain knowledge that *someone* would have to take care of Coresan until Haraket found another boy to tend her. And Coresan, at her best, was no Kashet. At her worst, well, she was evidently so unmanageable that Sobek had chosen disgrace over continuing to tend her.

This was the opportunity, all unlooked-for, that Vetch had not dared to hope would be granted to him. He leaped upon it and seized it with both hands. "Overseer?" he said, into the leaden silence. "I will tend Coresan along with Kashet, if someone else will mend harness, pound *tala,* and clean Jouster Ari's room for me. I will *need* that sort of help. Feeding, tending, and bathing two dragons will not be easy; it is hard enough at the best of times, but it will be much more difficult, when one of them is Coresan, a dragon newly-mated. But I will do it for her sake. There are no bad dragons here," he added boldly. "Only mishandled ones."

A collective sigh arose out of the huddle of dragon boys. They gazed at him in awe, and was it—in sudden respect? Yes, it was! Vetch kept his eyes on Haraket. Now was not the time to take advantage of *that.*

Haraket's brow cleared a trifle. "You? Coresan is no Kashet, boy. She has always been a handful for Sobek with that tail of hers, and as you said, she is going to lay eggs, which will make her even more difficult—"

"But I have been around females about to whelp all my life," he countered, raising his chin. "My father was a farmer. I believe that I can tame her a little. Perhaps more than a little." He allowed scorn to come into his tone, for the first time ever. But Sobek was now, in Haraket's mind at least, in utter and complete disgrace, just like his Jouster. Dragon boy and Jouster had both failed, and failed as badly as it was possible to fail and not die. Criticism of Sobek would fall on ears ready to hear it.

And it was such a relief to be able to abuse one of those wretched Tian boys without fear of being punished for it! Vetch waxed eloquent in his scorn. "Sobek never treated her properly; half the time he was afraid of her, and he never thought she was anything better than a dumb beast with a vicious streak. He never saw how clever she was, or treated her with any kindness. I'd have snapped at him myself, if I had been her; she's smart enough to bully anyone who gives way to her, but she's also smart enough to change her ways if she's treated right."

Haraket rubbed his shaven head with the palm of one hand, now looking worried. "Sobek was—not entirely in the wrong, boy," he admitted. "Perhaps he neglected his dragon, but that will make her all the more dangerous. Coresan could harm you, if you are not careful."

"Let me feed her, feed her now, Overseer," Vetch pleaded, urgently. The plan was rapidly forming in his mind, a beautiful plan that would give him everything he could possibly want, but he could only carry it out if *he* became Coresan's keeper, at least until she laid those eggs. "She's hungry now, and she'll be easier to win when she's hungry. Please! Watch and see if I can handle her!"

Haraket took a deep breath, and Vetch felt a surge of triumph, knowing he had won—at least so far. "Very well. You may feed her, but I and my helpers will be standing by to guard you. Ari will never forgive *me* if I let any harm come to you. We will see—"

Vetch did not wait for Haraket to have second thoughts. Haraket left to get help, while he seized a barrow, got it loaded with meat, and was out into the corridor before anyone could blink, his own footfalls making the walls echo as he ran—but not, like Sobek, for the outside world. He had a chance; he had to make the most of it. Unlike Sobek, he had nowhere to go, nothing to lose, and the world to gain if he succeeded. . . .

Haraket and two of the biggest of his slaves, trailing a curious and apprehensive crowd of dragon boys, intercepted him on the way to Coresan's pen. He was wheeling a barrow heaped with *tala*-treated meat, as much as he could manage, and double the ration that he usually gave Kashet. If Coresan was breeding, she'd be hungrier than usual even given the exertion of the mating flight as her body demanded the wherewithal to make eggs, and if Sobek had been neglecting her because he was afraid of her and impatient to get away, he might not have been feeding her properly for some time—and she'd be hungrier still. The way to a dragon's heart was ever through her stomach. There was no reason, no reason whatsoever, why he should not feed her to bursting. She wouldn't be flying any time soon—she *would* be making eggs. Why not stuff her, and soothe her with food?

Besides all of that, with a double ration of meat would come a double ration of *tala*, which, once it got into her, would gentle her even in her aroused state. With all of Ari's instruction, he knew what *tala* did. If he could get her to allow him to lay nurturing hands on her, with a full belly that *he* had supplied, and the tranquilizing effect of the drug making her see things in a pleasant light—

He would create a mighty contrast to Sobek, and it would be right in the forefront of her mind—

Well, he might truly tame her. She would never be a Kashet, but she might become one of the better dragons.

He heard her hissing before he even reached her pen, and looking up, saw her head up above the walls, watching the corridor, swaying back and forth at the end of her long neck.

She was gorgeous; if she hadn't been so angry, he'd have been able to appreciate her beauty more. Her color was a deep ruby, shading at the extremities and along the vanes of her wings to a turquoise-blue. But her scales looked dull, as if there was a haze of dust over them, and that made him frown.

She ignored him—except for a voracious glare down at his laden barrow. *He* was not Sobek; she did not expect feeding from *him*.

But when he appeared in the door of her pen with his barrow heaped with fresh, red meat, she reared up, her hiss of anger turning to a short bark of surprise. Then she went into a lunge that came up far short of where he stood, her chain snapping taut between her collar and the wall.

She was ravenous, and Vetch gritted his teeth when he realized that she was thin—not unhealthy, not yet, but that miserable excuse for a dragon boy Sobek truly hadn't been feeding her nearly enough, just as he'd suspected! Hadn't he *seen* how much hungrier she was?

Hadn't her Jouster?

Like Jouster, like dragon boy, it seemed; Sobek and Reaten deserved each other, for neither of them had noticed the changes in Coresan. Seftu's rider was evidently nearly as much in the wrong. As Ari had said, *none* of the trouble of this morning would have happened, if they had only been paying proper attention to their dragons!

Vetch didn't leave the poor thing straining at the end of her tether for any longer than it took him to get up beside the barrow and begin tossing the biggest chunks of meat in it in her direction. She was quick; she saw the first one coming and snatched it right out of the air, snaked her head around to catch the second, and the third—

She paused to swallow; he kept the meat coming. Only when the barrow was half empty did she pause, for a breath, then to turn her head to take a good long drink from her trough.

While she was drinking, he moved the barrow nearer her, and perforce, himself; when she looked up, the barrow was well within her reach, and Vetch stood behind it, making sounds that Kashet found soothing, a kind of "pish, pish" noise.

Now the *tala* that had been dusted over the meat she'd bolted had begun to take effect, taking the edge off her aggressiveness and the anger that must have been born of hunger. Oh, he understood that, all too well! He felt a surge of sympathy for her. He would see to it that she never had another hungry day in her life!

She had eaten as much as she usually did, too, and although she was still hungry, she was no longer ravenous, and her mood had mellowed considerably. She arched her back and her neck, and eyed him with a great deal more favor.

"Come, my beauty," he said to her, in a soft and coaxing voice. "See what I've brought you? There will be plenty of meat for you from now on, if you can be a good girl for me. *I* understand how you must be feeling! I know how much an empty belly hurts!"

Evidently she could, when she chose, move her head as fast as that whippy tail. She snaked her head at him with a lightning-strike, and snapped a pair of jaws that could have taken off his head—

If his head had been what she was aiming for.

The jaws clashed a good foot above his head. He never moved. *She* was trying to see if he rattled as easily as Sobek; if he flinched, she'd bully him at every possible opportunity. He'd seen her with Sobek at the grooming compound, where she looked at him out of the corner of her eye and lashed her tail at him, and he would jump and wince and insist that slaves put extra tethers on her. She reminded him of a goat on one of his masters' farms, who'd done the same to her herders until she got one who'd given her a good rap across the nose with his crook the first time she charged him.

"Come along, my beauty," he coaxed. "I'm tough and stringy. There's better fare for you in my barrow, if you're good."

She eyed him again, then abruptly buried her muzzle in the meat, and didn't stop until she'd eaten every morsel and licked the barrow clean. Only then did she raise her head and gaze at him with eyes that blinked with satiation and just a touch of sleepiness. So the *tala* was beginning to take hold. *Good.*

"*There's* a good girl," he told her, and taking the chance that the *tala* was coursing through her veins, further tranquilizing her, he moved down and loosened her chain from the wall. "Come on," he said, tugging at the chain. "I know you want a good bath, and a proper oiling, don't you? That wretched Sobek can't have given you one in an age."

She was more restive by far than Kashet, and never had Vetch felt the differences more keenly. And she kept snapping at the air above Vetch's head, as if she wanted to express irritation and anger, but not truly at *him*. She still allowed him to lead her to the grooming court without too much fuss.

Perhaps it was her bulging belly that was leading her . . . or just perhaps, in the depths of that odd mind, she was making comparisons between him and her former keeper, and deciding that she liked the change.

He fastened her to the nearest ring in the wall, and began buffing and oiling her. Flakes of dead skin fell away from the crevices of her wings as he rubbed, confirming his guess that Sobek hadn't been tending her properly. And *she* responded to his careful ministrations, slowly, but favorably, finally bending her head to permit him to tend to the delicate skin of her ears, her muzzle, and around her eyes. In fact, he felt her muscles relaxing under his hands, until at last she was allowing him to tend to even the most sensitive and ticklish places with her eyes closed and the breath coming quietly from her flaring nostrils. *Now* her scales glowed with the color of fine gems as they should have.

When he led her back to her pen, she ambled along quietly beside him, and dove into the sand pit to wallow as soon as they reached it. He chained her up—she was *still* no Kashet, and he wasn't going to trust to this good behavior until he knew how big a dose of *tala* he really needed to keep her tractable—but he gave her a much longer chain than ever Sobek had. She could reach every spot of her pen now; she just couldn't get out of it or fly off. She could bury herself in her hot sand, and roll and wallow, without the chain bringing her up short and making her uncomfortable.

Haraket had followed him every step of the way; as he left her to her nap in the warm sand and turned to leave the pen, Haraket gave him an approving slap on his back that staggered him.

"Well done!" the Overseer said gruffly. "You *do* know your business. You tend your Kashet and this virago; that's enough work for any man or boy. I'll see to it that your other tasks are taken care of."

Vetch ducked his head, and murmured his thanks, then headed back to the butchery to get Kashet's ration and his treat, for if ever a dragon deserved special tending today, it was Kashet. This would *not* be easy; Coresan was going to test him every single time he entered her pen. She was intelligent and crafty, and she had learned how to disobey. Disobedience was a habit it would be hard to break her of.

But if all went well—she would lay her eggs on *his* watch, and he would have every possible opportunity to spirit one away, if anyone could.

And then Vetch would have a dragon egg. And after that, well—then it would all depend on the gods of Alta, and whether here, in the heart of Tia, they would be strong enough to aid him. One step at a time; that was all he dared think about. For now— wait for the eggs. Then see.

TEN

WITHIN hours, Vetch found himself in an interesting position; no one envied him, but he was no longer the target of scorn either. In fact, some of the other dragon boys began to look at him as if they did not quite believe anyone was mad enough to do what he was doing. Curiously enough, it was the oldest boys who gave him the most respect. Maybe that was because they had the most experience with dragons; they knew what it was he had volunteered to do, and how much work it would be.

Others, however, if they did not scorn him, did not love him for what he had done either. Sobek might not have been universally beloved, and he certainly had brought his downfall upon himself, but those boys that had been his friends took it ill that Vetch should dare to take his place, dare to outdo him, even. A mere serf, lower even than a slave, had not only been accepted as a dragon boy, but had the audacity to claim that he could care for a difficult dragon better than a freeborn Tian? And to have the gall to say, in so many words, that the freeborn Tian had not been caring for the dragon properly in the first place? It was an insult that they took poorly, and never mind any doubts that might be creeping into their minds about Sobek's performance. Now they would never voice those doubts.

He consoled himself with the knowledge that at least none of them were looking at him as if he was some sort of insect any-more. Nor did they ignore him. And if he got black looks of resent-ment, he also got respect.

And it could have been worse, oh, very much worse than suspi-cious or worried looks and whispers. No one ventured to suggest that Vetch had somehow engineered all of this—which, had he been an adult instead of a child, *could* well have happened, and how would he defend himself against a charge that could neither be proved nor disproved?

That very thought was in his mind as he led a now-relaxed Coresan back to her pen, when he saw the odd pair of boys watching him and whispering to each other.

He'd seen just such a thing happen when the first new Tian overlord had taken the farm, back when he was still with his mother, grandmother, and sisters, slaving on what had been their own land. One of the village girls attracted the eye of a Tian offi-cer and rebuffed him. She had taken care to avoid him when he showed that he was disinclined to take "no" as an answer. She was no landowner, and the idea that a young maiden could "at-tack" a Tian officer was absurd, so he had taken his revenge in some other way. Before long, there were accusations of spells and curses, and within weeks of the refusal, she was taken up as an "Altan witch."

The officer started it, with a lurid story of how *he* had rebuffed *her*—blatant lie that it was—and how after that, she had come to him every night, sitting on his chest, and sucking out his breath (and, it was hinted, other things). Oh, that certainly did happen, and it might even have happened to the officer—but it couldn't have been poor little Artena who'd been the sorceress! And it was certainly *convenient* that none of these attacks were of the sort that would leave any visible marks!

That opened the floodgates, though. Soldier after soldier claimed that she had come to him in the night and "stolen his vitality," or brought him nightmares, or led evil wandering spirits in to attack him while he slept. No matter what anyone said, it came down to the fact that it was the word of Altans against Tians, and there was an end to it, especially once it was strongly implied that anyone who spoke up for her was liable to be charged with witchcraft as well. She was finally brought up before a Tian magistrate and sentenced—then she vanished from the village altogether in the custody of her accusers, and nothing whatsoever was ever said of her again.

The adults all went quiet if he or any of the other children asked what had happened to Artena, and he never did find out. Now, well, he knew it couldn't have been good, and he hoped it had been quick and not too horrible. At that time, though, it had been driven forcefully home to him that such unprovable charges could be just as potent as any real crime.

So it would not have been out of the question—had he been a little older—for someone to claim Vetch had managed to *make* the disaster of Coresan and Seftu happen. Never mind that if such a thing *could* have been done, it would have to have been by means of powerful magic. And why would so powerful a magician be wasting his time to supplant a dragon boy? For that matter, why would he remain a serf, when he could use such magic to escape to Alta rather than working like a dog in the Jousters' Compound?

The adults at least, and the older boys, dismissed such a notion out-of-hand.

But there were other possibilities, of course, and even if no one considered it possible that he had caused the accident, there was still Coresan's behavior with Sobek to consider, for she had not had the reputation of being difficult before this. Within hours, there were dark looks from the younger ones, and suggestions of curses, though they swiftly learned not to say anything of the sort where Haraket could hear them. Only once that day, as he was bringing Coresan her evening meal, had someone come to Hara-

ket with tales of magic, and the boy who had ventured such speculations had found himself sitting on the ground with one ear
ringing from the impact of Haraket's fist. Haraket was decidedly
unamused by such arrant nonsense, and said as much.

And fortunately, none of the boys knew about his father's
shrine, or certainly there *would* have been dark rumors of magic.

By nightfall, after experiencing an entire day of this new change
in attitude on the part of the other dragon boys, Vetch decided
that he did not particularly care what they thought, so long as
nothing bad came of it. He was, in fact, too busy to care—and
the rumors and veiled accusations of curses had an effect that
those who made them did not anticipate.

"That's ridiculous," said Haraket. And, *"Too stupid to be funny,
little brats, frightening themselves with bogeymen,"* said the older
boys, contemptuously. But—

But.

Maybe *Vetch* hadn't done anything, but he was Altan, and the
enemy, and the Altans had magic, too, just as the Tians did. A
new set of stories and speculations began to drift among the boys.
Maybe the magic that Altan sea witches were working against the
enemies of their land had elected to operate on Vetch's behalf. . . .

It was well known that magic did not always work as it was
supposed to. Curses went awry, and so did blessings, sometimes
alighting on targets that were related to the intended one, for the
magic had to go *somewhere*. Perhaps Vetch was attracting Altan
blessings, or providing a medium through which Altan curses
could operate.

Maybe it wasn't *Vetch* who was creating the curses—or blessings. Maybe it was the sea witches, and Tian magic was so effective at deflecting curses, blessings, or both, that the best outlet
the magic could find was to improve the life of a single serf turned
dragon boy.

And then, by nightfall, yet another variant emerged. There was
a more dangerous possibility than the magic of mere mortals as
the cause of Sobek's downfall, the injury of one Tian Jouster and

the disgrace of both. Maybe the Altan gods were striking back through him, or had taken an interest in his welfare. Sobek had been one of the boys who had been the most vocally contemptuous of Vetch, and his Jouster one of the Jousters most opposed to a serf as a dragon boy, and now—Sobek was dismissed in disgrace, Reaten lying in his bed with a cracked skull.

No one wanted to annoy a boy who *might* have attracted divine intervention. So even though the gossip was meant to hurt, in a way, it helped him.

As for Coresan, by nightfall, she was back to being a bit more even-tempered. She'd had two big meals, she'd been buffed, her chain lengthened, and when he was done with Kashet, Vetch perched cautiously nearby on the very edge of her wallow, and talked to her soothingly until dark. At first, she had been suspicious, but after a time, she accepted his presence, listening to him warily.

Given the rumors flying, he was pleased, rather than otherwise, that she didn't warm to him immediately. That she had lost that dangerous edge was enough, for now. He really did not want to add fuel to the rumors by taming Coresan down into a Kashet in the course of half a day.

She wouldn't settle down and go to sleep while he was there, however, so when his own stomach growled, he decided that he had given her enough attention for the first day, and he would leave her alone until morning.

When he arrived at the kitchen court, he paused for a moment in the entryway. And although conversation didn't *stop*, it paused for a moment, and everyone—literally, *everyone*—stopped to take a look at him.

Then they went back to their food. But in that brief moment, he had a sense of what had been going on while *he* had been shuttling between two dragons. The reaction his presence caused could not have been more remarkable. In those looks had been caution, respect, just a touch of fear, here and there. From the slaves and few fellow serfs, he saw pride, admiration. *No* contempt.

And when he sat down at his usual table, the two serfs and two slaves who shared it with him gave him quick, congratulatory smiles. No more than that, but those smiles, and the approving pat on his back from his favorite serving woman, created a surge of warmth inside him that took him by surprise. The serfs and slaves then turned the discussion—among themselves—to the rumors that they had been hearing. None of them mentioned Vetch, Sobek, or Coresan by name, nor did any of the conversationalists speak to Vetch directly, but it was clear that they were using this method to let him know just what was being said about him.

But best of all, truly the top to his day, was when a still-weary, but not-so-haggard-looking Ari arrived at Kashet's pen after sunset. And for once, Kashet could not be roused, not even by his beloved Jouster.

"We flew the equivalent of three combats today," Ari said, after calling the dragon's name and getting no response. "And to tell you the truth, he's not in fighting condition after the rains. So I'm not surprised he won't awaken." Ari stretched, and winced. "I'm not in fighting condition either, to be honest."

"You should get another massage," Vetch said severely, knowing by now that such boldness wouldn't even earn a rebuke from Ari. "It doesn't do me any good to take care of Kashet if my Jouster won't take care of himself."

Ari chuckled. "Truth to tell, I just wanted to come and tell you that you have done a very fine thing with Coresan today. It was brave of you to take her and stand firm and let her test you, and braver still to work with her afterward. You gave her nearly a full day of the best possible care, and I do think that she will respond to that."

Vetch felt himself flushing, with embarrassment, and pleasure. "Ah—" he stammered, "—I just didn't want to see her made into a mar dragon after you'd gone to all that difficulty in catching her.

And after all you've told me, I thought I could probably read her aright."

"If what I've told you is helping you to get her *properly* tamed, then I am well-rewarded," Ari said, with warmth. "You've done well, Vetch. It may be presumptuous of me to say this, but I'm quite proud of you."

"Oh. . . ." Vetch was quite taken aback, both by the praise and by his own reaction to it. "Ah, thank you." He tried to think of something else to say, and couldn't.

Ari didn't seem to mind. "It's been a cursed long day for all three of us," he said, into the awkward silence. "And I'm going to follow Kashet's example and your advice. You should probably do the same. Good night, Vetch."

He limped off, but Vetch did get the last word after all, for he called after the Jouster, "Get another massage!"

Ari's chuckle floated back in the darkness, making him feel warm inside.

Everyone seemed to take it as a given that Coresan *would* lay eggs, even though she'd only mated the once. Vetch could only shrug his shoulders at that; the only things with wings that *he* had any experience with were geese, ducks, and chickens. He would have thought, if dragons were a species that required multiple matings, that she would be mad to get at a male as soon as she'd slept off her enormous meals—and he was perfectly prepared for that, when morning came. He'd even shorten her chains if he had to, though he hoped it wouldn't come to that.

The next day, though, when the dragons flew overhead on their way to morning practice and the first patrols of the season, she yearned after them a little, but that could have been the eagerness to fly rather than to mate again. The moment that her meat appeared, she was much more interested in it than in the dragon shadows passing over her head.

Haraket could not tell Vetch if—or how many—of her eggs were likely to be fertile after just one mating. Ari, who might have known if one mating was enough for the eggs to be good, was, well, not really available. Vetch found out that morning that Ari was now flying two patrols, his own and Reaten's, just as he had expected would happen. Vetch vowed to manage on his own, with the information he already had, and not trouble his Jouster further. He knew from experience that Ari might well start to continue to talk on his favorite subject, then stay awake far too late to do so, in the hope that what he told Vetch would help him with Coresan.

And he didn't want to ask Ari for another reason, besides sparing him; Ari was sharp-witted, and might very well guess just what Vetch was planning from the tenor of Vetch's questions.

He wanted *no one*, not even Ari, to guess what his real goal had been in taking on Coresan's care. But how could anyone, having been exposed to Kashet, *not* fall under the spell of dragons, and want one like him?

He did not know how Ari would feel about that; if he'd been freeborn, there was no doubt that the Jouster would have encouraged him, but a serf? And a serf born free, born Altan? However Ari felt about the war, personally, he still fought Altans; how could he countenance putting another dragon in the hands of someone who could only be described as an enemy?

Even if the enemy himself didn't yet know what he would make of such a situation. . . .

But that was counting one's chickens—or in this case, dragons—long before they were laid, much less hatched. There were a great many obstacles to overcome before Vetch could find himself a-dragonback. And many more pitfalls, and a thousand ways in which the plan could go horribly wrong.

He also couldn't find anyone who could tell him how long after mating it would take a dragon to lay her eggs, which was a good thing, because it meant that no one would be expecting eggs on a given day. That was totally in his favor, for it meant that he had a measure of time in which he could act before he had to admit that there *were* eggs and allow the slaves to take them away to discard them.

The one thing that everyone agreed on was that Coresan would take her time about becoming a mother. Absolutely no one expected an egg the next day, or the one after that; eggs took time to form, after all, even in chickens. Especially something as big as a dragon egg.

Vetch had wondered, despite what Ari said, if he would have to compete with other Tians for the eggs, perhaps would-be Jousters who had not yet gotten a dragon, or even other boys who decided that *they* wanted to emulate Ari. It seemed logical, after all; maybe no one wanted to dare stealing eggs from wild clutches, but here was Coresan, about to go to nest, and the eggs were practically begging to be taken.

Surely there would be *one* boy (other than himself) here in the compound who would want to become a Jouster by getting himself a dragon.

But Ari had been right; no one rushed forward to claim an egg in order to repeat Ari's experiment.

Vetch couldn't understand it. *Especially* given what Kashet and Ari had done in saving Reaten. It should have been obvious to a blind man that Ari's way was the superior one. When you hatched and raised your own dragon, you got a beast that was so much easier to handle, and so much more cooperative! Why would anyone even think of taming a dragon any other way?

But no. And when he asked, cautiously, he got the same answer that Ari had given him. The Jousters much preferred the old ways—hunting the nests of dragonets about to fledge, trapping them, and confining them while they were tamed.

And it was clear, the more questions he asked, that they saw nothing obviously inferior in the way their dragons were trained, either. Dosing them with *tala,* training them until they were broken to the saddle and accepted a rider, and schooling them with increasingly heavy weights on their backs until they were grown enough to carry an adult Jouster, might be harder in the long run than Ari's way, but it meant that the Jousters *themselves* didn't have to do a thing until they were presented with a dragon already trained.

But this was hardly the way to tame a wild thing and turn its heart toward you. Even Vetch knew that.

What was more, besides knowing little or nothing about the taming, the Jousters weren't even involved in the primary training of their mounts. The poor things would pass through several hands before they came to a Jouster—one group of hunters to trap the fledglings, then a coterie of trainers to make them tractable, then a dragon boy to see to their needs. By the time they finished their training, it was yet another stranger who rode them and commanded them, Jousters who never saw them except when it was time to ride. Small wonder none of them loved their Jousters. Only Ari and Kashet had that bond of trust between them that made for more than a grudging service.

And not even a lowly dragon boy, much less a Jouster, seemed to understand how a bond like that enriched every moment of both of their lives.

But then again, Vetch had seen how the other Jousters lived, in quarters that were certainly better than Khefti-the-Fat's, with almost anything they could have wanted at their command. And in return for this, they rode patrols twice a day, fought Altan Jousters now and again, occasionally joined the Great King's armies in battle, and trained and drilled. Very light duty compared to, say, that of a spearman or a bowman. *Extremely* light work compared with almost any craftsman, or a laborer.

But to follow Ari's path, once the dragonet hatched, a Jouster would have to do the very considerable work of both a dragon boy and a trainer, work that would be demanding and might be considered beneath him.

Perhaps that was the real reason why none of them were interested.

But why wouldn't some other dragon boy seek to duplicate the feat?

Perhaps because, in the end, they were lazy. What had happened with Vetch and Coresan was very different in nature from taking on a dragonet. Coresan was a "productive" dragon, trained and ready for another Jouster once the eggs were laid. A dragonet would not be ready for patrol and combat for two to four years. Haraket would hardly allow any of the dragon boys to slack on their regular duties to take on the care and feeding of a second dragonet. At least, Vetch didn't think so. From Haraket's point of view, a dragon boy's duty came first, and a dragonet would be—a hobby. Something he could do if his duties permitted it, but *not* the sort of experiment that would permit him to shirk things like the leatherwork, the *tala* preservation, or the cleaning.

Even if, contrary to Vetch's expectations, Haraket *did* permit such a boy to devote himself only to his dragon and his dragonet, even with the other chores taken off his hands, that was still a lot of work. And as the dragonet grew, the burden would become greater, not smaller, for to those tasks would be added that of trainer. A dragon boy would have to be willing to do the work of three, which would leave him exactly no time for himself.

Yes, that might well be the answer; the others valued their own ease over the possibility of becoming another Ari, with another treasure such as Kashet.

Well, *let* them be shortsighted. That just made it easier to do what he wanted to do.

On that first day, as he had buffed and oiled his new charge, his mind had been entirely on what *he* might do and how to do it. Once it was obvious that the only thing he needed to guard against was discovery, not rivalry, nothing else particularly mattered.

The day after the rescue proved to be very interesting. With Ari off in the morning flying Reaten's patrol instead of training, Vetch devoted the time to Coresan, getting her used to being handled properly. That consisted of taking her around and around her pen on a lead, and teaching her that it was more pleasant to follow him than to fight him. He did not flinch when she snapped, he did not scream at her or prod her with an ox goad when she balked. He simply let her fight the collar, then learn that when she stopped fighting, all was well again. He took the lessons in short sessions, so as not to aggravate her, and he always ended them when she had done a complete circuit of the pen without misbehaving.

When Ari and Kashet returned, Vetch had already fed Coresan her midday meal. After Coresan had buried herself in her hot sand to drowse away her second meal of the day, Vetch fed and groomed Kashet to within an inch of his life. And before the grooming, Kashet got something he well deserved; Vetch had not forgotten his promise to Ari to reward Kashet with the treat of ox hearts. He'd gotten half a basket yesterday, and the butchers had promised Vetch more today.

With Coresan sleeping, Vetch and his empty barrow made the trek to the butchers, who practically fell all over themselves to cull out the delicacy for the dragon hero of the hour. By this time, everyone in the entire compound, from the old man who swept the corridors to the Commander of Dragons, had heard what Ari and Kashet had done; it made Vetch wonder just how much peace Ari was going to get, after all. Kashet got a full basket of his favorite treats, and he savored them; once fed, Vetch made sure that every inch of him gleamed with buffing and oil, telling him the whole time what a fine and brave, and above all, *clever* fellow he was.

If Kashet had been a cat, he would have purred, and not just because of Vetch's ministrations. People kept coming to the door of the grooming pens to admire him, and Vetch was sure that it wasn't his imagination that made him think there was a certain *posing* look about the great dragon whenever another admirer appeared. Nor did he think he was deluding himself that Kashet took care to display himself to best advantage on the side where people were.

And with every word of praise, he arched his neck a little more, and flashed his eyes at Vetch, and became even more relaxed and happy. There was no doubt that he enjoyed hearing the tone of Vetch's voice, but of late Vetch had to wonder just how much of the words he also understood. The more time he spent with Kashet, the more certain he became that the dragons were far more intelligent than any Jouster—except, perhaps, Ari—really guessed. In the happier days on the family farm, he'd seen their little donkey work the harder for praise, and admiration had doubled the number of mice laid out for inspection by the granary cat. Kashet was easily as intelligent as either beast.

Still, beast he was, for he showed no signs of the thinking ability of a man. Nor did any other dragon; well, if they had been *that* clever, they'd have all slipped their chains and flown far out of reach a long, long time ago.

But he could hardly begrudge Kashet his preening; he'd earned the right to preen. It had been an amazing thing that he and Ari had accomplished, and even the fact that it had been attempted at all was astonishing.

"I won't neglect you for Coresan, handsome one," he told the dragon, as they paced back to Kashet's pen, side by side. Kashet curved his sapphire neck, bringing his head down to Vetch's level as they walked. Vetch reached up and smoothed the skin of Kashet's golden nose and forehead, and the dragon breathed into his hair. "And I won't neglect you for—" He didn't say it—*my egg, my dragonet*—he didn't dare think that far. "—for anything else either," he promised. "As long as I'm here, I won't neglect you, I'll see you get the treatment you deserve."

As long as he was *here*. He could not promise more than that.

For though he tried not to think of it, because he did not want to give himself too much hope, too many dreams, to hatch and raise a dragon meant more than just echoing Ari's achievement. Ari was Tian; by raising Kashet, he had won an automatic place within the ranks of the Jousters. If you had a dragon, you were a Jouster, it was a simple equation. Tian custom, so resistant to change, had worked for Ari in that instance.

But Vetch was Altan, a serf, and not born into captivity; he had no loyalty to any Tian, and no reason to fight for the Tians. In fact, he had many, many compelling reasons to fight against them. So no matter what happened, if anyone discovered he had a dragonet, it would be taken from him; no sane Tian would leave such a dangerous weapon in the hands of an enemy.

That was the first, and most all-encompassing difficulty he would have to face, every moment of every day from the first instant of claiming an egg for his own. But if he could raise a dragonet to fledging—and teach it to carry him, so that, like Ari, his dragon's first flight was with *him* on its back—

—he could escape. And no one would be able to stop him. Not even another Jouster, if he could contrive for the flight to take place when they were all out on patrol.

He tried not to think of that. One step at a time, and be primed for disappointment. After all, if he failed, he would be no worse off than he was now. And there were so many ways in which the plan could fail, so few that would lead to success.

The first step: get an egg. And not just any egg; a *fertile* egg.

He went to sleep at night with his mind full of prayers for success.

For the next three days, he gave Coresan double rations, which (more than the *tala*, he suspected) greatly improved her temper. She swiftly put on weight until she was sleek again, and her scales shone with health and good care. On the second day, she stopped looking up when the other dragons flew overhead; she began to dig in her sand, as if she was looking for some perfect spot to nest. She had plenty of opportunity to do as she pleased, since she only left the pen with Vetch to be groomed. The rest of the time she was on a long leash and left to her own devices when he wasn't feeding her or trying to gentle her. He still had Kashet to tend, after all, and that left her plenty of time on her own.

She began taking him for granted, as a part of her landscape. It was tolerance rather than acceptance, but it was enough. She suffered him to clean her pen while she was in it, which was a mercy; the scheme would swiftly have fallen apart if he'd had to ask Haraket to get someone to clean the pen while he took her out of it. No matter what happened, he couldn't actually *take* an egg until after nightfall, which meant that it would have to stay in the pen from the time that she laid it until sundown. If someone else had been required to help him, then farewell secrecy!

After living the good life for several days, Coresan still snapped at strangers, and that agile tail of hers was guaranteed to deliver painful blows to the unwary. But she seemed to have decided that making life difficult for *him* was not going to change what she was being asked to do, and would only delay the rewards of food and grooming that she wanted. In fact, there were only two or three more attempts to intimidate *him* rather than strangers, and even then, the attempts were halfhearted, as if she didn't care if he didn't react. He had to wonder, then, what that fool of a Sobek had done with her, that she had gotten so ill-tempered.

Perhaps all it had taken was simple neglect, after all. Though why Sobek had neglected his charge, when Coresan had not been known for being a particularly difficult dragon, baffled Vetch. Maybe it had been fear; maybe he'd been afraid of her all along, and as a consequence, kept chaining and tying her closer and closer, so that the only time she was truly free to move was when she was under saddle. Maybe that was why she'd learned the trick of snapping her tail at everyone. Sobek hadn't ever acted as if he feared her until the last, but then, he was a blustering sort of boy, and maybe he couldn't have admitted his fear even to himself.

Well, in her position, as he'd thought and said before, he'd have acted the same way Coresan had. If Sobek *had* been chaining her short, she had certainly been partly cold all the time, since there was no way she could properly wallow on a short chain. He already knew that she'd been hungry, and that she hadn't been properly cleaned in an age. So, cold, hungry, and itchy—it was a wonder she hadn't tried to take off Sobek's head, fulfilling the fears that made him ill-treat her!

Or maybe it had just been laziness on Sobek's part, rather than fear. Certainly Haraket seemed to think so. It was a lot easier to bring a barrow full of whatever the butcher happened to put there and leaving it for the dragon to clean out, rather than carefully observing the dragon to see if it was still hungry after the first barrow. And it was easier to skimp on grooming if the dragon was fractious.

Or, just possibly, Sobek had stupidly thought that by keeping Coresan hungry, he would teach her not to fight him. Now, that *was* a technique that could work, but only if you made up for the short rations in reward morsels, tidbitting the dragon whenever she did something right, and making sure she got her full feed over the course of the day.

If the Overseer had thought that Sobek's fear of his dragon (rather than laziness) was the real reason for what had happened, he still wouldn't have hesitated to dismiss him, but it wouldn't have been in such complete disgrace.

Haraket, so Vetch had heard, had made it known that Sobek was a shirker, a slacker, totally incompetent and the kind of boy who would find any excuse to evade doing his duty. Now the officers of the army wouldn't have him, even in the lowliest of positions. That didn't leave much for him but manual labor, or perhaps the scribes or artists, and Sobek had not enough patience for the former, or talent for the latter.

Just deserts, in Vetch's mind. No dragon, no beast, could ever be successfully starved into submission.

Whether it was due to a full belly and a building layer of fat, due to the *tala*, due to kind treatment, or all three, Coresan confined her displays of temper to the most minor of outbursts with Vetch, snorts, hisses and head-tossing, spending most of her time lounging in the heat. Even those displays of pique were half-hearted, as if she was saying, *Yes, you see, I am a princess, and you are beneath me, and will render me my due or feel my wrath. See? I can punish you with my display. Now, you will fetch me some of those lambs or I will make you rue it by hissing at you again.* She was, in fact, turning into a creature that reminded him more of a spoiled, wealthy girl chit than a carnivorous monster.

Yes, tending her was a great deal of work, work he could not have done without a slave assigned to take over his other chores. Actually, his chores had been divided, with a slave cleaning Ari's quarters, and the chores in leather workshop and armory being taken up by the other dragon boys. It *was* more work than Kashet caused; Coresan was difficult to move about the compound, and required extra effort when he fed her and especially when he groomed her.

Nevertheless, she did not cause him as much work as Sobek had been put to, and Vetch was convinced it had all been because of *how* he had handled her. It was easier to pause at the doorway and throw the impatient dragon chunks of meat until the edge was off her hunger than try and fight past her to put the barrow next to her. It was easier to chain her in the grooming pen and wait out her head-tossing and fidgeting than to fight to chain her even shorter. It was easier in general to work around her than to fight her, and when she didn't get a fight, she lost interest in fighting. All perfectly logical, really.

Every morning Haraket asked if there were eggs yet. Every morning, Vetch answered in the negative, truthfully. Then, slightly more than a week after the mating, the first egg appeared; Coresan had laid it some time in the night.

He hadn't yet given up hope, but he'd begun to wonder if, perhaps, "everyone" was wrong, and a dragon wouldn't lay unless she'd mated more than once. But it had become habit to scan the sands of the wallow for any sign of an egg, paying close attention to parts of the pit that Coresan had been digging in the night before.

The egg, that precious egg, was indeed in a corner of the sand pit she had been paying special attention to last night, and if he had not been looking for it, he might not have seen it, for only the barest top curve showed above the sand. He didn't go near it, much as he wanted to; he fed her first, wanting to get some *tala* into her before he made any attempt to investigate it.

When she was sated, she returned to her wallow. He walked

around the pit cautiously, and with one eye always on her, in case she decided to take exception to his interest. But Coresan didn't seem to notice him, or that he was interested in her egg; she was buried in sand, dozing, when he finally crouched down next to the object of his desire, and brushed the sand away from the top.

The egg was exactly the same color as the sand, and the shell even had a similar texture to sandstone; it was very hard, like an enormously thick bird's egg, rather than leathery like a snake egg. He could get his arms around it easily enough, he thought; the question was, how much did it weigh? He uncovered it further, and slid his hand underneath it. He hefted it experimentally, with one hand steadying it and one under the shell, though he didn't try to lift it completely out of the sand that cradled it. It was as warm as the sand, and weighed about the same as a five-year-old child. Coresan didn't seem to mind that he handled it, perhaps because she wasn't yet brooding.

Or perhaps it was only because this was her very first egg. With barnyard fowl, first-time mothers weren't always very motherly.

He covered it back up again, quickly; he didn't want to chance it getting cold. And now the reality of it came home to him in a rush.

An egg! Coresan had laid his egg! His hands shook, and his insides felt as if he'd eaten live fish. He could hardly contain his excitement. An egg! Here it was, what he'd been waiting for—

He forced himself to calm down; he tried to look normal, although he felt anything but normal. The first person he had to get past was Haraket, when he arrived to get Coresan's morning feed. Sure enough, the Overseer was there, making sure the *tala* got properly measured out, that boys were getting *enough* meat for their charges. Haraket asked him about eggs when he dipped the scoop into the powdered *tala* to shake it over Coresan's rations, and he just shook his head, trying to keep from looking the Overseer in the eye. Haraket took that as "there is no egg yet" and didn't ask anything further, much to his relief. He didn't want to lie to Haraket, not if he could help it. The gods didn't like falsehood, and he needed the gods on his side in this. He also wasn't entirely sure that he *could* lie to Haraket. He wasn't good at lying, and the Overseer was uncannily good at knowing when someone was lying to him.

But the egg was on his mind all day as he divided his time between his two charges. He had a choice of several courses of action now, but he would have to decide what he was going to do soon. He had to get his egg before someone else decided to check Coresan's pen on the theory that Vetch wouldn't necessarily know what he was looking for, or that Coresan would have buried the eggs and not allowed Vetch to see them.

When it all came down to it, he was just a dragon boy and not even Haraket knew how much Ari had taught him about the great beasts. It was a logical supposition to presume that he wouldn't know what to look for; until last dry season, he'd never even seen a dragon that wasn't high in the sky. It wasn't likely that Ari would have told anyone how much the Jouster had been teaching Vetch about dragons. Why should he? It would make no difference to anyone, and was no one else's business.

They probably figured that the reason that he'd gotten Coresan to behave had more to do with being a farmer's son and knowing in general how to handle beasts than it had to do with his newly-won knowledge of the great creatures.

He knew from his experience with geese and Ari's stories about wild dragons that they didn't dare let Coresan go broody over her clutch.

So the very moment that eggs appeared, Haraket would, understandably, feel they had to take them *as* they appeared. For if she did go broody, they'd be in for nothing but trouble from her.

She might not even let them get *near* the eggs once she went broody. Someone might get hurt or even die trying to take the eggs, if her motherly instincts finally awoke. Hens were bad enough; all hens did was to peck the hand that tried to take their eggs from underneath them, and they frequently bruised or even drew blood. He did not even want to think about taking eggs from a broody dragon if their behavior was at all similar. Maybe you could do it at night, but given that he'd already seen Kashet awaken to accept attention from Ari long after he thought that the great beast was torpid, he wouldn't bet on a female dragon being unaware of what went on at night when she had eggs that she needed to tend.

Even if she didn't become protective of her clutch, if they waited to get her eggs away until after she went broody, they would probably have to give her infertile eggs, or dummy eggs to brood, or she would start looking for another mate with twice the energy she had used before. That was what happened in many birds, and if Coresan had been difficult before this—well, with the drive to mate in her at double strength, Vetch didn't think even he would be able to handle her.

So he could understand why Haraket would want to get each egg from her as she laid it, or shortly thereafter. He understood it, but that meant he would have to decide within a day or two what *he* was going to do.

Should he take this egg, for instance?

He could take the chance that the first egg would be fertile, and carry it off. He already knew when he could make his theft—at night, when the Jousters were in their quarters, the dragonboys at their recreations, and darkness would cover his actions. Coresan would be torpid, and would not notice him. More importantly, if she missed the egg in the morning, she would not know *who* had taken it.

And he knew where he would take it when he had it—one of the empty pens on either side of Kashet's. There were three times the number of pens than there were dragons, plenty of empty pens where an egg could incubate in the hot sands undisturbed. No one ever went into the empty pens, unless they happened to be storing something there. No one put two adult dragons next to one another, even if they appeared to get along, because of the chance that they would decide one day to fight one another. Or worse, chose one another as mates. Dragons were creatures that flocked together—sort of. They *did* spend a lot of time in a juvenile flock when they were young and not ready to mate, because clumsy juveniles working together were able to bring down prey that one alone couldn't manage. And when they weren't raising young, they also kept to a flock, but that could have been because natural hot places—natural sand wallows, sheltered places where the sun heated the sand, hot springs, and the like—were relatively few compared to the number of dragons. It could have been necessity that had them roosting together at night. But when they were fertile, they were like spotted hunting cats—sharing a territory just long enough to raise the dragonets to fledging, then parting again, and they would fight the dragon that had been a mate if there was a conflict over food, flock rank, or perches. So while there were plenty of extra pens, there was no need to take the risk of conflict by housing the beasts too closely together.

He would put the egg where it was easy to get to, and when it hatched (if it hatched), Kashet would probably ignore the dragonet as completely as he ignored other adult dragons. Just as he was alone among the other dragons in his affection for humans, he was alone in his indifference to his fellow dragons.

Now, instead of taking the first egg, he could wait, hope that no one noticed the growing clutch in the corner, and have his choice of eggs. Coresan could lay as many as four; he was giving her plenty of extra bone for the shells, which she would sorely need, to keep her hale and healthy. But the more eggs that appeared, the more likely it was that someone would get impatient and take a look for himself to see what Coresan was up to, and the more likely that she would go broody.

Take the first, or wait? He wavered between the two actions all day, the egg looming large in his mind the entire time. When Kashet and Ari came in, clearly tired from taking double patrols, he still had not decided. While the rest of the Jousters were still on the lighter duty of practice and patrol, *they* were on a full schedule; it was a good thing that Kashet was so strong and so willing.

"If I didn't know he was flying twice as far as the others every day, I wouldn't guess it," Vetch said, as Ari handed him a lance and dismounted, as usual, with a pat on the shoulder for Kashet. "He's *tired*, but not as exhausted as he could be. I think you're more tired than he is."

"Well, perhaps it's because he was first-laid," Ari said with a proud, if tired, smile. "They hatch in order of being laid, about two days apart. First-born is supposed to be strongest and the smartest, but when the young ones are taken by dragonet hunters out in the wild, firstborn has usually fledged and gone, so they get whatever is left."

Then Ari strode off without looking back, which was just as well, for Vetch was still standing there with his mouth open for a long moment after he was gone.

There it was, the deciding factor. *Firstborn is the strongest*. If Vetch was going to succeed, his dragon would have to be very big, very strong, and mature very quickly.

If that had not been enough, *all* of the conditions that night were perfect for him to move his egg. Most of the other dragon boys all went out that night, for it was a full moon, and the father of one of them, a fisherman, had promised to take them out for night fishing in the moonlight. The Jousters' quarters were full of music and voices; one of the others was holding festival with many of the Great King's nobles in attendance, and even Ari, as weary as he was, had consented to attend; the boys who were not out fishing had been pressed into service for the feast. The corridors outside the pens were flooded with light from the moon, and utterly deserted—and Coresan slept like a stone, probably exhausted from laying this, the first of her eggs.

Vetch dug the egg out of the hot sand with his bare hands. It was very warm, the texture very like that of a common pot, and unwieldy. He lifted it very carefully, transferred it to a sand-lined barrow, and trundled it to its new home without sight or sound of anyone or anything except a few bats flitting about the corridors in search of insects attracted by the torches. The spirits of the dead were supposed to take the form of bats. Was one of them his father, flitting like a silent guardian over his son? For a moment he paused, looking for a sign—

He sighed, as the bats went on with their hunting, paying no attention at all to him. They were probably just bats. If his father returned from the Summer Country, how could he *possibly* know that his Altan son was here, in the compound of the Tian Jousters? No, he would surely be flitting about the farm that had been stolen from him. Hopefully, if he had chosen to return, he was sending the worst possible dreams into the heads of those who had taken it.

Vetch reburied the egg in the corner of the empty pen least visible from the entrance. The sands were bake-oven hot, but he had gotten used to them by now. He knew, from Ari's stories of how he had raised Kashet, what he would have to do from this point. He would have to turn the egg at least twice a day to keep the growing dragonet from sticking to the inside of the shell. He would have to make certain that no one spotted him going into the pen. But that was the easy part.

For if the egg was fertile, if it hatched, he would have to get food to it several times a day, also without being seen—and keep the dragonet amused once it got old enough that it didn't sleep all the time when it wasn't eating. Then he would have to somehow train it as Ari had trained Kashet, to carry a burden of a saddle and a rider. He would have to keep anyone from seeing the dragonet—or at least, arrange things such that no one guessed that it wasn't one newly brought in from the wilds. If he could manage all of that—

If, if, if. There were a lot of "ifs" standing between him and a fragile hope of success. . . .

One thing at a time. One day at a time. There was no point in thinking past the next obstacle, which was how to slip away to turn the egg in the morning. . . .

One small step at a time, on the path to what was nothing more than a hope at this point. That was all he dared to do for now.

There were sixty mornings, sixty evenings, one hundred and twenty egg turnings to get through before he had to worry about a nestling. If there was a nestling. If the egg was fertile, if the sand was hot enough but not too hot, if no one discovered it. . . .

There were a very great many "ifs" between him and a dragonet, and most of them he had no control over.

But he had the will. And as Ari said, "Enough will, is will enough." He had to hope that in this, as in so many other things, Ari was right.

ELEVEN

WITH his precious egg tucked cozily in the hot sand in the empty pen, Vetch went back to his pallet in Kashet's pen. There was nothing more he could do for the egg at this point. It was hidden, it was warm, and if Ari was right, dragons themselves didn't take too much care about keeping their eggs perfectly warm until they actually started brooding them. Still, after he curled up on his pallet, listening to Kashet breathe, the egg lay heavily in his thoughts. He had to keep reminding himself that there really was not anything he could do right now. Nevertheless, he kept trying to think of some way he could hide the egg better, how he could manage to get extra meat to feed the dragonet, how he could keep the youngster quiet—

And training. I need to know how to train it. I need to get a saddle, guiding straps, harness—

Perhaps it was just as well that Kashet and Coresan together kept him running, because eventually the need to sleep caught up with him, and he dozed off in mid-thought.

Vetch woke just as dawn was coloring the sky to the east. A desert thrush was singing somewhere overhead, and the breeze from the direction of the Great Mother River smelled of wet mud and algae, with a hint of fish. The Flood was definitely over now, and the river was pulling in the hem of her robe. And he was just in time to slip over to the next pen and turn the egg before anyone else was awake.

He flung off his blanket and sprang up out of his pallet, not bothering to twist on a kilt. In the dim light, everything seemed painted in shades of blue, and the damp air was clammy and cool on his skin. He scuttled over to the next pen, feeling fairly secure that no one else would be awake at this hour.

He waded out into the hot sand, which felt exceptionally good on his chilled skin, and carefully dug around one side of the egg until he had uncovered enough to enable him to give it a half turn. Then he covered it back up again, except for a very small area at the very top, the merest curve of shell.

Then he sprinted back to Kashet's pen, and his pallet. Kashet had not moved a muscle, and until Kashet woke, there was no reason for him to get up either.

In fact, he managed to doze a little, before the rustling sound of sand moving against dragon scales warned him that he had better start his working day.

He was actually feeding Coresan four times daily now, giving her a final meal just before she went to sleep for the night. This meant that she would sleep longer in the morning than Kashet, and he could feed his primary charge first, get him saddled and ready for Ari by the time most of the other dragon boys were still queuing up for meat. This meant that when he came around with a barrow for Coresan, most of them were gone already.

When he reached her pen, she was scratching in an absent-minded way at the sand in the corner where her egg had been, but the moment that he appeared with her breakfast, she lost interest in that corner in favor of food. He went about the usual routine as though she had never laid an egg, and after another cursory search for it when she'd eaten, Coresan soon settled. She didn't so much give up, as lose interest in looking for it. A good sign, Vetch thought.

In fact, at noon she wolfed down meat until Vetch thought she was going to pop, then stretched herself out in the sun for a long doze, quite as if the egg had never existed.

Kashet came in that afternoon looking marginally better, and so did Ari, who took a look around the pen as Vetch divested the dragon of his saddle and harness. "I was afraid, doing double duty as you are, that all the work was going to be too much for you, Vetch," the Jouster said, with just the faintest overtones of surprise. "But I swear, if anything Kashet's pen is cleaner and neater than it was before. Are there two of you? Have you spawned a twin brother you haven't told me about?"

Vetch smiled to himself. "I'm used to doing more than my share," he said boldly. "It gets put on me, often as not. And don't think it's your fault, because it isn't! But so are you and Kashet, used to doing more than your share. And you don't have anyone to take the boring part of your work off your hands; at least I got that much advantage."

"Huh. You've certainly hit that target in the heart ring," Ari replied, with a raised eyebrow. "I suppose, though, it's always been true that those of us who are outsiders have to work twice as hard just to prove ourselves the equals of those on the inside. How's Coresan?"

"Fat and lazy, and getting fatter," he replied truthfully. "*I* figure, the fatter I get her, the less trouble she'll be, because she'll be too lazy to make trouble."

"The fat part is probably the eggs she's about to lay," Ari corrected. "And the lazy part because she's preoccupied with nesting and saving her energy for the eggs she'll lay. Has she been digging in her wallow?"

"All the time," Vetch said instantly, glad that now he needn't conceal anything in Coresan's pen. "One corner in particular, the one that gets sun all day."

Ari nodded. "Then she's about to lay. Good! Otherwise, is she behaving for you?"

"Better every day, by a little," Vetch said, feeling very proud of himself. "And I've been saving back the best meat from her meals to tidbit her with when she behaves herself."

"Then, once she's finished laying, I don't think it would be out of the question to reinforce that by making her meals of the shanks and inferior meat, and save the things she likes for tidbits only," Ari replied, squinting thoughtfully. "You don't want to starve her, but if you make it clear that she gets the finer things only when she's on good behavior, she'll come completely around. She *was* trained properly originally—well, as 'properly' as you can, when you're starting out to break a dragon, rather than really tame it."

"She'll never be a Kashet," Vetch stated, as he removed the last of the dragon's harness, and the great beast gave himself a shake and stepped down into his wallow.

Ari laughed. "No. You're right there. I'm afraid there will never be another Kashet."

And with that, the Jouster gave Vetch a wink, and left.

Vetch hid his smile. There would never be another Kashet? Well, that remained to be seen.

Perhaps for once Ari will be wrong, so long as the gods are with me.

And two days later, Coresan's second egg appeared in the same corner as the first, though this time Vetch found it in the afternoon rather than the morning. Actually, the appearance of the egg surprised him; he would have thought that it would be more of an effort for her to lay such enormous objects.

With great relief, Vetch went straight to Haraket and reported it. Finally he was not going to have to worry about evading Haraket's questions. Nor would he have to worry that the Overseer might begin to wonder *why* there weren't any eggs. Mind, Haraket hadn't shown any evidence of suspicion, but—well, Haraket wouldn't necessarily *show* anything. The Overseer was very good at keeping his ideas to himself when he chose. Vetch would never want to play the stone game against him, for there would be no reading anything in Haraket's face.

It took Vetch some time to actually track Haraket down; he wasn't with the butchers, inspecting occupied pens, discussing the work of the boys with the harness maker, or any other place where Vetch expected to find him. Finally, after asking everyone he met, Vetch discovered the Overseer in a little room just off the kitchen. He was sequestered with the Steward of the Household, who was in charge of supplying all of the food and clothing needs for the Jousters and the considerable staff it took to support them. Te-Velethat, apparently, was not in charge of this most vital of duties. Te-Velethat, from a remark that Vetch overheard before he made his presence known, considered the procurement of supplies to be entirely beneath him as an Overseer, and left it all up to Haraket. Haraket, who was already handling the procurement of everything associated with the dragons, got saddled with this job as well.

And as a consequence, it seemed, Te-Velethat had a great deal less power and influence within the compound than he *thought* he had . . . which was a bit of information that Vetch filed away, just in case he needed it at some time in the future.

"An egg! Finally!" the Overseer grunted, once Vetch had apprised him of the situation. "I was beginning to worry that she might be egg-bound."

"What would you like me to do, sir?" Vetch asked diffidently.

"Don't do anything; I'll handle this," Haraket said firmly. "Now, go back to her, and don't act any differently. Don't pay any attention to that egg, because we don't want her to have a go at you. She might, she might not, there's no telling at the moment. You'll have to leave her be, and if she acts possessive, leave her alone with it, just lengthen her chain and take a barrow of meat in to her and don't bother any further with her. As a first-time breeder, chances are she won't know what to do with it, but don't take any chances if she shows the *least* little sign of getting protective."

Vetch ducked his head. "Yes, sir," he said obediently. "I'll do that, but she didn't even act as if she cared about it at all. The way she acted, it could just as well have been one of her droppings."

"That could be a ruse, the way a plover plays broken-wing to lure you away," Haraket warned, "But as long as *she* doesn't think you know about it, she won't do anything to draw attention to it. You're too valuable for us to risk you getting injured by a broody she-dragon. I don't want you hurt."

"Yes, sir," Vetch repeated, knowing already that Coresan wasn't going to do anything about the second egg, since she hadn't been at all possessive about the first. He was safe enough with her, and given her indifference, perhaps it was just as well that they weren't going to give her the chance to be a mother.

Perhaps, though, he was doing her a disservice. Chickens didn't pay any attention to their eggs until after the full clutch had been laid. There was no telling but what, once her instincts awoke, she wouldn't have been a good mother after all.

And for a moment, he felt horribly guilty; here they were, taking her eggs from her, never giving her a chance to raise them. It didn't seem at all fair.

If the gods had meant her to breed, he told himself, *she'd have gotten away from Ari and Kashet and gone off into the hills. And she'd have found herself a handsome male and set herself right up, no doubt. What healthy dragon could have resisted such a scarlet beauty?* And he went back to his split duties, leaving Haraket and the Steward poring over tallies of wheat and barley.

He fed Coresan, then made sure that Coresan's pen was as spotless and tidy as Kashet's. If Haraket was going to arrive with a picked crew to purloin the egg, he wanted the pen to show just how diligent a worker he was. By the time he finished Coresan's pen, it was time for Kashet and Ari to come back from their second patrol, so it was on to the next round, feeding Kashet, buffing and oiling him, then giving Coresan the same treatment, and that fourth little meal that would hold her overnight until late morning. In all that time, there was no sign of Haraket, and the egg was still in the corner of Coresan's pen.

Then, just before going to bed himself, he slipped into the empty pen to turn *his* egg, as he had been doing for the past two mornings and nights.

When he went to feed Coresan the next morning, the egg was gone, so he guessed that Haraket had duplicated what he himself had done—taken the egg in the night, when Coresan was least likely to see and react to the theft of her potential progeny.

Ari lingered while Vetch unharnessed Kashet after the morning patrol, as if he was uncertain about something. Finally, though he made up his mind. "I thought you might like to know, Seftu's rider, Horeb, is back on his patrols."

"Ah?" Vetch said noncommittally. "So what came of his side of the mess, then?"

"First, a good long dressing-down from Haraket that practically pinned his ears back," Ari said, with a grim little smile. "I suspect that didn't impress him too much past the moment, but then he had an intense session with the Captain of Jousters, which of a certainty *did*. The Captain ordered an official inquiry and when that was over, he had an *interview*—" (Ari's tone and expression put a certain decided emphasis on the word) "—with the Commander of Dragons. I saw him leave, actually; he looked like a whipped cur."

"Is the Commander so fearsome?" Vetch asked wonderingly. This was the first time that he had heard of the Commander actually doing anything with the Jousters other than issuing orders.

"Oh, he's worse, I do pledge you," Ari said, "He does not hear excuses; we are weapons in his hand, and woe betide the weapon that fails. As a Commander of Hundreds expects each man to tend to his equipment and see that it is in top condition, the Commander of Dragons expects that we are to do the same with our beasts. It's bad enough to face him when he's giving you a commendation; it's got to be a thousand times worse when he's about take you apart. But the inquiry proved that Horeb was not as much to blame for the incident as Reaten was. Apparently Coresan had been proddy for the last week; Seftu only got interested when she went up in the air and he saw her start to display instead of obeying her rider."

"Huh." Sobek, of course, was just as guilty, but he'd already been punished to the extent that the arm of the Jousters reached, Vetch had to suppose. "So what's to do with Reaten, then?"

Ari cleared his throat, and it sounded embarrassed. "Well, here, you see, I have a dilemma. What happened to Horeb is very much public knowledge. Plenty of underlings knew about the interviews, and plenty more saw him going into and out of all three of them. The result of the inquiry is also public knowledge. However, the same cannot be said of what's to happen with Reaten. If I tell you, it's gossip that the—ah—"

"Serfs, slaves, and servants aren't supposed to know," Vetch supplied, the words leaving a bitter taste behind as he spoke them.

But this was Ari—and Ari was not like anyone else. "True. This is not the sort of thing that should be gossiped about—"

He winked. It was a very sly wink. "Well, as you know, I could just be talking to myself, or to my dragon. In fact, I believe I will talk to my dragon," was Ari's response, and he looked up at Kashet, who craned his neck around to stare into his Jouster's eyes, looking for all the world as if *he* wanted to hear this gossip himself. "Now, as for Reaten, when he recovers, it's rumored—just rumored, mind—that his interview will be at the hands of the Royal Commander himself. Isn't that fascinating, Kashet?"

The dragon snorted, as if he was skeptical of how much good a mere dressing-down would change Reaten's ways.

"Really? On the whole, I would tend to agree with you, Kashet, given what I know about Reaten." Oh, now Ari *did* look sly. "You see, Kashet, Reaten is noble, himself, and he seems to be under the impression that anyone of noble blood need not concern himself with orders and instructions. Fortunately I have it on more substantial authority that Reaten is going to be demoted back down to merest apprentice, no longer permitted to fly or fight until the end of the Floods. And that if the Great King didn't need Jousters so badly, he'd be sent packing after his dragon boy. And *furthermore*, since the Royal Commander is of sufficient rank to cow anyone other than the Great King, he has decided that Reaten's father is going to sit in on the dressing-down, just to give a bit of familial emphasis to it all."

While Ari didn't sound gleeful, there was no mistaking the satisfaction in his voice. "If you were to ask me, Kashet, I would say that the punishment is certainly fitting."

And serve him right, too, was Vetch's conclusion. Anyone who hadn't *noticed* that his dragon was looking to mate didn't deserve to be a Jouster, and if he'd been depending on his dragon boy to tell him what Coresan's condition was, he'd been completely a fool. He should have seen she was too thin, he should have immediately seen how restless she was and checked her over himself. Noble or not, when he undertook to become a Jouster, he took the same oaths to obey his superiors as any warrior or officer, and that meant *every* order, *every* rule, not just the ones that suited him. If he felt taking proper care of his dragon was beneath him, well, he should have just resigned and gone off to serve as an officer or something in the regular army.

And through his foolishness and Horeb's—the latter not having the good sense to *notice* when his he-dragon had begun a courtship flight!—Tia had nearly lost two Jousters and two dragons. That they hadn't, had been a miracle, due in no small part to Ari—who had been "rewarded" for his wisdom and skill by taking on the duties of Reaten and himself combined.

Well, that wasn't entirely true, as he learned that very afternoon.

"Well," Haraket said very quietly as Vetch obtained Coresan's dinner, "Your Jouster's done it again."

"Done what again?" Vetch asked, his eyebrows puckering in

confusion. Surely Haraket didn't know how much about Horeb and Reaten that Ari had told him. . . .

"He didn't tell you? Huh. Well, I'm not surprised." Haraket sighed. "He's been given quite a bit of recognition, in a ceremony last night. He's attracted the attention and the notice of the greatest and most powerful in the land, Vetch, and not for the first time. Ari was awarded the Gold of Honor at the hands of the Great King himself, two armlets and a full broad collar."

Vetch blinked. "He got a ceremony? By himself?" was all he could think of to say. If the Great King had held the Gold of Honor ceremony *just* for Ari—well, it was certain that Ari wouldn't be a mere Jouster much longer.

And then what would happen to Vetch and his plans?

"Well, no," Haraket admitted. "There were something like forty others. But still! Two armlets and a collar! Everyone else, or nearly, got just bees or armlets, and only one other person got more than Ari did, and *he* was a Commander of Hundreds. And do you *know* what he did with them?"

Vetch shook his head, but he already knew he was going to find out. He could tell from the vehemence that Haraket was showing that the Overseer was only using Vetch's presence as an excuse to vent his own exasperation. Though why he should be exasperated about Ari getting a great honor, Vetch could not imagine.

"I'll tell you what he did! He dropped all three of them in his clothes' chest, like—like an old kilt! The slave that cleans his rooms found them there, and I had to come and take them away to lock up for him! And what's more," Haraket continued in disbelief, "he did the same with the *other* awards he's won. They were *all* in there, packed up as if they were unsuitable presents from an inconvenient relative! Anybody would think he didn't care!"

It was perfectly clear to Vetch at this point that Haraket was both partly pleased because Ari was not puffed up by the awards, and exasperated that he seemed to count them of so little worth.

Vetch made sympathetic noises, but he didn't understand Ari's attitude either—

Yet somehow, it *felt* right. If Ari had been the type to search after the attention of the mighty, well—

—he wouldn't have been Ari.

The next day, Vetch thought he heard music at sunrise—the distant blare of trumpets and the pounding of drums, the shaking of sistrums. And for a moment, he couldn't imagine why. . . .

Then he closed his eyes and tried to reckon up days, and realized what it must be.

It was the beginning of the Planting Ceremony. The flood was officially over, and the Great King was standing in the stead of the god Siris, with the Chief Lady in the place of Iris, blessing the fields nearest the Palace to prepare them for sowing. All over Tia the priests of Siris and Iris were doing the same, and in Khefti's village, there would be a great festival with bread and beer distributed at the Temple to all comers. He had lost count of the days, working as hard as he was—

But then, Planting had never been more to him than the faint hope that he might be able to slip away from Khefti long enough to collect some of that bread and beer for himself. Altans celebrated four seasons, not the five of the Tians. By the time the Great Mother River got to Altan lands, she had spread out so wide in the swamps and delta that Flood was little more than a rise in the waters of an inch or two, and there was no real dry season, just one without rain. But now he remembered how quiet the compound had been last night—and it would be just as quiet tonight, for the Court of the Great King would be holding festival, and all of the Jousters would be invited.

Haraket appeared as Vetch tended to Kashet shortly after sunrise. He, at least, did not look the worse for wear, so either he had not attended last night's feast, or else he had been moderate in his appetites.

"How was Coresan before we took the egg from her?" he asked Vetch, without preamble.

"Fine, sir," Vetch said honestly. "No different than usual. If I hadn't known the egg was there, I wouldn't have guessed; she even went out for her buffing without any more trouble than usual. And I looked in on her this morning, and she's still fine. I don't think she's missing it, to tell the truth."

"Ah, good—" Haraket began, but looked up at a footstep just outside in the corridor.

Ari appeared in the doorway, also looking no worse for wear than Haraket. But Haraket soon proved who had been attending what last night with his next comment.

"You were missed at the feast last night," he said. "I was asked about you."

Ari shrugged. "And did you explain that double patrols do not leave a man with much desire to drink date wine, eat until he's sluggish, pursue pretty little dancers, and stay up far too late?" he replied.

"It is generally considered an honor to be asked to banquet with the Great King—" Haraket began.

"—along with a few hundred of his closest friends, indeed." Ari snorted. "If I was missed, it was only by the Vizier of the feast, who found himself with an empty place to conceal."

"I don't understand you at all," Haraket growled, as Ari checked Kashet's harness. "Last night you were invited to the Great King's own feast, three times you've been awarded the Gold of Honor, and no one would even *guess* it."

Ari shrugged. "I'm a practical man. All very well to be heaped with tokens of the Great King's esteem, but you can't sell Honor Gold, nor trade it; you can only wear it to show your valor and rank."

"And the fact that the Great King *favors* you, fool!" Haraket retorted with exasperation.

"And the Great King's favor gains me—what, precisely?" Ari replied mildly, with no more than a raised eyebrow. "I don't care to mingle with the nobles of the court, I'm not looking for a promotion, and I value nothing that is as ephemeral as fame."

Vetch kept his head down, hoping neither of them noticed him. This was a very interesting conversation, and he didn't want to be sent away in the middle of it.

"The Great King's favor can make you," Haraket said flatly.

"And break me." Now Ari's voice went as stone-hard as Haraket's. "Suppose I were to put myself forward. Then I must guard my tongue waking and sleeping, lest someone who wishes to be *more* favored takes some word of mine and twists it, and whispers it in the Great King's ear! I could not choose my own friends, my own pastimes, nothing, for fear that someone who does not love to see me raised on high may find a weapon to bring me down! I would be more of a prisoner than a serf, who at least may command his own thoughts. I think not; that sort of life is not for me. Now, if such honors would grant me the freedom to study dragons, rather than use them as weapons, *then*, they would be of value to me. As it is, they are worth less than sand in the dry season."

And with that, he nudged Kashet, who was already impatient to be gone, and they thundered into the sky. Haraket sheltered his eyes with his hand, and peered after him, shaking his head. Vetch didn't know what to think, but he stowed the words away in his memory to ponder later.

Coresan laid a total of three more eggs, one every three days, which were duly taken away from her before she had a chance to go broody. She didn't seem to miss them at all, any more than she'd missed the one that Vetch had taken. Vetch didn't know what had been done with those eggs, and tried not to think about them. After all, he had more than enough on his hands at the moment, tending to her, Kashet, and his own precious egg which—if he wasn't mistaken—was showing every sign of being fertile. When all the eggs had been laid, Coresan began to show signs of restlessness.

Dutifully, Vetch reported that to Haraket as well. The Overseer pulled on his lower lip and thought for a moment. "Reaten is going to be sent down, back to the ranks of the unflighted, until he learns better dragon husbandry," he said, in an absentminded tone that made Vetch assume he was thinking out loud. "But there's a likely lad coming up who might do well with Coresan, if she'll take him. . . ."

Haraket's voice trailed away, and Vetch wondered what he meant. Could a Jouster be taken from his dragon?

Maybe not Ari, for Vetch was certain Kashet would never, ever fly for anyone else . . . but would it make any difference to Coresan who flew her?

Probably not. And that was confirmed a moment later, when Haraket nodded briskly. "I'll do it," he said aloud, with satisfaction in his voice. "I'll switch their dragons. Hah! If he can get into trouble with *that* beast, I'll eat his saddle raw, without salt!"

That very evening, as Vetch was about to take away a half-barrowload of meat that Coresan suddenly didn't want—for all on her own, now that she had delivered herself of her clutch, she was cutting back on her food—Haraket appeared at the door to Coresan's pen with a strange young man in tow. This one could not have been out of his teens, but there was a no-nonsense look about him that made him seem very confident. And when he looked Coresan up and down, he was not at all afraid of her.

"And this is Coresan. Stand your ground with her," Haraket was saying. "Remember what I told you."

The young man nodded, and approached the dragon, who was peering down at him with great interest. But she didn't snap; her snappishness all seemed to have been due to her wanting to mate, and being about to go to nest. Now she was back to her old self, agreeable, but with mischief and rebellion in her. Her tail twitched, Vetch noticed, as if she was contemplating a sly and seemingly absentminded *thwack* across the newcomer's shins with it.

"Coresan!" the man shouted, before she had made up her mind about it. "Down!"

Vetch gritted his teeth on his own resentment as the young man reaped the benefits of Vetch's work with Coresan; perhaps she hadn't been flying, but *he* was the one who calculated that her bad humor was due in part to hunger, *he* was the one who'd been working with her basic commands, if only to make his own job easier, and *he* had been teaching her that both obedience and disobedience had consequences. She *had* been obeying only when she felt like it; now, after all his drilling, she did so automatically.

She knelt, and the newcomer gestured imperiously at Vetch. He wanted her saddle, of course; Vetch throttled his impulse to follow Coresan's unruly example before all that drilling and become selectively deaf and blind. Instead, he brought up the saddle and harness.

At least this fellow was competent enough to do his own saddling. Feeling very much as if *he* was the expert here, and the Jouster the interloper, Vetch watched the harnessing with a critical eye, and could find nothing to complain about.

But he felt better when, as the young man finished, he gave Coresan a rewarding slap on the shoulder. At least he didn't look on the dragon as a sort of flying chariot, insensate and insensible.

"Up, Coresan," the Jouster ordered, and then looked back over his shoulder at Haraket as she obeyed without complaint.

The Overseer nodded, and the new Jouster put one foot on Coresan's foreleg, and vaulted lightly into her saddle. He signaled to Vetch, who released the chain from around her neck, the chain that had kept her earthbound until this moment.

Coresan's training held, though she had not been ridden in nearly a moon; she stayed on the ground rather than going for the sky, although a few weeks ago, she'd have been up like a shot arrow once the chain was off. Instead, she was rock-steady until the new man gave her the nudge to send her up. She responded to his signal eagerly, throwing herself into the air, as Vetch and

Haraket shielded their eyes from the storm of sand and wind driven up by the fierce beats of her wings.

When the buffeting had ceased, Vetch looked up; Coresan was a tiny figure against the hot blue sky, still climbing, and still under control, back to her old self, but with a superior level of obedience as far as Vetch could tell. He glanced over at Haraket, who smiled with satisfaction.

"I think he'll do," the Overseer said aloud, and there was no mistaking the pleasure in it. "We'll see how Reaten does with Beskela."

Vetch's mouth dropped open at that. Beskela! The male was the oldest dragon in the compound, so old that the blue of his main color had deepened to near-black! If there was a lazier dragon here, Vetch had yet to hear about it. He had gotten rotated back to the new lot of Jousters because his old Jouster had been killed by a lucky arrow from an archer on the ground, and Beskela had elected to return to the compound rather than fly off to freedom as nearly any other dragon would have.

And that was a measure of how lazy he was. Beskela had learned the most key of lessons, which was *where the food came from*. He knew that—unlike the case of a dragon in the wild, who, when he failed make a kill, didn't eat—in the compound, meals arrived on time and in full supply whether a dragon exerted himself to the fullest or not. Beskela *liked* captivity, so long as no one made him work too hard. And it was rather difficult to force a creature the size of a dragon to do much of anything it didn't want to.

Vetch hid his smirk behind his hand. If there was ever a Jouster who deserved being assigned to Beskela, it was Reaten. Patrols would take twice as long to compete as Beskela lounged his way through the sky, and Reaten could pretty much forget about the Gold of Honor, for at the first sight of a fight in the offing, Beskela would do his best to keep as far away as possible from the combat. Failing that, he would hold back, and shy off every time his

Jouster tried to close in. That was assuming he didn't flee altogether, refusing to answer the guide reins.

Oh, yes, this was certainly a case of the right chickens coming home to roost.

On the other hand, if a Jouster couldn't master a dragon like Coresan, at least with Beskela he could get patrolling done and wouldn't get anyone else in trouble.

Vetch went back to work, his jealousy fading. Coresan had a good Jouster, it seemed, one of whom Haraket approved. For that, he was grateful. Coresan was no Kashet, but he had been getting rather fond of her.

Still, it rankled, to be treated as if he was nothing more than a mobile saddle rack, and otherwise ignored.

When Coresan came back in, it was very clear that her new Jouster was going to continue ignoring Vetch, and it was only because he had gotten to like Coresan that Vetch didn't go straight to Haraket and demand to be put back on his old duties, serving Ari only. This was like the treatment he had gotten from the other dragon boys, only worse. Why, he didn't even learn the Jouster's *name* for three days, and then only discovered it when he overheard another Jouster asking, "Well, Neftat, and how do you like our prime virago, Coresan? Or do you wish you had Beskela back?"

Neftat asked him *nothing* about Coresan—though he did examine every inch of her every time he took her out. He continued to act as if Vetch was a mere convenience, of no import except that he kept the dragon fed, watered, clean, and comfortable.

Still, he treated Coresan well, and paid as much heed to her moods as an attentive lover would have. She was out of shape, and he was putting her back *in* shape on a reasonable schedule, being neither too demanding nor too lax. He was a good rider for her.

But.

Finally, he couldn't stand it. He went to Haraket.

But once he got the Overseer's attention, he hesitated. How could he, a mere serf, complain about a Jouster?

He decided that it wouldn't be a *complaint*, exactly.

"Overseer," he said, choosing his words with the greatest of care, "What is my—my relationship to be to Coresan's Jouster?"

"Relationship?" Haraket asked, with a lifted brow. "None, and I told him as much. You aren't Coresan's boy—you're Kashet's. I don't want him giving you orders that may conflict with something Ari's asked you to do, so I told him to leave you alone while I find Coresan a good boy."

Suddenly, Vetch was very glad that he hadn't voiced an actual complaint, for he would have looked very stupid. "Thank you, Overseer," he said, with utmost politeness. "I—ah—wasn't sure what I should be doing, with regard to Jouster Neftat." And he bowed properly, and got out of Haraket's way as quickly as he could, thanking the gods that he had learned to think before he blurted something out. How much less trouble he would have been in, if only he had kept his mouth shut over the years! He took care to smile at Neftat from then on, even if the latter didn't appear to take any notice.

At least with both Coresan and Seftu back on patrol, Ari could stop doing double-duty. Vetch had the idea that he was sleeping a good deal. Certainly Kashet was!

Haraket was as good as his word, too. By the time the planting season was over, in fact, within a moon, Haraket found another dragon boy for Coresan, another serf from a stolen farm like Vetch.

Presumably, having found that Vetch was such a good worker, Haraket was willing to try another of the same type.

Haraket brought the replacement in one afternoon, without any fanfare, though he had taken the time to get the new boy cleaned up, kilted, and all before he brought him to the pen. With any dragon, that was a good idea; they were used to Jousters and dragon boys in their uniform kilts and kit, and dragons were creatures of habit. Even the few servants like Haraket and the slaves wore pretty much the same uniforms, which varied only in quality of materials. Presumably a dragon couldn't tell the difference between coarse linen and fine, and the similarity of costume told the dragons who "belonged" here, and who didn't.

However, just the previous day Coresan had reacted poorly to the presence of a pretty woman friend of Coresan's Jouster, Neftat. The bright fluttering gauze of her gown, the high voice, the jangling jewelry—whatever it was had made Coresan rear up and hiss angrily, her tail giving one of those vicious lashes that Vetch had not quite managed to train her out of.

Neftat had in his turn reacted as Vetch would have wanted, shooing his lady friend outside. This was one of the only times when Neftat actually *spoke* to Vetch.

"Keep her company for a moment," he'd ordered (rather than requested). The tone made Vetch grind his teeth, but he obeyed, though he had no idea how to amuse a *lady*. He listened to Neftat soothing his dragon with one ear, while he directed the lady's attention to the carvings on the walls, the construction of the pens, even the dragons peering over the pens with interest at them— babbling foolishly whatever came into his head in an effort to distract her.

Fortunately, Neftat finally came out and apologized to the lady. Vetch hadn't even waited to hear what he said.

But now—it looked as if his patience wasn't going to be on trial for much longer.

"Vetch, this is Fisk," Haraket said shortly. "He's a serf; I want him for Coresan's boy. If you can train him to take Coresan, do it." And he left, with the two boys staring awkwardly at one another.

It was Fisk who made the first move, though. "Ah," he said, ducking his head in unconscious submission. "Could be you'd give me your name?"

Vetch had to smile, then; *he* knew in part how Fisk must be feeling, but poor Fisk knew nothing about his would-be mentor, perhaps not even that Vetch was a serf! The hair should tell him, but Fisk might not know that only Altan serfs wore their hair long as a sign of their indentured nature. "Vetch," he replied. "And I'm a serf, too." He looked the other boy up and down; could it be that Fisk had been a farmer's boy, too? "Well, if I'm to teach you about Coresan, what do you know about animals in general?"

"Ah. Mostly I've tended goats," Fisk ventured, and looked up at Coresan, who looked curiously down at him. "That be a mighty big goat. . . ."

For a heart-stopping moment, Vetch thought the other boy was feeble-minded, but then he saw the slow grin, and realized with relief that Fisk was joking.

And it soon was apparent that Haraket had chosen well, so far as Coresan was concerned, for Fisk was not afraid of her, and had more experience with intractable creatures than Vetch ever had. For one thing, he was two years older than Vetch—and what was more, Fisk had actually been a goatherd in charge of a large number of animals, and goats could be the most stubborn and evil-minded domestic creatures ever created; he might not be very bright, but he was eminently practical, and he had a good rapport with beasts. Unlike Vetch, *he* hadn't had a family to lose, as he was already an orphan when the Tians came, tending the herd of goats for a surly uncle. As a consequence, life in the Jouster's compound was more than an improvement, it was an improvement without any previous loss attached. He had never really known what it was like to be free or to have a close-knit family, for his father was dead and his mother had been her brother-in-law's servant. While she loved her son, she had been able to give him nothing but her love while her brother-in-law worked her to death and bid fair to repeat his treatment with her son.

Now, with only a single, nonwandering creature to be in charge of, good treatment, and much better food, Fisk was convinced he'd fallen into a honey pot. He'd understood *exactly* what Vetch meant when he described Coresan's quirks and personality, and he didn't let her bully him.

More to the point, to both Vetch's and Haraket's delight, Fisk and Coresan took to each other with a great deal of mutual respect and even affection. It was nothing like the bond Vetch had with Kashet, but it was as close to that as any other dragon boy's, and closer than most.

That released Vetch from his duties to Coresan, which was a great relief. Coresan needed someone who understood her and *cared* about her, and Vetch's heart was given to the creature growing inside his egg and to Kashet. Haraket was overjoyed, and within the week, Vetch overheard him speaking with Ari about finding more goatherd serfs in the future to use as dragon boys.

As for Vetch—Fisk might not be anyone he could have a deep and meaningful conversation with, but he *was* friendly, and he *was* another serf, so at least now he had someone who would share a meal and a joke with him. The cold shoulders of the other dragon boys weren't so hard to take when there were two to face them instead of one alone.

Gratefully, he went back to his old chores, which, after all the work of tending Coresan, Kashet *and* a dragon-in-egg, seemed infinitely lighter. The growing season was well underway, and the increasing heat would surely be the trigger to hatch his egg, and soon he would need all the extra time he could get.

He certainly completed his round of ordinary chores faster than he had before he'd been doing double-duty with Coresan. Or perhaps it was just that he was putting on muscle and strength himself. He practically flew through his cleaning chores, and as for the others, the old leather worker and the Weapons Overseer had taken to giving him an allotment of work, so that the others wouldn't shirk theirs, knowing they could load it onto him when he finished the sooner.

All this came just in time.

The egg was starting to move.

TWELVE

THE egg was starting to move because the developing dragon inside was shifting restlessly. It was *definitely* fertile, and was going to hatch if nothing went wrong with the dragonet, there was no doubt whatsoever about that. Though how long it would be before the egg really hatched now that it was starting to move, well, he didn't know, and he wasn't sure that even Ari did. It could be days; it might be weeks. The only thing he could be absolutely sure of was that it would be within the moon.

The timetable seemed about right as well, given what he'd learned from Ari, though it did not seem possible that so much time had passed so quickly. By *his* reckoning, it should barely have been time for the Planting Festival.

But there it was; caught up in the peculiar schedule of the Jousters' compound and as busy as he was, time was all distorted. Among the Jousters, there were only two real "seasons"—the season of the rains (which included part, but not all, of flood season) when the Jousters and dragons could rest a little, and the season of no-rain, which meant full patrols and everyone working flat-out. The Temple-regulated festivals of the seasons, so important when he'd been working for Khefti-the-Fat, had slipped by him without noticing. Now growing season was well under way, the plants were all sprouting in the fields, and he hadn't even noticed. If Ari was right, eggs hatched well inside Growing season, giving the richest time of the year, so far as game was concerned, for the critical first weeks of a dragonet's life. Then, when the little one was old enough not to need feeding so often, came Dry season—and in the heat of Dry, the dragonet could grow and develop without needing to be kept warm by a parent.

Soon. The egg must surely hatch soon.

He slipped away every night as soon as it was quiet to turn it and speak softly to the dragonet within the shell, and woke before dawn to turn it again. So far, no one had caught him at his tending—but then, there wasn't anyone about that early or that late. Not even the most diligent of Jousters rose any earlier than he had to—and who could blame them when they were flying long patrols to prevent Altans from sabotaging the crops in the fields? Burning crops was an easy way to strike back at the hated enemy; you left no traces behind if you were clever, and every field burned was more grain that the enemy would have to purchase with precious gold—which in turn, could not be used to hire and equip soldiers. Altan serfs, and those Altans who still retained possession of their own farms through some miracle, would not burn their own crops—they'd starve if they did, for they would get cold charity from the Tian masters. But that wouldn't stop Altan insurgents from firing the fields, regardless of who owned them. About the only relief there was from *that* threat was that Altans, like the Tians, could not be persuaded to go out into the fields at night, when homeless, hungry ghosts were a-prowl. Not even the rebels would take that risk, a very real one, and not the sort of thing that even Haraket dared. Unhomed spirits were very real, and it never seemed to occur to the Tians that their rigor in denying slaughtered Altans the proper rites and funerary shrines only made *more* angry ghosts to plague their nights. It was dangerous enough to walk the streets of a village, where the protection of the Temples held sway, and the lights and lamps drove the ghosts out. Only a priest or a witch would dare venture into open fields by night, and what priest or witch would trouble to fire a field when their time was better served making magic? But every so often, someone too foolhardy or desperate or sure of his protections went out at night, beyond the protections of the streets, and was found dead in the morning. Usually there wasn't a mark on him, but his face was generally contorted with pain or horror.

No, the rebels were bold enough, but not *that* bold. They did their work between the first hint of dawn and the last light of dusk.

So the Jousters were in the air whenever possible, reminding those below that the Great King had more than just soldiers to enforce his will, scanning the fields at dawn and dusk for creeping forms that should not be there. That meant more time in the sky, tired dragons and Jousters, and the most profound of silences from sunset to sunrise within the walls of the compound. No time for festivities now—oh, no! Once in a very great while, Vetch would hear music coming over the walls, but it was all quiet music, harp and flute, and never went much past the time that a late dinner would be. Probably some of the more aristocratic Jousters were having music with their dinner.

So Vetch's ventures were secure. Not even Ari caught him, even though the Jouster came to the pen nearly every night, for at least a little while. At least now that Neftat was taking up patrols on Coresan, Ari had been able to cut back his territory, which gave him a little time of his own again. He spent most of it with Kashet, and Vetch had to wonder if Ari was as lonely as *he* was. Certainly he didn't spend much time with his fellow Jousters.

Sometimes Vetch wished that he was just a bit older, more Ari's age. Often, as he listened to Ari talk softly in the darkness, to Kashet and to him, he wondered if *he* was the closest thing to a friend that Ari had, other than Haraket. Did he ever talk to Haraket like this? Maybe not—there were things he said to Vetch that Vetch didn't think Haraket would ever accept tamely. Ari could criticize his own leaders and his own people freely with Vetch; Haraket might well feel he had to report such "disloyal" talk.

Maybe that was why he spent some time every night here. He had to unburden himself to *someone*, and Vetch was safe.

And he wished one other thing—a wish that he could never have imagined himself making before he'd come here. He wished, for Ari's sake, that he was Tian. For if he had not been Altan, and a serf, he could have confided his egg theft to Ari, who would have been delighted, and would surely have helped him when the egg hatched. If he had been Tian, he could *have* a dragonet openly, and become a Jouster, joining the ranks of the rest.

He could become Ari's friend, and not—what he was. Whatever that was, now. Dragon boy, serf, mostly Altan, no longer able to unthinkingly hate his Tian masters—but knowing that nothing would ever induce them to accept him either, with a life that was a strange mixture of the bitter and the sweet, with nothing in between.

And it occurred to him the same night, as he lay thinking about that wish and staring up at the stars, that the one time when his anger stopped gnawing at him altogether was when Ari was around. With everyone else, except maybe Haraket, there was always that edge, the feeling that underneath it all, if a choice had to be made between him and a Tian, well, he'd come out second-best.

And even Ari and Haraket, if the choice had to be made publicly, would probably favor the Tian.

Maybe that wasn't true, but it was something he didn't want to have to put to the test.

It was an unpalatable thought.

He resolutely shoved it away. He would just have to make certain it never came to that.

Besides, he had another worry that he ought to be concentrating on. That egg would hatch within days, and that would bring the next hurdle, a successful hatching. He *had* to be there. He daren't take any chances. Baby chickens thought that the first thing that *they* saw was their mother—the same might be true of a dragonet—

And that was when, once again, it seemed as if the Altan gods *had* heard him and were answering him with subtle aid.

The second half of the growing season was always dry—not the Dry of the dry season, when the air sucked every bit of moisture out of everything, but usually there weren't any kind of heavy rainstorms. Instead, there was just enough rain to keep the crops from dying, and that usually in the early morning or early evening. Storms that were not hard, didn't do much, and were never very long.

In fact, they tended to be rather warm and muggy rains, bringing sticky humidity rather than refreshment to the air. And the one thing that it was possible to count on was that they would *not* be the violent storms that broke at the end of dry season.

There had been a feeling of a storm coming the day that Vetch was sure the egg was close, very close, to hatching. Vetch was checking it as often as he dared, and as he did, he couldn't help notice that the air felt heavy and wet. So just to be on the safe side, he pulled the canvas over the empty pens on both sides of Kashet's pen, including the one that held his egg. After all, if a storm *did* break, whoever was nearest would start dashing around pulling awnings, and the last thing he wanted them to do was to stumble into *that* pen. He even freed up the awning over Kashet's pen to be ready, just in case.

Then, in the middle of afternoon patrol time, he noticed that the sky on the horizon seemed unusually cloudy out to the north. The clouds themselves were thick and tall, or at least they looked like it from inside the walls of the compound. He congratulated himself on taking the precaution of pulling those canvas coverings early. It looked as if there was going to be a good solid rain rather than a mere sprinkle.

He thought no more about it, except to wonder if the rain

would be bad enough to bring the Jousters back early, so he reckoned that he had better see to it that Kashet's pen was done as early as possible. Haraket and the other Overseers, even Te-Velethat, trusted him to get his work done in whatever order he happened to do it, and not necessarily on a set schedule anymore. He could always do his quota of leather work later, and if he *really* needed to clean Ari's rooms, Ari had no problem these days with having Vetch in to see to it whether or not the Jouster himself was in the suite.

So Vetch was in the middle of cleaning out Kashet's pen and he didn't think anything more about rain, until he heard something that sounded like the rumbling of a thousand chariot wheels, and looked up again sharply, into the north.

The clouds were boiling up before his very eyes, and with bottoms as black as the soil the floods laid on the fields. As if the hand of a god was shoving them along, they were speeding toward Mefis in a way that boded no good for anything caught in their path.

What was more, he could *see* the colorful specks that were the Jousters on their dragons, running along ahead of the storm front. For that storm was powerful enough to send the dragons back on the gust front itself, frantic to get out of the sky before the lightnings and winds caught them, winging ahead of the fury lashing the ground behind them, as fast as their muscles could send them.

He stood there with his mouth wide open for a bit, then it suddenly came home to him that this was going to be no ordinary storm.

He wasn't the only servant to have realized what was happening; a moment later Haraket ran through the compound shouting for the boys to run for the landing court, slaves to cover the pens, and cursing everyone in his path. Dragon boys and every other servant that happened to be free ran for the landing court, for there was no way that most of the dragons were going to be able to land in their pens with that wind behind them. In fact, they'd be lucky to get down without any injuries.

Vetch was right behind Haraket, and the Overseer thrust chained collars into his hands without regard for who he was or which dragon he served. Well enough; Kashet and Ari wouldn't need him, but Seftu and Coresan, and perhaps another half-dozen other dragons he'd gotten to know, and which probably would trust him, certainly would.

The first of the dragons came plunging down into the courtyard just as Haraket, Vetch, and the others got there themselves; already wind, chill as the winds of midwinter, whipped through the open space, sending dragons skewing sideways as they tried to get down to the ground. This wasn't the wind of the Dry, the *kamiseen*, that always blew in the same direction—no, this was a nasty wind, a demon wind, that twisted and writhed unpredictably. The landings were chaotic; with the exception of Kashet, the dragons were clearly fighting their Jousters. They wanted, more than anything, to get back to safety *on the ground* before the storm struck, and if they'd had a choice they would have landed *anywhere* they thought they could find shelter rather than take the chance on speeding for home. There were near collisions in the air above the landing court, actual collisions on the ground, as hard gusts blew dragons aside and into each others' paths. If it hadn't been that their eyes were on the coming storm and not on each other, there might have been fights among the dragons as they competed for the limited landing space; Vetch and two or three of the braver boys dashed in with chains and collars to fasten around their throats. They found themselves scrambling among the fearsome claws, to snap the collars around the first throat that presented itself, then drop the end of the chain in the hands of one of the servants or slaves. Coresan recognized him as he ducked under her nose, and actually pulled back her claws in mid-lash so that they skimmed along his back, barely stinging; he handed off the chain to Fisk, who had been behind him. He helped Seftu's boy get the leads on Seftu, but they didn't need them; Seftu was so grateful to be down that he was actually whimpering, and was crouching so low that his belly dragged the ground. The rest of the boys spread out along the walls and shouted to attract the attention of their Jousters, so that the dragons could get separated and steered over to the proper handler, and taken back to their pens.

The chaos began to sort itself out, so Vetch stayed where he was, knowing Ari and Kashet, knowing that *they* would come in as they always did, as if the sun god stood high in the sky, untroubled by storms. And sure enough, he saw them, Kashet's powerful wing beats holding course against the wicked winds, coming in last of them all. He saw then that Kashet, secure and nothing near as nervous as the rest, was going to land in his own pen as always. That was when Vetch abandoned the mess in the landing court and headed for his proper place—

He got there just as they landed, and it was clear from Ari's wet hair and the rain streaks on Kashet's flanks that the rain wasn't far behind. At that point, no one cared about duty or protocol (not that Ari ever truly did); Ari helped Vetch to strip Kashet of his saddle and harness and pull the canvas canopy over the sand pit just as the first warning drops of the torrent to come splattered into it. Then Ari raced for his own quarters, as splatters turned to downpour.

The canopies were clever devices, just like the awnings that shaded the human inhabitants of the compound from the rays of the sun, fastened to fat bronze rings which were strung on two ropes of wire, running along two opposite walls of a pen. You grasped two hanging straps and pulled the canopy on its wires across to the other side of the pit, where you fastened the straps to rings at the other end. Then you had a "roof" over the sand pit that protected it from rain. This was the only way to keep the sand pits from turning into hot sand soup during the rainy season—or now.

Kashet burrowed down into the sand as the rain poured down onto the canvas, sheeting down along the sides and into the drains along the edges of his pit.

And Vetch sprinted for the next pen.

He thanked his gods that he had pulled the canvas over the tops of the "unused" pens. No one had barged into his pen to protect it. And his egg was safe from the downpour.

But so close to hatching as it was—he had to see.

It was almost not worth it. In the brief time it took to get from one pen to the other, he was soaked to the skin. He peered through the murk from his vantage point in the doorway—and thought that his egg was rocking, but it was hard to tell. Without getting into the pen, all he could see was that it was all right, that the canopy was keeping it and the sand-pit dry.

Back he ran to Kashet's pen. He peeled off his sodden kilt and changed to a new one in the shelter of his own little awning. The edges of the awnings had become waterfalls, and the sky was so dark it seemed to be dusk, not mid-afternoon. Lightning flickered constantly, seeming to freeze droplets in midair for a moment, and thunder drowned out every other sound.

He was just grateful that the gust front had been the only wind. A good blow could rip the canvas from its moorings, soaking and cooling the sands, and *that* might have spelled an end to his hopes. If a chicken egg got chilled as it was about to hatch, the chick died before it could be born. Would the same be true of a dragon? He rather thought so—

The storm would have terrified him, if he hadn't been so preoccupied with thoughts of his egg. Fortunately, such fury couldn't last long; before he became too impatient to wait any longer before returning to his egg, the sky lightened, the torrent lessened, the lightning and thunder passed into the distance, leaving behind only a steady, heavy rain, interrupted by brief surges of a real pelting.

But his first concern *had* to be for his primary charge; Kashet could have gotten injuries that neither he nor Ari saw in their haste to get him unharnessed before the storm burst. Vetch dashed across to the sand pit in Kashet's pen, the edges of which steamed from the rainwater that had escaped the drains to soak into the sand along the perimeter.

Kashet was fine. He was securely wallowed in the middle, buried up to his flanks, his neck stretched along the top of the sand with his eyes closed. Vetch knew that pose. Nothing was going to get Kashet out of his warm wallow; not the sweetest bit of meat, not the coaxing of Ari, not the promise of a grooming and burnishing and oiling. Nothing. And at the moment, every other dragon in the compound was probably taking the same pose as Kashet.

No one would interfere with him or come looking for him. Not until the rain let up, anyway.

Back he ran to his egg.

It *was* rocking! In fact, it had rocked itself right up out of the sand! It must be hatching!

No one was going anywhere in this mess; the dragons wouldn't stir, and the Jousters and dragon boys were all in their respective quarters at this point. Vetch waded out into the hot sand to the egg, which now was rocking madly. He steadied it with his hands, and murmured to the dragonet inside. It paused for a moment, then he heard the dragonet inside knocking furiously at the shell. He passed his hands over the outside, and after examining it carefully, he spotted a place where it was cracking.

Ari had said that mother dragons had to help their little ones hatch; a shell hard enough to protect something as big as a developing dragonet was too thick and hard for them to break by themselves. Ari had helped Kashet; now it was Vetch's turn to help his baby.

He'd heard the story from Ari a dozen times; he knew what to do, and he didn't stop to think about it, he just did what he'd been planning in his mind for weeks, now.

He took the hilt of his tiny work knife and pounded at the cracking spot from his side of the shell. This seemed to encourage the dragonet, and it redoubled its efforts to crack through.

He pounded, the dragonet pounded, and it was a good thing that the steady growl of thunder drowned out most sounds, or they would surely have been caught by all the noise they made together. To his ears, it sounded like a pair of carpenters or stonemasons at work, and if it hadn't been for the storm, so much banging and tapping would certainly have attracted anyone within earshot.

Finally, just when he thought that the egg was never going to actually break, the dragonet punched through!

Two big flakes of shell fell away. A bronze-gold nostril poked up through the new breathing hole, and the dragonet rested for a while. Vetch let it be, just picking bits of broken shell away from the hole and snapping the jagged edges off to enlarge it. That was harder than it sounded; the shell was like stone and the edges of the bits of shell were sharp. But the more he opened the hole, the more of the dragonet's muzzle protruded out, the nostrils flaring as it pulled in its first breaths of fresh air. The egg-tooth, a hard little knob between the nostrils on top of the nose, like a flattened cone, was clearly visible. The dragonet would slough that within a day of hatching, but it was needed in order to break out.

When the muzzle withdrew from the breathing hole, the rocking and hammering started again from within the egg. Vetch watched to see where the cracks were appearing, and helped again, pounding with the hilt of his knife, and grateful that the thunder and rain didn't look as if they were going to stop any time soon. Despite the cold, damp wind, Vetch was sweating, and he kept up a steady murmur of encouragement to the baby within the shell.

Vetch confined himself to helping cracks along and chipping bits away from the air hole. He wasn't certain how much—beyond that little—he could help the dragonet without hurting it by forcing the hatch; this wasn't one of his mother's chickens, after all, and even she had been careful with hatching eggs. There was a difference between *assisting* a hatch, and *forcing* it, a difference which could mean a dead chick or a live one.

He had to run off at one point to feed Kashet—the dragon's appetite wasn't diminished by the rain. The entire time he watched Kashet, he worried; what if the dragonet got into trouble? What if the egg fell over, and the breathing hole was blocked by the sand? What if it hatched, and floundered out of the sand and got chilled?

But this was also an opportunity. He loaded his barrow with more meat than Kashet could eat now that he was out of that growth spurt. The top was the usual big chunks, but on the bottom was a thick layer of the smaller scraps and chopped bits that he got from troughs near where the butchers worked. They called this stuff "porridge." When a dragon needed a heavier dose of *tala* than you could get into it just by dusting the big pieces with the powder, the other dragon boys would mix it with the chopped pieces and blood—

Well, that wasn't what he needed the "porridge" for, and the butchers weren't curious enough to notice what he loaded his barrow with. *They* were too busy listening to the rain and thunder outside, and talking about it in nervous voices. Under any other circumstances, he'd have stayed to listen.

But not today.

He fed Kashet to satiation, while the rain drummed on the canvas awning; it didn't take long, the dragon wanted to go back into his wallow and didn't dawdle over his food. Kashet yawned and dug himself back into his hot sand when he was done, and was asleep in moments. Vetch quickly checked the corridor for the presence of anyone else before he whisked the barrow out of Kashet's pen through the cold rain, and into the one next door.

And found himself looking at a limp and exhausted scarlet dragonet, sprawled on the sand, limbs and damp wings going in all directions in an awkward mirror of Kashet's pose. The damp wings were half under the poor thing, and at his entrance, the dragonet looked up at him and *meeped* pathetically. It could barely raise its rounded, big-eyed head on its long neck; the bronzy-gold and scarlet head wavered back and forth like a heavy flower on a slender stalk, the huge old-bronze eyes barely open, as if the lids were too heavy to lift. To either side, the halves of the egg lay, red-veined on the inside, with a membrane still clinging to them.

Vetch parked the barrow under the awning and floundered out

into the sand to the dragonet's side. It was bigger than he was, and heavier—twice his size and weighing about as much as a young child, he thought, though it was hard to tell for certain. It was going to get a lot bigger before it was finished growing, though. He dug a trench in the hot sand and helped it to slide in, tucking the clumsy, weak limbs into comfortable positions, and spreading the wings out to dry on the surface.

It sighed, as it lowered its head down onto its foreclaws; already the anxiety it had shown when it realized that it was alone was ebbing. It was going to be a crimson red, like both its parents, but unlike Coresan, the extremities were going to be some shade of gold or bronze; until it got a little older, its delicate skin was going to tear and bruise easily if he wasn't careful with it. Right now, the skin was as delicate as his own—more so, in places—and soft as the thinnest lambskin. He petted the dragonet's head and neck for a moment, marveling at the softness of the skin. Then he left the dragonet to bask in the heat and rest from the effort of hatching, heaped a bucket with the chopped meat, and returned to its side.

It opened its eyes when he returned to it, and its nostrils twitched as it caught the scent of the meat. Its head wavered up; the poor thing looked so weak! But the mouth opened, and the thin hiss that emerged was anything but weak, and had a great deal of *demand* in it. The mouth gaped wide. It had a formidable set of teeth already, no surprise in such a carnivore. Openmouthed, it hissed again, and whined at him, red tongue flicking out in entreaty.

He laughed. "All right, baby—don't be impatient!" he whispered, and dropped a piece the size of his palm in the open mouth.

He'd worried about whether the dragonet would be difficult to feed—in the next several minutes, he knew that this, at least, was *not* going to be a problem. The little one snapped its jaws shut on the meat and swallowed; he watched the lump going down its throat with remarkable speed. Then the jaws opened up again.

They quickly fell into a rhythm. The baby gaped, he dropped

meat and bone in, the jaws snapped shut and the throat worked, and the mouth gaped. It was so easy to feed the little one that literally anyone could have done it. In fact, before it was sated, it had eaten nearly its own weight in meat! It ate until its belly was round, the skin tight, and Vetch could not imagine how it could cram another morsel in.

That was when it stopped; it closed its mouth and *looked* at him, really looked at him for the first time since it had hatched. The big, dark eyes seemed all pupil—he could see that they weren't, though, that the iris was simply so dark a color that it was nearly black, but the huge, dark eyes seemed to draw him in and hold him. He couldn't look away, and didn't want to, for those eyes seemed to him to be the most wonderful things he had ever gazed into. And then it sighed, laid its head in his lap with complete and utter trust, and closed its eyes and went immediately to sleep, without a care or a worry in the world.

He was here, and he was now the center of the dragonet's world. So long as he was here, there could be nothing wrong.

He thought his heart was going to melt. A pent-up flood of emotion threatened to overwhelm him; he squeezed his eyes shut to keep from crying, and just whispered tender nonsense into the ruby and bronze shells that were the dragonet's ears, while he stroked the soft skin of the head and neck with a hand that shook.

But he couldn't hold the tears back for very long; finally they started, and he wept silently, anger and grief that he had held in for so very long, mingling together with joy and relief in those tears, and nothing left to hold them back.

How long he cried, he couldn't have told. He cried until his eyes were sore, his nose clogged, his belly sore from sobbing. He cried until his throat was raw and scratchy, crying for all he'd lost, and all he *could* lose now, crying that his mother and father weren't here to see him, in his first moment of triumph since the Tians came.

It couldn't have been long, or he'd have heard Kashet hissing for his supper. Certainly it wasn't as long as it felt.

But finally, even he ran out of tears. He wiped his eyes with the back of his hand, careful not to get sand in them, and sniffed.

He felt odd. Felt as if he had cried something *out* of himself, and now there was just a hollow where it had been.

"Can you see me, father?" he whispered into the rain, into the vast space between himself and the Summer Country. "Can you see what I've done? Isn't this baby a beauty, the most wonderful thing you've ever seen?"

The dragonet stirred a little in sleep, and hissed softly.

Carefully, so as not to wake it, he began to stroke the head and ears, and as he petted the delicate skin of the brows, he knew that his dragonet was a female, for it did not have the bumps beneath the skin that would eventually form into a pair of skin-covered "horns" that marked the males.

"What shall I call you, baby?" he murmured to it. This wasn't a question he took lightly. Words had power, and names were the most powerful of all words. Words where what the gods used to shape the world, and whatever he named this little dragonet would shape her.

Then it came to him; from her colors, shading from yellow on her belly, through the scarlet of her body, to a deep plum along her spine and at the end of her tail while her ears and muzzle went to that brazen-gold. Like the colors of a sunrise—

"Avatre," he murmured. "Fire of the dawn. I name you for that."

She stirred in her sleep and pushed her forehead against his stomach, as though in approval. Avatre it was.

"Avatre," he sighed with content, and with rain drumming on the canvas above them, caressed the head that rested so trustingly in his lap.

Now for the next hurdles. Keeping her presence secret—and *keeping* her. . . .

But for now—now it was enough to cradle her, and listen to her breathing, softly, in the rain.

* * *

He had to feed Kashet again, eventually, of course. But the rain was still coming down, and he knew that not even Ari would come out of his quarters in this out-of-season downpour. So tonight, well, tonight he would *not* be sleeping in Kashet's pen.

He eased the baby's head off his lap and she woke and looked at him, then yawned, her tongue waggling comically before she shut her mouth. She stared at him for a moment, then made a small noise that he had no difficulty in interpreting as a demand.

He had to chuckle at that. Fortunately, there was enough left in his barrow to line her belly, if not fill it; enough to hold her while he went to fetch more food for her and for Kashet. Then it was the same routine again, except that already she was getting the idea that biting down on the hand that was feeding her was not going to get the meat pieces to arrive any sooner, and in fact caused a delay in delivery as the owner of the hand made funny sounds and waggled the hand in the air. This was entertaining, perhaps, but did nothing for a hungry belly. So she quickly learned to be gentle, and learned that when she sucked at the hand instead of clamping down on it, sometimes it would bring a cargo of delicious wet stuff that lubricated the throat and tongue and tasted sublime.

The "wet stuff," of course, consisted of bits of the livers, hearts, and lungs; prime treats for every dragon because of their rich blood-content, but difficult to maneuver once they were cut up unless the dragonet was cooperating. Avatre was a fast learner, even fresh out of the egg as she was, and when he was done he hardly needed to wash his hands, for she had wrapped her tongue around them and sucked on them until every bit of blood and juice she could get had gone down that voracious little throat.

She fell asleep again immediately, and now that her wings were dry, he tucked them in against her body and heaped sand around her to keep her warm and supported. Then he took his barrow back to the butchery.

But just as he was leaving the butchery, he overheard something that made him pause for a moment.

"—witchery!" one of the butchers was saying, darkly. "Altan witchery! The Haras priest Urkat-re told me himself; he and the other Haras priests had all they could do to hold the storm back enough that the dragons could land without killing themselves and their Jousters!"

"I don't much like the sound of that," one of the others murmured uneasily. "The sea witches have never been able to reach so far before. . . ."

"Because they never tried to do so on the wings of a storm before."

Vetch jumped; that was Haraket's voice!

"Overseer, have *you* heard anything more than that?" asked the first butcher humbly.

"No. You seem to have gotten all the tidings there are to hear, Tho-teret. But I don't doubt you, nor do I think what you've said is mere idle speculation. I have *never* seen a storm like that in growing season, and since the Altan sea witches' powers are of the wind and water, it stands to reason that *they* called it up, all out of season." Haraket seemed very sure of himself, and Vetch saw no reason to doubt him. "It makes every sense, too, when you think what their strategy must be. They have fewer dragons and less-experienced Jousters than we; they can no longer meet us man-to-man. So they must get us out of the sky and thin our numbers somehow. What better way than to smash our dragons to earth with an unnatural storm?"

Vetch nodded to himself; it made perfect sense. Doubtless the sea witches who had conjured the tempest were even now lying spent within the walls of their temples, and would not be able to move from their couches for days or weeks—but the damage had been done.

"And the damage has been done," Haraket said, in an uncanny echo of Vetch's own thoughts. "No one was killed, thanks only to the grace of Haras and the skill of *our* priests, but there are torn wing webs and sprained muscles in dragons all over the compound. A dozen will not fly without days of rest, and by then, the witches will be ready to send another storm against us."

"They will?" gasped a butcher.

"Of course they will! It is by far the most effective weapon they have now!" Haraket said, with scorn for the man's obtuseness. "They will hardly abandon it! And I fear *we* will now have to cease our scouting forays over *their* land; if a dragon is driven to earth over their territory—"

He did not need to elaborate. Even Vetch knew what would become of a Tian Jouster caught by Altan foot soldiers on the ground.

He moved off silently, using the door to the barrow storage room to make his exit. At the moment, he had rather that Haraket did not know what he had overheard.

He couldn't but help feel some elation; among other things, if Haraket was right, Ari stood at far less risk of being hurt or killed now in the course of his duties. *Kashet* was bigger and stronger than any other dragon in the compound, now, and he had always been a better and more skilled flyer; it would take more than a witch-conjured storm to hurt him. And if the Altans were going to use storms against dragons, they must have pulled their own Jousters back so as to avoid harming them accidentally. Which meant that Ari would not be facing anyone in a Joust until the Dry came, and not even the most powerful of witches could conjure up a storm.

He trotted back to his pens with the rain drumming on his wet hair; he checked on Avatre, but saw she was sleeping as soundly as a dragon could—which was very soundly indeed. So just in case Ari turned up, he curled up on his pallet in the unseasonable gloom.

He would have a lot of chores to catch up on tomorrow. But he didn't think anyone would complain or take him to task for them. He'd been all over that courtyard, and he could always claim he'd sprained something, helping bring the dragons in, and had taken to Kashet's sands to bake the aches out. . . .

Huh. Maybe he'd better lend verisimilitude to that claim by moving his pallet there now.

It didn't take a moment, even in the twilight gloom and the rain, he was so used to doing so after the rainy season. And he was glad that he had, when not long after, he heard Ari's step outside the pen.

"Vetch?" the Jouster called into the dimness of the pen.

"Here!" he called back. Kashet didn't even stir. "I sprained my shoulder getting chains onto some of those dragons."

"I thought you might have—one of them marked you, too. Do you need something for the scratches?" Ari made a dash across the open, rain-filled space and got in under the shelter of Kashet's awning.

"It was Coresan, and she pulled her blow when she saw it was me," he replied, feeling oddly touched that Ari had *noticed* in the midst of all the chaos. "I've gotten worse from thorns, or the stuff Khefti made me sleep on."

Ari sighed, and sat down on the edge of the wallow. "Just bake out the sprain, then. You won't be the only one tending injury. There are sprains and even a dislocated shoulder or two all over the compound, and that's just among the Jousters; I expect anyone in the landing court is probably nursing some sort of hurt, and the dragons themselves may have gotten sprains when they landed. We won't field but half the dragons tomorrow, nor the day after. It appears that your countrymen have found an effective weapon to ground us."

His heart leaped at that. So it was definitely true, then! Haraket had been right! But he didn't say anything, and Ari didn't seem to expect a comment.

"Well, I won't complain," Ari continued. "There won't be any double patrols to fly, when we daren't take any dragons over Altan lands. Just the simple runs over our own land, until the

Great King decides to break the truce and send the armies out again."

Vetch's heart dropped as fast as it had risen. Ari had said "when," not "if"—

"But since the King has not chosen to favor me with his plans for conquest," Ari continued, still sounding oddly cheerful, "*I am not going to concern myself over that until the day dawns. Nor should you.* Instead, I am for my honest bed; there is no point in doing anything but follow Kashet's example and catch up on rest. Good night, Vetch."

"Good night, Jouster," he called off after the retreating form that sprinted out through the door, in the rain.

And he waited just long enough to be certain that Ari was not going to return, before gathering up a blanket and abandoning Kashet to sleep alone.

For tonight—and for every night that he could manage it—he would be sleeping beside *his* dragon.

She stirred ever so slightly as he laid his blanket down on the sand beside her, and fitted his body around hers. And she nestled her head in next to his outstretched arm with a movement that brought a smile to his lips and a lump to his throat.

Help me, he whispered to the Altan gods—who, it seemed, *could* reach into this Tian stronghold, after all. *Help me, keep her secret, keep her safe. . . .*

And the prayer murmured on into his dreams, a prayer that surely, surely, they *must* answer.

THIRTEEN

VETCH was helplessly, hopelessly, in love. He had never felt like this before, and yet the emotion was one he recognized immediately. There was nothing he would not have done, would not have sacrificed for his beloved. His heart was lost to him, and he didn't care.

Of course, if all of the love songs he'd heard wafting out of the Jousters' quarters during feasts and festivals were true, that was pretty much how he *should* feel.

From the moment that Avatre curled her body to fit the curve of his, he was in love. And it didn't matter, at all, that at the moment *probably* all he was to her was to be the bringer-of-food and the one who made sure her itches were soothed and her messes cleaned away. He loved her with a passion the like of which he had never felt before, a passion that shook him to his bones. It frightened him, if he stopped to think about it. He had never had so much to lose before. If he lost Avatre—

He wouldn't think about that, couldn't waste the time that would be lost if he thought about it and froze in an agony of fear and indecision. He had to concentrate on how to keep her, not on what would happen if he lost her.

He'd had some small inkling of how deeply he had fallen that night, when he went to sleep curled protectively around her, with his last thoughts before slumber being a prayer for her safety. It really came home to him when he woke in the first light of dawning, still curved around her, and looked at the oddly endearing creature that had been entrusted by the gods to his care, and his *first* thought was a prayer for her safety. Her hot little body was the exact temperature of the sand under both of them, and as she breathed in and out, he felt himself changing the pattern of his breathing to match hers.

Then, when she woke, just a little, and blinked at him trustingly before going back to sleep again, he knew that he was forever lost to her.

Was this how Ari had felt, when he first looked into Kashet's eyes?

Rain still pattered lightly on the canvas overhead; it was very peaceful and comfortable, and he wanted to go back to sleep—but he didn't dare. He would have so much work today, it didn't bear thinking about, except that he would have to think about it very hard indeed, and right now, in order to plan things properly. Every moment, between dawn and dusk, would have to be planned and accounted for, if he was to get his work done and give her the kind of attention she required.

Both Avatre and Kashet would need feeding as soon as it got light enough for them to wake properly, so he would have to manage to crowd both activities into the same amount of time he normally took for Kashet. Now, even if she was awake, he couldn't feed Avatre now; no one would be at the butchery yet, and neither Kashet nor Avatre would want their breakfast until they were thoroughly awake and their appetites were roused. But there were other things he could do *now* in order to get them out of the way. For instance, he *could* slip over to the leather room, light a lamp, and get his quota for yesterday and today done early. *Then* he could get the food for both dragon and dragonet, feed Avatre first, then Kashet—and if the rain cleared enough that Ari showed up for a morning patrol, Vetch would be where he belonged, in Kashet's pen. Then he'd have to clean Kashet's pen in half the time he usually took, possibly feed Avatre again and certainly clean *her* messes up, and be ready for when Kashet and Ari came back . . . oh, and at some point during all that, he should get himself bathed and fed, somehow. He *should*—but he knew very well that if anyone went short, it wouldn't be his charges.

I can bathe in the water from Kashet's trough. I can eat something on the run.

He eased himself away from Avatre, heaped some hot sand up where he had been in order to support her, and went off to get a clean kilt and get to work. He was glad enough of the lamps in their sheltered niches along the corridors; someone must have come along and substituted the rainy-season lamps for the torches that had been placed there after the rains were supposedly over. Though the sky overhead was getting lighter, it was dark down between the walls. It was strange to be the only one in the leather room; it was quite peaceful, actually, and he found that when he wasn't distracted by the gossip of the other boys, he actually got things done a little faster. By the time he put the last of his pieces in the "finished" piles, though it was still raining and overcast, he could tell that it was late enough that he would be able to get meat for his charges. He wasn't the first at the butchery, but he was certainly among the earliest, and as he stood in line in the gloom of that overcast morning, listening to the rain fall in the corridor outside, he paid close attention while the butchers and the other boys talked. Now, more than ever, he needed to know what was going on and being said in the rest of the compound. What were the Jousters going to do in this out-of-season rain? And if there was talk of Altan witchery, would anyone connect it with him?

Their conversations, punctuated by the *chack* of the cleavers on the chopping blocks, revealed just how much damage had been done to dragons and riders in that frantic dash for home yesterday afternoon. That no one had been killed or even *seriously* hurt was deemed a miracle, but there were sprains, pulled muscles, and strains a-plenty, and as Ari had told him, even a couple of dislocated shoulders among the Jousters. He got his meat without any comment from anyone about what he was taking—they were all too busy recounting the near-misses and providential escapes, and speculating on what might come next. It was at that point that Vetch decided he ought to leave. He felt the long hair that marked him as an Altan serf brushing against his back with a shiver. . . .

He quickly took his burden out, shoving it along in front of himself as fast as he could manage without spilling it. In fact, some of that damage to the dragons was proving out rather audibly, as the dragons of the compound awoke for the day. As he wheeled his barrow back to Avatre's pen, he could hear the injured dragons as they hissed and whined in pain when they tried to move. From what the other boys said, there were plenty of riders who were just as damaged, including several who would probably choose to see a Healing-Priest. In the course of that mad dash, dragons had been tossed around in the air like so many dead leaves, and some Jousters had held to their seats only at the cost of injury. And here he was divided in his emotions; he was immensely pleased that *finally* Alta had struck a blow against Tia, but these dragons were not to blame for what was going on, and he knew many of them personally. He hated to see them hurt.

At least their injuries were only temporary. And Ari and Kashet had come home fine. He soothed his conscience by telling himself that if Alta had sent a storm with more lightning, or could have directed it, there would be a lot worse than sprains and strains.

He fed Avatre quickly; she was more than pleased to cooperate in that regard, swallowing as fast as he popped pieces into her mouth, until the skin was tight enough over her belly to drum on. Then she gave an enormous yawn, blinked, and plopped herself down into the sand to sleep.

By then, the rain had faded to nothing, but he left the canopy over the pen anyway. It wouldn't hurt anything, no one would particularly care, and it would keep anyone flying over the compound from seeing her.

Kashet was not only no worse for wear, he was happy to see Vetch, feeling playful—and in good temper and appetite. He buried his muzzle in the barrow, and Vetch went to get his harness. Sure enough, Ari *did* appear, just as Kashet was finishing, his flying helmet dangling from one hand.

"No more than half of the Jousters are going out on morning patrol," Ari said. And at Vetch's worried look, he added, with a little nod, "Don't be too concerned. It's going to be a short one. We're just checking to see that no troops moved in or sabotage was done under cover of the storm."

By then, Vetch had finished the harnessing, but rather than have Vetch pull the canopy back so they could take off from the pen, Ari motioned to him to leave it alone, and led Kashet out to the landing court.

Is he thinking there is going to be more rain? He might well be, actually. *But if the patrol is going to be short—*

Then he'd better get busy if he was going to clean up after Kashet *and* Avatre, feed the dragonet again, *and* take care of his other chores.

He ran for breakfast, bolted it down, ran back to the pens, glad for all the good feeding he'd been getting, for he was much stronger now, even if he wasn't much taller. He cleaned the pens, filled the barrow, ran with it to the place where the droppings were left. He checked on Avatre, and he woke her to stuff her again, though her belly clearly wasn't empty. Still, his mother always said that a baby could always eat, and she was no exception to that truism. Then he cleaned *her* pen and ran the barrow out again, hiding the much smaller droppings among the rest, adding them to the running tally so that no one would wonder why there were *more* than had been accounted for. Then he was back in Kashet's pen, and just in time, for even as he checked to make certain that he hadn't forgotten anything, he heard the dragons coming back in, wings flapping heavily in the still air.

They were *very* early. It was a good thing he'd gone everywhere at the run. . . .

When Ari brought Kashet in, the latter was almost as fresh as when he'd gone out. "Leave the canopies on," Ari said, as the dragon ducked his head to come in under the canvas. "We're in for a rather wet season of growing, I'm afraid—not that I think it's going to harm anything."

"It won't," Vetch replied, out of his own experience. "It'll just save farmers needing to open the irrigation ditches as often. At least, it won't as long as it's just rain."

"Let's hope, then, that the sea witches can't conjure hail out of the clouds, then," Ari said soberly. "You should be ready for us to come back early this afternoon, too. Until we're ordered otherwise by the Commander of Dragons, the senior Jousters have decided that no patrol is going to go outside of the borders established by the last truce."

Yes, and wasn't that the point of the last truce, that you weren't *to fly outside the boundaries?* Vetch asked in his mind, and some of that anger he'd managed to keep bottled up stirred restlessly again. *Maybe if you'd stayed inside them, this wouldn't have happened? Maybe if you didn't keep pushing past those boundaries, taking what isn't yours?*

He shoved the anger back down, and just nodded. It wasn't Ari's fault, and Ari was troubled, more than troubled, by the greedy land grabs among those who wanted the borders pushed back still further. "So, short patrols, then?" he asked instead, lifting the saddle onto its rack.

"Just over our own lands, looking for trouble," Ari replied, with a twitch to the corner of his mouth. Vetch cast a sharp glance at him, and it occurred to him that Ari didn't seem to be at all displeased about that.

But of course, he wouldn't say so, not where he could be overheard.

And he had to always remember, *always*, that no matter what, no matter how kind Ari was to him or what the Jouster confided to him, *he* was still an Altan serf, and Ari was a Tian Jouster.

And if he wanted to keep Avatre, he must never forget that.

As Vetch labored mightily to get all of his work done *and* keep Avatre's belly full that day, the compound itself was full of activity, a great deal of it rather disorganized and smacking of controlled panic.

He was getting a hasty bath just before lunch when he heard chanting approaching the bathing room, and just as he started to leave, he had to duck back inside to avoid colliding with a procession of what must have been fully half the priests of the Great Temple of Haras on Temple Road. Chanting and setting spells of protection, accompanied by little priestesses with sistrums and boys with drums, it appeared that they were determined to cover every corridor of the compound, and in the process, get in everyone's way. Every priest wore a striped headcloth with the mask of Haras gleaming from the front, and a falcon pectoral in gold with a matching belt across his snowy white robe. The priestesses all were in filmy gowns of mist linen with wide collars of gold, carnelian, and lapis beads and gold cords around their waists, their wigs done in hundreds of tiny braids, each one ending in a bead, and a *latas* flower centered just over each one's brow with the stem trailing down her back. Behind them came six slaves bearing feather fans on long poles, though what *they* were supposed to do in the chill, and the damp, Vetch had no idea.

They weren't the only ones either. Racing from cleaning Ari's rooms, Vetch ran into a procession of the priests of Siris and Iris, who, not to be outdone, arrived to replicate the first effort! The same sort of procession, with music and magical chanting, only the costumes differed. The priestesses of Iris wore the horns of the moon on their brows, and their gowns were tight sheaths of red linen that ended just below their breasts, with wide bands of embroidered and beaded material that served as straps running over their breasts and shoulders, while the priests wore helmets much like the Great King's war crown and intricately wrapped kilts with heavy, beaded belts.

And not an hour later, *they* were followed by the priests of Nuthis and Thet and Hamun, each in their own variations on priestly dress, who all trooped past Kashet's pen while he was feeding Kashet and Avatre—

"A man can't turn to fart without blowing stink into a meddling priest's face today," growled one of the butchers to another while Vetch was collecting Avatre-sized bits for another feeding. Vetch smothered a laugh and quickly; it was funny, but not to the butcher. By now it was clear that virtually everyone else in the compound but Vetch was worried sick about the way that Altan sea witches had managed to wreak havoc on the Tian Jousters so far within the borders of Tia itself, and he didn't want to draw attention to himself while people were so unsettled. And unfortunately, nothing that the priests were doing was giving anyone any real confidence that the compound had any more protection on it than it had *before* all the chanting and the processions. Everyone knew that the real, truly powerful magic went on in the holy sanctuaries, without witnesses, and this was just something to make people feel better. Whether that was true or not, Vetch had no idea.

Part of him was fiendishly glad that the witches had done their work so well—part of him wanted to see more damage and fear—just retribution, by his way of thinking. It would be a fine thing for these Tians to get a taste of fear for a change!

But of course, once they started to get over their fear, it would mean trouble for every Altan serf inside the borders of Tia.

Not that all that much real damage had been done, when you came to think about it. It was only because no one had predicted what was coming, or guessed the fury of the storm ahead of time that anyone had gotten hurt at all! No one was likely to be even slightly injured the next time the sea witches sent a storm, because now everyone would fly for home the moment that thunderheads appeared on the horizon. And as he'd pointed out to Ari, rain was not going to cause any harm to the crops.

No point in trying to tell that to anyone here, though. They weren't likely to listen; nerves were on edge, and people were all too ready to imagine that the sea witches could do all manner of dreadful things.

What if they call lightning to strike the compound—or the Great King's Palace! What if they shower us with hailstones the size of pomegranates! What if they make the Great Mother River to run backward!

What if, what if, what if—

What if they make pigs to fly and shit on your heads from above? he thought at last, in irritation, overhearing yet another frightened and wild speculation over a hastily-snatched dinner. *That's just as likely, if not more so.*

For it didn't seem to occur to anyone that the sea witches had not had much luck at controlling the storm that they had created; they had simply set it in motion and shoved it across the border. Vetch was a farmer's child, and he knew, better than most, just how much worse it could have been if the Altans had any amount of *control* over that storm. It was, after all, the season of growing, and Altan saboteurs had already made it perfectly clear that the ruin of Tian crops was high on their list of priorities. If the sea witches had had real control over that storm, it would have been hail, not rain, that pounded down on Tian fields. The crops would spring back from the heavy rain and wind. Hail would have ruined them. Why attack the Great King's Palace with lightning, when you could make his whole land starve? For that matter—he didn't much want to think what a hailstorm would have done to dragons and Jousters in the air. There *would* have been deaths.

Still, all the fuss was of benefit to *him*. No one paid any attention to what he was doing, how many barrows of meat he took, how many barrows of droppings he left, or where he was when he wasn't where he was supposed to be.

Avatre ate and slept and woke and ate and slept again, like virtually any other baby. By day's end, she was demonstrably bigger and heavier—in a way, it was gratifying to see that all of the work he'd done hauling all that meat had a visible effect!—and Vetch purloined some soft cloths and a jar of oil from the buffing pens to keep her skin soft and supple while she grew. Dragons didn't shed their whole skins at once as they got bigger; instead, they shed their skins a little bit all the time, old skin flaking and falling off, exposing new skin underneath; tiny scales grew larger, and new scales formed along the edges of old ones. Vetch didn't know how a mother dragon kept a dragonet from itching as it grew and shed, but he would have to keep Avatre oiled and buffed, or she'd be driven mad with itching.

Her pen was a still pool in the middle of all the chaos, and he went to it as to a refuge. She murmured sleepily as he took an oil-soaked rag and waded into the hot sand with her, to stretch out her wings and coat them with oil that soaked into them the way the first rain after the Dry soaked into the earth. The scales of her body were tiny, hardly bigger than the grains of sand around her, but they would grow, as she grew. He buffed them gently and rubbed the rag over her, and she lifted her head and gave him another of those wavering, limpid gazes, before settling back down to sleep again. He could hardly bear to leave her, but he had work to do, and it was risk enough taking this much time during the daylight hours with her.

By nightfall, when all the priests had finally finished their bespelling and prayers, less hysterical personalities managed to prevail within the compound. Haraket kept his head the whole time, of course, and Ari and the more senior Jousters seemed to have kept the panic all around from infecting *them*. Interestingly, just after supper, some of the older priests of various gods turned up to help soothe some of the hysteria, and that helped. One of the most helpful was the High Priest of Hamun, who actually turned up at both the kitchen court and the Jousters' quarters, and pointed out many of the same things that Vetch himself had been thinking all this time. He arrived in his full regalia, leopard-skin cloak with the snarling head over his right shoulder, freshly-shaved head, two standard bearers standing behind him, and bedecked with so much gold jewelry it made Vetch's back ache in sympathy just to look at it. Supposedly he was the Great King's uncle; he certainly had the kingly manner, and that alone seemed to set peoples' minds moving into calmer channels. So at least, by the time that the sun set, a measure of quiet had returned to the Jousters' compound, if not peace.

Things were still edgy and chaotic the next day, and the next, which was all to the good so far as Vetch was concerned. The more people were focusing their attention on what was going on—or presumed to be going on—*out*side the compound, the less they would notice what was going on *in*side.

Even Ari was so preoccupied that if Vetch hadn't made a point during his cleaning of snatching away the dirty garments as soon as Ari shed them and making sure the linen chest was full of clean ones, he probably would have worn the same kilt three days running. He wasn't in his quarters or out on Kashet much, and Vetch could only assume that he and the other senior Jousters were engaged in some sort of council with important leaders of the army and the government.

Vetch himself was certainly doing enough running. He ran everywhere he went; it was the only way to make everything fit into the day. He worked with one ear cocked nervously for a sound in Avatre's pen, he worried that Kashet might betray what was going on with his mild interest in what was on the other side of the wall. . . .

Kashet surely scented something, or heard it. He tried several times to peer over the wall to see what was there, but the canvas awning on the other side foiled his attempt to look into the wallow, and much to Vetch's relief, he finally gave it up.

And Avatre ate, and slept, and grew, definitely bigger every day . . . and the compound held its collective breath, and waited to see if the sea witches were going to be able to repeat their attack.

Sure enough, on the fourth day, another of those monster storms roared up out of the North, sending the dragons flying for home before it.

This time, though, there were no injuries. As Vetch had figured, the first sight of a thunderhead building up was enough to send the dragons all back well in advance of the gust front.

This storm was a little different, too; with a great deal of wind and lightning, but the initial downpour was much shorter, and the light rain and overcast persisted longer, forcing the dragons to stay in their pens all that day and the next, except for brief patrols over Tian lands and even briefer practice sessions. The exercise was just enough to take the edge off their restlessness.

There was nothing to take the edge off the restlessness of their Jousters. This was *not* the season of rains, they were *not* working on the ragged remains of their strength and happy to have the time to rest; quite to the contrary, they were fit and itching for action, and to be held confined to the compound by a pack of *witches*—

Well, it rankled. They badly needed something to do. Vetch sensed it in the sour looks, sour tempers, and growing tension. He heard wild parties at night in the Jousters' quarters, and heard rumors of scandalous escapades among the dancing girls, and of broken furniture. He started taking the most out-of-the-way corridors when he had to go anywhere, and so did the rest of the serfs. He'd seen this mood before, and when tempers flared, well—

If it is a choice between Tian and an Altan serf—no matter who is in the wrong, it is always the Altan who pays.

He redoubled his efforts at stealth. He bit his nails to the quick in worry over Avatre. The tension could not last. Something would break, and soon. But he *knew* that. And he kept telling himself that all he could do was to stay out of the way, and hope that it did not break over him—

* * *

Vetch was eating his noon meal in the farthest corner of the kitchen court, when the noise from the corridor made him whirl and look at the blank wall behind him in alarm. A shiver of fear gripped him as he wondered if the all of the stress he'd sensed had finally found an outlet, for it sounded like a mob in full cry—

And he wondered who or what was the target for all that pent-up tension—

—or if they could be coming for *him*—

But then, one of the slaves dashed into the court, his eyes wide with excitement and not fear. "A dragonet!" he shouted. "Two of the Jousters have brought in a wild dragonet! Come and see!"

He dashed out again, followed by a stream of quicker-witted folks or more curious dragon boys and servants, as a new fear held Vetch paralyzed in his seat for a moment.

Have they found Avatre?

He broke the paralysis in the next instant—he had to know! With the others who were more slow to react, he shoved his way to the door, just as the procession of two of the younger Jousters and a small army of slaves came triumphantly by. They were, indeed, hauling a squalling, protesting, *blue* dragonet, encased in a net and bundled onto a palanquin carried on the shoulders of a team of eight or ten slaves. This was a much, much older drag-onet than Avatre; it was easily the size of one of the huge, sacrifi-cial bulls of Hamun. Its claws had been encased in padding and bags, its legs tied together, its mouth trussed shut. It looked abso-lutely furious, and Vetch did not want to be the person who cut it loose.

"Where are they going?" he blurted, not thinking, not really expecting an answer.

"Oh, they'll put the beast in one of the open pens and one of the trainers will come care for it until it's tame," came the answer from above and behind him. "Tame enough for a dragon boy to look after, anyway. Haraket won't be pleased! He'll be the fellow who will have to find a boy, and all out-of-season."

Vetch looked quickly around behind him, and saw that the

speaker was one of the slaves, one that had been reasonably civil to him from the time he arrived. "Why?" he asked, feeling bewildered. "I mean, I don't mean why are they doing that, I mean why did the Jousters go out after a dragonet, and why go after one that isn't even fledged yet?"

The slave grinned down at him and winked. "You've been keeping yourself to yourself these few days, or you'd have heard. The Great King sent down a decree to the Jousters. If Alta is going to try to ground our Jousters, then the Great King wants more of them—too many to keep on the ground, no matter how many storms the sea witches raise! So." He nodded after the mob, which had turned a corner, leaving only the noise behind. "Now the most restless of the Jousters are going to help the trackers and trappers out, as they used to when there were fewer of them."

Vetch blinked. "More dragons?" he asked.

"More *dragonets*, more Jousters in training, both," the slave corrected. "And the King's Vizier made the little suggestion that since the Jousters are grounded, perhaps *they* ought to be the ones hunting the new dragonets."

"But—" Vetch thought about the fury in that young thing's eyes, and pictured to himself the fury of the *mother* if she happened to return while her babies were being abducted. "Isn't that dangerous?"

"Entirely," the slave replied callously. "And so long as no one tells *me* to go along on one of these hunts, I care not. Whatever it takes to get the young hotheads' minds off making trouble around here is perfectly fine. You would not *believe* what they've been getting up to in their quarters. The wrestling matches that end in broken furniture are bad enough, and the drunken parties, and the wild adventures with all of the dancing girls, but there are four *very* angry nobles who had to drag their daughters out of rooms in the compound that they should never have been in, and several more who've been asking pointed questions about where their wives have been, and with whom." The slave snickered.

"Which is probably why the King's 'suggestion' was phrased so near to an order."

Vetch could certainly agree with that, but he had to know more, and he decided to go in search of Haraket.

Haraket, it seemed, was already in search of *him*. He spotted Vetch coming around a corner, and shouted his name. Vetch hurried toward him.

"I've three—gods save us, three!—spitting and yowling dragonets, and more to come, and I need you and Fisk to help train new serf boys," he growled, as soon as Vetch came within earshot. He was accompanied by a tall, aristocratic man in a fine kilt, striped headdress, and a simple, but very rich, neckpiece and armlets. "Gods help us! If we don't have some of them killed before this is over—" He shook his head. "Well, it'll be the stupid ones, or the ones with more bravado than sense, so, small loss, I suppose."

"No loss," said the stranger, who had the deep-set eyes, the beaky nose, and the stern look of one of the statues of the Great King. He looked down at Vetch. "So, this is your little serf boy, Haraket? The one who makes dragons love him?"

"The very one," Haraket replied, with a hint of a smile.

Vetch, meanwhile, felt himself held in the man's powerful gaze. Whoever this was, Vetch felt like a mouse between the paws of a cat. He knew he should avert his gaze and stare at the ground in respect, but he *couldn't* look away! He was fascinated and terrified at the same time by this man—a powerful man, an *important* man—

A man who could order my death and be obeyed on the spot—

How he knew that, he didn't know, but he knew instantly that it was nothing less than the truth.

It felt as if his mind was being rummaged through. Desperately, he kept his thoughts on Kashet, on Coresan, on all of the dragons he had been making friends with, a little at a time. . . .

"So, boy," the man said, speaking directly to Vetch, as *no* Tian noble had ever done before, "How do you make dragons love you? Is it some witchery?"

Vetch gulped. Witchery! Oh, gods, that was the *last* thing he wanted anyone to think! "I'm—good to them—lord," he whispered. "Patient. Careful. I—give them treats—show them the pleasures of being obedient—let them become my friend—I coax them to be good—" He fumbled for the words to describe what he was doing, and failed. "I—like them," he said desperately.

To his shock, the man tossed back his head in a bellow of laughter, freeing him from that paralyzing gaze. The stranger slapped Haraket's back; Haraket actually staggered.

"A good answer! A true answer!" the man said, still laughing. "So speaks any good tamer of animals! Well enough, Haraket, find me more such as this boy, and I authorize you to take as many boys, be they free, slave or serf, as you need for the new Jouster Hundred. You undertake that—I will find you Jousters who are neither too bold nor too foolish, even if *I* have to take them from the fields and the quarries to find sensible men of courage to fill those saddles. And if our nobles are offended by this, and feel I have demeaned their feckless sons by allowing peasants and laborers to serve alongside them—well, they can come and quarrel with *me*."

With that, the man strode away through the mist and rain, paying so little heed to the weather that it might as well have been bone dry.

"That, young Vetch," Haraket said with satisfaction, "is the Commander of Dragons, who just happens to also be the Great King's seventh son by one of his Lesser Wives. And if our young hotheads can actually manage to steal so many dragonets from the nest—and I am forbidding them to take more than one from any one nest—then we are about to double our strength to a full Hundred, and perhaps more. Though—where I'm to find so many dragon boys—boys who have experience—boys who are not intimidated or afraid of dragons—"

"Shouldn't they just love animals and understand them?" Vetch said, without thinking.

"What?" Haraket said, startled.

"Someone like Fisk—" Once again, he knew what he wanted to say, but didn't have the words for it. "He loved his goats—he knew how to see what they were going to do by the way they acted—" He floundered, but Haraket's eyes lit up. "It's not like dragonets are as big as grown dragons. Even one the size of an ox is still just a baby, after all! And he said you could take serfs or slaves—and serfs and slaves are *always* doing the dirty work around animals."

"You could be right, boy," Haraket mused aloud. "Perhaps— dog boys, the ones that tend the hunting packs. *They* live, sleep, even eat with their packs. Dog boys will know how to care for a young thing, even a dragon. By the gods, I see what you mean. They're out there, invisible, because none of us ever look at them!" Haraket exclaimed. "The boys that tend camels, the ones that care for the sacred animals in the Temples, or the Great King's menagerie! Good gods, all those slaves and serfs we never even look at, living under our very noses! The boys that tend the Khephis bulls are surely no strangers to big, dangerous beasts, and Hamun can spare us a few of *them*, I should think!" He nodded with satisfaction. "Good! I'll find the boys. You get back to *your* duties, and when I've gotten a clutch, you and Fisk can pick out the ones that are any good."

Vetch went back to his duties with most of his questions answered, and as he went to get meat for Kashet and Avatre, he encountered a harried-looking *adult* in the doorway of the butchery. The man was pushing a barrow filled with small chunks, none bigger than his hand, and Vetch realized that this must be one of the dragon trainers, men he had not yet actually seen, the ones who were to tend to the dragonets until Haraket could find boys to take over the job. He did not look happy. Vetch could well imagine why. This was, more-or-less, *his* season of leisure and it had been seriously curtailed.

At least this was more confusion to hide what *he* was doing.

Provided, of course, that someone didn't try to put a dragonet in the pen that Avatre was already in, and find her, and start to ask questions. So—subtract one worry, add another—

By nightfall, there were five dragonets in pens in the compound, none of them nearly as young as Avatre, but not near fledging yet either. Vetch didn't have to time to look at any of them, though he heard that they were all about the size of the first one, as wild as lion cubs and as ready to take off limbs before their first taste of *tala* calmed them.

Coresan must have mated late in the season, if these were the size of the dragonets out in the wild. By nightfall too, Haraket had found a round dozen new dragon boys, and to Vetch's great relief, he and Fisk were not going to have to train all of them. Half, in fact, were freeborn, and Haraket deemed it more appropriate that they be trained by their peers instead. The ones that Fisk and Vetch met with the next day were all from the Great King's Palace, and the households of one or two of his nobles, and all were dog boys but one, who tended the Great King's falcons.

This was a much, much older boy, not even a *boy*, really, for he must have been at least seventeen or eighteen. And he proved to be a great surprise to all concerned.

Haraket brought them all to the pen containing a young dragonet of a rich golden-brown color, again roughly the size of a fully-grown bull, that had been chained in place and was ignoring the barrow full of meat within his reach. His eyes were furious, and even Vetch was taken aback by the intelligent rage that was in them.

But the older boy wasn't in the least fearful.

"So, this's a dragonet?" he asked, looking at the young beast measuringly. "My lord Haraket, I *asked* to come here. I had some thoughts, you see, and I wanted to see if I was right. If you would let me?"

Much to everyone's shock, including Haraket's, *he* had come prepared with a novel approach to taming a young dragonet, and he was fully prepared to test it. When Haraket nodded, speechlessly, he looked immensely satisfied.

"Thank you, my lord," he said. Then he simply walked into the pen with the young dragonet with great steadiness and aplomb, fixing it with a challenging gaze. This clearly took the young thing aback; as it fanned its wings wide in confusion, and backed away from him, the boy took three swift steps and a lunge, and popped a bag with a hole in it over the surprised creature's head. While it went rigid in surprise, he worked the hole around to where the dragonet's muzzle was, got the golden-brown muzzle poking out of the bag so the dragonet could breathe, and tied the bag's mouth around the dragonet's neck to keep it in place.

It went suddenly still, and Vetch and the others could see its muscles relaxing.

"Good," the boy said with satisfaction. "They *are* like falcons, then. My lord, falcons rely on sight, and I guess these beasts do, too. If they can't see, they don't fight you." And he picked up a piece of *tala*-dusted meat and slid it along the dragonet's mouth, teasing the corner of the mouth until the jaws opened a little, then popped the juicy chunk inside.

There was a sound of surprise, then the mouth snapped shut and the throat worked.

By now, even the trainer was watching in shock. "He hasn't eaten all day!" the man exclaimed.

The boy just shrugged. "No more do some falcons, taken from the nest too old to decide that a man's just a funny sort of mother. This works with them, though we use a leather thing that we call a hood instead of a bag; 'tween the bag and *tala*, they'll tame in a week, I guess, and maybe sooner."

The trainer shook his head, though in amazement rather than disbelief. "Let me get the others," he said, and when he returned, it was with at least ten trainers. By that time, the rest of the boys had gathered around this older one, who was slowly feeding the dragon bits of meat, talking all the while in a calm voice.

"The falcons haven't the mind of these fellows," he said, "They just go straight into a trance when the hood's on their heads. Look! He's figured out already that I've got food, and now that he can't see me, he isn't afraid anymore, and his gut's telling him how hungry he is."

Sure enough, the dragonet no longer had his jaws clamped shut; as soon as he swallowed the last bit, he gaped again for the next one to come.

"He's not in a trance, but as long as he can't *see* me, it's not so bad for him," the young man continued. "He's hungry enough that he'll put up with my voice so long as he keeps getting fed. Now, if *I* were the one in charge, that's what I'd say to do; treat them like young eyases, keep them hooded for the next couple of days, only feed them when they're in the hood, and after a couple of feedings, start to handle them all over between each bite so they get used to hands as well as voices."

"And then?" Haraket's voice boomed from behind Vetch.

"Then I'd make him skip a meal so he's good and hungry, then take the hood off, and make it pretty clear that if he doesn't take the food from *me,* he won't get any." The young man seemed pretty sure of his course of action, and Vetch was quite impressed. "Never had *tala* to use on falcons, but if it works like you say, lord, he may tame down in a day or two, not a week."

"Try it, Baken," Haraket ordered instantly. "And if he tames as well as you say, *you* will be in charge of training these others. What's more, at the end of the year, if the training of dragonets and boys works out properly, I'll free you and you'll begin serving here at a freedman's pay."

The young man's eyes gleamed in a way that Vetch understood perfectly well, and a wave of raw envy came over him that nearly made him sick. Freed! Haraket was going to *free* this boy! How much would Vetch do if only he could have freedom at the end of it—

But of course, he never would, never could.

"You won't get any Kashets out of this," Baken warned. "I've *heard* about that Kashet. At best, these dragons will be proper-tamed, like the best of the ones you've got."

"That will do," the Overseer replied. "That will certainly do.

Now, explain to the boys and the trainers how you handle the young falcons, and how you think it should apply to the dragonets. Vetch, Fisk, you can go back to your duties."

Vetch was not sorry to go back, for he was already worried about Avatre again—but mingled with relief was such bitter envy at Baken's good fortune that it tasted like bile in his throat. That wasn't fair to Baken. He didn't know the young man, and Baken was clearly kind to the falcons in his charge, competent, and eager to tame the dragonets in the most humane way possible. But it was so cruel, to see freedom offered to someone so nearly in his *own* circumstances, and know it would never be offered to him!

But he won't have Avatre, he reminded himself, as he took a quick peek into her pen and assured himself that she was still asleep. *He doesn't have her. And I have to make sure he never shall.*

FOURTEEN

OVER the next half moon, as the sea witches sent storms about every four or five days, Avatre grew at a rate that would have been alarming if Vetch hadn't expected it. Dragons flew for the first time at the end of the dry season, for they absolutely required heat, and the nests that lay in the full sunlight during the dry season would be fully exposed to the rains and cold winds of the winter wet. They were by no means able to hunt and kill for themselves; indeed, their mothers and fathers fed them for the next two years, but they *had* to be mobile by that time. A young dragon had to be up and out of his nest before the rain and wind came, so that he could follow his mother down into the warm volcanic caves for the winter.

Then he would spend the next two years reaching his adult size—or at least, that was how long it took in the pens. In the wild it often took even longer than that, for his growth depended on how well he ate. Here in the compound, of course, a dragonet never lacked for food, so he would achieve his full size in the minimum possible time.

And as a consequence of all that good food, Avatre doubled her weight nearly every day. Vetch oiled and buffed her morning and evening now, not only to keep her from itching too much, but to keep her skin supple and prevent it from tearing as she grew. There was never enough time, yet somehow he managed to squeeze everything in, by running everywhere, doing everything at full speed. Ari had always been easy to clean up after, now he was so seldom in his quarters that there was almost nothing to do. Vetch did his leather work by lantern light, and only needed to turn up on time for the inspection of the weapons, but the Jousters were going out so seldom, and then never seeing combat, that the inspection hardly took any time at all. It wasn't easy, but at least, it wasn't impossible.

There were twenty new dragonets in the compound now, and he was learning an enormous amount by eavesdropping on the trainers. Sometimes he even eavesdropped on the former falcon keeper, Baken, but although what the young man had to say was interesting, it didn't really apply to Avatre, since everything *he* knew pertained to wild or half-wild beasts, not one being hand-raised like Avatre.

He breathed a little easier with every new dragonet that came into the compound, especially when another of the new ones was also a red—and he felt more at ease with every new doubling of Avatre's weight, for she looked more and more like the other new ones.

Another factor was working in his favor. It was getting impossible for anyone but Haraket to know which new dragonet belonged with which new dragon boy, or in which pen, and Haraket was so busy that unless something actually went wrong, he left the new boys and dragonets to Baken and the trainers.

He was not doing triple duty, after all, which *would* have been impossible. It was Baken, not Vetch and Fisk, who weeded out the unsuitable boys from the ones that would take proper care of their dragonets. It was Baken who taught them what to do, and was turning into Haraket's right-hand assistant. Suddenly, the soon-to-be-former slave's star was very high indeed, and Vetch's was quite eclipsed. Not that he went back to being the outcast. There were far too many new people thronging the compound now for the freeborn boys to single him out—far, far too many serfs and slaves being made into dragon boys for them to say or do much about his status anymore. But there was no doubt that the admiring glances followed Baken now, and it seemed that every other sentence he overheard these days started with "Baken says. . . ."

And Vetch couldn't hate him, though it would have been easy to. Baken was genuinely *good* with beasts; he tried to understand how they thought and why they did the things that they did. Before he'd been assigned to the falcons, he'd handled both dogs and horses, and once had been given a sick lion cub to nurse. He was both firm and gentle with the creatures under his care. He tried to puzzle out what he called their "language"—what was important to them, what made them what they were, what poses and calls they used to communicate with each other—and he used that "language" to win their trust and cooperation. If he'd wanted to, Vetch had no doubt whatsoever that he could raise another Kashet and become a Jouster as good as Ari.

If he'd wanted to. But if Vetch was any judge, that was absolutely the last thing that Baket wanted. To be free, certainly! To become the Overseer of the entire compound, possibly. To become a Jouster—never. There was a look in his eyes whenever a Jouster was about, a bland look that spoke more of scorn than respect. . . .

Well, that was none of Vetch's business. Nor was it any of Vetch's concern. He had enough to worry about without concerning himself with Baken and *his* plans, when he had plans of his own. Maybe that was the reason why he couldn't hate Baken; he didn't have time or energy to spare to hate anyone.

First and foremost of his concerns was Avatre, and she was his last thought at night, the first every morning. It was true enough that the older she got, the more she blended in with the growing number of dragonets. But growing older and bigger meant becom-

ing more and more active as well. By the end of that half moon,
she was no longer just eating and sleeping. Whenever he cleaned
her pen, she watched him alertly, bobbing her head in a way that
made him laugh. When he buffed her, she stretched and crooned
and bumped her head against his hand, begging for further caresses. She was moving a little around the sand—not much, but it
was a portent of things to come as she took tentative, wobbling
steps. With every day, she showed more personality, and with
every day, he loved her more.

He thanked the gods whenever he had a moment to spare, for
surely they were protecting her. Between the storms and the influx of dragonets, there was too much going on in the compound
for anyone to be paying any attention to Vetch's activities as long
as he went out of his way to draw *no* attention to himself, in any
way, for any reason. Perhaps, given his reputation of being able
to handle most dragons, people assumed he was spending his free
time making friends with the new dragonets and those boys that
were serfs, like him. Actually, he wished that he could.

But he didn't dare; for one thing, Avatre needed every spare
moment, and for another, if he made friends, he increased the
possibility that a new friend would come looking for him and discover him with her, and he was *Kashet's* boy, not the keeper of a
dragonet. It was something of a torment, actually. He'd been so
lonely up until now, with the others shutting him out. If this had
happened *before* he'd hatched Avatre—

*I could have had friends. I probably would never even consider
trying to run.*

Well, that was how the gods had decided things. And he could
put up with a great deal of loneliness if it meant having her.

Everything conspired to help him, it seemed. The butchers kept
plenty of small-chopped meat on hand now, and no one seemed
to notice that Vetch was taking some at each feeding, even
though Kashet was long past needing anything that small.

And, luckily, no one was keeping track of the sheer *amount* of
meat he was taking. Even Haraket was too busy to supervise the

dispensing of dragon meat; he left it to the butchers to make sure that the boys were leaving with completely filled barrows. Nobody ever asked about overfilled ones.

Ari wasn't paying a lot of attention to what he was doing either. The Jouster was working so hard of late that when he turned up at night to spend time with Kashet, he seldom spoke, just sat there, wearily, caressing the dragon's head in the silence. He had been recruited by Haraket to help train the new Jousters that the Commander of Dragons was bringing in, and when that duty was added to his own training and patrols, Vetch reckoned that Ari was stretched nearly as thin as his dragon boy was. That was all to the good; it kept him from noticing that Vetch was in and out of the pen next to Kashet's all the time.

Excitement kept him from feeling too exhausted. And if his day was crowded from dawn to dusk, well, it was crowded with good things rather than miseries.

The only *bad* thing was that now, instead of enjoying his meals, he had to bolt two of the three as fast as he could in order to keep on his frantic schedule. Since he'd taken to delaying his evening meal until after he'd given Avatre her last feeding for the day, that was the only one where he could actually sit down and taste what he ate. It wasn't too difficult to arrange for that either. With so many new dragon boys *and* additional servants and slaves to support them in the compound, it wasn't possible to feed them all at once, and there was more competition for getting your meals first than last.

The influx of servants and boys and trainers—and, eventually, it must be presumed, Jousters and yet *more* servants—had yet another effect on the compound. New slaves and servants meant more slaves and servants that needed training, monitoring, housing, feeding. Te-Velethat was absolutely frantic, for his charge was the domestic side of the compound, and although the Great King's Vizier had made ample provision for wages and slave purchases, the new staff still had to be acquired, fitted in, and trained. And provisions needed to be gotten for them, which meant more work in the stores and record keeping. He couldn't put all of *that* on Haraket anymore, not when the Vizier was looking over his shoulder to be sure his accounts were honest.

Vetch almost felt sorry for the man. But he was getting his own "come-uppance," as Vetch's mother used to say. If he hadn't been so concerned with his own status and lording it over all of his underlings, he would have had plenty of cooperation from people who were already trained and knew their business. Look at Haraket, for instance! Though the Overseer had a wicked temper, and never hesitated to use his tongue, fist, and very rarely, his whip where it was warranted, he was fair, honest, and never lorded it over anyone. And once you'd proved yourself to Haraket, he was perfectly ready to make allowances for your honest mistakes, or when you were just having a bad day. As a consequence, Haraket's people were falling over themselves to take on extra duties and train the new people.

On a clear night, six hands of days after that first horrible storm, Vetch put Avatre to bed with a full belly, and stayed with her until her eyes had closed and she was breathing deeply. The last of the sun god's radiance was gone from the sky; to the west, it was a lovely azure, to the east, the color of fine lapis, and overhead, stars were beginning to come out. A clear night meant that the sea witches would probably conjure a storm tomorrow, or next day at the latest; which meant that the Jousters would go out after more dragonets and there would be yet another influx of youngsters. Vetch headed for the kitchen court, feeling slightly melancholy.

The slaves and serfs who served the latecomers, when things were slower and mistakes easier to rectify, were all new to Vetch, and *they* didn't know him from any of the new serf boys. He probably would have missed his friendly serving woman more than he did, but by the time he sat down to dinner, he was usually so tired he could hardly think.

Still, when he took his place in that out-of-the-way corner tonight, he wished she would move to doing the late serving. The

slave who left him a jar of beer and a platter of bread did so without even looking at him. He sighed, reached for a loaf, and tore
off a piece with his fingers, hoping that there was someone still
grilling fresh meat, and he'd get a plate of that, instead of cold
leftovers. And *that* thought made him realize just how far he'd
come. Last year at this time, he'd have done nearly anything for
a *scrap* of meat, burned hard enough to need pounding between
two rocks before he could actually eat it!

A shadow fell over his table; a tall one. He looked up.

"Well, Vetch," said an unsmiling Baken. The slave must have
just gotten a bath; his hair was wet, and slicked neatly back, his
hands were clean, his kilt fresh. Vetch noted without surprise that
Baken wore a hawk-eye talisman made, not of the usual pottery,
but one like Haraket sported, cast from silver and inlaid with
enamel. Never had it been so obvious that Baken was *not* from
Tia—he had a Tian's black hair, but it was curly, and not all the
water in the world could make it lie straight on his head. His eyes
were a disconcerting blue, and his complexion, beneath his tan,
was a fine olive-color rather than Tian bronze or Altan ivory. His
features were mathematically symmetrical; deep-set eyes, promi-
nent cheekbones, small nose, generous mouth, chiseled chin with
a cleft in it. Definitely not Tian, nor Altan.

Vetch blinked at him, taken by surprise by the young man's
appearance at his table. "Well," he replied, not knowing what else
to say. Baken seemed to take that as an invitation to sit down,
because he did so, sliding onto the bench opposite Vetch's.

"So, you're Kashet's boy, I'm told," the young man said, taking
a small loaf, but just holding it in his hands, rather than tearing it
open to eat it. "You're the serf. The first serf to be made a dragon
boy. The one that gave serfs a good reputation as dragon boys."

Vetch nodded warily. What was this leading up to? Did he have
something against serfs?

"So it's largely thanks to *you* that I'm here at all." Baken regarded him steadily, the torchlight in the court illuminating only

one side of his face, and once again Vetch nodded, feeling even more alarmed.

"So why do you hate me?" Baken asked, as calmly as if he was asking why Vetch was eating bread instead of an onion.

Vetch started. "I—I don't *hate* you," Vetch protested, feeling horribly guilty, and caught completely off-guard by the unexpected question.

"Then in that case, just what is it that makes your eyes go so dark and angry when you see me?" Baken persisted, pressing his advantage like a hunting cat trying to flush a pigeon, and with every bit of that intensity. "I'd like to know. I don't *make* enemies, and if someone has decided on his own that he wants to *be* my enemy, I want to know why."

Since Vetch had thought he was keeping his feelings securely to himself, Baken's accusation made him tense and nervous. What *else* wasn't he keeping secret? And why was Baken confronting him about this, anyway? It wasn't as if he was trying to make himself into Baken's rival. He didn't *want* to be Haraket's assistant—he didn't even want to be here! "I'm not your enemy," he said brusquely, looking away. "I don't wish you ill. How could I? You take better care of the dragons than anybody but me!"

Baken's head lifted at that, like a hound on a scent, and Vetch felt another pang of alarm. *Now* what had he given away? "Anybody but you. Is that jealousy I hear?"

"No!" Vetch snapped. Then honesty drove the truth out of him. "Well—not jealousy. Envy."

Baken's eyes lit, and he nodded; at that moment, he looked like one of the falcons he had once taken care of, with prey in sight. And Vetch already knew what prey felt like; it was a familiar sensation, a helplessness that—oh, yes—he was certainly feeling now. "Ah . . . envy. Let me see—what have you learned or seen or heard that could possibly make you envious of me? I'm not your rival for Kashet. Jouster Ari would never accept another boy even if Kashet might. You're far too young to consider yourself as a potential assistant to Haraket, but Haraket offered me a great deal else besides that position. . . ."

Vetch winced a little at the mention of Haraket's promises, and the falcon stooped on the prey that had just been flushed before its eager eyes.

"Ah. I see. In that case—would it be that promise of freedom that Lord Haraket made me?"

Freedom. Vetch felt his gut twist up inside him, and he set the bread aside, uneaten. Why was Baken tormenting him like this? It wasn't fair! "Yes," he replied, biting off the word, making it a challenge. *Leave me alone!* he thought angrily. *Why twist the knife in the wound? What have I done to you to deserve this?*

The falcon looked at the prey in its claws—and then, unexpectedly opened its grip. Baken sighed, relaxed, and shook his head. "I'm sorry, Vetch," he said, sounding genuinely apologetic. "I can't help what I am, nor what you are. When a slave is offered freedom, well—"

"I'm more of a slave than you are, or ever could be," Vetch grated. "A serf is *less* than a slave, for all that the masters pretend otherwise. I don't hate you, but don't expect me to love you for it either."

Baken closed his eyes for a moment, and there seemed to be a pocket of unexpected stillness holding both of them. "I know that. I also know why our masters will offer freedom to a slave, but not a serf, though I doubt it would be of any interest to you. Still." He pondered a moment, then continued. "I'll try and explain it to you, as my last, and most worthy master explained it to me. Slaves are either born that way, from those Tians who are born into slavery, or are Tians sold into slavery to pay debts, or they are brought as slaves from countries Tia has never conquered. Take me, for instance, I come from a very distant land indeed, so far that there is no chance my people could ever be the enemies of the Tians, so it is safe enough to free me. I have always been treated well, and have no one to revenge myself on. I've nowhere to go, freed—no reason to go to Tia's enemies, and every reason to stay here and continue to serve at the same place, but for a wage. Whereas you—" He shrugged. "Serf, you are an enemy. Freed, you are still an enemy, but there is no control over you or your actions anymore. I am sorry. If I could change things, I would."

Vetch's gut twisted a little harder. "It's not fair," he whispered.

"No," Baken agreed. "It's not. It's even less fair, because I am certain that Lord Haraket would offer *you* freedom if it was in his power, for how you took over the dragon Coresan and tamed her without frightening or hurting her. You *are* the one who has the reputation for making dragons love him."

The knot in Vetch's gut eased. "You know about that?" he asked. He hadn't thought Baken cared, actually. The young man had been very much involved with his own doings.

Baken smiled, and his set of large, even, and very white teeth gleamed in the torchlight; they were startling, not the least because Vetch had never seen Baken smile before. "Lord Haraket is very much impressed with your dedication and abilities; he told me all about it when he told me *why* he changed his mind about having serfs and slaves as dragon boys."

"Oh." Now Vetch felt guilty all over again, and felt he had to defend himself. "Well, I don't *hate* you, Baken. But you can't blame me for—"

"Of course I can't, and I don't," Baken replied, interrupting him. "I just didn't want the most skilled dragon boy in the compound to be my enemy, that's all. Here. In my country, when men agree to be comrades, they shake hands." He thrust out his hand.

Vetch shook it, gladly—and gladder still that Baken hadn't said "friends." Of all of the people in the entire compound, Baken was the *last* one he dared to have as a friend, for he was the one most likely to uncover the secret of Avatre's existence. "I don't mind that you're getting all the attention, that Haraket's depending on you, and that—well—you've taken over the new boys," he said, earnestly. "Honest, I don't. The freeborn boys probably *do* hate you, though."

Once again, that gleaming, toothy grin. "Let them. The boys I've picked are all like you and me—well, maybe without our gods-bestowed gift for understanding animals, but they're just as hard-working and they like their charges. They *aren't* freeborn boys with plenty of choices ahead of them, and plenty of arrogance to match their choices. They already know that there are many, many worse places to serve, and they're learning that this is one of the best, and they do *not* want to lose their places. Pretty soon, our kind will outnumber theirs, and I *know* we'll outlast them. So let them stew in their own juices until they can't even stand themselves. Just so long as you and I have gotten things straight between us. There shouldn't be any animosity between men of our kind."

Men! That was sheerest flattery, and Vetch knew it. Still, it was sweet to hear, even if it *was* flattery. "You need to meet Ari," Vetch said at last. "He's—different. You'll admire him, you know, he's not like any other Jouster in the compound, maybe not like any other, ever."

"So Lord Haraket says." Baken nodded. "He seems very different, and everything I've heard is good. He might change *my* mind about—"

He stopped abruptly, but now it was Vetch's turn to pounce alertly on an incautious phrase. If Baken had forced *him* into an uncomfortable place, well, turnabout was fair play. "About Jousters, you mean? Just why don't *you* like the Jousters?"

He whispered that; he didn't want to get Baken in any trouble, just because he wanted to know one of Baken's secrets. Baken frowned, fiercely, but he couldn't conceal his own unease.

Ha! Got you!

"What makes you think that I don't—" Baken began aggressively, but stopped, and gave a self-conscious laugh. "You're pretty observant as well as clever, Vetch."

"Maybe. But I want to know," Vetch replied, not allowing himself to be deflected. "Ari is—I don't want anyone around him who *doesn't* like Jousters and might do or say something that would give him trouble. Unless you've got an awfully good reason for it."

And it had better be an astonishingly good reason.

"You have a point." Baken studied him for a moment. "And all right; I think I can trust you, so I'll tell you—though it isn't merely that I don't like Jousters, it goes further than that. It isn't because of what they do, it's because of what they are." He paused a moment, and signaled to a server, who plunked down a platter of still-sizzling meat and another of onions between them, with an undisguised look of hero worship for Baken, who answered it with a wink. "You eat, though, while I talk. You look starved enough as it is."

"All right," Vetch agreed—since now that his gut had unknot-ted, it was growling. He plucked a hot piece of meat from the platter and dropped it quickly on the bread, adding an onion slice; he waited only a few moments for it to cool before biting off a mouthful.

"It isn't that they're the masters either. It's more complicated than that." Baken took an empty beer jar from the table and brooded down at it. "As I said, I've always been treated well; I don't think anyone ever realized how I feel. As I'm sure you've noticed, no one ever pays any attention to the feelings of serfs and slaves."

Vetch waited, patient as a cat at a mouse-hole with only one entrance.

"What do you call a man who calls up his servants, has hunting birds brought out to him, takes one on his fist, unhoods and casts it, and basks in the admiration of his peers when it takes a fat duck?" Baken asked, after a time.

"Um—" Vetch replied, and shook his head. "Um—a noble? A rich man?" he hazarded.

"Ah. Good answer. But not the one that makes me angry." Baken's lip curled. "You see, what he calls *himself* is 'falconer.' He has not caught the birds nor taken them at great hazard from the nest, scaling the cliffs to find them and bring them down. He has not tended them, he does not feed them, he has not trained them." The bitterness in Baken's voice made Vetch blink in surprise. "If the bird flies away, his wrath is only for the loss of a valuable *possession*, not because he is losing something he has invested a part of his life and self in. If it is recovered, he is pleased only because his *possession* is returned to him, not because he has gotten back something that is near as dear as a child. But the man who *has* done all those things, *is* all those things, is not called a 'falconer.' He is called slave, servant, and he has not even the right to challenge the master when the master says 'I will have this bird,' and he knows that the bird is not fit to fly that day."

There was a story behind that—perhaps many. Vetch didn't want to know them. There was already enough pain in his own short life; he didn't want to add the burden of Baken's to his own. Already he had three people besides himself in his prayers—his father, Ari, and Avatre. If he added any more, the gods might begin to wonder what was wrong with him, that he assailed their ears with so many pleas.

"Now—at least there is a separate name for the man who takes a dragon who is cared for by someone else, trained by someone else—who mounts into the saddle and flies it off, caring nothing except that it do what it is trained to do and bring him glory," Baken continued, his jaw rigid. "And at least he is named for what he *does*, and not the good beast that he treats as he would a mere chariot."

Vetch started, hearing his own thoughts echoed so exactly.

"He takes a creature that would, on its own, serve him in— say—hunting, and he turns it into a weapon, a horrible weapon, and exposes it to the spears and arrows of enemies with his only thought being where he would get another if this one fell." Baken's gaze smoldered. "And which of these *Jousters* truly knows his dragon, or has studied its ways and made it his friend, or has even cared for his own beast for so much as a day?"

"Ari has," Vetch said, stoutly, raising his chin. "Ari raised Kashet, trained him all by himself, and comes to be with him nearly every night. And he *would* tend Kashet himself, now, if he had the time. And he doesn't trust Kashet's care to just anyone either!"

Baken's rigid expression softened, and he patted Vetch on the head like a small child. Vetch bristled a little, but kept his resentment on a tight leash. To Baken, doubtless, he *was* a small child. That was the hazard of being so little. "So I have been told, and see no reason to disbelieve it. So your Ari is a single paragon among the Jousters, as the Commander of Dragons is a paragon among the nobles, given that he *has* taken, cared for, and trained his own birds, dogs, and horses." Now there was plain admiration in Baken's voice, and Vetch guessed that of all of Baken's masters or the men those masters consorted with, the Commander of Dragons had been the only one who had earned Baken's highest regard. "Such men are worth serving, and serving well. Our Haraket is another such. But such men are few, and often given names they do not deserve, when they take the praise that is rightly given to men that they think beneath their notice."

Oh, there are many *stories there,* Vetch thought, somberly, and now wanted to hear them even less. Stories—and heartbreak. *And I have troubles of my own.* "Thank you for explaining," he said, carefully. "I—I won't tell anyone."

Baken nodded, accepting his word. "Now, that isn't the only reason why I wanted to see you," he continued, his tone now so light, his expression so casual, that Vetch could hardly believe what he'd looked like mere moments before. "I have need of your help, you see. I'm training one of the dragonets myself."

Vetch blinked. "You are?" That was unheard of! Trainers were trainers, and dragon boys—whether or not they were Haraket's assistants—were merely dragon boys, not to be entrusted with the training!

"Haraket wishes to see if my methods—things that I have learned from training both horses and falcons—produce a better beast than the methods used now," Baken explained, with an ironic lift of his eyebrow. "As I said, another remarkable man, our Overseer. He does not answer a question of 'why' with the answer 'because we have done it thus-and-so for ten hundred years'."

Vetch stifled a laugh with his food.

"I need *you*, young Vetch, because you are four things. You are brave, you are agile, you know and like dragons, and you are small," he continued. And smiled. "And if you will agree to take time to help me, you will see why I need someone who is all these things."

Vetch could ill spare the time—but—

But he was going to have to begin training Avatre himself in another moon. And if he could learn how to do so by helping Baken. . . .

"What's more, Haraket says that there is absolutely no need for you to keep on with the leather work and the weapons' inspection. You know very well how to do both, and there are more than enough new boys who *need* to learn to make up for you not being there." Baken cocked his head to the side. "Will that give you time enough?"

This time, he did not even need to think for a moment about his answer. "When do you need me?" he asked.

The blue dragonet that Vetch and Baken now faced—the very *first* one brought to the compound—was an entirely different creature from the hissing, snarling thing that had been brought in a mere handful of days ago. Vetch would not have believed it, if he hadn't seen it with his own eyes.

Mind, it was no Avatre, much less a Kashet, but although it eyed both of them with an expression both alert and wary, it was not prepared to rip off their limbs and eat them. Instead, it accepted their presence and eventually was relatively relaxed as first Baken, then Vetch handled it. This one was a solid, sky-blue from nose to tail, the same color, deepening on the extremities, rather than shading into a different color altogether. Sky-blue, *latas*-blue, he was a wonderful beast to look upon.

"I've got him used to saddle, harness, and guide straps," the young man said, as he buckled those accouterments in place. "I've even got him used to bearing weight on his back. But that was a sack of grain, and a sack of grain is not a human—and a stranger, at that."

Now Vetch understood entirely what Baken had meant last night by "brave, agile, and small." He would need to be brave, because this dragonet *didn't know him* and might turn on him if he tried to mount. He needed to be agile to get out of the way if it did. And he needed to be small, because, big as this blue dragonet was, it couldn't bear the weight of a man yet, or probably even one of the larger dragon boys. Their growing spines were surprisingly fragile, and could not bear too much stress.

The dragonet's harness had been fastened to four ropes that were in turn fastened to four rings in the pen wall. Vetch wasn't sure what those were for—

Well, he was about to find out. He'd made friends with the dragonet as Baken had shown him. Now he was about to shock it. As Baken stood back from his handiwork, Vetch strode across the sand with confidence and calm, both of which were going to be very important to keep the youngster from feeling uneasy as he approached. He greeted the dragon as Baken had shown him, as an adult greeted a subadult, with a breathy trill and a head bump, then without a pause, he vaulted up into the saddle.

He had to vault—this dragonet hadn't learned "down" and "up" yet, and he stood about as tall as one of the great god bulls. Baken had taught him the maneuver this morning, practicing on a saddle strapped to a beam supported on legs, mounted at about the right height out in the landing court. Both hands on the saddle, a jump, and a twist as he shoved his own weight up with his arms—

—and he was in place, balanced on the thin pad of leather, for the first time, with a dragon underneath him and *him* in the saddle instead of face-down over it.

Then, with another quick movement, he wedged his legs under and around the leg-hold straps, and grabbed the front of the saddle with both hands. There were no guide straps yet to hang onto; Baken deemed this confusing and disorienting enough for the poor young thing.

The dragonet went rigid with shock. Vetch felt its muscles tensing under his legs, and braced himself for its inevitable reaction.

It was as well that he did, for it tried at that moment to take off.

Thanks to the ropes, and the fact that it really wasn't old enough to fledge yet, it succeeded only in crow-hopping upward a few feet, flapping its wings clumsily. But that was unnerving enough—clearly another reason why Baken wanted someone brave!—and Vetch was very, *very* glad of the restraining ropes! It bounced about at the end of the ropes, bucking very much like the family's little donkey when startled, and Vetch clung on with grim determination and teeth rattling in his head. He couldn't even think, really—his very thoughts were bounced out of him! The straps cut into his legs with every bounce, and the saddle felt as if it was going to pop off at any moment.

But it couldn't keep such fighting up forever, though, and the moment it stopped, in a flash, Baken was at the dragonet's head, soothing it, comforting it, telling it what a wonderful beast it was. It didn't *want* to be soothed, but gentle hands, a soft voice, and a liberal allocation of tasty tidbits made it stand still, though it trembled like a leaf, and kept rolling its eye and twisting its head to look at him.

"Now, then, handsome one—" Vetch murmured, when he was sure it wasn't going to go off again under him, and added one hand—*one*—to Baken's caresses. Baken gave him an approving look. "Now, then, you'll be used to this soon enough. It will all be fine—"

He murmured other such nonsense, reaching places to rub that

Baken couldn't from his stand on the ground at the dragonet's shoulder. And, slowly, the dragonet relaxed.

"You see?" Vetch murmured to him. "I'm not some strange monster on your back. I'm not up here to hurt you—I'm not a lion, come to break your neck and eat you! I'm just Vetch, you know me now, don't you?"

"Slide down now, Vetch," Baken murmured after some small time, while the dragonet was engaged in getting his eye ridges rubbed. "Then get back on him again."

Vetch unwrapped his legs, threw the right over the dragonet's neck, and slid down even faster than he'd vaulted up. The dragonet reacted to his absence with a start of surprise, but didn't hop about this time.

And before it could get too used to him being gone, Vetch jumped back into the saddle again.

This time, it only hopped once, and when it stopped, it wasn't shaking. Now it only looked indignant, and that was a great improvement over terrified.

They played this game four more times, until Baken decreed that the dragonet's developing spine had gotten enough stress for the day. He unharnessed and freed the youngster of everything but the single chain holding him around his neck, rewarded and praised him a little more, then both of them left the pen.

Once outside, Baken slapped Vetch on the back with a hearty grin. "By the gods, it works! I thought it might, but I wasn't sure. I'd like you here just before feeding, twice a day, so he's good and hungry, and he'll work for his tidbits; we'll play this little game on him until he takes you as easily as Kashet takes Ari, and until we've taught him 'up' and 'down,' and how you'll use both to mount, and we've taught him the use of the guide straps. Then, when he can actually get off the ground with you on his back, I'll get one of the heavier boys to help me, and work my way up until he can carry a very light man."

Hmm. Like you, Baken?

Well, why not? If Baken wanted to add himself to the roster of trainers, why not?

Vetch nodded, seeing the good sense in the planning. Trainers did *something* like this, only they started much, much later, when the dragonet *could* carry a man, and they didn't precede it with the gentling process. They just tied the dragonet down, threw a saddle on him, and jumped on, letting the dragonet wear itself out on the ropes and "breaking" it to saddle.

Small wonder that dragons did not love their riders. . . .

And now, thanks to Baken, Vetch knew how to train Avatre without having to ask Ari. *Exactly* how to train her. Only he would be starting very early indeed, with nothing more than a few straps to get her used to things being bound around her body.

And when she flew—it would not be with ropes holding her to the earth.

Gods willing. Gods willing. . . .

FIFTEEN

T HE expected sea-witch–sent storm did not come that day, nor the next. The tension built once again; fear and anxiety becoming as much or more of a weapon wielded against the Tians than the storm itself. Finally, another one—again, with a great deal of wind and lightning, but with less rain than the last—struck on the sixth day after the last storm had ended. And the next storm arrived *seven* days after that.

Were the sea witches getting weary of their sport? Or were they only toying with the Jousters, hoping to set them off-guard? Vetch dreaded both, and yet at the same time, hoped this was so. That Alta at last had the strength to fight back! The sea witches had not been as numerous or as strong as the magicians of Tia within living memory. Had something happened to change this? Had they learned new magics, had their numbers increased? Or had the priests of Alta also found a way to add their magic to that of the sea witches, as the priests of every Tian god could join their forces into a massive whole?

Or was this only a brief, hectic flare of power before the end, like the dying of a fire? Something that could not be repeated?

Were the sea witches' powers once again on the wane? This was what Vetch dreaded.

The rumors spread throughout the compound, causing at least as much unease as the storms themselves. The priests said nothing, perhaps fearing that if they took credit for the weakening of the storms, the witches would turn their words to ashes in their mouths and prove their boasts to be lies.

The Jousters were reluctant to go farther afield despite the changing conditions, and it seemed that the Commander of Dragons agreed with them, for he issued no new orders. But further rumors told of convocations of the priests in every temple on Temple Row and throughout, not only the city, but all of Tia, as magicians and Seers attempted to pierce the veils of magic concealing the seats of Altan power, and discover what their counterparts in Alta were planning. Evidently, however, no matter *what* the strength of the sea witch power was, the protections still held; there were no revelations coming from the Seers of Tia.

And in the end, it was that most necessary of creatures that brought the real news—

—a spy.

It was Haraket that spread the word of a massive, compoundwide meeting to the dragon boys, at morning feeding, as each of them collected the meat for their dragons. "Everyone to the landing-court at noon," he repeated, over and over. "No exceptions. The Commander wishes to address us." And of course, that only created more rumors rather than stilling the existing ones.

If some of the others had time enough to buzz and whisper over the rumors, Vetch did not. The only time he might have said anything was to Baken—and Baken was not inclined to talk about anything other than the progress of the blue dragonet.

"So much smarter than a horse—" he was muttering cheerfully as Vetch arrived to help him, only to find him harnessing the youngster. He looked up when Vetch arrived with a satisfied smile on his face. "Vetch, you have no idea. The best qualities of a falcon, with the intelligence of a fine hound, and you can tame him like a wild horse—look at him! Mere days since he was brought in, and look at him!"

Indeed, the dragonet regarded both of them with aloof tolerance, standing calmly, and registering displeasure with a hiss only when he didn't care for something that one or another of them did. Sometimes, it was when Vetch moved a little too quickly, once, when Baken accidentally pinched a fold of skin while harnessing him. "I might gentle a wild horse that fast, but I wouldn't lay money on it," Baken continued, "And a horse is not a hunter, it is a social animal that craves its herd around it. It is harder to tame a creature that takes prey; by their nature they are competitive and wary. It is also harder to tame one that, in the wild, is not part of a herd."

"You wouldn't have been able to if he'd ever eaten man," Vetch reminded him. "You got a chance at him while he was still impressionable. He thinks we are mightier than he—if he'd ever eaten man flesh, he'd still be thinking of us as dinner."

Baken nodded, knowing, as Vetch knew, that anything as small as a man was generally killed and carried whole to the nest by the mother dragon, so the young dragonets got a good idea what their prey should look like.

"All the more reason to start taking youngsters earlier than first flight. What's happened here with him, by the accident of the Jousters going out and robbing nests *far* earlier than they've ever done before, is to repeat what we falconers usually do with eyas falcons," Baken replied. "We take them old enough to know that they are falcons, but young enough to tame quickly."

"Well—yes, it's true that's successful. But it was at the cost of eight Jousters so far," Vetch reminded him. "Mother dragons aren't like falcons. When *they* defend their nests, it's the humans that lose the fight."

Baken snorted. "And there are two would-be Jousters eager to replace every one stupid one that tries to haul off a dragonet with the mother too near," he replied. "It is easy to replace Jousters.

It's a lot harder to replace a dragon, especially a properly-tamed one. Better that they get themselves killed off *now*, than that they get themselves killed in a joust or accident and lose a trained dragon."

It was clear that his opinion of the Jousters hadn't changed. Well, Vetch shared it. As far as he was concerned none of the fools who'd become dragonet dinner was much of a loss.

Besides, every one that goes down a dragon's throat is one less to attack Alta. . . .

"There!" Baken said in triumph, and stood a little away. "Last strap. Now—today, we'll teach him 'up' and 'down.'%%" He laughed. "This isn't my training, though. I asked the other trainers how they do it. But I need you, Vetch, because this is a two-man job."

He passed the end of a jousting lance to Vetch, holding onto the other end himself. "Now, we fit this right into the crook of the elbow on his front legs. When I say the command, push down and in on his lower legs. They'll collapse, especially since he won't be ready for this, and he'll go down. When he does, get the lance away so it doesn't hurt him or stop him from going all the way down, and shove down on his shoulders."

That was clear enough, and clever, too. Vetch nodded. Together they pushed the lance in on the dragonet's forelegs. "Down!" Baken ordered, and they both pushed the blue dragonet's legs with the lance shaft. Now, if they had tried to *force* him down, *starting* with a shove on his shoulders instead of with the lance, he would have fought them—and he'd have won. Young as he was, he was still stronger than they were. But this caught him off-guard, like a man tackled from behind at the knees. With a snort of surprise, the dragonet felt his own legs giving way underneath him, and he was too startled to fight. He went down—and to Vetch's pleasure, he also folded his rear legs under him as well. It was accidental, but this would set the mark for what "down" meant.

"Good boy!" Baket crowed, rewarded the young beast with a

tidbit immediately. "Very good boy!" He caught the slight move-ment of the dragonet as it prepared to scramble back up to it's feet, and shouted "Up!" just as it made up its mind to get up. More praise, another tidbit, and the dragonet's eyes were sud-denly very bright. Was it too much to say, there was speculation in them? He'd been taught here that there were things he would have to do that he didn't necessarily think of for himself. Did he now realize that here were two of those things that he actually needed to learn?

Again, Baken signaled to Vetch to use the stick. "Down." "Up." "Down." "Up."

Dragons didn't have very expressive faces, but Vetch had learned to read subtle signs in the skin around their eyes, and the set of their heads. The dragonet was definitely thinking, and think-ing hard.

But this would be the first time that it had been asked to learn that those strange sounds coming from its captors meant that it was supposed to do something. That was a difficult concept for an animal to learn, for in the wild, they certainly didn't issue com-mands to each other. . . .

It was too much to hope that the youngster would learn "down" and "up" in a single session, but he did understand the physical part of the command by the time they finished with him for that session. The moment he felt pressure on the lance shaft, he went down, and when the pressure went away, he came up.

"That's good progress for a morning," Baken said in satisfac-tion, when the dragonet started to show signs of waning interest and irritation. "I'll see you before afternoon feeding."

"Have you named him yet?" Vetch asked, curiously, for Baken had never yet referred to the dragonet by anything other than "the youngster," or some other generic name.

"No," Baken replied instantly. "And I won't, until he first flies free and comes back. I never name a falcon that hasn't made a free flight."

Well, Vetch could understand that, because that moment of

free flight was the risky one, when the falcon or dragonet realized that he *was* free and he *could* fly off, never to be seen again. Names had power.

But a name can pull something back to you again. He'd felt that instinctively when he named Avatre; he had bound her to him with a name—or so he hoped. Well, maybe that was on purpose, too. Maybe Baken was unwilling to use *anything* to pull a falcon—or dragonet—back to him, other than training and whatever affection was possible from a falcon.

He'll find, if he can win it, there's a lot more coming from a dragonet. . . .

"Did you ever try to tame flappers?" he asked curiously, referring to the winged lizards of the desert that looked so much like miniature versions of dragons.

Baken laughed. "What boy hasn't?" he replied. "But boy or man, there is *no* taming those wretched beasts! All you ever get for your pains are lacerated fingers and a view of it vanishing into the sky the moment the cage door is open. I suppose, if you could actually *find* a nest, you might be able to get one to fix on you the way a baby chicken can, if you hatch it yourself—but I wouldn't even bet on that. There's no room for anything in those heads but killing and meanness."

Vetch had to laugh, for although *he* had never had the leisure to try and catch and tame a flapper, every one of Khefti's apprentices had tried, and every one of them had gotten the same result—fingers slashed to the bone, and eventually, an empty cage, since the little beasts could never be kept confined for long. He'd never seen anything for the ferocity of a flapper; it was a good thing that they were uncommon, shunned humans, and lived only where people didn't, or no domestic fowl would be safe.

"Don't forget the meeting," Vetch reminded Baken, who grimaced, but nodded. Vetch glanced up at the sun; it was near enough to noon that he decided to make a quick run of food to Avatre, then sprint for the landing court.

In stark contrast to the wild dragonet, Avatre was overjoyed to see him, and it occurred to him that he had better find something for her to *do* when he wasn't around. She was old enough now that she could get bored if he wasn't there to play with. He needed to find dragonet toys. Perhaps she'd enjoy gnawing on a bone, like a dog?

The butchery was deserted, the butchers already at the meeting place, which gave him a free hand there. So when he got her meal of the usual small pieces, he also took possession of a huge leg bone from an ox and brought it with him. It had been stripped clean by the butchers already, which made it ideal for his purposes; there wasn't any meat on it to putrefy and make her ill. Once she was stuffed, he left the bone beside her, and she was already tentatively biting at it out of curiosity as he left.

He was one of the last to reach the landing court, and as he entered the gate, all he could see were the backs and heads of people in front of him. As short as he was, he hadn't a prayer of actually seeing anything *but* the backs of heads. He looked around for something to stand on, and decided that his best bet was to climb up on the base of the pillars carved at either side of the gate itself. The sandstone was smoothed as well as sandstone could be, but he was used to climbing, and swarmed up it like a monkey. It didn't take long to get himself up there on the top of the pedestal that supported the pillar, and once in place, balancing on the tiny ledge where the square base ended and the round pillar began, he gaped in astonishment at the sheer *number* of people gathered within those four, high walls. He'd had no idea that there were that many people housed within the compound!

Obviously, the Commander of Dragons knew, though, which was why he had set the meeting here, for there wouldn't have been any place else able to hold all of them all at once, not even the Jousters' Hall where Vetch had been freed from Khefti.

The sun shone down on a sea of heads—heads in simple, striped headcloths, shaved heads, heads with the hair cut short and precise, and here and there, the shaggy, long-haired head of a serf. The colors of the wall paintings blazed in the sun, and there was a murmur of voices, a hum that filled the space between the walls.

At the far side of the court, a simple, head-high platform had been set up. Standing up there were the Commander of Dragons and several priests in formal attire—the sort of robes and jewels and regalia they had worn when they had led spell-casting processions around the compound after the first storm. Other than the wall paintings, they supplied the only spots of color in the courtyard, for the garb of nearly everyone from the compound itself was uniformly made of sun-bleached linen. Very few wore ornaments other than the hawk-eye talisman either.

The Commander stood with his hands on his hips with the bright sun shining full down on him, surveying the crowd below him, looking remarkably casual and completely at ease. Once again, he was dressed simply, with none of the showy jewels usually sported by the nobility, and only the Haras pectoral spreading jeweled wings at his bare throat, and the royal vulture at the front of his blue, close-fitting war helmet, marked him as any higher rank than a senior Jouster. Seeing him so very calm evidently was having an effect on the inhabitants of the compound; some of the tension was out of the air, and the murmurous sound of many conversations did not have that frantic edge to it that Vetch had expected.

Finally, the Commander held both hands up peremptorily for silence, and he got it, as the crowd hushed.

"Hear the words of the priests of the gods of Tia," the Commander said, his words ringing out, strong and deep, into the quiet. "The gods of Tia are stronger than the gods of Alta; her priests are wiser and more powerful, and in no way can the Altan magicians hope to prevail over those of this land. The gods of our land will prevail."

"Which only means the shave-skulls haven't figured out what the sea witches are doing, nor how to prevent it," someone muttered below Vetch, and his neighbors nodded in agreement.

Vetch had to agree with that; if the priests had successfully countered the sea witches' magic, they'd have boasted about it here and now. If they'd been able to find Seers who could get past the protections that hedged in Altan places of power, they'd have trumpeted their findings. This was all empty air.

But the Commander wasn't finished. "The priests of our land are wise, learned, and powerful," he continued, and Vetch thought he heard just a tinge of irony in the man's voice, "But no man goes hunting with only duck arrows in his quiver, when he does not know what other quarry he might encounter. The Great King, may he live a thousand years, also sent eyes and ears that walk upon two bare feet into the land of the Altans, and this is what he found—"

Vetch found himself leaning forward and holding his breath, and he was not the only one.

"The sea witches have a new magic, but as it is Wind and Water magic, it is subject to the season and the conditions of the season," the Commander told them, making sure each word was plain and unambiguous. "As the season progresses from Growing to Dry, there will be less water in the air, less-favorable winds. The storms will come farther and farther apart, and lose strength as the days pass and the Dry comes upon us, until at last, they will fade to a memory and we need cope only with the Dry, as ever. Perhaps the Dry holds terror for the enemy of the North, but *we* know it as an old neighbor. And our priests strive to see that we can learn to turn it against them, as they have sent their sea-born storms against us."

A collective sigh of relief arose from the crowd; if, like Vetch, some of the other Altan serfs felt disappointment, they were careful not to show it.

Now there were some murmurs beginning, and in a moment, they would probably be in full roar of conversation. Once again, the Commander raised his arms for silence.

"This is not to say that the sea witches may not find ways of raising storms in the Dry," he cautioned. "I do not need to do more than mention the Midnight *kamiseen*, I think. . . ."

His words had a chilling effect upon the crowd. The Midnight *kamiseen* was so named, not that it arrived in the dark of the night, but because it threw so much sand in the air, with such terrible winds, that it blotted out the sun. When such a storm blew up, it was as dark as midnight at midday. There was little hope for anyone caught without shelter in such a sandstorm, for it was literally impossible to breathe. One could actually drown in sand.

"Nevertheless, this is a magic of Wind only!" the Commander added. "And the sea witches' power has ever been that of *Water*, not Wind alone. Haras of the all-seeing eye is the guardian of the winds of Tia, and of the Jousters, too, and you can rest assured that His hand is over the Jousters and their dragons, and all those who serve them! And since it is a creature of Haras, the priests of Haras intend to learn to turn it northward, and give the witches a taste of true power!"

Small comfort, that, to those gathered below Vetch. Still, it did not do to say so aloud. The priests might hear—and withhold their protection from the grumblers.

It was always a chancy thing, to arouse the enmity of the priests. They might choose to ignore you, or they might not.

Vetch knew, however, as did every other Altan-born serf, that the sea witches' power was so integrally tied in with water that it was highly unlikely they could call up a Midnight *kamiseen*. Still—if the storms that had been brought had kept the dragons close to home, perhaps the threat of powerful sandstorms would do the same.

"The Great King," the Commander continued, "has mighty plans for us, my Jousters. I may not tell you what they are, but I am certain you may guess that as your numbers increase, you become a still more powerful weapon in his quiver. So I will leave you with that. Trust in the gods and their priests, and dream of the Gold of Honor!"

That was enough to evoke a cheer from the assemblage—all but Vetch, who was covering the fact that he was not cheering by climbing down from his perch. He knew, as did everyone else here, what those "plans" were. The truce, which was being eroded at every possible opportunity by both sides, would fill. And once again, Tia would hammer northward, with the Jousters at the forefront of the challenge.

But if the gods are with me, by then I will be gone. . . .

Eventually, as the storms weakened and took longer and longer to appear, he pulled back the awning over Avatre's pen. That gave Kashet a good look at her, and she at him, and within a day Kashet got bored with his neighbor and stopped spending so much time peering at her. His one regret was that he didn't dare ask Ari for advice. If only he could have! But he could take no chance that *anyone* might learn of Avatre, and of all of the people in the compound, he had the most to fear from Ari. Avatre was in the pen next to Kashet's, Ari knew very well that he had *not* been assigned a dragonet to care for, and—Ari was Tian. There was *always* that. So Vetch had to blunder through on his own, with common sense, what he learned from Baken, and what he overheard from the trainers.

He learned by eavesdropping that the dragons weren't allowed to carry a grown man until they were three, but that even a male fledgling, smaller than a female, could carry the weight of a small boy. By the time the dragon could fly, its backbone could bear up under that much weight with no problem.

In the old style of training, for the first two years that they were in captivity, the young dragons were given saddles and harnesses, then taken out on long leads and goaded to fly with the dead weight of sandbags in the saddle. This strengthened their flying, and got them used to harness, saddle, and weight on their backs.

Baken, of course, was going for a much more tractable dragon. He had no intention whatsoever of using goads on the new dragonets, and after a lot of convincing (and based on his success so far) the other trainers agreed to follow his lead.

Baken would follow their example, insofar as using the long leads and the sandbags went for early flying practice—but in the safety of the pens and on the four tethers, he would keep putting boys on the dragonets' backs to get them used to living weight. Furthermore, he was going to use a technique of flight training from falconry, and he planned to teach the dragonets to fly on those long leads from one end of the training field to the other on command. His plan was to teach them to fly between him and another trainer, as a dog was taught to "come" on command; this would be in return for rewards, rather than goading them into the air. This was a training technique he knew well, and the dragon trainers were mightily impressed with the ploys that Baken had used so far.

Vetch was not going to be able to do that; he could hardly take Avatre out of the pen without being discovered. He would have to strengthen her in some other way, so that her first flight would be a strong, high, and fast one. Because, by necessity, it would be with him. . . .

This would be an all-or-nothing cast of the bones. They would either succeed, or fail horribly.

He would not think of failure, or its consequences.

So as soon as she was romping around the sands of her pen, he began getting her used to a weight on her back, improvising a harness and a small sandbag at first, then when he discovered where the dragonet harnesses were kept, purloining one and using that. He actually kept a weight on her for about half of the day when he was sure it wouldn't tire her.

She certainly was anything but quiet; in fact, he had to make her, not one, but several toys to keep her amused. He brought her bones. He made her a big ball of rawhide stuffed with grasses, which she would pursue like a kitten with a ball of thread. Taking a cue from kittens, he rigged a rope with a scrap of silk on the end to a pole he stuck in the sand of her wallow, so she could bat at it with her foreclaws as it moved in the wind. He wrestled with her, teaching her to stop attacking when he commanded her to do so, and enforcing that she must be gentle with him, because he knew that if he did not do this *now*, while she was small, he could never control her behavior when she was big. The closer it got to the Dry season, the faster she seemed to grow, strong and agile.

The complement of dragonets was now at the fifty that the Great King had stipulated, with as many new boys—at a cost of thirteen Jousters and several dragon hunters that were not themselves Jousters. There was talk, now, of enlarging the compound—because the Great King had gotten wind of the new training techniques, and if they worked, he wanted still *more* Jousters and dragons. . . .

This did not bode well for Alta. Vetch could only pray that the Altans had spies abroad to hear such things.

At just about the time when the magic-spawned storms stopped altogether, Baken stopped needing Vetch's help, for now there were two or three of the new boys that weren't any larger than he was that he could use as "riders" to get the youngsters used to the presence of a human on their backs. Half of the dragonets had learned "up" and "down," and the blue dragonet was at the stage of learning to fly short distances on a lead. Vetch stole time to watch whenever he could get a moment, trying to make out how he could adapt all of this to training Avatre.

It was just as well that Vetch didn't need to help Baken anymore because Avatre was taking more and more of his time. He had thought he had been busy when all she did was sleep. Now that she was active, she *needed* attention.

Fortunately, Ari didn't know that he wasn't helping Baken now, and Vetch didn't intend to tell him. As long as Ari presumed that he was off helping the other dragon boy whenever he was missing, there would be nothing at issue.

He never saw Haraket anymore and Ari only in passing. He was worried about Ari, though; the Jouster was thinner, and looked as if he was not sleeping well. But there wasn't much that Vetch could do to help him—

—and besides, if Ari learned about Avatre—

Vetch slept entirely too well, but that was hardly surprising, considering how much work he was doing over the course of the day. He was so used to doing things at the run, that he wasn't sure now if he'd ever be able to do them at a more leisurely pace without feeling that something was wrong.

He sometimes surprised himself by how strong he had gotten, when he found that he had absentmindedly lifted some weight that would have been so far beyond his strength a few moons ago that he would not have considered trying to heft it. He hadn't gotten all that much *taller,* and he certainly wasn't a little barrel of muscle in the way that one or two of the other boys were. He was still wiry and lean, but it seemed that all the good food and hard work had strengthened every single muscle fiber to an amazing degree.

Avatre was also a great deal stronger than he would have guessed; when he loaded her with a sandbag that was nearly his equivalent, she hardly noticed the weight, and there was nothing to tell by looking at her that she *hadn't* been wild-caught like the others. He had to wonder, given how lively and big she was, if giving *tala* to the growing youngsters did more than simply make them easier to handle—if, perhaps, it actually slowed their growth. Certainly Kashet was the biggest male in the compound, nearly as big as any of the females, and he had never gotten *tala.* Avatre was going to be huge; bigger than her mother Coresan, for certain, and females were always bigger than the males.

She was not as vocal as the other youngsters either; they *meeped* all the time, their tone rising in shrillness the closer it got to feeding time. Avatre only gurgled happily when he appeared in the doorway, hissed if something alarmed her, and made no other sounds but a soft chuckling when she settled down for a nap with her head in his lap. So the last of Growing season was spent, with Vetch so busy that he could not have told how many days had passed from storm to weakening storm.

At last, one day, he woke to find that all of the *tala* bushes planted within the compound had blossomed overnight. The air was filled with their peculiar fragrance, sweet, but with a bitter undertone, like myrrh, carried through the corridors by an arid wind that must have begun in the night, coming from off the desert.

The kamiseen——*the Dry just began*—he recognized with a start, as he awoke with the scent in his nostrils, out of an uneasy dream of laboring at Khefti's wells, and heard the wind whining around the corners of the walls of Avatre's pen. He had been here a year!

Although these pampered bushes within the compound always blossomed a day or so before any others, this, and the wind, were the signals that the Dry had officially begun. Unless the sea witches had some new and profoundly powerful magic, there would be no more storms to keep the dragons inside the borders of Tia.

The Commander took the coming of the Dry as his sign as well, and ordered that the Jousters resume their overflights of Altan territory.

He sweetened this order with another: to signal the start of the new patrols, he decreed a two-day festival within the walls of the compound, and provisioned it himself, from his own treasure houses.

Work hardly stopped, of course, but the Jousters were not to go on patrol at all during the festival, and the servants and dragon boys were given leave to partake when their duties were done. Anything in the way of chores that did not immediately pertain to the care of the dragons was suspended for those two days—no leather work, no housekeeping (Palace slaves were brought in to take care of it), even the dragonets were given a reprieve from training (somewhat to Baken's displeasure). The landing court was laid out for the celebration with a bazaar full of merchants selling trash and treasures, and food and drink tents, jugglers, acrobats, musicians, and dancers, games of chance and games of skill.

The Jousters had their own games, out on the training field, in which they were to compete with each other. They made passes at a ring suspended from a thread which they were to catch on their lances, they swooped down to snatch up bags of straw which they were to drop again on a target painted on the ground, they had races for speed only, and races where speed and agility counted equally.

The landing court was set up the day before, and on dawn of the first festival day, the entertainers were in place, the tents set up, and food of every sort was set out temptingly. The festival began at dawn exactly, with a fanfare of trumpets from the musicians, as those servants who had been freed from duties entirely—and the Jousters, of course—were summoned to the celebrations. Vetch was already awake, of course, but the trumpets startled and frightened Avatre, and he began the day feeling annoyed and irritated.

Then Vetch found himself dodging boys who were suddenly as quick as he to get their feeding and cleaning chores done. Never had the corridors been so congested, so early. And worse was to come—so far as *he* was concerned, who had no reason to love this festival. The kitchen court was closed, all the servants, serfs, and slaves getting their own holiday, with everyone expected to go to the festival site to get their meals. Once he was out of the area of the pens—which swiftly emptied, as the dragon boys finished their duties and fled to the delights in the landing court—the place was full of strangers.

Once he sent Ari and Kashet off, he slouched off in a sour mood to get himself breakfast. He didn't even trouble to get a bath—*he* wasn't going to compete with the little popinjays who were using up all the water in order to try and impress some girl or other! No, he would wait until the afternoon, when there was no one to compete with, and he could get a bath without some stranger poking his nose in the door and staring at him.

For his privacy was gone along with the quiet; nobles practically swarmed the place, especially the Jousters' quarters. It was a repetition of the usual scene at the training field, only within the compound itself. The glitter of gold, the gleam of jewels, and the sheen of expensive fabrics made him glower with disgust at the amount of show. There were so many women, young and old, draped in flowers, with perfume cones atop their elaborate wigs, that the air was sometimes chokingly sweet with their scent. He was glad that all visitors had been barred from the pens on account of the dragonets, who were easily startled. The fluttering ribbons, the high, shrill voices, and the idiotic babbling would have left the place in an uproar that would take a week to undo.

The only place where Vetch could get away from the press of the curious and the fawning was in the pens themselves. Not feeling in the least like celebrating when he knew very well that what was being celebrated was the start of more aggression on his own people, he found the pens far more congenial.

So that was where he took himself, after a brief visit to the landing court where he got fried fish—a delicacy that seldom graced the tables of the dragon boys—and some date-stuffed honey pastries for breakfast. The corridors were, by then, thankfully, echoingly, empty.

He wasn't surprised to find Kashet still gone. Ari was a senior Jouster, and at this point his skill and Kashet's were near-legendary. He would, no doubt, be competing in the games for most of the day—or perhaps demonstrating that falling-man-catch trick for an admiring audience, but done with a dummy instead of a man. But as Avatre was finally having a nap, worn out from fretting at the unaccustomed noises, and he didn't want to disturb her, he settled down in Kashet's pen for his meal.

He had just about finished it and was licking the last of the honey from his fingers, when, much to his surprise, a shadow darkened the sun above the pen, and when he looked up, he saw that Ari and Kashet were returning.

He leaped to his feet—*very* glad now that Ari had found him here, and not in the other pen. He sent a brief thanks to the gods for sending Avatre that bout of sleepiness as he waited for Kashet to settle, then trotted over to the great dragon's side.

"Unharness him," Ari said, with shocking brusqueness, as he threw his leg over the saddle and slid down to the ground. "We won't be going back out. The cursed games can go on without us. And I hope they all choke on fish bones."

Vetch stared at him with an open mouth; Ari's face was white, his mouth pinched, and that last had been said with such savagery that Vetch was sure Ari meant every word. *"Why?"* he blurted.

"You don't want to know," Ari replied, and started to stalk off.

But something inside Vetch made him act without thinking; he grabbed the Jouster by the elbow and wouldn't let him go. "Yes, I do," he said firmly, shocking himself with this insane act of audacity, but unable to stop himself. "Or maybe I don't—but if you don't tell someone, you're going to snap, and then where will Kashet be?"

Perhaps nothing other than the stark truth that if *Ari* failed, his dragon would suffer, got through to him. He resisted for just a moment, then his shoulders sagged, and he turned back to Vetch. His eyes were bleak, his mouth twisted, and his skin so pale beneath his tan that it looked as if every bit of blood had been drained from him.

"You don't want to know. And I want *you* to know that I didn't have anything to do with what happened. If I'd been *ordered* to do it, I swear, either I would have stopped it, or I would have flown Kashet into the wilderness instead and never come back—"

That shocked Vetch even more. Ari? Threatening to *desert?* "Tell me—" he just barely managed.

Ari took a deep breath. "There's a date orchard, just over the border. The Altans haven't bothered to even try to protect it for seasons and seasons, I don't know why, I suppose it isn't profitable enough. There's a Tian village of settlers right on the edge of the orchard right across the border; when the dates ripen, they harass the Altans and grab the dates for themselves. It's happened every year, like the Flood. But this year—maybe because of the sea-witch-sent storms, the rightful owners got up some courage, they fought back. I mean, *really* fought; they chased off or wounded most of the Tian settlers who tried to steal their fruit, and even killed two. So yesterday, instead of going out on patrol, one of the senior Jousters decided to teach them a lesson. He led an entire wing of Jousters to the village, where they stooped down on the villagers in their fields, grabbed whoever they could get, carried them up—and dropped them."

Just like on the battlefield, Vetch thought, his heart growing cold inside him. Only—these weren't enemy commanders being smashed on the rocks. These were simple farmers, who'd done nothing except defend what belonged to them, who had only tried to protect what had been stolen year after year, in defiance of laws and treaties.

"They didn't stop until there wasn't anyone left in the open. They—weren't even all men—" Ari got out between clenched teeth. "There were women. And some children."

Dropped, to plummet to the earth and die, smashed like eggs. They hadn't had a chance. Vetch wanted to scream, weep—he couldn't even breathe.

"I didn't find out about it until today. When the target game started." Ari grated, each word wrung from him, each phrase drenched in pain and anguish. "When they started boasting about it—and saying that the *next* time they went out—they should stop long enough to paint a target on the ground for more *sport!*"

Vetch's anger, so long dormant, erupted within him like a volcano, and filled him with such rage, that if Ari's voice hadn't been flooded with outrage and pain that nearly matched his, he'd have gone for the Jouster's throat, just because he was Tian. As it was, he swayed where he stood, going cold and hot by turns, red mists passing between him and the rest of the world as he tried to hold the anger in check.

"I will *not make war on children!*" Ari shrieked—and broke away from Vetch, and ran.

Vetch felt his knees giving, and he dropped to the ground like a stunned bird, his pain finding vent in a howl of his own, and a flood of tears that he could not stop, and did not want to.

* * *

He came to his senses only when his eyes were swollen and gummy, his cheeks raw, and he was so dehydrated from weeping and the *kamiseen* that his lips were cracked and his tongue cleaving to the roof of his mouth. Something snuffled his head—and the back of his neck.

He looked up through blurring eyes, to see that not only was Kashet whuffing at his hair in concern, but *Avatre* had managed to make her way out of her own pen and into this one. She whimpered in sympathy and no little fear, though not of Kashet, apparently, who was dividing his attention between Vetch and her.

"It's—all right—little one," he said thickly, even though it wasn't, but she couldn't know, couldn't understand what had happened, and neither could poor Kashet, who only understood that the center of his universe had screamed and run away, and the other source of his comfort was suffering, too.

He got unsteadily to his feet, and went over to Kashet's trough, and plunged his entire head under the water, keeping it there for as long as his breath held out. He came up with a gasp, and wiped his eyes.

He couldn't help Ari; Ari would have to find his own solution to his conflict. But certainly his absence from the games would not go unnoticed.

What Ari does about it is Ari's business.

He finished unharnessing Kashet with fingers that shook; he tried to comfort the unsettled creature as best he could. Avatre kept butting her head against him, anxiously, and he had to pause frequently to try and give her comfort, too.

What comfort he had to offer, anyway.

Snatches of raucous music came wafting incongruously from the landing court; muffled shouts from the training field where the games were still going on. His stomach turned over. He was glad that he didn't know the names of the Jousters who had participated in the atrocity; he didn't think he'd be able to restrain himself from trying to take some sort of revenge if he knew. Which would gain him nothing, of course; he'd be caught and probably executed, and then what would happen to Avatre?

Poison? Where could he get hold of poison? Or at least, where could he get hold of poison that he could actually use? Nowhere, of course; there were plenty of things in the compound that were poisonous, but they tasted or smelled foul, or were only poisonous in such large quantities as to make their administration impractical. Knives in the dark? He snorted at that. As small as *he* was, even an ambush was out of the question, and he was no trained assassin, to sneak into the Jousters' quarters undetected to slit the throats of sleepers—

—though the vision conjured up by that thought was vastly satisfying.

No—he could do nothing for revenge.

And he could do nothing for his own people either, not as he was now.

But if he and Avatre could get away—

I hold the knowledge of how to raise and train the most superior Jousters and dragons in the world in my head. What would happen to the Tians if every Altan Jouster was as good as Ari and Kashet?

Until this moment, he'd had no real idea of what he was going to do with Avatre besides escape. *Now* he had a goal, a mission. He would go north, to Alta, to Bato, the heart of the ringed capital of the kingdom. He would present himself to the Altan Commander of Dragons. They surely knew about Ari already; tales of such a legendary Jouster would have come not only from their spies, and their Seers, but from their own Jousters who encountered him. Vetch would have the proof, in the form of Avatre, not only of how Ari had trained such a perfect dragon, but that the training could be duplicated.

"It's all right," he reassured the anxious dragon and dragonet, taking a deep, unsteady breath. "Or, at least it will be."

SIXTEEN

I f Vetch had little stomach for the festival before, he had even less now. He could not bear to look at those cheerful faces and wonder which one of them knew what Ari had just revealed. Or worse—which ones had participated in some way.

Or worse still, which ones approved.

He led Avatre back to her pen, and as she settled anxiously back into her wallow, he wondered briefly if he was going to have to begin tethering her there to keep her from following him. But he soon realized, when she displayed no further interest in the entrance, that she had only come looking for him because she had heard his deep distress and had followed the sound of his voice; she had wanted to comfort him as he had so often comforted her.

The very echoes of the celebrations made him feel ill. How could there be a festival going on, how could people be having a good time, when a massacre of innocents had just taken place? How could the people who had *participated* in it be joking about it and planning to make a game of killing the next time? How could they even bear to *imagine* a "next time?" And the part of him that longed for revenge writhed inside, urging him to go *do* something, *now*, while his enemies were all unwary.

Was it weakness, or was it wisdom, that offered the counter to that anger in his soul? *If I do that, I am no better than they are. . . .*

He hoped it was the latter, for the thought held him for a moment.

Suppose he *should* go and do something horrible, not to the Jousters who had been the murderers, but to ordinary folk? That would be *exact* revenge—but that wouldn't be right either. And if he did something horrible, just how much worse would the next Tian atrocity be to "make the Altans pay?"

He saw poor Kashet peering anxiously over the wall, and resolutely turned his heart away from vengeance. Ari's dragon was just as distressed as little Avatre; his rider had acted *quite* out-of-keeping with anything Kashet had come to expect, had run off from the games, been in deep anguish, had not paid any attention to Kashet, and had run off after shouting at Kashet's dragon boy. The bottom was out of Kashet's universe.

Fortunately, Vetch knew what would make things at least partially right again, at least for the dragon and the dragonet.

Because the butchers were going to have a holiday along with everyone else, priest-magicians had come yesterday to create the reverse of the magic that they worked on the dragon sands, taking the heat *away* from a huge room at the back of the butchery, presumably sending that heat into one of the pens. Or—perhaps putting it into one of the cook tents, to keep the hot food there warm without the use of charcoal or other fire. The butchers had worked at a frenzied pace to fill that room, and the result was that two days' worth of dragon fodder was stockpiled in the ensorcelled storage area, a curious place in which it was so cold that one could see one's breath, hanging in the air! This was no new thing, or so Vetch had been told; the Palace kitchens had such a place. But the magic was seldom used outside of the Palace, except for occasions such as this; it was much simpler just to have butchers to deal with the steady stream of carcasses that always came from Temple Row.

The way to soothe a dragon's heart ran through his belly. Vetch went to get Kashet's favorite treats.

He brought some for Avatre, too, the hearts of smaller beasts than cattle. Although it was not feeding time, Kashet always had room for beef hearts, and his favorite food relaxed and comforted him. When he finished his snack, he looked up at the sun speculatively, and yawned—then waded out into his wallow, and instead of burying himself as he did during the winter rains, he spread himself out to bask in the hot sun, with his wings stretched to their fullest extent.

This was a contented dragon, and Vetch knew it was safe to leave him.

He returned to Avatre, and introduced *her* to the delights of Kashet's favorite. She was dubious at first, but one taste convinced her. Rather than relaxing her, though, the snack energized her, and she began exercising her wings, flapping hard and making little jumps into the air.

Unlike birds, who had to grow feathers *and* skin and bone before they could fly, dragons only had to grow enough skin and bone—the bone forming the support, the skin forming the wing surface. And unlike birds, whose feathers were fragile while they were growing, dragonets began hopping and flapping fairly early in their development. But they hovered far better than most birds could, and Vetch knew, from watching the older dragonets, that at some point Avatre would be able to hover for a few moments in place, even with extra weight on her back. When *that* happened, he would know that the moment for first flight was close.

He watched her closely, and realized that the day was not far off. It was time to keep the harness on her during daylight hours, except when he was giving her a bath. And it was time to start edging the weight she was carrying upward, until it was heavier than he was.

That way, when she actually made that first flight, she would have built up her strength to carry more than Vetch, and as a consequence, she should be able to go higher and farther than a dragonet of similar age. He had to plan on pursuit; he hoped it would not come until he and Avatre were out of sight, and those who came looking for him would cast their nets far short of where he and she eventually had to come to ground. With luck, pursuers would assume they had no more strength and endurance than the average dragonet at first flight, and as a consequence, would never guess how far they *could* go.

The best way to strengthen her was through play, so until she grew tired and wanted another nap, he resolutely closed his ears to the unwelcome noise of celebration and chased her around the pen until she tired of that, then let her chase *him*. The play was good for him, too—though he felt guilty at *playing* when he knew what he knew. . . .

But Avatre didn't know, and wouldn't understand if she knew. There was no reason to deprive her of the fun and exercise she needed.

Like a puppy or a kitten, her energy seemed boundless right up until the point where she suddenly tired, flopped down where she stood, and was instantly asleep. At that point, he left the pens for what (he had already decided) would be his last foray out to the landing court until the festival was over.

He brought a clean barrow with him, and wandered among the food tents, picking out items that would not need to be eaten warm. No one questioned him, oddly enough. Perhaps they assumed he had been sent to get provisions for several of the other boys over at the games. When he had enough to hold him for two days, he returned to the pens, and went straight to the butchery, stashing his provisions in that cold room. There he would not need to worry about them spoiling—and he would not have to venture among the celebrants in order to eat.

Which was just as well, because to do so would have put the temptation to wreak anonymous harm too near to resist. It had come very, very close, as he had made his way around all of that unguarded food. . . .

The easiest, and safest route to revenge *would* be at the festival, through the medium of poison. If the droppings of dragons burned the skin, what would they do if ground as fine as flour and stirred into food? Put into a stew heavily flavored with pepper, onion, and garlic, it probably wouldn't even be tasted until too late.

Ari was far away from the festival—and he could be certain that the only people who ate the poison would be those from within the Jousters' compound.

But what if I poisoned Baken by accident? Or Haraket? Or one of the other serfs? That was the problem with such a plan; he *knew* the people who might be hurt, and there was no way to strike at the perpetrators without knowing who they really were. And if he went after them specifically, he couldn't act anonymously. It all got very complicated, and he could entirely sympathize with Ari's anguished cry of *I do not make war on children!*

And he couldn't help remembering another plaint of Ari's. *Haraket says I think too much.*

Maybe that was Vetch's problem, too. People who didn't think didn't seem to have any complicated and inconvenient problems of conscience.

Kashet had gotten a full holiday out of it, after all; Ari did not return to the dragon pens until after the celebration was over. And when he did, he was close-mouthed and grim. Vetch wondered where he had been all that time; he hadn't been in his quarters when Vetch went to look, and Kashet had missed him sorely.

He appeared, as usual, one of the first Jousters to come for his dragon on the morning after the festival. What was *not* usual was that he was wearing his helmet, rather than carrying it. It was difficult to see his face, impossible to make out his expression, but he didn't say anything at all as he inspected the harness and lance. Vetch didn't mind that—how could he? He knew Ari, and knew what it was like to have no recourse to the world's hurt but to retreat from it, put on a mask, hide anguish within. He couldn't blame Ari at all for retreating even (or especially?) from him. But what did bother him was that Kashet had so clearly missed those evening visits these past two nights, and Vetch had a good idea that the reason Ari had not come was because of *his* presence in Kashet's pen.

What was more, he would be willing to hazard that Ari was in desperate need of the silent comfort of his dragon, too. As long as Ari thought he had to avoid Vetch, he wouldn't come to Kashet. And he wouldn't ask Vetch to absent himself either. It was up to Vetch to give Ari a way around the problem that salvaged his self-esteem.

So before Ari could mount up and fly off on patrol that first morning after the festival, Vetch caught his Jouster's arm long enough to make Ari pause for a moment, his foot on Kashet's shoulder.

"Sir, Baken wants me to sleep in the pen of one of the dragonets," he lied. "He doesn't want just anyone, he wants someone who's used to it, so that the dragonet isn't startled by someone who doesn't know how to act around them in the dark. It's the one they put in next to Kashet, so I'll still be *here* if Kashet needs me. He thinks she's so young that she'll tame amazingly if she accepts me as a kind of nest mate."

"The little scarlet, over there?" Ari replied, with a tilt of his head, as he considered the request for a moment. "Well, I suppose I've no objection. I wanted you sleeping in here initially both to keep Kashet company and to keep you out of the reach of the other boys so they couldn't easily torment you—but Kashet will be able to scent you over the wall, you *will* be here if he calls out, and you'll still be out of reach of the other boys." He paused a moment. "Yes, I've no objection at all. Go ahead and move your gear."

"Thank you—" Vetch began, but Ari had already mounted, and before he could say more than that, Kashet was in the air.

Huh. He thought that, under that veneer of coolness, he'd sensed relief in Ari's voice. Well, now he had every excuse to be with Avatre between sunset and sunrise, which was a help to him, too. This wasn't entirely bad; in all of the wretchedness he and Ari were feeling, there was one small grain of good, for at least he wouldn't have to wake up before first light to be in Kashet's pen by the time the sun crested the horizon anymore.

And hopefully, Kashet would get his Jouster's attentions again. No matter *what* he felt, or Ari, the poor dragon shouldn't have to suffer. How could Kashet understand what was wrong? All he knew was that something was the matter, and that he was lonely.

That night, as he lay along Avatre's side, waiting for sleep, he thought he heard Ari's footsteps outside in the corridor—and a few moments later, he definitely heard the Jouster's voice murmuring on the other side of the wall, though he couldn't make out the words. He sighed, and felt some tension move out of him. That was it; either Ari was embarrassed at having betrayed his feelings to a mere serf and dragon boy, or he was still so ashamed of what had been done to that Altan village that he found it difficult to face Vetch, another Altan. Or probably it was even more complicated than that, but whatever was wrong, it *had* been Vetch's presence that was keeping the Jouster from his nightly visits to the dragon.

Vetch certainly found it hard to face Ari. No matter what Ari had *said*, the fact remained that he might well be in the next party ordered to "pacify" an Altan village in the same way. It was possible that, despite his anguished outburst, Ari *would* countenance such an atrocity if only by passive silence. Vetch didn't *think* he would—

But he couldn't be sure.

How much was Ari bound to his duty? How far did loyalty to orders go? What would really happen when *he* was caught between obedience and conscience?

And Vetch was caught on the horns of a dilemma, because if that happened, on one hand he didn't want to *know* what Ari's ultimate decision about obeying such an order would be, but on the other—

Knowing the truth about someone was important.

But having your illusions smashed was painful.

He couldn't pretend that nothing had happened if Ari *did* simply go along with more horrors.

But losing what you thought was a friendship—even if it was only an odd sort of friendship—was more painful still.

But did he want to maintain it when it was based on false perceptions? *He* didn't know what decisions Ari had come to, all by himself, over the past two days. Ari was clearly not going to tell him either. Except that he was going out on his usual patrol—

—a patrol intended to keep innocent Tian farmers and their crops safe—

—but at what cost?

He had to concentrate on what he *could* affect, or he would go mad.

And maybe that's how Ari feels.

At least now Kashet wasn't being deprived of Ari's attentions. That was something, anyway. It wasn't enough for Kashet to "just" get general petting and attention—a certain amount of that petting and attention had to come from *his* person, the one he had bonded to from the moment of hatching. And if the only way that Kashet could get that attention was for Vetch to absent himself into the next pen—well, that was all right. Curious, though, that Ari had known about Avatre, even identified her by her color. He wouldn't have thought that Ari'd had time to notice.

I wonder if Ari guesses about Avatre— he thought, suddenly, alarm making him sit straight up in the darkness. Avatre murmured her objections to his movement, and he lay back down again, mind racing, as he went over every question or comment that Ari had made in the last few days, trying to divine whether there was a clue in what he'd said, some hint that Ari was probing, trying to discover if Vetch had followed in the Jouster's footsteps and hatched his own dragonet. *Ah, don't be stupid*, he thought at last, after he'd been over every detail that he could remember at least twice. As busy as the Jouster had been, how could Ari possibly guess? *He just saw Avatre over the wall when he came in at some point. He hasn't said a word about her, and he hasn't caught me here with her. How could he guess that she's my hatchling?*

Still, it would be a good idea to take extra care from here on in. Ari saw more than most, and was disconcertingly good at putting facts together into a whole. Vetch filed that in the back of his mind, for caution was now certainly the order of the day.

But as time went on, the Dry progressed, and the days got hotter and hotter, Ari said nothing. Vetch elected not to return to sleeping in Kashet's pen, and Ari said nothing about that either. The fact was, Ari wasn't talking about much of anything, not to him, not to Haraket—but he was doing *something*. What, Vetch couldn't guess, but he was spending every waking moment when he was not in the air or with Kashet off somewhere.

That was all to the good. It was keeping the one person who was likeliest to guess just what the "little scarlet in the next pen" was far away from the scene.

He was increasingly afraid of leaving Avatre alone, lest she make that first flight in his absence. He rushed through the chores that took him away from the pens. Heart in mouth, he listened all the time for some sign she had been discovered to be something other than one of the "official" dragonets, or worse, that she had made her flight without him.

And yet, though that would be "worse" for him, it was not necessarily so for her. At least she would be free, even if he were not.

He was so close to his goal, and yet, at any moment, the prize could be snatched away from him.

And for the first time since his father had been killed, he prayed, not only to the Altan gods, but to any god that would listen, that she *not* be discovered and taken from him—or that, if she was discovered, at least let it be that she escaped into the free skies—

Even if *he* could not.

And perhaps the gods, aloof in the Land Beyond the Horizon, actually listened to him.

Because the moment of discovery—and the moment of first flight—both came at the same moment, and it was when he was with her.

He was, in fact, sitting on her back—in a purloined saddle. That saddle was one of the small ones in the compound, made precisely for dragonets, and one that he had been eying for days, waiting for the dragonet who was using it to outgrow it. He had his legs braced in the harness, his hand locked into the hand brace at the top of the saddle, the guide straps, which she had learned to obey beautifully, tied to the brace, while she made little bounds up and down the sands of her pen, flapping her wings enthusiastically the whole time. *He* had come to enjoy these wild rides, even though he'd been terrified at first, for unlike the dragonets that he had ridden for Baken, *she* was not tethered. He remembered, all too well, his very first ride a-dragonback, face-down over the front of Ari's saddle. He'd sworn then that he would never, ever ride on a dragon again, but that had been before Avatre. Now—well, he was guiding the dragon, the exhilaration had overcome the terror and now he was able to join in the sense of *fun* she had in these exercises.

He thought that she was building up to that burst that would take her truly up into the air, but he wasn't actually *expecting* anything other than her first hover. She was right in the middle of her pen, about to make a really big bound; he thought that this might be the moment when she really went airborne with him, rather than just jumping about with wing-assistance, and he was braced for it—

When a wild shout from the doorway of the pen startled them both.

"Hoi!" shouted one of the older dragon boys, staring at them. *He* knew Vetch, he knew very well that Vetch wasn't assigned to a dragonet, and he knew that Vetch should not have been sitting in the saddle on an untethered dragonet's back. He didn't know

what Vetch was up to, but one thing he did know. It wasn't what Vetch was supposed to be doing.

"Haraket!" he shouted. *"Haraket! Come quick!"*

Vetch didn't even think what to do; he just reacted, by punching Avatre in the shoulders with his heels. *She,* already startled and alarmed by the shout, and even more so by a strange human in her pen, a thing she had never seen before, also just reacted—by leaping, not jumping; leaping for the sky, eyes focused up, neck outstretched, and wings working purposefully. She was frightened now, truly frightened, and she wanted away before any more people shouted at her and jammed their heels into her! *One* wing flap. *Two.*

She was off the ground, with *him* still on her back. Not a hover, this; no, it was the first wing beats of real flight.

"Dragonets are often startled into their first flights," he heard Ari's voice in memory. *"They get very nervy about the time they're about to take that big leap. Maybe it's the gods' way of making sure they get off the ground that first time, because if nothing startled them into flying, they'd be too afraid to try. . . ."*

She was making good, strong wing beats now, not flaps. And she wasn't just fleeing, she was climbing, with determination. *She* wasn't afraid to fly, not Avatre! She surged upward in that way he recalled from riding Kashet, a jerky, lunging motion, throwing him back each time she made another wing beat, until he bent over the saddle, crouching, to get himself in balance with what she was doing. He was just the rider now; Avatre was the one in control. All he could do was to hold on and try not to hamper her.

She was above the walls. Then *higher* than the walls—

There was more shouting down below; he clutched at the harness in sudden fear—

He heard Haraket's voice; he heard the voices of other men, loud, excited, angry, down below and behind him; he looked back and saw a crowd of men in Avatre's pen, Haraket at their center, gesturing and shouting—but not at him.

That sent a chill down his back.

They weren't calling his name.

Instead of ordering him back, demanding he return then and there, as they would have been if they thought this flight was purely accidental, they were shouting at each other, issuing confusing and probably contradictory orders. But none of those orders was shouted at *him*.

That was when he knew he was in deep trouble.

They knew what this was about; they *knew*—knew he'd "stolen" a dragonet, though they didn't yet know it wasn't one of the new ones. They knew that this wasn't just the result of a wager or a boyish prank.

They understood that he was going to try to escape, that he intended to fly off on Avatre in order to do so.

And they weren't going to let him get away. He wasn't a dragon boy now; he was an Altan enemy, stealing a precious dragonet.

Avatre craned her neck around and looked down at the waving, yelling humans below her as she beat her wings down in a stroke more powerful than the last had been. Then she glanced back at him, her eyes pinning with alarm; she seemed to understand the fear in him, and redoubled her efforts, which were showing more skill with every passing second. For the first time, Vetch was glad, *glad* that he was such a skinny weed. He was lighter than the sandbags he'd been training her with, and she was having no trouble carrying him. He felt her deep, easy breathing under his legs; he felt powerful muscles under his hands driving her upward. The compound spun away under him; she caught sight of the hills in the east, and they must have awakened some deep instinct in her, for she drove for them.

Now she was over the city, wings pumping furiously as she continued to seek for height and the winds above. The *kamiseen* would aid her in this direction; it drove for those same eastern hills, giving her speed she could never have reached on her own. He clung on to her back more by instinct than skill, crouching down over her neck, trying to move with her. He told himself not to look down.

He couldn't help it, though; as she leveled out and stretched her wings in a gliding stroke, he looked down and saw only the broad, flat, gray-green expanse of the Great Mother River below, a boat like a child's toy being towed against the current, going upriver, pulled by a team of oxen seemingly as small as the ones in his father's funerary shrine.

The shrine—

Too late to think of that, too late to consider all the things that he'd hoped to take with him. If they escaped, he would have to survive and keep them both alive with what he had with him.

If they escaped.

They *had* to.

Then they were over the fields, once green, now brown in the dry, with here and there a small square of dusty green still being irrigated by hand to provide some special crop. Vegetables, or perhaps even *tala*.

Tala—for dragons.

The only way anyone would be able to catch him would be on a dragon.

How many Jousters had been in the compound? How many could get their dragons saddled and into the air quickly? How many were just back from a patrol, or about to leave on one? Ari wasn't back yet, but he'd been due out of the north at any moment. There were others who had surely beaten him back in; Ari was generally the first to leave and the last to return.

That alone might save him; this was the *end* of a patrol, not the beginning, and dragons were coming in tired and hungry. It might be hard to get them into the air, and they'd be irritated, sluggish, and reluctant to obey.

But he had to look back over his shoulder and saw behind him what he'd feared to see—the bright vees of color against the hard blue of the sky—dragons and Jousters in pursuit. Tiny in the distance, but there were several of them who'd managed to get their mounts airborne; experienced fliers, experienced riders.

If they caught him—they would never let him keep Avatre. They'd never let him near another dragon again, probably, even if my some miracle he convinced them that this *had* all been an accident. . . .

If he claimed that, could he make them believe him? But then, how would he explain purloining the egg and hatching her? That he was raising her for Ari, as a surprise?

Would anyone believe a tale that tall?

Even if they did, how could that make any difference? They'd still take Avatre from him!

Nothing mattered against the enormity of losing Avatre.

He would rather die than give her up. She was everything to him now; without her, it wouldn't matter what they did to him.

He made up his mind at that moment that if they caught him, if they started to force them down, he would jump. Better dead than lose the only thing he loved, the only family he had now. The harness and saddle were not of such tough stuff that she could not eventually get them off; without tending, the leather would quickly dry out and become brittle in the sun. Within weeks, at most, the last pieces would fall off her.

He would never let them take her. He would rather die and set her free.

Sobs welled up in his throat, he choked them down. His heart felt as tight as if there were copper bands around it, and he prayed wordlessly. Surely the gods had not brought him this far only to snatch everything away from him!

He looked back again; there were three dragons in pursuit of him now, for all the rest had dropped out of the race. But these three were obeying their Jousters, and he thought they looked a little nearer, though not near enough to tell who they were. Just the colors; a scarlet, a green, and a blue.

He looked down; they were over the desert, which undulated beneath them in waves of pale sand, broken by rocky outcrops.

The breath of the desert, hot, dusty, and so arid it parched his lips, wafted up to them. He bent over Avatre's neck, and shouted encouragement to her.

He'd had no idea where to go, but she, guided by instinct alone, was heading for the same hills that her mother had sought at the end of the mating flight. Those hills were riddled with caves and rich with game—and they marked the boundary of the lands that could truly be called "Tian." Out there, although Tia claimed the earth, it really belonged to the dragons and the wild, wandering tribesmen of the Baydu, the Blue People, the Veiled Ones who called no man "king." If they could reach the hills, they could hide there. They could stay under cover until the hunters had given up.

But the hills were a long way away, and there were three trained dragons in pursuit. He crouched lower over Avatre's neck, and willed his own strength into her. His long hair whipped into his face; he ignored it, and tried to wish himself lighter than he already was.

When they were halfway between the hills and the Great Mother River, he looked back again. Avatre was still flying strongly, showing no signs of tiring. And now there were only two dragons following. One, the scarlet, had dropped down and was gliding behind the other two, making a long, slow turn to return to the compound.

His heart leaped. One gone—could they outdistance the other two?

"Go, my love, my beauty!" he shouted at Avatre's head. "Go! We are small and light as down; ride the wind, my heart! Take us to freedom!"

He thought she responded to his encouragement with a little more power.

One gone—two to go.

But they were two Jousters, and he was only a dragon boy on First Flight. They had strength and experience on their side; all he had was hope and heart, and the valor of a very young dragonet.

He looked down again; the sand was interrupted by more and larger outcroppings of rock. They were getting closer to the hills. He redoubled his prayers.

With every wing beat, they drew nearer to escape. When they reached the hills, he looked back again.

One of the two remaining dragons had turned back!

But the third was still in hot pursuit, and was closing the gap between them.

And now he could see, with pitiless clarity, that the third was Kashet.

His heart felt as if it was being squeezed, and for a moment, he was blinded by tears. But he leaned over her neck again and begged Avatre to fly faster, harder—

She heard him, and he felt her trying to do as he asked. They topped the first set of hills—

But below them he saw the ground of the second rising to meet them, closer than it should have been—

She was losing relative height and *real* height as well. He felt her muscles beginning to tremble, and knew then that she was running out of strength and endurance.

And a shadow passed over them, between them and the sun, the superior position for a Jouster to force another dragon to earth.

He knew without looking up that it was Kashet.

It was over.

Ari had caught them, and he would force them down, take them both captive. The teams of trainers and soldiers that Haraket had surely sent after them would come and take them back, bound and chained.

They would take Avatre away from him, if he allowed that to happen. Avatre was at the end of her strength, and there was nothing more that she could give him.

It was time to give *her* a gift—her freedom.

And with a sob, he pulled his legs free of the harness, he leaned down over her neck.

"Good-bye, beloved, my light, my love," he murmured to her. He squeezed his eyes tight; he couldn't look at the ground. But this was the only way. Better this, better lose life, than lose everything that made life worth having.

Let me wander as a hungry ghost. Better that, than a slave without her.

He took a long, last, deep breath.

Then he deliberately overbalanced, and let go.

It was horrible.

He screamed in utter terror as he fell, tumbling over and over in a macabre parody of an acrobat. The screaming just burst out of his mouth without any thought. He waited for the scream and the horror to end in a terrible blow, and blackness.

Something hard struck him in the stomach instead, knocking what was left of his breath out of him and ending his scream in a gasp. He slid face-down along something hard and smooth and hot—then impacted a second time, and felt a strong arm grab him around his waist.

And he screamed again, this time in thwarted rage and heartbreak, as he realized that Ari and Kashet had plucked him out of the sky, as they had saved Reaten. Only he didn't *want* to be saved, and they had rescued him only to haul him back to a wretched existence not worth the living!

He screamed and tried to fight, but he was lying in a difficult position, he could only strike at Kashet. Ari was three times his size and double his strength, and was not about to let him land a blow. He cursed the Jouster in every way he could think of, tears blinding him, as he changed his tactics and tried to squirm out of Ari's grip to resume the plunge to death that they had interrupted.

That was just about as successful as trying to fight them.

He felt Kashet sideslipping and losing height quickly; his stomach lurched with the renewed sense of falling, but he knew that this "fall" would not end in blessed blackness, but in captivity, and he howled his anguish.

Avatre cried out above him—he'd never heard her cry before,

it sounded like a hawk—and she followed them down, floundering wearily through the air, as Ari and Kashet brought him down to the earth. As they spiraled down into a little valley, he just gave up and went limp. *He* was crying, uncontrollably, sobbing with rage and thwarted hope, and the death of everything he had hoped for. He couldn't see, blinded by the tears as they landed, as Ari slid off first, then pulled him down to the ground—

—and held him while he wept.

He wanted to fight, but all the fight was out of him. There was nothing, literally nothing left but grief and hopelessness. He was all alone, and there was nothing left to him but a bleak future of pain and emptiness.

Or so he thought—until Ari took his shoulders and gave him a good hard shake, stopping his hysterical sobs for just an instant.

And that moment was all that Ari needed. *"Stop it!"* the Jouster commanded into the hot silence. "You don't really think I'm going to take you back, do you?"

For a moment, the words made no sense. Then when he *did* get the sense of them, he was so shocked that all he could do was stare, eyes still streaming, throat still choked on a sob.

"I have no intention of bringing you back," Ari repeated, wearily. "Especially not after seeing you try and kill yourself to keep from being caught. I may be a monster, but at least I'm not that sort of monster."

He might have said more, but just then Avatre came charging toward them, knocking Ari aside with her head, and clumsily putting herself between the Jouster and Vetch, hissing defiance. Ari put up both his hands, placatingly, but laughing all the same, as Vetch instinctively threw his arms around her neck.

"There. How can I possibly take you back? She'd only come and carry you off again, and probably tear the rest of us to shreds doing it!" he chuckled.

Vetch held his arms tight around her neck, to steady himself as well as to keep her from some clumsy attempt to attack Ari. He still couldn't believe what he'd just heard.

He's not taking us back? How can he not take us back? Isn't it his duty?

But it was Ari, who had never told Vetch a lie—

Then Kashet, full of dignity and twice the size of Avatre, interposed himself between the dragonet and his Jouster, looking down at her with an expression of weary condescension. Avatre, who had never seen another dragon but Kashet except as a head over a wall, or a shape in the sky overhead, just hissed at the bigger dragon, defying him along with his Jouster.

"Very brave," Ari chuckled. "I hardly think I need to worry about you encountering trouble. She'll certainly protect you from anything and everything, or die trying. And at the moment, there isn't much that will be able to take her on except humans."

Vetch swallowed. Hard. "You're—" he began.

"I am *not* taking you back. I never intended to," Ari replied. That was when Vetch's legs failed him, and he sat down hard on the ground.

Avatre stood over him, making it very clear that she was not going to allow anyone or anything near him.

The Jouster looked at both of them for a long moment, then sighed, shaking his head. "Look," he said. "We're in the middle of the Dry, practically midday, and it's damned hot out here in the sun." He beckoned. "If you can get up, follow us."

Vetch struggled to his feet. Ari and Kashet were already halfway down the slope, heading for the dry streambed that cut down the wadi. Evidently, he knew where he was going, and Vetch took hold of Avatre's harness and followed behind. Avatre resisted at first, not wanting to follow the creature that had threatened Vetch, but at his insistence, she reluctantly and suspiciously plodded after Kashet.

Ari turned down a crack in the earth so narrow that Kashet's folded wings brushed both sides of the wind- and water-sculpted passage. The sun might be right overhead, but here, everything was still in shadow, and it was a lot cooler. It was deep, too; they might have been going down one of the corridors between the pens, except that the farther they went, the taller the "walls" became.

The sandstone was carved in weird, smooth, many-layered curves that twisted and turned without any rhyme or reason. This tormented, contorted passage was far wider at the bottom than it was at the top; above them, the crack couldn't be wider than a two feet or so, while down below Kashet was able to squeeze along without too much difficulty. The floor was a thin layer of sand over a harder rock; Vetch felt it under the hard soles of his bare feet. It was strangely beautiful here, and completely without the mark of man on it.

Then, with no warning, the walls opened up into a sort of pocket about the size of a dragon pen, again, with only a small opening to the sky overhead. The rock of the ceiling framed the irregular oblong of turquoise sky like a gold mounting surrounding a gem. At the far end of the pocket was a patch of green where sun must fall during some part of the day—a twisted, ancient tree, a few flourishing bushes, some grasses—all surrounding a tiny pool of water fed by a mere drip of a spring that trickled down the side of the rock through that hole above.

Ari bent and drank a palmful; he gestured to Vetch to come up beside him. With his tongue cleaving to the roof of his mouth and his eyes as dry as sand, and sore with weeping, Vetch didn't have to be asked twice.

But first, he let Avatre drink her fill.

She drank down the basin to about half its depth, and only when she was satisfied did he drink, and take a handful of water to carefully wash his eyes.

Ari watched him with tired satisfaction; Kashet with benevolence.

When he had drunk and cleared his eyes, Vetch looked up at the Jouster with one question in his mind. He felt such a whirlwind of contradictory emotions that he literally shook with them—relief, anger, gratitude, defiance, hope, disbelief—

He distilled it all down to one word.

"Why?" he demanded.

Ari sighed, and looked around for a place to sit, choosing eventually a smooth outcropping wind-sculpted into a shape vaguely like a toad. He sat down on its flat top, and Kashet folded his own legs underneath him.

"That's two questions, I think. Or, perhaps three. Why did I save you, why did I follow you, and why did I do so, intending to help you make your escape?"

Vetch nodded; his legs were still shaking, his knees still weak, so he followed Ari's example, except that since there was no outcropping to sit on, he sat down on the ground.

"I was just coming in as *you* took off," the Jouster said meditatively. "I'd had my suspicions about that little scarlet dragonet ever since you asked to sleep in her pen, by the way. How did you manage to purloin her away from Baken?"

Vetch managed a shaky smile of triumph. "I didn't," he said proudly. "I hatched her from Coresan's first egg, just like you did with Kashet."

"Great Haras!" Ari exploded, looking astonished and delighted at the same time. "No *wonder* she follows you like a puppy! Is that why you volunteered to take Coresan in the first place? And she's been in the pen next to Kashet all this time?"

He nodded, and smiled. At least he had managed to deceive Ari in *that* much! That was no mean feat.

"By Sheshet's belly! I can scarcely believe it! And you tended and hatched the egg *and* tended Kashet *and* Coresan? When did you *sleep?"* the Jouster asked incredulously, then waved off the answer, while Avatre gave a huge sigh and flopped down beside Vetch. "What do you call her?"

"Avatre," he said proudly, and she raised her head at the sound of her name.

"Fire of the dawn—" Ari smiled at the dragonet. "Well . . . to continue, we were coming in to land after our patrol; Haraket waved us off, after another couple of Jousters, and pretty soon it was clear enough why we were in pursuit. I recognized you, of course, and the little scarlet, and at first I thought this was some sort of accident, that you'd been exercising her for Baken and she'd broken the tether or something. But by the time we were halfway across the desert, it was clear enough to me that it was no accident, and that you were trying to escape with her." He took a deep breath, and shook his head. "What was going to happen when you were caught—well, it was pretty obvious, too. So when the second rider dropped out of the chase, I kept it up; I'd already decided to help you, but I wasn't sure yet what I was going to do. I figured I'd force you two to ground and work that out once I got you down. I didn't expect you to do what you did."

He leveled an accusatory look at Vetch. Vetch matched him with defiance. "I would rather die than lose her," he said, quietly. "She's all that I have."

"You made that abundantly clear," Ari said dryly. "And you nearly turned my hair white when you rolled over her shoulder like that. I wasn't sure we could catch you."

Vetch remained silent. Ari examined him closely; Vetch put his arm over Avatre's shoulder, and wondered what, if anything, Ari saw in his expression.

"Well, no one is going to find us down here," Ari said at last. "You can overfly this place as much as you like and you'll never spot it. I only found it by accident because I was following a dragonet one day and I couldn't work out why he had dived into a crack in the hill. So, we have time enough to work out what we're going to do."

"We?" Vetch repeated, incredulously.

"Yes," Ari replied, settling back against the rock. "We. Let's start with where you think you're going to go from here."

SEVENTEEN

WITH those words, Vetch wondered wildly if Ari was going to come *with* him, and a strange, wild hope rose within him. It was not just that it would be so much *easier* to make his way northward with Ari—no, it was that he would not lose his friend—-

But Ari's next question dashed that thought, and that hope, to the ground and broke them.

"First of all, where are you going?" Ari asked. "To the—ah—'Great Devil, Alta,' I presume?"

Ah. Of course. He can't go with us to Alta; he wouldn't be welcomed, he'd be killed. So unless Ari had a different destination in mind for both of them, though what that could be, Vetch had no clue, Ari would not be making an escape along with Vetch.

And Vetch felt horribly trapped by the question. Once Ari knew that Alta was his final destination, surely now Ari would stop him—

But Ari only shrugged, and answered his own question, as if it had been entirely rhetorical. "Of course you are; what else is there for you? They'll welcome you, certainly—an escaped serf with a dragonet bonded to him—I can guarantee that they'll welcome you. Now, you'll probably have to prove that Avatre won't fly for anyone else, because they'll assume she's like every other dragonet and try to take her from you, but I don't believe you'll have any trouble convincing them that the two of you come only as a pairing."

Vetch shrugged, helplessly, but underneath it, he was dismayed, because he hadn't considered *that* possibility!

"Don't worry too much about that, Vetch," Ari said, in a kindly tone. "You're both still youngsters. Now, if she was Kashet's size, they'd make more of an effort to take her, but as it stands, they'll know very well she won't be useful to them as a fighting dragon for another couple of years, and by then—well, so will you."

Unless I can be useful to them in another way altogether, Vetch thought somberly. Still, Ari was right; they probably wouldn't fight too hard over a dragonet. And if the Altan Jousters were as reactionary as the Tian ones were, well, it would probably take years to convince them that *hatching* dragons made more sense than *catching* dragons, anyway. . . .

"So, it's Alta. Unless you plan to wander with your dragon in the wilderness—" Ari shook his head. "Take it as read, don't even consider that option. I do not advise that course at all, because sooner or later one of us will run across you, and you can't expect to outrun us twice."

Vetch nodded, knowing that Ari probably was a better judge of that than he was, given his years of experience.

But I'd try it anyway, if he'd come with us. . . .

"First things first," Ari continued briskly. "Do you even know how to get across the Border from here without following the Great Mother River?"

Vetch could only shake his head.

"Have you provisions? Clothing? Tools?" Ari persisted. "What were you going to eat? What were you going to feed her?"

"I thought we'd hunt," Vetch said weakly. Ari shook his head ruefully.

"Mind, since I know you must have had a lot of experience in foraging for yourself, you aren't as ill-prepared to fend for yourselves as some of those idiot boys back at the compound," he said graciously. "And I know you weren't exactly thinking that this would be First Flight when you got on her back this morning, so how could you be prepared? Still—no, this is no way to send you off. You need a great deal more than you've got." He stood up. "You two stay here, and don't move from this place. I need to make some arrangements, and neither of you are going to be able to help in the least."

"Arrangements?" he asked weakly.

"Arrangements . . . and one is going to have to be immediate." Ari glanced over at Vetch's exhausted dragonet. "First thing of all, we need to do something about little Avatre—she's expended a lot of energy, and when she gets over being too tired to move, she'll be hungry."

He stood up; Kashet took that as a signal, and got to his feet. *"Don't move,"* Ari repeated, as he led Kashet out down that twisting passage.

Vetch had known the first time that Ari said "stay here" that his knees were too shaky to hold him. *As if I could move. . . .* he thought ruefully.

Then Vetch and Avatre were alone. He looked down at her, and saw that she was asleep in the pool of sunlight that came down through the hole in the ceiling. He slid to the ground and lay down beside her, feeling absolutely drained to the point of numbness. He couldn't even think properly, and the silence down here was so profound that it seemed to echo in his head. The hills broke up the *kamiseen* winds, so that there was nothing down in this crevice, not even that omnipresent whine. Even that trickle of water slid over the rock without making a sound.

It was never silent in the compound; it had never been silent on the farm. He found it a novel experience, and closed his eyes, trying to pick out anything besides his own breathing and Avatre's. And in listening to the silence—silence of a quality that he had never before experienced—he fell asleep without having any intention of doing anything of the kind.

He woke to a strange, grating, dragging noise; he shoved himself upright in alarm, as Avatre beside him shot her head up, eyes pinning.

But it was Ari who emerged into the pocket, followed by Kashet—who was wearing only the collar of his harness *as* a harness, as the rest of the straps had been unbuckled and reassembled into a peculiar sort of drag arrangement. That was the scraping sound—Kashet dragging three very dead goats underneath him.

"It's not Jousting fare, but if she's hungry—" Ari began, as he unbuckled the first and dragged it into the pocket, leaving it on the ground while he went to get the next.

He didn't get a chance to finish that statement, for Avatre pounced on the carcass and began tearing into it as if she ate whole wild game every day.

"Evidently," he chuckled, "she's hungry."

Vetch blinked, for there wasn't a mark on any of the three bodies. "How did you—"

Ari laughed, and took off his belt—which wasn't a belt at all, but a sling.

"Maybe other people have trouble using missile weapons on dragonback," he said, with something as close to a smug look as Ari ever got, "but I don't. Then again, our Noble Warriors do think that a sling is beneath them to use. . . ."

"The more fools, they," Vetch replied, with scorn.

Ari smiled. "And I strongly suggest that if you haven't already got skill with a sling, you acquire it. Well, that takes care of your little girl. Are *you* starving?"

He shook his head; curiously, he wasn't even hungry. Then again, his stomach was still roiling from all he'd been through and the gamut of emotional states he'd run.

"That's just as well; wild goat broiled on a knifetip over a scrap of fire bears a close family resemblance to burned sandal, and that's all I have to offer you," Ari told him, with a raised eyebrow, inviting his reaction.

Vetch blinked at him for a moment, then managed a smile.

"You just let her eat and doze in the sun; *you* drink plenty of water, and wait for us to get back," Ari ordered. "Rest, if you can, because it will be the last uninterrupted rest you'll get for a long while. Your journey is going to be long and hard, even with my help."

Vetch couldn't imagine what Ari was going to do, but he nodded, and helped Ari drag the corpses of the other two goats over to Avatre, who was nearly finished with the first.

Once again, Ari and Kashet vanished down that tall crack in the earth. Avatre was busy with her meal—the first she'd ever eaten that hadn't been cut up neatly for her, but she was doing perfectly well, and didn't need *his* help. Evidently there would be no need for a "how to eat whole wild goat" lesson.

Vetch lay back down on the ground to watch her with his back against the crevice wall, and pillowed his head on his arms for just a moment. He really didn't intend to sleep, but his eyes were still sore, and he still felt as drained as a wineskin of the first vintage at the end of a festival. No, he really didn't intend to sleep. . . .

When he woke, the pool of sun was all the way across the floor, and what woke him was the sound of voices overhead.

His heart leaped in his chest with fear. *Voices! Can anyone see down here?*

He pressed himself back against overhanging wall of the pocket, and peered up. He couldn't see anything, but some peculiarity of the shape of the pocket brought the voices clearly down to him.

". . . saw him fall about there," came Ari's voice.

The terror of discovery held him pinned against the wall.

And his first thought was that Ari had betrayed him, betrayed them both—

He should have lied! He should have told Ari that he was going west, east, south—anything but admitting he was going to try to make it to Alta! Now Ari had brought people from the compound, guards or soldiers—

But before he could move a strange voice answered.

"Not a sign of him. Not that the jackals would leave anything, and they probably dragged the body off to a den, anyway," came that other voice. "And the dragonet flew off?"

Ari again. "That way."

"Towards the breeding valleys. Well, she'll be back with her mother by now, and we won't see her again. By now, the other dragons will have chewed the harness and saddle off her, and no captured dragonet ever gets caught twice. You're right, Ari. It had to have been an accident, poor boy, and we jumped to an unwarranted conclusion. If he'd been planning to steal a dragon, he'd have taken one of the older ones, not an unflighted dragonet."

"Of course he would have; of what use is a first-year dragonet to the Altans? They can't carry a man for at least another two years," Ari replied, sounding mournful. "My Kashet would have carried him. I wouldn't be the least surprised to find that Coresan would have, or a half dozen others. What's more, you saw for yourself that there was nothing about his gear that looked as if he was getting ready to run away. There were no provisions, nothing packed, and he didn't even have a firestarter or a waterskin. He didn't even take the funerary shrine."

"No, he didn't—and if nothing else, that's a pretty convincing argument for pure accident. Poor child. He must have underestimated how close that dragonet was to First Flight. Baken is shattered; he thinks it's his fault, showing the youngster how to train the dragonets to carry a man. He thinks Vetch was trying to find a way to prove to Haraket that *he* deserved the same sort of reward that Baken had been promised."

"It's more like to be mine," Ari said, and if Vetch hadn't known better, he'd have believed in his own demise, Ari was doing so good a job of sounding guilty. "If I'd just *followed* at a distance instead of chasing him, when the dragonet got tired, I could have retrieved him. Instead, I frightened her into throwing him before I was close enough to catch him. Which is why—"

A long silence.

"Ah. I'd wondered. Well, the Great King is hardly likely to begrudge you *that*."

"Indeed. Well, I've brought the shrine, and I got another figure for it. You head on back. I'll see if I can find something like remains, and even if I can't, I'll still place the shrine and the offerings for the boy and his father. It's the least I can do."

"And you don't want to find yourself haunted either," the voice said shrewdly. "I don't blame you. No, get that shrine placed out here so his spirit won't try to come back to the compound. I don't want to see any wandering ghosts in the corridors! See you back at the compound."

Vetch sat there with his mouth falling open, hardly able to believe what he was hearing. Was—Ari had reported him *dead?* And had he just heard Ari and another Jouster agreeing that he was?

A shadow passed across the opening above, and the familiar sound of dragon wings echoed down where Vetch waited.

And for some time, nothing more happened, as Vetch strained his ears and his nerves went tight as lute string. Then, when he was ready to scream with the tension, he heard something in the passage. It sounded like footfalls. Two light feet, and four very, very heavy ones.

That "something" was indeed Ari and Kashet. The dragon had a large bag strapped across the back of his saddle.

"Ah, awake. I don't suppose you overheard me up there?" Ari said cheerfully. "Down, Kashet."

The dragon stretched himself alongside Avatre, who was still sleeping.

"Uh—most of it. I'm dead?" Vetch hazarded.

"As the god-king Arsani-kat-hamun," Ari agreed. He took the bag from the back of his saddle and tossed it to Vetch; it was a *lot* heavier than it looked. "Your grave goods. I told everyone you'd been thrown and the dragonet escaped, then suggested that I

ought to go set up a funerary shrine to you and your father where
I last saw your body. So to avoid having you come back to haunt
us, virtually everyone in the compound rushed to put together a
rather motley assortment of funerary offerings. I, of course, put
together a very select assortment of my own choosing as well,
but I saw no reason to refuse their gifts. There might actually be
something worth keeping in them."

He felt rather as if he'd been run over by a chariot. Why had
he not confided in Ari in the first place? His fears seemed baseless
now. Ari had taken a chaotic situation in hand, and had taken
care of every possible consideration. "You want me to leave these
things for my father?" he hazarded.

"Some of them," Ari said cryptically. "There's another bag
back up there—" he jerked his head at the opening, "—where the
obliging Dethet-re left it. And yes, I did bring your father's shrine,
but I strongly suggest that you set it up here and leave it, or you'll
only have to hunt a place to leave it later, and *that* place will not
be nearly as secure. You'll find, I think, that it isn't the sort of item
you can afford to take along on a journey the length of the one
you have elected to make."

"I can always set up another for him when I get there," Vetch
said, after a pause.

"Indeed. Now, I'll go get the other bag, you rummage through
that and see what's useful. What isn't—that, you can just leave
for your father's spirit."

Ari strode off down the crevice. Kashet remained where he
was, since Ari hadn't ordered him to his feet. Vetch knelt down
beside the coarse canvas bag and opened it.

On the top of the bag was a roll of his own bedding, with something hard and squarish in it. The shrine? Yes, he discovered as he
carefully unrolled the bedding, that the shrine was wrapped in it,
so his first act was to deal with it. Ari had been marvelously careful; he quickly set the shrine to rights and looked around the little
refuge for somewhere to put it. Finally he climbed up to a kind of
shallow niche, high above what he hoped would be the high-water

mark in the rainy season. He set the shrine on that ledge, after chasing out sand, a few dead leaves, and the shell of a beetle or two.

He scrambled down from his perch, and returned to unpacking the bag. Under the bedding were the woolen cape he'd been given for cold weather, and the canvas rain cape, both of which he had kept with his bedding. Tied up in a square of cloth were the little treasures he had accumulated while he was at the compound. There weren't many of them, some faience amulets, a carved knife-handle that someone had discarded, a horn spoon he'd made himself, a very small oil lamp he had modeled from clay. A little box proved to be a tinder-box with a firestriker; then came a couple of small knives—a sling and a pouch of stones—a wineskin that sloshed when he shook it. And on the bottom, barley bread and honey cakes, a bit squashed, but he wasn't going to complain.

Ari reappeared with that second bag. "I have no idea what's in this one," he said, bringing it over to where Vetch had spread out his loot. "I packed the first one; the gods only know what the others thought was suitable as your grave goods." He chuckled. "I'm afraid that your fellow dragon boys recalled that rumor about you being the focus for Altan sea witch magic, and stuffed anything they could think of in there to placate your spirit, because it's cursed heavy!"

The first thing out of the top was a gameboard and counters. "Well, that's useful," Ari said sarcastically. "But I'm sure your father's spirit will appreciate it. "Now what—ah, that's more like it! Someone was feeling very guilty, indeed!"

He pulled out two more wineskins, both full. "Pour those out, rinse them, and fill them with water," Ari directed. "Avatre can't drink wine, and in the desert, water is more precious than the Great King's own vintages." After a moment of thought, Vetch emptied and refilled all three. He had never much liked wine, anyway, and the water here was very clear and good.

A net bag full of more bread. A flute—a pair of sandals far too big for Vetch—a set of jackstones, a set of dice—

"—evidently they hope you will occupy your spectral time with drinking and gaming rather than haunting—"

—a cone of perfume and a bundle of incense—a set of twelve *abshati* slaves, meant to serve tirelessly in the afterlife—

"—and apparently, with a dozen slaves to work for you, you'll have the leisure to gamble and drink—"

Kilts, and loincloths, which Ari shook his head over. "Not that Haraket would grudge them, but he's going to have the head of whoever had the audacity to take these from stores without asking. Still, at least you'll have some spare clothing. And speaking of heads, here's some headcloths. Good; you'll need them to keep the sun off you in the desert."

Yet another net bag of bread, a jar of oil, a clay lamp and some wicks, a bow and a quiver of hunting arrows.

"Can you shoot?" Ari asked, and when Vetch shook his head, he laid the bow aside with the objects deemed useless. "Don't bother taking this. Not only can you master the sling a great deal more quickly, but the ammunition is just stones, or clay pellets you can bake in your evening fire. You won't have to worry about losing or breaking arrows or arrowheads, and any fool can roll clay pellets. It takes a master hand to knap arrowheads and fletch the shafts."

Fishing line and hooks, a fishing net. "Not much use in the desert—but they're small and light, so you might as well take them."

Another knife, this one rather longer, a small ax. And last of all, in the very bottom of the back, a small sack that—jingled.

"What's this?" Ari said in surprise as he poured out the contents.

Coins and a little jewelry. Copper coins, copper rings, a copper bracelet, two very small silver pieces, several amulets of different gods made of enameled copper or soapstone or some other stone. Vetch expected Ari to deem that useless as well, but after pouring it all back in the pouch, he put it with the rest of the gear. "You might need that when you're across the border, to buy provisions," the Jouster said. "Now, let's get you packed, because I'll have to bring the bags back with me, if I'm going to maintain the story about laying all this out as grave offerings."

In the end, the clothing went rolled into the bedding, all but the two capes, which Ari fashioned into crude bags to hold the rest of the goods. One knife went on Vetch's belt, the others into the bags. When they tried the bags experimentally on Avatre, she didn't like them, but it appeared she would tolerate them. She craned her neck around to stare at the offending objects, quite affronted by their presence, sniffed them, then decided to ignore them. Vetch climbed back up to the niche, and Ari handed up the things they had decided to leave. When Vetch climbed back down again, the niche was tightly packed, and Vetch was satisfied that his father's spirit was going to be rather pleased, for though the leavings might be impractical stuff for *his* journey, they were fine funerary goods.

"Time to go," Ari decreed. "We need to go east, far and fast, to get out of patrol range before the next scouting wave goes out today."

"East?" Vetch asked, now supremely puzzled. Of course, Avatre had gone east, into these hills, but he'd had no choice about where she went. Alta was in the north, not the east. "But—"

"Whether you make up your mind to go to Alta, or elect to live in the wilderness after all of my warnings, you need to get out of where we're patrolling, or you'll only be caught," Ari said firmly. He nodded, as Vetch bit his lip. "So you'll have to go east before you can go north. Besides— Well, never mind. You'll see when we get there."

"We?" he asked.

"I'm going to take you somewhere," he said, again surprising Vetch, who thought he had come to the end of surprises. "Just follow me and Kashet, and don't drop back; it's going to be cursed hot, and you're going to want to get out of the sky, but that's the last thing we can afford to do. Up, Kashet."

The great dragon rose; Ari led him into the crevice. Vetch called to Avatre, and followed.

Instead of taking immediately into the hard, blue sky as Vetch had expected, Ari took hold of Kashet's harness and led them on foot. Outside that crevice, the sun beat down on Vetch's head with unrelenting heat; under his bare feet, that he had thought were callused and toughened, the hard, baked soil, full of stones and hotter than the sands of the wallows, was very difficult to climb. But he didn't complain—how could he? He owed Ari much, much more than simple obedience without complaint, and it appeared that before this day was over, he was going to owe him a great deal more.

Both of them laboring in the heat, sweating like lathered horses, they led their dragons over the top of next ridge. Only there, just below the crest, did Ari mount up. Sweat poured down his face, but he ignored it.

"Remember what I said. Don't lag," he cautioned, as Vetch clambered into Avatre's saddle. "Now, let's get going. We have a long way to go."

At his signal, Kashet spread his wings, and leaped—forward, not up. Avatre, purely by instinct, followed, both of them coasting down the slope of the hill like a pair of ducks skimming over the surface of the Great Mother River.

Up the following slope and down the next, Kashet skimmed along the surface of the hills, staying low, and after some confusion, Vetch thought he knew the reason. If they went *up*, there was the chance that someone might spot them in the distance, even if all they could see were two dots, and wonder why there were two dragons in the place where there should be only one.

Despite the concerns that Ari had voiced, he wasn't pressing Kashet to any great speed. Avatre fell in behind him, just off his right wing, and it seemed as if it was easier for her to fly there, in his wake. It occurred to Vetch that flocks of geese and ducks flew that way, in formation. Did dragons? Well, why not?

It was, as Ari said, "cursed hot." Avatre seemed to revel in the heat, taking new strength from it, but it wasn't long before Vetch was thinking longingly of the bathing pools of the compound.

Ari and Kashet set up a kind of pattern in their flying that Ava-tre imitated—heavy, jouncing wing beats on the upslopes, and a long glide down the other side. Whenever the *kamiseen* came roaring down a draw or around a hill, and caught them unexpect-edly, they side-slipped in a way that sent Vetch's stomach into a tumble. None of these modes of flying was especially comfortable for the rider, and Vetch found a new respect for the Jousters, who did this day after day, twice a day, for most of the year. No wonder they were as muscular as the best warriors!

They went on—forever, it seemed—up one slope, down an-other, on and on, as the sun god's boat slowly crawled across the heavens, and Vetch began to wonder just how far was *far enough*.

Then they topped another rise, and this time there was nothing more in front of them but the long slope, down into arid, rock-strewn wilderness and more desert—

Except that off in the distance, there *did* seem to be a little green—

Now Kashet took a bit more height, and Avatre followed him, Vetch clutching the saddle, his stomach lurching all the way. Once aloft, Kashet began a long, stately glide, spiraled up a thermal, then took a glide down until he reached the next thermal to spiral up it, all of it taking them indirectly toward that speck of green.

It was farther away than Vetch had thought; distances were deceptive in the clear desert air. Which was probably why Kashet had gotten the height to enable him to glide in; laboring that far, wing beat by wing beat, was a lot harder than getting up to where he could maneuver from one thermal to another, even if it was the longer route, measured in distance.

That speck of green eventually resolved itself into trees. Not just any trees; Vetch soon recognized them for what they were. Date palms.

It was an orchard around an oasis.

And there were people there, and tents—people garbed head to toe in long, indigo-blue robes—

The Veiled Ones! he realized, as they began a final spiral down.

He didn't know much about the Bedu, but he knew that much—their customary garb, and the fact that they made their home out here, where there was nothing that a Tian would recognize as civilization. He was able to make out their flocks, now, sheep and goats, a few donkeys.

So here was his first glimpse of the mysterious desert nomads of which he had only heard, who had no king and no land of their own. He wished he wasn't so preoccupied with flying; he would have liked to pay more attention to the exotic encampment.

They didn't seem particularly surprised to see two dragons coming to land at their camping place, although there was some pointing going on down there. Vetch was just glad to see the well that irrigated the date palms. At the moment, his mouth was as dry as the desert sands they were about to land in.

Definitely, "about to land"—the ground was coming up a lot faster than he had realized. And just about the time, as Kashet backwinged to a graceful stop, he also remembered that Avatre had never landed with him on her back—had, in fact only actually *landed* once in her whole life—and he hadn't been on her back at the time either.

Which was just about the time when she blundered right down onto the ground, stumbling in a tangle of legs and wings, and he went somersaulting over her shoulder again, this time entirely by accident, and this time hitting the ground instead of Kashet's neck.

Hard.

Very hard.

So it *was* true that when you hit your head, you saw stars. . . .

Fortunately for the shredded remains of his dignity, if any of the Bedu were laughing, they were doing so silently, behind their veils. He didn't actually break anything, although he did indeed see stars for a moment. By the time he picked himself up off the ground and dusted himself off, one of the Bedu had approached Ari, apparently to act as spokesperson for the group. Male or female, there was no telling; they all dressed alike in those robes, and all wore headcloths and veils that showed only their eyes.

"I see you, Jouster of Tia," said a voice from behind the veil—either a high male voice, or a low female; Vetch couldn't tell which.

"I see you, Mouth of the People," Ari replied respectfully, briefly touching first his chest, then lips, then forehead with his first two fingers. "I come in peace."

"I greet you in peace," the Bedu answered, returning his salutation. "Do you seek aught here, from us, besides peace?"

"Water, and a bargain, in service, not goods." Ari sketched another little bow, this time in Vetch's direction. Awkwardly, Vetch copied his salute of respect. "My apprentice is of Alta."

There were murmurs from behind the veils of the other Bedu gathering around them, but no one spoke aloud but the one designated as the "Mouth."

"Of Alta." The Mouth feigned no surprise. "He has the look of it. Well, Jouster of Tia, Apprentice of Alta, what is it that you bargain for?"

Ari took a deep breath; Vetch held his. Ari looked squarely into the eyes behind the veil.

"My apprentice would go home."

Vetch had the feeling that no matter *what* Ari had told the Mouth of the Bedu, that personage would have at least *appeared* as if it was all perfectly expected and ordinary. Then again, perhaps it was. There were Seers enough in the Temples, so perhaps this person was a Seer as well as spokesperson. Perhaps he—or she—had known for some time that they were coming, and what they would ask.

Whether a Seer or not, the Mouth, however, was a shrewd bargainer, and proceeded to make it very plain that the services of the Bedu were not to be had cheaply.

Ari, for his part, made it equally clear that he expected a great deal out of the Bedu for their payment, and that *he* was no green goose fresh from the farmyard to be plucked.

He drank from his own waterskin, though the well was in plain

sight, and stood under the broiling sun as if it were the coolest of
days in the winter rains. "Passage-right, for this mere child and his
beast, two *debeks*," Ari began.

The Mouth chuckled richly. "You take us for unsophisticated
rustics, perhaps. A fugitive, with a *dragon*, going to your enemies?
Twenty."

"Five," Ari countered. "It is no dragon, but a dragonet, and not
even one that was on the roster."

"Eighteen. He will need hiding. How does one hide a dragon?"

So the bargaining went; first passage-right, then hunting-right,
shelter-right, water-right, then something called lead-on, forage-
and-feed, cover-right . . . every one of these things was considered, bargained over, hotly contested, then agreed to. And Vetch
had no idea whatsoever what these things meant, how much they
were going to cost, or—most importantly, how they were going
to be paid for. There surely wasn't enough in that little pouch of
jewelry and coin to cover even *one* of these "rights"! Was he expected to go into another kind of servitude to pay for his passage?
But how could anything he knew be reckoned of enough worth to
pay it in any reasonable length of time?

He, at least, could use Avatre as a shade, and followed Ari's
example in drinking from one of the three waterskins he'd filled.
He offered some to Avatre, but she wasn't interested, so he
scooped up handfuls of sand and gave her a buffing as they waited
and listened. The rest of the Bedu remained encircling them,
watching and listening just as avidly.

Finally, after an endless amount of bargaining, while the barge
of the sun god crept toward the west, Ari and the Mouth finished
their negotiations.

"All rights, all guides," the Mouth said, as Ari wiped his sweating forehead with the back of his hand. "One *lek*, twenty *alleks*,
seven *debeks*."

"Done." Ari seemed satisfied, but Vetch's head reeled. That
was enough to provision an entire village for six moons! Where
was he supposed to find that much money?

But Ari was rummaging in a leather pouch hanging off the front of Kashet's saddle. "I believe that you will find these are easily the equivalent of that sum," he said, stepping forward, and placing a necklet and two heavy armlets in the Mouth's outstretched hands. Vetch recognized, first the yellow glitter of gold—then, with a sense of shock, the Gold of Honor. Engraved with the Haras-hawk, and the royal vulture, how could it be anything else?

"The Gold of Honor, Jouster?" the Mouth said at the same moment. "Will the Great King not be incensed that it comes into profane hands? Will we not be courting his anger?"

"Do not seek to gull me into thinking you less than shrewd, Veiled One," Are retorted. "You will melt it down or pound it out, of course. I care not, so long as it buys my apprentice those rights."

"And has the Great King not forbidden any such thing?" the Mouth countered. "The Gold of Honor is not to be defaced, according to his laws."

"Since when have the People ever bent to the laws and will of the Great King of Tia?" Ari retorted, acerbically. "What matters it to you? There is no curse on such a thing, if you are concerned. It is law, not magic, that marks what may and may not be done with Honor Gold."

Then he raised one eyebrow, and his expression went from acerbic, to sardonic. "I had never thought to hear that the Bedu feared the wrath of Tia's King."

"Then the bargain is struck, Jouster," the Mouth said smoothly, apparently not in the least stung by Ari's jab. "Be pleased to accept our hospitality."

Then, and only then, as the gold jewels disappeared into the Mouth's robes, did the circle of onlookers break. Yet another of the robed creatures beckoned to both of them, and they followed, into the oasis.

There, on a wool carpet spread in front of one of the tents, they were offered dates, stewed lamb, flatbread, and water in brass cups. Their servers did not speak to them, and once they sat down to eat, the servers vanished.

Vetch, however, could not eat. He was still reeling from the shock of seeing Ari hand over his Gold of Honor to these nomads.

Ari paused with a bite of the lamb in a scoop of flatbread halfway to his mouth, and frowned. "What's wrong, Vetch?"

"The Gold of Honor," he whispered, and gulped. "You gave up the Gold of Honor—"

"Which I cannot sell, nor trade, nor melt down inside the bounds of Tia," Ari pointed out. "What good did it do me? I could wear it, if I chose to flaunt myself. I could put it in a chest and keep it. I could display it on a table. *Very* useful."

"But won't the Great King be angry if he asks you to wear it, and you don't have it anymore?" Vetch asked, nervously.

But Ari only smiled. "*I* told Haraket to fetch it for me, that I was feeling guilty about your death, and I was going to leave it as *my* funerary gift. That, at least, is permitted—one *can* leave the wretched stuff in a tomb, a shrine, or as a temple offering! Haraket seemed to think this was a sensible plan, and I have no doubt that a scroll telling some fool scribe in the Palace of what I have done is on its way to the Treasury now. And the King will probably insist on replacing the wretched baubles with ones even larger and in poorer taste." Ari sighed gustily, surprising Vetch into a laugh.

"There! Much better. Now eat—" he prodded Vetch with a piece of flatbread. "You and Avatre will need strength; you'll be leaving this camp at the same time that I leave to return home."

"Indeed," said the Mouth, who seemed to materialize out of nowhere at just that moment. "It is too dangerous for you to remain here for very long. Hear what your master has bought you, apprentice. You will have safe passage across the face of the desert, and water at every oasis. You have the right to hunt and forage, and if you cannot find food on your own, then we will supply it, but as our resources are limited, you will be required to try hunting first. There will be a message going ahead of you, and a guide to the places where you will be spending your nights. Not human, no—" the Mouth told him, anticipating his question. "Here is the first one."

He handed Vetch a cord with a blackened bead strung on it— but curiously, the cord did not hang straight, it slanted toward the east, as if something was pulling it. And when he took the cord from the Mouth, that was, indeed, what it felt like.

"At each stopping place, you will surrender your guide, and get another like this, that will lead you on to the next oasis," the Mouth said. "And if by some fearful accident, you are taken by your enemies, you must pledge on your soul's survival that you will release the bead to fly home without you!"

The Mouth was clearly waiting for an answer in the affirmative; Vetch quickly stammered agreement, and put the cord around his neck.

"As I told you, you have hunting-right, to hunt for whatever you see wild on the way, to feed your dragon and yourself. But you also have hearth-right, giving you both food from our stores if you cannot catch anything—though I will warn you. We are not a wealthy people, and you both may go hungry if you count upon this."

"I won't—" Vetch began, but the Mouth wasn't listening.

"Last of all, you have water-right, which of itself, is worth twice what this bandit bargained from me." The Mouth's tone gave the lie to his words, though. He didn't sound angry or even annoyed. "So—the message is sped, and so should you be. A man on a camel can reach the next point on your journey by full dark; you should have no difficulty."

With that, the Mouth stalked off again, leaving Vetch to stare after him.

"Don't look for friendship from them," Ari warned. "We made a bargain; that's all. The Bedu don't care for our little wars, nor our pretensions at holding dominion over the land."

"You sound as if you admire them," Vetch ventured.

"Say, rather, that I envy them. Their only enemies are the land

and the weather, and they are the freest people in the world, though they pay a heavy price for freedom." He sighed. "And the Mouth is right; finish that meal, and we will both be on our separate ways."

So there it was—the moment he knew was coming. But he had never thought that it would be like this.

"Master—" he began.

"Ari," the Jouster corrected firmly. "I am no longer your master. Though I'll have a hell of a time replacing you."

Vetch winced, and hung his head. He felt horrible, leaving Ari in the lurch like this. But what could he do? He couldn't go back. . . .

"I'd try to get Baken, but Haraket would fight me for him. I think I'll exercise my rank and purloin one of those youngsters that Baken is training," Ari continued. "Though I think not a serf, this time. If another dragon boy gets it into his head to emulate me, I at least want to get another Jouster out of the situation."

Vetch looked up, and caught a twinkle in Ari's eye, and felt a little better. Not much, but a little. "I wouldn't have run—except they'd have taken her away from me," he said softly. "And I knew it would break her heart. And mine—"

"That's how you should be thinking, from this moment on. Whatever you decide, do it for *her* sake," Ari replied, firmly. "Nothing else. Nothing less."

"I won't," Vetch said, drawing himself up and looking Ari straight in the eyes.

"Good." There was a long moment of very awkward silence—awkward on Vetch's part anyway.

"Can't you come with me?" he asked finally. "We don't have to go to Alta—we could go east, to Beshylos—"

"No we couldn't," Ari said, sadly, but firmly. "I took certain oaths, and I will do my duty. I must. I wish—well, it can't be otherwise."

"I'm sorry, Ari," he said, overcome with guilt. "I—"

"Don't be. *I'm* not." For the very first time in all of the time that Vetch had known him, Ari broke into a broad and unshadowed smile. "It's the best thing in the world, to see a young thing fly free. I suppose—I suppose I should give you all sorts of advice now, but I can't think of very much." He sighed and shrugged his shoulders.

Finally, Vetch got the courage to ask the question that had been in his mind all along, since the first day Ari had plucked him out of Khefti's yard. "Ari—*why?* Why—everything?"

Ari looked at him quizzically. "I'm not sure myself." He looked up into the hard, cloudless blue bowl of the sky. "When I first saw you, so angry with me for stealing your water, I thought you were amusing, like a kitten that's ready to attack a lion for some imagined offense. Then, when that fat idiot of a master of yours came out and you turned from angry to terrified, it wasn't so amusing, and when he laid the lash on you, I knew I couldn't leave you there. And I *did* need a dragon boy."

"But the rest of it—" Vetch suddenly had to know, desperately. "Finding me a shrine—"

"Because it was right. Because I never had a younger brother. I'm the youngest in my family. Because—" He sighed, and looked inexpressibly sad. "Because *I* feel guilty for all of the wretched things that are being done to Altans, and perhaps at first I thought I could assuage some of that guilt by being good to you. But after a while, Vetch, you *earned* your place, and everything I did for you. By the time that wretch Khefti showed up again, you'd earned it. The other boys may not have liked you, but they could never claim you hadn't earned your place. And—I don't know, but I'm a man who believes in the gods, and I've had a feeling all along that the gods have some purpose in mind for you, and I was just the means to that purpose."

Vetch sighed; that was another dark fear put to rest. In the back of his mind, he'd wondered all along if Ari had a darker purpose for him.

But no. It was all as simple, and as complicated, as guilt, faith— and just maybe, friendship.

"Now, I have a question," Ari said into the silence. "You aren't *really* named Vetch, are you?"

He smiled; he almost had to. "No—that's something we Altan peasant farmers do, to protect precious boy babies. We name them something awful, so that the demons think they aren't worth taking in the night."

"So, just what *is* your real name?" Ari asked. "No—wait, let me guess. Kiron. Like your father."

Vetch nodded, and felt a sudden sting in his eyes that he blinked away.

The bead suddenly tugged at Vetch's neck, just as the Mouth materialized again, looking significantly at the sun. Ari nodded, got to his feet, and whistled sharply for Kashet.

The dragon raised himself from where he'd been basking in the heat, beside Avatre, and moved toward his beloved Jouster. Ari swung up into his saddle without asking Kashet to drop to the sand, and from that lofty perch, looked down at Vetch.

"Whatever you do—try not to get on the opposite end of a Joust with me. I still have my duty, and I will hold to it."

He nodded. "I understand."

Ari smiled again. "I thought you would. Your gods go with you, in whatever you decide, *Kiron*."

And he sent Kashet up into the sky, leaving Vetch—no, *Kiron*—and Avatre to watch, as they disappeared into the heavens that were, at last, no less bright than his hopes, and no lighter than his heart.

EPILOGUE

"**W**ELL, young Kiron," the Mouth of the Bedu said. "One more day, and you will be where you wished to be—across the border, in Alta. I hope that this proves to be truly what you desired."

Kiron—he had told the Bedu at the beginning of his journey that *this* was his name, and how he wished to be addressed, so as to get himself used to the shape of a name he had not used in years all over again—looked out over the desert, and saw, in the far western distance, the faint haze that marked the beginning of land where things could grow. He licked dry lips. "It has to be, doesn't it?" he replied, as straightforward as the Bedu had been. "There's no place else for me to go."

It had been a long journey, one in which he had lost track of the days, as he zigzagged from one oasis to another, following the pull of the little beads he'd been given. At each oasis, he would surrender the bead that had brought him there, to receive a new one. He and Avatre had learned, together, how to hunt, for only at an oasis—and only if they had not been at all successful in their attempts to find food on their own—would the Bedu supply them.

This was not out of greed; when an oasis held herds and flocks that numbered, not in the hundreds, but in the handfuls of animals, it was very clear that the Bedu were not a wealthy people. Honorable, yes. True to their word, without a doubt. But not wealthy.

He and Avatre honed their hunting skills quickly. He could not bear to see the big eyes of the unveiled children watching every bite he took as if it was coming out of their own portions. Which it probably was. . . .

Sometimes he went hungry, though he never, ever let Avatre go without.

That was all right; he was used to hunger.

There had been nights spent in the open desert, the two of them huddled together against the cold, Kiron's bedding pulled over the two of them. There had been days when he'd rationed out water by the sip, as they crossed expanses of desert. But the Bedu had never misled him, nor miscalled the distances, nor failed to provide him with at least enough water to get from oasis to oasis. But the closer they drew to Alta by their circuitous route, the better he and Avatre had gotten at hunting, and the more game there had been to hunt. Until now—they never went hungry at all. He was tougher; *she* was tougher, stronger, and much bigger than when they had fled the Jousters' compound.

Mind, what they caught and ate might not be very palatable now, and they might be eking out their meals one scrawny hare at a time, but they never went hungry anymore. They were self-sufficient, and it felt rather good.

He had come to know as much of the Bedu as they ever allowed outsiders to see, and he came to admire what he saw. Not that he had a chance to see very much, for only the Mouths were permitted to speak with outsiders. Still, they were generous within their means, and they never once led him astray. When he slept within their encampments, they found means to give Avatre a warm wallow, by digging a pit, lining it with rocks, and letting a fire burn to ashes atop them before covering the hot rocks with sand. They gave generously of what they had, and he quickly came to the conclusion that they were not the barbarians he'd always been told that they were—not if a "barbarian" was a wild and lawless creature devoid of the understanding of honor, without religion, without wisdom, without learning. All these things, they had in plenty. It was only in material goods that they were lacking.

He mounted into Avatre's saddle, and wrapped his legs into the bracing straps. He would not need a guide bead now, with his goal within sight.

"You undertake a different sort of trial, when you cross that border, young Kiron," the Mouth persisted. "And perhaps things will not always be to your liking. We of the desert know little of the dwellers in the marshy delta of the Great Mother River, for they have little to do with us. I cannot tell you what to expect."

"But I will be free," he said softly, with one hand on Avatre's neck. "And so will she."

The Mouth bowed his head slightly. "This is so." He stared with Vetch to that distant haze of green. "Then, I can only say, may your gods go with you."

Kiron touched his brow, his lips, and his heart in thanks and farewell, and gave Avatre the signal; with a tremendous shove of her legs, she launched for the sky.

The free, and open sky, and the beginning of a new life for them both.